MARDAN'S MARK

MARDAN'S MARK EPIC FANTASY ADVENTURE SERIES

KATHRESE MCKEE

Mardan's Mark: Mardan's Mark Epic Fantasy Adventure Series
Copyright © 2014 by Kathrese McKee
All Rights Reserved

Copyeditor: Sally Bradley, Bradley Writing and Editing Services,
    http://www.sallybradley.com
Cover design: Robin Ludwig Design Inc., http://www.gobookcoverdesign.com/
Compass rose: http://www.123rf.com/profile_lightwise
Logo design: James Mbewe
Formatting: Polgarus Studio, http://www.polgarusstudio.com

This is a work of fiction. All of the characters, organizations, and events portrayed in this novel are either products of the author's imagination or are used fictitiously.

All rights reserved. This book was self-published by Kathrese McKee under Word Marker Books. No part of this publication may be reproduced, distributed, or transmitted in any form or by any means, including photocopying, recording, or other electronic or mechanical methods, without the prior written permission of the publisher, except in the case of brief quotations embodied in critical reviews and certain other noncommercial uses permitted by copyright law.

Word Marker Books
Houston, TX

For permission requests, foreign and subsidiary rights, contact the author or her representative via http://www.kathresemckee.com

Scripture quotations are from The Holy Bible, English Standard Version®(ESV®), copyright © 2001 by Crossway, a publishing ministry of Good News Publishers. Used by permission. All rights reserved.

Printed in the United States of America
ISBN 978-0-9863578-1-7

DEDICATION

To my husband, Lynn, and my children, who inspired this story: Matt and Sarah Neely, Kelly, Sharon, and James.

To my parents, Joe and Oleta Coleman, who never said a discouraging word when I quit my job to write. And to my sister, Latricia, who is the best kind of cheerleader. Thank you.

Also, I would like to honor the Reading team at Dean Middle School in Cypress-Fairbanks Independent School District, especially my mentor — the doyenne of reading instructors — Mrs. Robin Casteel, who taught me how to teach. Reading teachers are the hope of future generations. Thank you for working on the front lines to save our students.

And to my loyal writing companions, Snickers and Champ, who gave me many judgmental looks during the writing of this book. Good dogs! I miss you both so much. Rest in peace.

ACKNOWLEDGMENTS

This book would never have reached completion without my outstanding critique partner, Laura Anderson Kurk. She pushed me, kicking and screaming with fright, through the door marked Author. Thanks, too, to my critique group for years of encouragement and gentle corrections. I want to acknowledge the input of: Azalea Dabill, Scott J. Abel, Karen DeBlieck, Sarah Ayres Grimm, Terri Proksch, Precarious Yates, Jennifer Rogers, Aaron Schlegel, Katie Patton Clark, Loraine Kemp, Sarah Witenhafer, and Tami ONeal.

Thanks to my alpha team: Sarah Neely, Oleta Coleman, Trish See, Sharon McKee, and Lynn McKee, who put everything aside to help me get this ready for prime time. I appreciate the kind encouragement and outstanding advice from Jeff Gerke. You, sir, are a fount of knowledge.

Thanks to Lisa Gefrides (aka Lisa Godfrees), Stacey Zink, Mary Hamilton, Sarah Grimm, and Cheryl Dawson for volunteering to be my beta readers; the story found its final form due to your invaluable feedback.

Finally, I appreciate the help of my editor, Sally Bradley, for helping me polish this manuscript, and Robin Ludwig, for a stunning book cover design. Thanks to Jason and Marina Anderson of Pogarus Studio for the lovely interior design and to James Mbewe for the logo. You guys are the best!

Even the captives of the mighty shall be taken,
and the prey of the tyrant be rescued,
for I will contend with those who contend with you,
and I will save your children.
— *Isaiah 49:25*

PROLOGUE

Kaedan Palace, Kingdom of Southern Marst

The king knelt at the feet of Azor, the alligator god, staring at the idol's jagged teeth and narrowed eyes. Incense smoke shrouded the cramped stone crypt.

Azor's priest, clad in black with an alligator tattoo on his right cheekbone, stood near the wall. "Drink more of the potion, Your Majesty. It will open your mind to the truth."

The king lifted a silver goblet to his lips with trembling hands, never looking away from the god's likeness. Embers burned in a hammered bronze brazier, casting more shadows than light. A witch, as shriveled as old shoe leather, sat on the floor behind the statue, chanting as she drew symbols on the floor with a charred stick.

"Azor is bright," the king said. He set the goblet aside and reached toward the idol. "He shines."

The priest moved closer. "Your Majesty, whom do you wish to consult?"

"I want to see Mardan, the first king."

The witch waited for the priest to translate the request into Norlan and then added "Mardan" to her chants.

The priest prodded the burning coals, and brilliance flared up on the brazier, sending up a dark cloud of smoke. The sickly sweet aroma in the vault increased a hundredfold.

"You must add your voice, King Baydan," the priest said.

"Mardan. Mardan." Baydan's voice croaked, halting and slurred.

"Mardan."

A form took shape in the haze. At first there were only stray wisps of smoke, but as the moments passed, the specter condensed and took on color. Baydan's eyes rounded. "Mardan."

Baydan seemed oblivious to the witch's horrified cry and the priest's hoarse shout.

The apparition grew to the size of a tall man, robed in splendid garments. Bright blue eyes, piercing and awful, glared down at Baydan. The spirit's voice thundered around the room. "Who dares to call me?"

"I I I . . . am King Baydan, my . . . my lord."

The fire in the brazier flared high, then dimmed.

"My son, you are cursed for seeking counsel from spirits. Since you have bowed the knee to Azor, El has turned his face from you."

Mardan's spirit vanished without a trace. Baydan stared at the statue of Azor as though seeing it for the first time. Silence fell like a pall over the room's occupants.

The priest ventured to speak. "Your Majesty—"

"No!" Baydan stood on shaky legs and faced the man. His voice rose in a frenzied shriek. "No, I won't do as you ask. You can't make me!"

"Your Majesty, wait—"

"No! No! You're evil!" Baydan pressed his palms over his eyes, and a loud moan escaped his white lips. "What have I done?"

A cool voice from the far corner spoke for the first time. "Kill him."

Baydan flung his hands from his face and whirled, groping for the sword at his waist. "You would not dare—"

A short scuffle ensued, but King Baydan was no match for the priest.

The cool voice continued. "You make a convincing priest, Captain Rozar."

Rozar didn't look up as he wiped his dagger on Baydan's tunic. "That's not surprising. I used to be a priest when I was young and naïve."

"Not so young and naïve now, eh?" The voice paused. "There is one other minor problem to deal with. After that, board your ship and leave quickly. We will communicate in the usual way." He sighed. "It's a pity about Baydan, but this will work to our advantage."

Excerpt from *Histories of the Twin Kingdoms*

>King Mardan begat twin sons, Kaedan and Kaeson, and because of his love for each, he gave Southern Marst to Kaedan and the territory north of the Marst River to Kaeson as Northern Marst. The Twin Kingdoms have thus passed to their heirs without a break for three centuries, until King Baydan of Southern Marst bent the knee to Azor, god of Norland.

CHAPTER ONE

Twelve years later, The Cathartid, *off the coast of Southern Marst*

Aldan crept past the sleeping crew members drooping in their hammocks, his bare feet soundless on the well-worn boards. One of the men mumbled. Aldan froze, the daggers hidden in the belt beneath his ragged tunic pressing into the small of his back. The pirate turned his head, but his eyes stayed closed.

Keep moving. The skin between his shoulders itched. *Nobody's there. Stop imagining things.*

Dawn's dull gray fingers poked through the latticework of the hatch in the deck above — barely enough light to maneuver around the sea chests and discarded clothing littering the deck.

Aldan ducked into the dark passageway and down to the pitch-black hold. The hot, musty air closed in around him.

He stopped and held his breath. The skitter and scrape of a ship's rat in the beams reassured him. The gulf slipped past the ship's hull, a constant rush of water. Satisfied, he hurried to the forsaken space reserved for Captain Rozar's slaves in the hold near the stern, picking his way by memory through the maze of barrels, crates, bolts of sailcloth, and coils of rope.

"Sam. Linus. Wake up." He shook Sam's shoulder and received a grunt in reply. Aldan pushed harder. "Get up."

"Go away."

"You've got to see this." He reached out to wake Linus and found an empty hammock. "Where's Linus?"

A quiet voice answered near his ear. "I'm behind you."

Aldan whirled around with a hiss. "Don't *do* that." He sagged onto the foot of Sam's hammock. "I think my heart stopped beating."

Sam's bass voice rumbled in the darkness. "How's a man supposed to get any sleep around here?"

"Never mind sleep. Linus, light the lamp so you can see what I found."

A tiny spark jumped from the flint to the char cloth, sizzling bright in the depths of the hold. A single point of red light glowed, followed by the birth of flame in the lamp as Linus held the cloth to the wick.

Aldan looked into the obsidian glitter of Linus's eyes. "Where have you been?"

"Behind you."

"How long?"

"The whole time."

Aldan blew out a breath and pushed his hair away from his forehead. "I woke you?"

"Indeed."

Aldan shook his head and dropped the subject — Linus would do whatever Linus would do. "Look." He drew three daggers from the back of his belt and handed one to each of his fellow slaves. He unsheathed the remaining blade and ran his thumb along the edge.

"I could do some damage with this," Sam whispered. He struggled to swing his legs over the side of his hammock and straightened to his full height. Sam was the most heavily muscled of the group and the oldest at twenty-three summers, but he wasn't as tall as Aldan, four years his junior.

Linus, younger and taller than the others, re-sheathed his dagger and made no comment. He reached into his tunic's neckline and drew out a small leather pouch. He loosened the cord, and five gold pieces clinked into his palm. They gleamed against his brown-black skin.

Aldan jumped to his feet. "Where did you get that?"

"Fratz's sea chest."

"What?" Aldan and Sam asked in unison.

Linus shrugged. "I saw Fratz steal it from Biscuits."

A grin split Sam's face, and his red beard bristled. "So Fratz can't cry about losing the gold pieces he wasn't supposed to have in the first place." Sam punched Linus's arm. "Well done."

Aldan frowned. "Are you out of your mind? What if you'd been caught?"

Linus leveled a meaningful stare. "What if *you'd* been caught?"

"It's not the same," Aldan said. "Nobody's counted the weapons we captured yesterday. Not Captain Rozar. Not Scar. So nobody will know they're missing. But even if he can't say anything, Fratz will know the gold is missing. And he's going to look for it."

Linus shrugged again. "I'm good at hiding things."

"He's got you there," Sam said, and he grinned. "That means we've got weapons and gold. Now all we have to do is figure out how to get ashore."

Aldan rubbed the stubble on his chin. "Aye, that's the problem, isn't it?"

"You think? We're stranded in the Great Gulf, leagues from any shore." Sam's mouth pulled down at the corners. "Our chances of getting off this cursed ship are almost nil."

"We'll think of a way. We must." Aldan took the dagger from Sam's hand and gave both weapons to Linus. "Hide these and the gold. I've got to get things ready for Rozar before Scar figures out I'm not where I'm supposed to be."

"That sea serpent." Sam's fists clenched at his sides. "Scar's getting bolder every day and the men listen to him. Rozar had better watch his back, and we'd better be gone by the time Scar makes his move. Once he's the captain, we're dead."

Linus nodded. "Indeed."

Aldan swallowed and looked away. *And I'm at the top of Scar's list.*

"Aldan, bring wine!"

Aldan stopped polishing the brass lantern in his hands and hung it back on its hook. Wine? In the middle of the day?

A watchful silence fell over the pirates on deck. Captain Rozar rarely drank and never before nightfall. Aldan turned to see what held the crew's attention and noticed a tiny sailboat approaching from the west.

Rozar glared around at his men. "Get back to work, you lot." The captain's attention swung back to the sailboat. Scar, the first mate, was out of sight. Aldan took the chance to linger near the hatch.

The craft drew up along *Cathartid's* port side, and a stranger in riding boots and a green tunic climbed the ship's ladder, greeted the captain like an old friend, and spoke near Rozar's ear. A wicked smile bloomed across the captain's face.

Aldan slid down the ladder without touching the rungs and hurried to fetch wine and two goblets on a tray from the galley. Biscuits, the cook, delayed him with questions, but Aldan broke away, promising to talk later. He reached the captain's stout door and listened hard. The door masked most of the words, but they were speaking in Marstan instead of Norlan. He knocked on the door, waited for Rozar's answer, and swung it open.

"Ah, Aldan. Come in, come in." Rozar laughed and rubbed his palms together.

Aldan set the tray on the captain's table and backed into the corner to watch, as stealthy as a ship's rat, taking care not to rap his head against the angled beams.

Rozar poured a liberal amount of wine into each vessel. "Join me in a toast, my friend."

"With pleasure," Green Tunic said. He took the proffered drink and waited.

"You've brought me the best possible news at exactly the right time." Rozar set aside the flagon and lifted his goblet. "To Fortune! May she shine as brightly on you and me as Sol shines today."

"Hear, hear," Green Tunic said, lifting his glass to touch Rozar's. "To your success."

Rozar took a long sip. "Mmm," he murmured.

Wait until Sam and Linus heard about this. Aldan dug his bare toes into the captain's prized silk rug and relished the cool sea breeze flowing through the open porthole. He studied the stranger, memorizing every detail. A golden wolf's head adorned his uniform's left breast. What was the man's name? If the stranger was Rozar's friend, why hadn't they seen him before?

Rozar took another swig of wine and thumped his goblet down. "Please, sit with me a few moments before you cast off again." His dark gaze darted to Aldan, and he snapped his fingers. "You. Out. Wait outside the cabin door until I call."

Aldan bowed himself out of the cabin and pulled the door closed. He didn't dare listen through the keyhole. No news was worth a thrashing. He put his back to the beam across from Rozar's cabin and listened to the sounds of the pirate ship and her crew.

Cathartid creaked and groaned around him, complaining about being too close to land when she could be hunting in the Great Gulf. A shadow fell over him, and he ducked in time to avoid Scar's beefy fist.

"You got time to stand around, do you? I know you have work to be doing, you layabout." The first mate grabbed Aldan's wrist and gave it a vicious twist. "Well? Why are you still standing here?"

"Captain Rozar's orders," Aldan said through gritted teeth. He met Scar's bloodshot eyes glare for glare. Every detail of the mate's disfigured face sprang into sharp focus, including Azor, the alligator god, tattooed on his cheekbone.

"Oh, that's likely." Scar gave his arm a wrenching yank and let go. "You know Marstan. What did they say?"

Aldan shook his head. "They drank a toast to Fortune, and Rozar told me to get out and wait here. That's all I know."

"Don't know much, do you?" Scar spit at his feet.

Aldan didn't answer or move a muscle.

"Stupid slave." The first mate turned on his heel and ascended the nearby ladder to the deck above.

Aldan checked both ways before he grimaced and rubbed his throbbing wrist. A whisper of sound captured his attention.

Linus emerged from the space beneath the ladder. He wore unrelieved black. Combined with his ebony skin, his clothing acted like camouflage in the ship's gloomy interior.

Linus paused, tilting his head to listen. "That one is the son of a devil," he said.

Aldan nodded. "His mother was a squid."

"Indeed." Linus gestured to Rozar's closed door. "No news?"

"Not yet. Rozar's half-crazed, he's so excited."

His friend heaved a solemn sigh. "Someone will suffer."

"Better clear out before anyone sees you, Brother." But Linus was already out of sight, gone without a sound.

An hour passed while the captain entertained his guest. Rozar called Aldan to clear away the drink tray and the empty flagon. Green Tunic departed, and as soon as the visitor's sailboat pulled away, the captain shouted orders to set the ship in motion.

"Bring her about, north by northeast. Look alive, you worthless curs! Scar! Get those sails trimmed." Rozar didn't quit giving orders until he'd set every hand to work. "Aldan, come here." He lowered his voice. "Get me down the ladder. Don't know why I ever touch wine."

Aldan half-supported, half-carried the captain to his cabin. Rozar hummed a tune under his breath and settled onto his berth with a muzzy smile. "Ish good you've grown up a bit or I'd be . . . hmm . . . hmm."

Aldan stared at the captain who'd fallen asleep the moment his head hit the pillow. "It's a good thing I'm the same size as you or you'd have broken your neck coming down that ladder."

He stole a moment to watch the waves through the porthole. *Cathartid's* hull vibrated with life under his hand. The ship possessed a soul of her own, an evil soul set on destruction.

Cathartid made the most of the wind in her swept-back sails, slipping through the waters of the Great Gulf like the deadly predator she was, barracuda swift and shark hungry, the fastest ship in King Dzor's pirate fleet with a captain and crew to match her ruthless nature.

A short nap later, Captain Rozar took the helm. Aldan took his normal place — out of reach but near enough to take orders. Rozar summoned him with a snap of his fingers.

"Find Sam and clear out the cabin across from mine. Tell the cook to make a fresh batch of the sleeping potion. Don't make me wait."

Aldan found Sam in the galley. No surprise there. His best friend had long ago discovered he could earn extra food scraps if he acted as cook's drudge. Sam needed all the help he could get maintaining his extra-large form.

Mirza, the ship's resident witch, was in the galley too, preparing some unspeakable sacrifice of fish entrails, strong spices, and spoiled eggs for Azor. The stench was unbearable.

Aldan's stomach rolled over, and he tried not to breathe through his nose. He relayed the captain's orders to Biscuits in one breath.

"Sam. Come with me." Swallowing a gulp of air, Aldan raced through the narrow space to reach the fresh breeze flowing through the hatch overhead.

Sam emerged a few moments later, munching on a stale piece of bread. He held more pieces in his other hand.

Aldan stared as Sam popped another crust into his mouth with relish. "How can you eat when she's making Azor's stew? That's disgusting."

"Mirza's disgusting, but the bread's pretty good. I'm hungry. Besides, it's not even moldy."

Aldan snorted. "I'm so glad the bread isn't moldy. It's your ability to eat around Mirza that's disgusting. Hurry up."

Sam walked at his side, bumping Aldan's shoulder with every other step in the narrow passageway. "I have two more pieces. Want one?"

Aldan looked at the bread. His stomach rumbled. "Oh, all right." He snatched a crust from Sam's hand and stuffed it into his mouth. "Thanks."

"Do you have to walk so fast?"

"Just hurry," Aldan said. "If Rozar decides to check on us, we'd better be done."

⁂

Ten bells rang after Sol went to bed beneath the western horizon. Aldan leaned over the stern railing to savor the end of the day. The surface of the

Great Gulf rolled back from the hull, murky and mysterious with traces of luminescence from the *Cathartid's* wake.

Rozar's shrill whistle echoed through the ship. Aldan turned from the railing, ran to the captain's cabin, and knocked once on the frame of the open door.

"Help me out of this coat," Rozar said with a snap. "Where were you?"

He didn't answer. Long experience told him the question was probably rhetorical. As soon as the door was closed, the captain launched into his nightly soliloquy in Marstan. Rozar enjoyed talking to him as if they were friends. As if they were more than jailor and captive, master and slave.

"What a day. Can you believe it? We're to take the richest prize imaginable in two weeks. Our provisions will be stretched, to be sure, but this will be the most profitable voyage of my life."

Aldan strove to keep the interest from showing on his face. Perhaps Rozar would say what was going on. He reached out and grasped the collar and one sleeve of Rozar's finest coat as the captain tried to shrug out of it.

"Have a care, boy. That's my hair you're pulling."

"Sorry."

Rozar extracted his other arm from the fitted garment. "I'll make you sorry." The threat sounded half-hearted at best.

Aldan placed the garment on the bed, bundled his master into a dressing gown of scarlet silk, and waited as the captain sank into his favorite chair.

Rozar chuckled. "Yes. King Dzor, Azor bless his soul, will likely give me the deed to my family's old estate as a reward."

Aldan knelt and grasped Rozar's boot in his hands, and the captain allowed him to pull it off. He put it aside and took the other boot Rozar pushed off. With the boots in one hand, Aldan retrieved the boot blacking from a shelf on the wall, sat on a low stool, and set to work.

The captain chuckled. "You just don't have a clue, do you, Aldan?"

He glanced up.

Rozar's dark eyes twinkled with malice. "You remember nothing before you came to me. Isn't that right?"

Aldan looked down at the leather of the boot he'd been buffing. *It's true.*

Hadn't he tried hundreds of times to remember his life before becoming Rozar's slave? Marstan was his native language. He'd learned Norlan from the crew in the school of hard fists and swift kicks. Rozar used Marstan with Aldan "to stay in practice."

"Well, boy? You've been aboard my ship a dozen years. Don't you remember yet?"

The captain usually didn't want or expect answers. Apparently, he did now. "I only remember the language."

"Ha! What a jest!" Rozar laughed again. "If only you knew— But no, I don't believe I'll tell you. Suffice it to say, there's nothing like being paid twice for the same work. In your case, I might be paid more than twice if the stars align the right way."

Aldan's eyes widened. Had someone paid to make him a slave?

"I've really confused you now." The captain gasped and sputtered, pounding his knee in apparent glee. "You should see your face."

A knock at the door cut the captain's laughter short. "Enter." The alligator tattoo on Rozar's cheek seemed to bristle with outrage.

Linus came in bearing a tray laden with food, and Rozar's dark expression lightened.

"About time."

Linus placed the tray on the table at the captain's elbow. The smell of wonderful, spicy soup filled the air, and Aldan's mouth watered. Linus poured the captain's favorite tea into a heavy mug.

"Out." One word, in Norlan.

Aldan hid a smile as Linus closed one eye in a sly wink, and his spirits rose. The joke was on Rozar. Linus and Sam had learned Marstan long since, but the captain always used Norlan for their benefit.

Linus let himself out of the cabin, and the door latch clicked quietly into place. Aldan finished with the first boot and moved to the second one.

"Bet you didn't know I was raised to be a farmer," Rozar said. "That's how I plan to spend my old age, just watching the crops grow on my father's old property. I can afford to pull down the manor and build a new one. Who knows? Maybe I'll even get a wife or two and father some brats."

Similar nonsense followed. About different crops. About horses and cattle. Such a strange state of mind — the captain had become more unpredictable each passing year. What would happen to them when Rozar went completely mad?

How did I become the one he talks to? He's already mad.

Rozar mopped up his soup with a crust of bread. "It all depends on Dzor and what he thinks of my prize, of course." The captain switched topics to the weather, sails, and supplies.

After completing his duties, Aldan closed the door and let out a deep breath. What prize would Rozar be so eager to take? A rival pirate's treasure? A shipment of slaves? A rich merchant ship? Now he had more questions than ever.

///

Aldan saved the scraps from Rozar's meal and wheedled more food from Biscuits in exchange for pleasant speculation about the meaning of the new orders. The cook lived for gossip of all kinds. Tonight, Biscuits doled out food for the brothers with a generous hand, and Aldan paid close attention to everything the cook had to say. Especially anything about Scar. At last, he left the galley and descended to the hold where Sam and Linus waited.

"You should have heard Rozar going on and on about cows and sheep and such," Aldan said. "I think he means to give up the ship if King Dzor grants his wish to get his land back."

Sam frowned. "Makes you wonder what he plans to do with us."

"Yes, it does."

"I'll tell you one thing," Sam said, lowering his voice and switching to Marstan. "I'll drown myself before I stay aboard with Scar. We have got to get away from this ship."

Aldan nodded. "Scar will feed us to the sharks, one piece at a time."

Linus, who sat right up against Aldan's side on the hammock, shuddered. "Indeed."

"I know we've talked about getting away before," Aldan said. "We have to do it soon. I feel it. If King Dzor is pleased with this prize Rozar means to take, there's no telling what will happen to us." He rubbed his forehead. "Maybe Rozar plans to take us with him to his estate, but more than likely, he means to take me. Only me."

Linus pressed closer to his side in silent protest.

Aldan hesitated. "Of course, he could mean to sell us in Port Azor, but it sounds like he has plans for me."

"I sure wish I understood what he meant about being paid twice," Sam said. "But I don't think Rozar has that much time left. Scar has to hold off until we capture this great prize Rozar's raving about. But after that . . ."

"You're probably right. We can't wait until we get close to Port Azor. We have to figure out a way to get one of the longboats over the side without getting killed or captured."

"We can't row across the Great Gulf."

"You just said you'd rather drown than be under Scar's command." Aldan glared at Sam and then at Linus. "So we'll take the boat and take our chances. Unless you have a better idea."

CHAPTER TWO

Kaeson Palace, Kingdom of Northern Marst

"A storm is coming, Your Highness."

Srilani turned to the freckled youth beside her. "This is the last arrow. We'll be inside the palace before the rain gets here."

She drew back the string of her bow, pulling it to the corner of her mouth, and aimed at the farthest target. A gust of gulf wind brushed her cheek, and she waited for a moment of calm. *Breathe out, breathe in, hold . . . release.* The arrow flew to the target and hit the center with a satisfying thud.

Srilani glanced to the east. The brilliant light of Sol sparkled on the Great Gulf's waves, but a line of dark clouds swarmed toward Kaeson Palace. Typical. The moment she had some free time, a summer shower would force her indoors.

"Now you may retrieve the arrows," she said.

Her assistant, aged six, galloped down the range with his dog close at his heels.

Srilani called after him. "Please be careful of the fletching!"

Behind her, Captain Olson's voice sounded amused. "How much do you pay him?"

"Olson!" She spun to face her good friend and sometimes teacher. "When did you return?"

Sunlight burnished the captain's iron gray, close-cropped hair and highlighted the light brown eyes beneath his bushy brows. "Just now. Please excuse my dirt, Your Highness."

"If you'll excuse mine."

The dog barked and drew their attention to the boy for a moment.

"How much, Blue Eyes?"

Srilani's lips lifted at the corners. How long had it been since she'd heard that nickname? "He's satisfied with sweets from the kitchens. I've worked out an arrangement with the head cook."

"I remember paying you the same wage when you were a little girl."

She laughed. "I learned from the best."

He coughed and looked pleased, but then his grin faded. "I need to report to your father. Can you arrange for Judge Elison to be present at two bells this afternoon?"

"It's that important?"

"I'm afraid so."

"I'll do my best." With an effort, she kept worry from showing on her face. "His Honor has good days and bad days. Hopefully, he'll feel well enough to attend."

Olson held out his arm, and she clasped it in the traditional salute of the Palace Guard. "I know I can depend on you, Daughter." He released her forearm. "Even if Judge Elison isn't able to attend, please come to act as his eyes and ears."

"I'll be there." Life would be much easier if Olson really was her father. She pushed back a strand of blonde hair and tucked it into her braid. "Thank you for including me. You know how Father is."

"I do." Olson's voice turned gruff. "Your father is blind where you're concerned."

⋀

Two hours later, Srilani dipped the tip of her quill into the ink pot and resumed taking notes. She sat at Judge Elison's elbow in the War Room and listened intently. Outside, the promised storm had arrived, and the small window set high in the stone wall streamed with rain.

Captain Olson's report concerned his covert mission along the Norland border and down the coast. He spread his hands out to his sides and let them fall. "Your Majesty, I know you have other worries, but the facts are alarming. My men and I have verified over one hundred people taken by the Norlan troops and pirates in border and coastal raids."

Srilani could remain silent no longer. "One hundred? Since the winter solstice?"

"Yes, Your Highness."

She pulled the quill's feathery end through her fingers as she did some quick calculations in her head. "That's almost one per day."

The captain nodded, his brows forming a deep *V*. "Not counting the scores of reports we haven't been able to verify."

Srilani glanced at her father. King Terson sat near the middle of the long table, looking across its surface at the captain. Usually, he discouraged her from taking an active part in his meetings. He hadn't objected to her first question, so she pressed on. "Is there any kind of pattern to the raids? Do the locations have anything in common? Whom do they prefer to abduct?"

Judge Elison, her law teacher and mentor, nodded. He'd taught her to pay attention to details, to analyze facts, to think logically, and to ask questions like a master of the law.

Olson paced in front of the table. "In fact, the raids concentrate on villages far from the barons' estates."

That made sense — go where the people lived but stay away from the protected areas.

The captain continued, "Occasionally, the Norlanders take random people from the countryside, probably as they have the opportunity. As far as the types of people, the raiders usually steal men and women fifteen to twenty-five years old. Young, strong, and fit for hard labor."

Srilani's stomach clenched. They might enslave the young men to work in their fields, but the young women would be lucky if that was all they were made to do. She'd heard whispered tales of captivity in brothels. *El, why are people so cruel?*

She feigned interest in writing her notes, but all her attention was focused on her father. The silence stretched out, punctuated by a rumble of thunder.

She suppressed the urge to fidget.

From under her lashes, Srilani watched her younger brother, Prince Jamson. He sat at their father's right hand, inching a piece of parchment back and forth. Jamson was a thirteen-year-old version of Father — straight brown hair, strong jaw, and snapping greenish-brown eyes. His face gave every indication that he was following the conversation with interest, but Srilani would bet her prized longbow that his mind was far, far away from the War Room. He was too young to care about these issues.

At last, her father spoke. "What are your recommendations, Captain?" His voice sounded disinterested. Remote.

How could he be so detached about this?

"With all due respect, Your Majesty, the barons need extra men to help them guard the northern border. Invest more of your men at the Cauldron Fortress. Assign extra patrols for a few of your ships. At least that would make those twice-cursed Norlan pirates more cautious about approaching our shores. We might even sink a few of their ships."

Srilani finished writing the last point and raised her quill, ready for more. Olson's suggestions made perfect sense. A flash of light outside highlighted her father's face for an instant, and a crackle of thunder followed. Why didn't he say something? What was he waiting for?

King Terson lowered his eyes to the parchments, maps, and scrolls that covered the table. "We're already stretched thin because of the Southern threat, Captain. I don't believe I can dedicate more resources away from the capital city and the Marst River forts."

Her father's words repeated in her mind. Just like that? Hadn't he heard anything Olson was saying? Pressure built behind her eyes.

King Terson turned to Judge Elison. "What say you, Your Honor?"

Elison's ancient, milky eyes were hooded, his wizened face pinched with pain.

Srilani bit her lip. Surely, Father would heed Elison.

Elison looked in the king's direction even though he was now completely blind. "Captain Olson has given you wise suggestions, my son." The counselor spoke with authority. "I've told you that my visions show a son of

Mardan uniting the Twin Kingdoms. I've told you this before. The true threat is from our old enemy, King Dzor of Norland."

The corners of Terson's mouth turned down, and his gaze briefly went to Jamson's face. He shook his head. "I believe what you say is true, Your Honor, but it was you who taught me that El's timing doesn't always line up the way we want."

Elison's hands tightened on the head of his cane, but he didn't interrupt.

"Currently, the only living son of Mardan is either me or my son," Terson said. "It seems unlikely that either of us has the ability to unite the Twin Kingdoms. Perhaps your visions are about Jamson's son or grandson."

He straightened the parchments in front of him. "One thing is clear — Habidan is gathering an army in Southern Marst, and their only possible target is us. Many Southerners grew up hearing stories of the Twin Kingdoms War. Some of the old Southerners took part in the fighting. There are still so many hard feelings."

A fire ignited deep inside Srilani. How could her father brush off a vision from El? If she hadn't been present to hear him say the words, she would never have believed it. He'd directly contradicted Judge Elison. She clamped her lips together and tried to recite genealogies. *Mardan begat twin sons, Kaedan and Kaeson. Kaedan begat a son and three daughters.*

Captain Olson clasped his hands behind his back and rocked from his heels to his toes. "What will you do to stop the raids, Sire?"

Her father rapped his knuckles on the table like he always did before he made a royal pronouncement. "We will take your recommendations into consideration, Captain Olson, and make our decision after the Solstice Festival."

"No!" The objection burst from Srilani's lips before she could stop it. Judge Elison flinched at her side, and the captain froze. Terson and Jamson stared, two pairs of hazel eyes boring into her face.

She shook her head. "You can't possibly mean to wait that long, Father."

His expression hardened, and she rushed to make her point. "The Solstice Festival is almost three weeks away and more people will be stolen. It's like condemning them to death — only worse." The fire inside raged and the words boiled up. "Why can't we ask for volunteers to ride the frontiers? What would it hurt? We can't stand by and let this situation continue unchallenged."

"This requires thought and planning, Srilani."

"I know. I know it does, but you're consciously choosing to delay." She waved her hand in Elison's direction. "And how can you contradict Judge Elison?"

"I don't appreciate your tone, Daughter." A vein throbbed in her father's temple. "And I didn't contradict Judge Elison."

"You did. When he said the threat is from Norland, you said it was from Southern Marst."

"Obviously, there are two threats, Daughter." He bit off each word. *Daughter* sounded more like a curse than an endearment. "I said I would take Olson's recommendations into consideration."

"But—"

"You're out of line."

She stared at her father's forbidding expression. When had he decided she wasn't worthy? Why didn't her opinions count? He'd insisted on educating her to think like a leader, but he didn't want her to act like one. He wouldn't even listen to her ideas.

"How? How am I out of line?" Srilani's heart beat so hard that it hurt her ears. She'd never spoken to her father in this way. "All I'm saying is that you shouldn't wait so long. Our people need our help."

"What's clear to me—"

She raised her voice over his. "To wait is negligent. It's a terrible thing to do — practically criminal." Her fingers bent the quill until it snapped, splattering her hand and wrist with ink.

Terson's chair flew back as he stood up. "Out." His voice was low, controlled, and coldly furious. A long rumble of thunder reverberated through the floor and walls as if to emphasize her father's anger. "Get out of my sight."

She stared at the black ink drops dripping like old blood onto her pale skin.

Captain Olson came to her side, brought out a handkerchief, and wrapped it around her hand. He urged her to rise with a hand beneath her elbow. "Come, Daughter. Let's go find your maid."

Her father picked up her notes and passed them to Jamson. His voice was noticeably warmer as he said, "Get a fresh quill and finish the notes, Son."

She raised her chin and straightened her shoulders. She refused to look in her father's direction as Olson led her out into the corridor, but once the doors were shut, she stopped and her shoulders slumped. Unshed tears brimmed, and she stared hard at the beamed ceiling above, blinking rapidly.

"What did I do?"

Olson gave a weak chuckle. "You said what I wanted to say." His fingers squeezed her wrist. "May El bless you, Princess."

※

"No, Ana, not this dress. I'm meeting Lieutenant Greyson today, and this dress . . . I'm sorry. Let's make it the one with the lace at the neckline." Srilani turned away from her looking glass as she unfastened the gown. She sighed. White. The curse of being a princess of Marst — white clothes.

Ana bit her lip and lowered her eyes. "Yes, my lady."

"Be careful of my hair. It's perfect like it is."

"Yes, my lady."

Ana worked efficiently to exchange the first dress for the second, and Srilani peered at her reflection in the mirror. After she was married, she would never wear white clothes again. *Praise El.*

Would Greyson like her? Would she like him? Her father seemed exceptionally pleased with himself this time, and soon she would have to make her final choice.

Since her sixteenth summer, King Terson had introduced her to one potential husband after another at every Third Day banquet. Some of the men were as young as she, some were older, and one had been nearly as old as her parents. She suppressed a shudder. What had they been thinking?

Now that she was seventeen, her time to choose was almost up. She would turn eighteen in the autumn, an old maid by most standards.

A soft knock drew Ana to the door of Srilani's sitting room. She admitted sixteen-year-old René carrying their baby sister, Audrilan. René's maid followed them inside.

"Shur-ee! Shur-ee!" Audrilan held out her arms, straining toward Srilani. René set the little girl on her feet.

"Audri. Come here to Sister," Srilani said, crouching with outstretched hands. She scooped Audri into a hug, kissed her plump cheeks, and stroked her blonde curls. "How's my favorite girl?"

Audrilan launched into an unintelligible story. Srilani sat with the child in her lap. She asked silly questions to make Audri laugh and stole more kisses.

René laughed too. "Nobody at court would recognize you if they saw you playing with Audri. You're like an entirely different person in this room."

"The court expects me to act like a princess." Srilani pulled Audri close. "This is the real me. How was your day? I miss having lessons with you."

"Not as much as I miss you. Maelan only cares about horses, dogs, and the garden." René rolled her eyes. "She's a wretched student. They should have paired her with Jamson so they could compete against each other." She leaned forward and studied the lace on Srilani's gown. "This is lovely. Are you excited to meet Greyson again?"

"Yes. Although Greyson would be a better match for you than for me. You're both so beautiful."

"Don't call me that." René's brilliant blue eyes narrowed. "I can't help the way I look. And don't — whatever you do — call Greyson beautiful. He's a man." She grinned and raised one slender brow. "Possibly the best-looking man who has ever walked on the earth, but not beautiful."

Srilani smiled back at René. "But is he smart? Can he make me laugh? Do we have other things in common?"

"For your sake, I hope so. I think Father is growing impatient." René turned to the maid who stood nearby. "Ana, you did a wonderful job of dressing Srilani this evening. I love the way you arranged her hair."

"Thank you, my lady."

Srilani's brow puckered. Had she even thanked Ana? Why couldn't she be as thoughtful and gracious as René? Audrilan snuggled her head into Srilani's shoulder, and she bent to kiss the child's forehead.

"We'd better go. Father sent a message that I'm supposed to arrive early."

Srilani, René, Audri, and the maids entered the Solarium together. The afternoon storm had passed and the evening's warm rays bathed the room's soaring white walls and arches in rich amber. Many chairs, couches, and benches were arranged in small groups among the columns supporting the high ceiling. Tall windows facing the north, south, and east framed the room.

Lady Kaelan, their mother, looked up from her customary rocking chair. She had married their father while his mother was still queen, and she had never been comfortable with the title of queen even after Grandmother had passed away. She held out her arms to receive Audrilan. "My dears, you all look lovely."

"Thank you, Mother," Srilani said. Her eyes drifted to her father who sat in the large armchair next to her mother. "May El bless you, Father."

Slowly, his eyes rose to her face. His usual expression had altered in some subtle way she couldn't identify. He set aside the roll of parchment he'd been reading. "Your mother reminded me of an item that was overlooked after your grandmother passed away." His voice, too, seemed cool to her.

Srilani's heart skipped a beat. "I beg your pardon?"

Her father stood, took her elbow, and guided her to a spot by the windows away from the others. She studied his face. Was the coolness she sensed a product of her imagination or the lingering effects of their confrontation?

He cleared his throat. "When my mother died, you were so young that we put this away." He drew a leather pouch from his pocket and poured a lovely silver chain into her hand. "I believe you should have it now."

A large oval aquamarine pendant, framed with crystals and pearls, winked back at her. "I remember this necklace," she said. "Grandmother used to let me play with this in her dressing room."

He glanced out the window toward the Great Gulf, visible from this vantage point, even though it was a couple of leagues away. "I had forgotten it entirely, but as I said, your mother brought it to my attention."

She hesitated. "Would you fasten it for me?"

"Of course." She turned around, and he worked the clasp.

She twisted the pendant back and forth to catch the light in the stone — fire trapped in pale blue ice. She turned back to her father. "I love it."

"My mother specifically willed it to you." His voice sounded solemn. "You are very like her."

"Thank you, Father." She reached out to him, and he permitted her a brief embrace.

"There's something else, Srilani."

She stepped back, but he retained one of her hands. "You're almost eighteen. You need to make a choice from the men I've presented to you." His voice seemed to come from a long way off. "Lieutenant Greyson is the last one I plan to introduce. If there is another man you would like to meet, you must let me know. If you cannot choose by the time you turn eighteen, then I will choose a husband for you. Do you understand?"

She nodded. He would take the choice out of her hands. Her lips firmed. Not if she could help it.

"Do you understand?" Terson repeated.

"Yes, Father. I understand."

Sol's golden light faded to mauve, and Srilani struggled to be patient. Soon, eight bells would toll — time to go into the Great Hall. She turned to her parents. "Where are the twins?"

"Late, as usual," Terson said. His fingers beat a tattoo on the arm of his chair.

"Well, don't blame Patience," Kaelan said. A mischievous smile lit her beautiful face. "She's dealing with Maelan. Your daughter is just like you, you know."

Terson's hazel eyes twinkled as he met Kaelan's glance. "Maelan has my coloring, but she inherited her sauciness from you, my dear."

Srilani's fingers closed around the pendant of her grandmother's necklace. Her parents' marriage was a love match, not an arranged marriage like the one she faced. The difference between being a prince and a princess came down to choice — her father had been free to choose a wife for himself. He spoke of her "choice" of husband, then gave her a deadline for love. If only El granted her request for a marriage founded on mutual respect. Certainly, she prayed for more respect than she received from Father.

The guards opened the Solarium doors to admit the twins and Patience, their nurse turned keeper. Jamson looked irked and out of sorts. Maelan, his twin, wore an identical expression on her face.

Jamson stationed himself in front of his mother. "Why do we have to go to the banquet?"

Maelan stood at his side and pushed her straight brown hair behind her ears. "We were watching Midnight Star have her foal, and—"

Jamson finished Maelan's sentence. " — we don't even know if it's a colt or a filly."

"I wonder if it's black like Midnight Star."

"Or chestnut like Sol's Light."

"When can we go back to see it?"

"Hush, and let Mother answer," Srilani said with a snap.

Lady Kaelan stood and handed Audrilan to the nurse. "Thank you, Patience. You've lived up to your name once more."

"You're welcome, Madame." Patience's rich, soothing alto voice belied her iron will. She gave the twins a stern look. "Mind your manners. Nobody would guess you're almost fourteen, the way you're acting. I will ask someone to find out about the foal for you, and you may visit Midnight Star and her new baby after breakfast tomorrow."

Maelan opened her mouth to object, and Patience held up a hand for silence. "No arguments, or you'll wait longer." She joggled Audrilan on her hip and left the room like a ship under full sail.

Srilani's eyes met René's, and they shared a smile. Jamson was heir to the kingdom, but Patience still ruled the nursery.

The giant bell in the center tower tolled — eight slow strokes echoed through the palace. Their mother smoothed Maelan's hair and examined Jamson's appearance one last time. "Come along," she said. "It's rude to be late."

Jamson's mouth formed a mutinous line. The twins put their heads together as they followed their parents out of the Solarium and started an intense conversation in undertones.

René shook her head. "Were we ever that young?"

"Oh, like you're such an old lady at sixteen," Srilani said. "You'll need a cane soon."

The sisters followed their parents and younger siblings up the middle aisle between the long rows of tables arranged in the Great Hall. The hall was full. Barons, their families, visiting dignitaries, servants — all the people stopped their activities to rise and pay homage to the royal family.

Srilani ignored the crowd. Instead, she searched the small group of Palace Guard officers standing on the dais. Her great friend, General Bertson, came to attention beside Lieutenant Greyson's father, Captain Corson. Next to the captain, interested in everything around him, stood Greyson — blond, breathtaking, and mysterious.

"There he is," René whispered.

"I know." The thumping of Srilani's heart behind her breastbone reached an uncomfortable velocity, and her lungs burned. She released her breath in a quiet whoosh, working hard to keep her face serene.

René leaned toward her. "Enjoy the banquet. Give me the sign if you want to be rescued."

Srilani took her place behind her chair, keeping her eyes lowered. Greyson's boots were shiny and new-looking. Her sleeve was a bare inch from his. His hands folded together and she almost missed her cue. She pressed her hands together and raised them to her forehead as Judge Elison proclaimed the benediction.

The prayer ended, but Greyson continued to pray for some moments longer. Then his eyes — blue as the sea — opened and stared directly into hers.

Unbelievable. The man was even more glorious up close.

"Daughter, you've met Lieutenant Greyson before, I believe."

Her father's voice brought her back to earth, and she broke away from Greyson's spell.

"Yes, Father." She gathered her wits and extended her hand to Greyson. "It is a pleasure to meet you again after so long, Lieutenant."

He took her hand to his lips, the lightest of salutes, and released it with an admiring smile. "The pleasure is mine, Your Highness. May El bless you."

Training came to her rescue. "May El bless you." *Stop staring like a child of four and follow the routine.*

Greyson pulled out her chair. She sank down onto it and busied herself with the meal, stealing occasional glimpses at her dinner companion. Of course, Elison had briefed her about the lieutenant — twenty-three years old, heir to Merripan, latecomer to the Palace Guard.

She possessed a ready store of conversational gambits but let the moments pass until the servants brought the second course. "Do you like the barracks? Are they comfortable?"

Face serious, he turned in his chair. "Naturally, I miss Merripan, but I do enjoy living in the barracks. Besides, home doesn't seem like home without Grandfather. He was my best friend."

Srilani's fingers tightened on her napkin. Just her luck to choose a poor topic right off. "I've heard of your loss, and I am sorry if I caused you pain by reminding you."

"Don't worry. Grandfather's murder grieves me, but I like to talk about him, to remember the time we had together."

"You must take comfort that your father is in the Palace Guard with you."

"No." Greyson shook his head. His lips thinned and his face looked severe, almost angry. "My father and I agree on nothing. Not one thing."

Srilani lifted her goblet of wine and took a sip, a way to let the moment pass. At least she could relate to Greyson's apparent conflict with his father.

Greyson ate a few bites of the meal before he continued in a warmer tone. "I have enjoyed being here among those my own age." He lowered his voice. "Our steward had no sons, and all the other boys my age were servants, working with their fathers. Hanna, the steward's daughter, was the only friend my age."

"I met Hanna a couple of years ago," Srilani said. Was he trying to hint her away because he had an affection for Hanna?

"Grandfather didn't permit us to spend much time together because . . . Well, he had his reasons. Besides, she left the estate when she married at fifteen."

"I thought she was widowed."

Greyson shrugged. "Yes and no — her first husband died during their first year together, but fortunately for Hanna, another man offered for her."

Greyson didn't seem to miss the company of Hanna the steward's daughter. Good. "You are new to the Palace Guard. I haven't seen you on duty yet."

A flush worked its way across his smooth cheeks. "The sergeants have to break me first."

She smiled at his rueful look.

"You know what breaking involves, I see," he said and gave her a conspiratorial grin. "This is the first time I've been allowed to eat a full meal in weeks."

Srilani laughed. "I do know. My father has told me of his experiences in the Guard." She raised her glass and met his eyes over the rim. "To a full meal."

She allowed him to savor the food for several minutes before launching into a new topic. "What do you think of Kaeson?"

Third Day banquets extended long into the evening hours — course after course — but this night, the time flew by. Terson and Kaelan rose from their places at the head table and descended from the dais to signal the end of the meal.

René stood ready to rescue her if Greyson turned out to be a bore, but Srilani shook her head ever so slightly. René would tease her later, but spending more time with Greyson would be worth the aggravation. Before she could ask him to escort her around the Great Hall, Greyson made his own request.

"Princess Srilani, would you do me a favor? Would you introduce me to some of the other guests?"

Her eyes narrowed. Was he being clever? If he thought to use her because she was First Princess, she would be sure to correct him. Greyson's eyes were clear and guileless as he waited for her answer.

"Fine." She placed her fingertips on his extended arm. Better to give him the benefit of the doubt. Her maid trailed them around the enormous hall, a silent witness to every conversation. Better not to think of the awkwardness of that fact.

Tonight, everyone seemed determined to greet her and her handsome escort. Avid curiosity permeated each short encounter. Captain Corson, Greyson's father, and a stately older woman approached them near the back doors.

"Do you know Lady Goslan, my father's cousin?" Greyson said.

"Yes, I do. She's a frequent visitor at court."

Srilani was seven years old when she figured out the true reasons for the Third Day banquets — to maintain power, to stay close to friends, and to keep an eye on potential enemies. Each week, Judge Elison took pains to advise her on topics for discussion and how to approach the most difficult personalities of the court.

Greyson offered a small bow to the captain. "Father."

Corson nodded once, his answer clipped and cool. "Greyson."

"How do you do, Cousin?" Greyson bowed over Lady Goslan's bony hand.

Srilani hid a smile. He moved with innate dignity at odds with his age, as if an old man were trapped inside his young man's body.

"I am well, Cousin Greyson." Her bright eyes were on Srilani as she spoke. "Your Highness, I'm happy to see you in such good looks tonight." The older woman dipped into a curtsy. "May El bless you."

"Thank you." Srilani had always admired Goslan's poise and sense of style. The baroness was handsome in a severe way, every hair in place, dressed in an elegant gown that disguised her twig-thin figure.

Goslan's watchful gaze slid back to Greyson. "Corson, you didn't mention that your son had grown so very delightfully handsome. It's been far, far too long since I've seen you, young man." She stepped back to study him from head to toe. "You couldn't choose a better looking man as your lover, Princess."

Srilani inhaled sharply, and the blood drained from her face. Greyson's arm grew taut beneath her fingers. Behind them, Ana's gasp sounded like the hiss of a cat.

Lover. Not beloved. Not suitor. Srilani stiffened her knees to keep from swaying. Outrageous. Insufferable.

Goslan smoothed the sleeve of Greyson's other arm. "No, no, Cousin, relax. I meant no offense. I was merely commenting on what a striking couple you make — you both have such a look of Mardan about you."

Greyson extracted his arm from beneath his cousin's hand. "You are embarrassing the princess, Lady Goslan. Please excuse us — there are others waiting to speak to Her Highness." He bowed to his cousin and father. "Good night."

Srilani allowed him to lead her away. The old biddy. Surely Lady Goslan knew that rumors about a princess could prove fatal. If officers of the Palace Guard thought the gossip was true, she could be executed without so much as a trial.

Greyson covered her hand on his arm. "I apologize for my relatives, my lady. My father is a cold fish, and Lady Goslan always says exactly what she thinks. Now I remember why I try to avoid her."

"I would never—" Shame choked off Srilani's response.

"I know."

"How could she—"

"I'm sorry."

Srilani forced her emotions into the secret place where she hid them from public view. Bitter experience had taught her that most people wanted to believe the worst of her without the least bit of evidence. She raised her eyes to search his. Nothing in his steady gaze suggested doubts about her purity. Gallant to the end.

"Thank you," she said.

"You're welcome, my lady." Greyson cleared his throat. "So . . . I haven't met the general, yet. Would you introduce us?"

CHAPTER THREE

Srilani stooped to turn over a shark's eye shell, perfect and unbroken, at the edge of the surf. She picked it up and handed it to René.

The sea shimmered like glass on Sol's brightest, longest day. Far to the south, the pavilions of the Solstice Festival, tiny and colorful, flickered in the waves of heat rising from the white beach sand. To the north, a wall of limestone shielded their destination, the private grotto reserved for the royal family.

Her earliest recollection of this place was from before she could read. Her father and mother and her grandmother, too, had come to the grotto to play in the surf. The memories seemed unreal now, especially after the last three weeks of silence from her father. He'd spoken to her only when necessary.

"Why the long face?" René dropped the shell into her drawstring bag. "Are you sad Greyson isn't part of our escort today?"

"Not in front of the twins," Srilani whispered. "And not when *he's* around."

"The twins aren't listening." René glanced over her shoulder at Captain Corson, trailing them as they walked. He was one of four guards — a small group by normal standards. "He's too far behind us to hear."

"Still. Don't talk about Greyson in front of his father."

René lowered her voice. "The captain can't read lips. I think General Bertson fixed the duty roster so Greyson would be assigned to you every day." She grinned. "Well, every day until today. I never suspected the general of being a romantic person."

Srilani sighed. René couldn't leave the topic of Greyson alone — no detail, no look or touch escaped her attention. "Be realistic," she said. "If Bertson altered the duty roster, his reasons were more rational than promoting true love."

"Huh. The end result would be the same."

"You're forgetting that Captain Corson is the officer of the watch this quarter. Corson created the duty roster."

"So?" René grinned. "General Bertson approved it."

"Can we talk about something else?" Srilani bent down to examine another group of shells. The opinions of the senior officers had to be factored into her decision about accepting or rejecting a marriage proposal from Greyson. Bertson probably did approve of Greyson or he would have reassigned the lieutenant to other duties. Greyson's father, too, must approve of the match. She couldn't read Captain Corson — he rarely spoke to her and never put himself forward in her presence.

She stood and brushed the sand from her hands. "Do you want to sail out in the *Skylark* before the day is over?"

"Yes. If Mother and Father ever return. They love that boat." René shook her head. "I like sailing, but I don't love it. Not like they do."

Srilani shrugged and adjusted her belt to keep her linen tunic from billowing in the warm sea breeze. "Sailing in the *Skylark* reminds them of their courtship. They love the memories, so they love sailing."

René's beautiful smile turned mischievous. "So years from now, you'll love the Third Day banquets. Right?"

"Hush. You know, not many people would suspect how annoying you can be. Let's catch up with General Bertson and the twins."

Jamson and Maelan flanked the general on the path ahead. Their other two guards reached the entryway and vanished around the bend. Srilani and René struggled to make up the distance.

Srilani glanced back. Captain Corson walked twenty paces behind them, close enough to see them but far enough away to give them privacy. They reached the wall of rock leading to the grotto. The limestone rose into the sky, standing between them and the surf line and cutting off the breeze.

René fanned her face. "I've changed my mind — I would love to be out on the *Skylark* with the wind in my face."

Srilani kept her thoughts to herself. Sailing couldn't compare with a cool bath in the shade of her room and preparing for the Third Day Banquet tonight. Greyson would dine with her again — a special feast since it coincided with the end of the Solstice Festival.

Not that she loved Greyson in a romantic way — yet — but his friendship and respect were better than any of her other options. Perhaps love would develop over time. Her brow crinkled. Greyson's behavior indicated a growing and warm affection toward her. Was it fair to encourage him? What if she were a cold person by nature?

"Stop."

"What?"

René hopped a couple of times on one foot. "I have a pebble caught in my sandal and it really hurts."

"Oh, sorry. Here, hold onto me and shake out your shoe."

By the time René finished, General Bertson and the twins were out of sight. Srilani looked behind them. Corson had stopped too, maintaining his distance.

A scream echoed among the rocks. *Maelan!*

Srilani broke into a run, laboring over the deep sand. René panted at her heels. They reached the entry to the hidden bay.

One of their guards — Luke? — sprawled, face to the ground, dead or dying. His crimson blood glistened on the dirt. Their other guard fought against two large men. Bertson was pitted against three, valiantly trying to reach the twins.

Jamson and Maelan struggled against a pair of brigands apiece. The men held them down on the ground, binding them with blankets and ropes. Two longboats rested nearby.

"Pirates." Srilani looked for Corson. He hadn't entered the grotto yet. She raised her voice. "Corson! Help!" She shoved René. "Run. Get away from here."

Srilani raced to Luke's body and grabbed his sword from the damp sand.

Surprise was on her side, and she managed to wound one of the ruffians attacking Bertson. Her blade left his flesh with a squishing sound, and bile rose in her throat. The pirate fell to his knees, cursing and grasping his sword arm.

René screamed. She screamed again.

Srilani blocked a blow from another pirate. Sweat streamed down his naked torso as he feinted toward her with a wicked-looking dagger. In his other hand, he brandished a stout club that he used to parry her counter-attack. She skipped back, circling to the right, trying to take in the situation. Bertson's tunic was ripped and bloody. He staggered.

Her opponent lunged at her again. A huff of pain announced the defeat of their fourth and last guard, and Srilani fought with renewed desperation. She retreated a few steps to draw the pirates away from the officers.

Jamson shouted. "Look out!"

Hairy arms encircled her from behind, and a club struck her temple. Black darkness pulled her into a never-ending void.

The Cathartid, *off the coast of Northern Marst*

Aldan leaned over the ship's railing. Three figures, cocooned in bright Norlander blankets and secured with ropes, reposed in the bottom of the first longboat. Two girls and a boy. The second longboat held another young woman, bound like the rest. He released the rail and turned away. All around him, the crew gloated and jeered over their latest haul.

Sam joined him at the rail. He let out a low whistle. "Take a look at those girls. Have you ever seen the like?"

"No." Aldan frowned and kept his back to the action below.

"What? That's all you have to say?" Sam punched his shoulder. "I haven't seen women like those since I was a boy in Port Azor. It doesn't hurt to look, does it?"

"Not as long as Rozar doesn't catch you."

"It'd be worth a thrashing for a closer look. What's wrong with you?"

Aldan turned to watch the crew raise the younger boy and girl over the side of the ship in a net. The brother and sister were copies of one another. Twins, fast asleep thanks to the captain's sleeping potion.

Of course. It wouldn't do to damage the merchandise.

The twins were lowered to the deck. Several seamen moved away from their vicinity, and one man waved his hand in a warding gesture. Why were twins considered such a bad omen? Aldan snorted. The numerous, conflicting superstitions of the crew were entirely illogical.

The next captive appeared to be a very young woman, perhaps fifteen or sixteen summers, and without a doubt, the most beautiful female Aldan had ever seen — fair, blonde, and curved in all the right places. Her head lolled back as they placed her beside the others.

"They've ruined her life," he said. He glared at Sam. "Don't you feel any pity?"

Sam shrugged. "I guess."

"I know, I know. Pity does them no good, but I hate this." He pointed. "They injured that one."

The last girl, older than the rest, had a purplish bump forming on her temple, just beneath long blonde curls. Her eyes were closed, but Aldan would bet his next meal they were blue. Fair hair and light-colored eyes, uncommon along the coast of the Great Gulf, brought the highest prices in the slave market.

"Yeah, well . . . I heard she put up a fight. She'll recover."

Captain Rozar glowed with triumph as he stood over his prizes. "Step lively. Get those longboats aboard. We need to be in Port Azor yesterday." The men responded with a roar of excitement. The captain scanned the crowd of men and beckoned to Aldan and Sam.

"Samazor, you take that one. Aldan, take the boy." He paused, frowning. "Where's Linus?"

"Here."

Rozar spun about with a snarl. "Drat you, Linus. Always were a sneaking, black shadow. Take the youngest girl." Rozar sent another man to fetch Mirza.

"I'll do the honors with this beauty. Follow me." The captain lifted the young woman with the bump on her forehead. Without ceremony, he slung his burden over one shoulder and descended the ladder.

Aldan eased the boy into position. Below deck, he laid the boy in the cabin they'd prepared weeks ago. Sam entered the cabin and seemed to take extra care not to thump the girl's head on the planks as he put her down. Linus brought up the rear with the other twin. The captives bore a strong family resemblance in spite of the difference in hair color.

Rozar ran an experimental finger over the knot on the oldest girl's forehead. His walnut skin grew dark with temper. "I should flog that good-for-nothing Fratz for hitting her. We're lucky he didn't kill her, but now she has a bruise."

The captain had reached boiling point by the time Mirza shuffled into the cabin in her usual lethargic fashion. "Witch! If you weighed more, I'd use you for an anchor. You know I hate to wait." He jabbed a finger at her skinny chest. "Take care of my prizes."

"But—"

"It has to be you because you're the only woman aboard. Earn your keep. And don't jabber on about your so-called spiritual duties. We both know you're a fraud."

Rozar strode to the door before turning to his slaves. "Aldan, stay here and make yourself useful. Samazor and Linus, why are you just standing there? If you don't have enough work, just say so. Out."

Mirza took the only chair in the cabin and settled back for a nap.

"Shouldn't we unwrap them?" Aldan said.

"Boy, when I want your advice, I'll ask. Be quiet and let me rest."

"Like always."

"Shut it, or I'll make your life a misery."

"Like always."

She glared at him for a moment, then shut her eyes.

He slouched against the wall by the door, closed his eyes, and woke with a start, drenched in sweat. He glanced at the captives. The young beauty moaned. Aldan pushed off the floor and poked Mirza's shoulder.

"What? Oh, it's you." Her mouth screwed up in a lemony pucker. "Why'd you wake me up for?"

"One of them is awake."

"So?"

"They'll all be awake soon, and they're getting too hot in those blankets. Rozar will be angry if they smother to death because you left them wrapped up."

Mirza's laugh sounded more like a cough. "So unwrap them."

"I'm not getting a beating for your laziness, Mirza."

"Afraid to touch them, *eh*?" She grinned, showing all of her missing teeth. "I could say you did anyway."

Aldan adopted a casual stance, arms crossed, leaning against the door. "Rozar wouldn't believe you."

The witch cocked her head to the side like a crow, studying him with her beady black eyes. He refused to look away, and after a few tense moments, she gave in. "Oh, all right! Get away from me. Can't a body get no rest around here?"

CHAPTER FOUR

Excerpt from *Histories of the Twin Kingdoms*
Written by the hand of Corson, Baron of Merripan
Captain of the Palace Guard in Kaeson

To His Sovereign Majesty, Terson
Baron of Kaeson
King of Mardan's Northern Domain

May it please Your Majesty, forgive your humble servant for communicating bad news.

It is my sad duty to write an account of the events of the day of the Solstice Festival, to the full extent of my knowledge and memory. Your servant was assigned to accompany the four eldest royal children throughout that day. I was one of four officers on the detail. To my eternal shame, I am the sole survivor of that group.

The deceased officers are: His Excellency, General Bertson, Commander of the forces of Northern Marst; and Captain Luke, son of Soleste Barony; and Lieutenant Evan, son and heir of Caldera Barony. Though it seems strange in hindsight, General Bertson, having a strong affection for the royal children, volunteered for this duty assignment. He died valiantly as befits a general officer. May our brothers rest in peace. Their loss is greatly mourned.

As is their custom on every Solstice Festival, the royal children elected to go to the hidden bay north of Kaeson, well known to Your Majesty. Captain Luke and Lieutenant Evan took point and reached the grotto first. General Bertson stayed with Prince Jamson and Princess Maelan. I took rear guard behind First Princess Srilani and Princess Renélan. During the course of the day, the eldest daughters lingered a fair distance behind the others.

Those officers on point entered the grotto, followed shortly thereafter by the general and the twins. At that time, we heard screams, whereupon we went to their aid. Unfortunately, we were not in time to help.

The eldest daughters ran ahead of me, heedless of danger. I arrived soon after, but the damage was already done. Ten pirates in two longboats ambushed our men and the children as soon as they entered the sheltered area. I saw that the three officers were dead and the three youngest children had been taken offshore in one of the longboats. I also saw a man strike down First Princess Srilani, who had bravely attempted a defense. Initially, I feared the worst had befallen her, but the pirates bound her for captivity and put her in their boat. We may conclude from their behavior that, if it be the will of El, your eldest daughter still lives.

My decision at that time, for which I accept full responsibility, was to make haste to Kaeson. There, I immediately communicated the situation to my brothers in the Palace Guard and assisted in the initial attempts to rescue the royal children.

CHAPTER FIVE

The Cathartid, *Great Gulf*

Srilani slogged over a dune of white, blistering sand. Sol's heat burned her, and thirst glued her tongue to the roof of her mouth. A vulture swooped low and blotted out the light. Its wings brushed her face.

The vulture squawked. "Finally. She's awake."

Srilani squinted at the bird. She was nose-to-nose with a shriveled brown face framed by a black headdress. Not a bird — a crone, missing several teeth and speaking Norlan. Filthy gray hair hung in untidy wisps beside beetle-bright eyes.

"Well, my fine lady. Made me miss my supper, you did."

The woman's stench was overpowering. Did she never wash? Her face disappeared from Srilani's line of vision.

A moment passed, and then a familiar voice spoke near her ear. "I'm so glad you're alive."

Srilani turned her head, and dizzying pain stabbed into her temple. Black dots threatened to obscure her view of René's tear-stained features. They were side-by-side on a plank floor in a gray, gritty room. A heaving motion, accompanied by a bouquet of musty oak, salty brine, and sweat, told her they were aboard a sailing ship.

"I was afraid you were going to die," René whispered. "How does your head feel?"

Srilani's voice was a dry husk. "Hurts. Where are we?"

"We're on a pirate ship."

Srilani closed her eyes. *El, why?* Nothing could be worse than falling into the hands of Norlan pirates — except for everything that was sure to follow. Her stomach flipped over and she choked back the urge to vomit. A paroxysm of coughing racked her body.

The cabin door slapped open, and a tall man wearing clothes of unrelieved black strode into the compartment. The tattoo of an angry alligator poised to strike snarled on his cheekbone, the mark of Azor, god of their enemies. His gaze swept over the group and zeroed in on Srilani.

She struggled to suppress her coughs.

"They're awake," the man said. "Aldan, fetch water. Make it quick." His voice was a steely rasp. His lips thinned into a cruel line, and he turned on the old woman. "Why are they still wrapped up? You were supposed to take care of my prizes, not keep them tied up, you good-for-nothing hag!"

Srilani had difficulty interpreting his words. His rapid Norlan speech didn't sound anything like her tutor back home.

"They are too many for me. I was afraid."

"Ha! You're just lazy, Mirza." He towered over her. "Aldan was here. They couldn't possibly overpower you both in their present condition."

Another spate of coughs shook Srilani's body, and pain spiked into her brain. Hurried footsteps heralded the return of the servant named Aldan. He handed the man a cup of water.

The pirate stooped and slid his arm beneath Srilani's shoulders, lifting her head from the floor and placing the cup at her lips. His coat brushed against her face, and the scent of fine musk and cloves wafted into her nostrils.

The cool water soothed her scratchy throat and stilled the cough. She stared at him over the rim, and his eyes gleamed down at her, lustrous as black pearls. His face was creased and stained dark by years at sea, beard short and sharply trimmed.

"Welcome to my ship," he said in Marstan. "I am Rozar." He tilted the cup further, and she drank the rest.

His lips spread into an oily smile, and his voice dropped low. "Sweet Kaeson plum. I wish I could have a taste of you."

As if he sensed her revulsion, his smile widened. He handed the empty cup to Aldan and bent closer to smooth the hair from her forehead.

Was he going to kiss her after all?

Long, tanned fingers examined her temple. "Fratz will pay for this." He set her head down gently and rose to his full height.

Srilani sagged against the floor.

Captain Rozar advanced on Mirza and switched to Norlan. "Listen close, witch. Get them up. Feed them. We'll be in Port Azor in three days. If my prizes aren't in perfect condition, I'll throw you overboard."

Mirza's voice took on an obnoxious, wheedling tone. "Yes, Captain Rozar. As you say, sir. As you say."

He turned back to the sisters and bowed. "You have but to command, my ladies, and the *Cathartid* will provide. Don't worry. Only the best will do for you. King Dzor will be pleased to make your acquaintance. Perhaps you'll even get to join his concubines."

Rozar walked to the cot against the wall and peered down at the twins. He nodded. "These two are just right for servants of the court. We'll get a fortune for them from the nobles back home."

The captain addressed his servant. "Aldan, see if you can fit cots in here for our guests. Bring food and more water and see to their needs." He left the cabin without a backward glance. Aldan left too. The clatter of the door's iron latch falling into place sounded as final and hopeless as a death knell.

⋀⋀

Aldan's fists clenched as the door latch fell into its slot. So Sam was right. Rozar meant to give the young women to King Dzor. He schooled his expression, hiding any hint of emotion. At least he could make their voyage easier since Rozar had put them under his care.

A shout penetrated through the deck above. "There's a ship!" Other voices joined in. "Ship. Ship to starboard."

Captain Rozar sprinted along the corridor and ascended the ladder. Aldan followed at his heels. In moments, they reached the railing. Rozar pulled out his glass, snapped it open, and peered over the water. Long moments passed as Rozar studied the horizon. The noise on deck hushed as the *Cathartid* held her breath.

Aldan didn't need the glass. Two masts, as thin as needles, floated above the ocean. They were swept back, marking the craft as Norlan in design.

Aldan measured Sol's passage in the sky. He'd lost track of time since the captives arrived. At least two more hours before evening arrived. Enough light to see and be seen. Enough time for anything to happen. He found Sam and Linus among the crew on deck. And Scar. Aldan's eyes narrowed on Scar's face.

The burly first mate's expression was a quandary of warring emotions as he watched the captain observe the other ship through the glass — excitement, contempt, uncertainty. Hope? Now that the captives were safely on board, Scar could choose to make his move to take command at any time.

Rozar tucked the glass into his belt with a growl. "The *Falcon*, and she's coming 'round." The men who stood closest repeated his words in low murmurs, and the tension and restless anticipation on deck increased a hundredfold. The *Cathartid* lived to fight and take treasure. What was hers, was hers forever, and Azor curse the ship who thought to take it from her.

The captain put his back to the railing. All eyes focused on him as he drew his sword from its scabbard. "Fortune smiles on us — two treasures in one day." He swept the sword around in an arc and shouted, "To arms!"

The crew thundered their approval, and Aldan's heart echoed the thunder in his ears. His attention returned to the first mate.

Scar, as second-in-command, took up Rozar's shout. "To arms! To arms!" The two men worked in tandem to prepare the crew and ship for combat. Every hand pitched in to clear the deck of any impediment to action, every extra piece of gear, and anything of value.

Rozar beckoned to Aldan and pressed a key into his palm. "Keep it safe. I'll want it back when this is over."

Aldan raced to Rozar's cabin with the key and unlocked the lid of the captain's sea chest. The captain armed his slaves to defend the ship. In the early days, Aldan used to hide Linus, enslaved at the tender age of four or five, until the fighting was over, but Rozar put an end to that as soon as Linus could swing a weapon.

Aldan chose a sword and a dagger for himself from Rozar's stash. Sam and Linus entered the cabin as Aldan strapped the scabbard around his waist and laid the dagger aside.

Sam pressed close. "What do you have for us?"

Aldan selected another sword and an axe from the hoard and handed them to Sam.

"Wish we could keep these," Sam said. He examined the edge on his axe.

"You know Rozar always checks his weapons when the fighting's over." Aldan rummaged through the chest. "Just be glad we get to defend the ship. I'd go crazy if they locked us below."

"You defend the ship," Sam said with a snort. "I'll defend myself."

"It's the same thing." Aldan chose a mace and glanced at Linus with a raised brow.

Linus nodded and took the mace, a nasty club with metal flanges on top. His dark skin was off-color, a sickly gray, and sweat beaded on his upper lip.

"Stay with me, Linus. We'll watch each other's back," Aldan said. He tried for an encouraging tone. "You always do well in these fights."

Sam cuffed Linus on the shoulder. "Cheer up. If it's dark before it's over, you'll be invisible."

Linus jerked away with a glare, and Aldan frowned at Sam. "Someday, you'll go too far and he'll make you pay."

"What's he going to do?" Sam lifted his chin. "Smother me with silence?"

Aldan slammed the sea chest shut. "This isn't the time for your kind of humor."

Sam shrugged and stomped to the door.

"Wait," Aldan said. This wasn't the way they should part. "There's something else."

Sam turned, hand on the door handle. "Make it quick."

"Keep an eye on Scar. My gut says he's about to make his move. What better time than now?"

Sam's hand dropped, and his mouth thinned. "Too right." One shoulder lifted and his eyes glittered. "Rozar's not the only one who can have an accident during a battle."

Sam's off-hand remark chilled Aldan. Linus coughed, but it sounded more like a choke of laughter. Aldan glanced at his "little brother," but as usual, Linus's expression gave nothing away. Aldan changed the subject. "This is our chance to get more weapons and other things if we're careful about it."

"What do you have in mind?"

Mirza sneered at Srilani's prone form and gave her a sharp kick in the ribs. The witch addressed Srilani in Norlan as if speaking to an idiot, her words loud and slow. "Time to get up, your ladyship. Rise and shine." The hag tugged at the rope around Srilani's blanket and rolled her across the hard wooden planks a couple of times. "Help your sister."

Srilani fought her way out of the suffocating cocoon. The pain in her head surged, and she stumbled to her feet, dodging the lantern swinging from the center beam. Pins and needles shot down her arms and legs.

Through the deck above came the clear sounds of an uproar. Feet rumbled on the boards, sending down a dust cloud from the rafters. Mirza listened intently. "They're getting ready for a fight."

A thrill raced through Srilani. Could one of their father's ships be this close already?

The witch stalked to the door, gave the handle a useless tug, and cursed. "We're under attack, and I'm stuck here with you." She rounded on Srilani and screeched, still in Norlan, "Unwrap her!"

Srilani put a puzzled look on her face, feigning ignorance. Mirza pushed and shoved her about, making signs and repeating her instructions in stilted Marstan. Srilani reached down and untied the rope that secured René in her blanket.

René rose on shaky legs and wiped her face with the blanket. She threw herself into Srilani's arms. "Thank you. I couldn't bear that even one more minute. Are the twins uninjured?"

Srilani knelt with René beside the cot near the wall. The twins' breathing seemed smooth and natural.

The ship heeled over in a long turn. Were the pirates trying to flee? Could the pirates outrun their pursuers? *Oh please, El. Please rescue us.*

She sat on the low cot and pulled Maelan's head into her lap. René squeezed onto the other end, hefting Jamson across her lap with an effort. Mirza returned to her seat, her pinched face the only sign she might be worried.

The shouts and sounds grew louder, and several people ran back and forth in the corridor outside their cell. Did Rozar always tolerate this lack of discipline in his crew?

Maelan stirred and whimpered. "My head hurts."

"Shh, Maelan," Srilani said. "You'll feel better soon."

René's voice shook. "What do you think is happening?"

"I'm hoping for a rescue," Srilani whispered.

"I thought you told me all of father's ships were out of port."

"Yes, but I'm praying that I was wrong."

⋀⋀

Aldan stood beside Linus and Sam near the hatch as the *Falcon* raced toward them. The *Cathartid* rushed to meet her foe, and the ships closed the gap with breathtaking swiftness. The *Falcon*'s crew made ready with boarding ropes. Aldan shifted his sword to his left hand to wipe the palm of his right hand on his shirt.

When the *Cathartid* preyed on a merchant ship, the merchant crew, once subdued, could stand aside with fair certainty they'd be allowed to sail away empty-handed. Battles between pirate ships, natural rivals, were deadly matters. Such encounters often ended in the destruction of the defeated ship and her crew.

Aldan's thoughts touched on the innocent, helpless captives beneath his feet. What would happen to them if the *Falcon* won? Aldan squared his shoulders. *That is not going to happen.*

The *Cathartid* stole the wind from the *Falcon's* sails, and the decisive moment arrived. Aldan moved the sword to his right hand and braced his feet for impact. Both crews howled like a chorus of demons, and Aldan's voice joined the unholy racket. The *Falcon* careened into the *Cathartid's* side, splintering the railing with rage and fury and flinging men off their feet. Moments later, the boarding party swarmed across to the *Cathartid's* deck.

A massive tremor rattled through the ship's frame, and everyone in the cabin was thrown to the floor. Mirza squawked as her chair pitched over and she landed in a heap against the wall. Srilani shielded Maelan with her body. The severe impact of their fall woke Jamson, and René pulled him into her arms.

"Where are we?" he asked. "What's happening?"

Cries and shouts, thumps and running feet, screams, curses, agony, and glee blended together overhead.

René whispered to the twins, but Srilani could only listen to the raging battle.

CHAPTER SIX

"Look out!"

Sam's shout penetrated the melee, and Aldan dropped to the deck. A breeze ruffled his hair as an enormous club swung past his temple. The man who wielded the weapon matched its size, his bulk plunging Aldan into deep shade.

"Oh no you don't." Sam threw his considerable weight, shoulder first, into the man's chest. Like a towering oak, the man crashed to the planks. Sam landed hard nearby.

Aldan rolled out of reach, jumping to his feet. Linus brought his mace down on the man's head with a sickening crunch.

Another *Falcon* crew member stepped forward to take his mate's place. Aldan rushed to intercept him and parried a sword thrust, shoving the weapon aside with his blade. A surge of adrenaline infused him with unnatural speed. The crowded deck blurred. Time slowed. His voice stretched out into elongated syllables, echoing in his ears. "Sam, get out of the way."

Aldan smashed his left fist into the attacker's face. The man fell back a step. Aldan lashed out with his sword. A line of blood appeared across the pirate's bare chest. He followed up with a blow under the man's chin. His opponent crumpled to the deck.

"Thanks, Brother," Sam said, panting. He regained his feet, and the friends regrouped with backs together to face any new threat.

Fierce battle heat consumed Aldan, driving out his fears. He launched himself into the fight. Who cared about the danger? If he lost the *Cathartid*, he lost his home and only means to stay alive. He could dwell on his hatred for *Cathartid* another day, but for these brief moments, she was his, and the gods help anyone who tried to take her away.

Sam fought by his side. Linus stayed behind him, covering his back. Bravado and desperation substituted for expertise. Minutes later, Aldan and Linus were separated from Sam.

"Here come two more." Linus's voice sounded detached and calm, as if he stood outside of the action.

Aldan spun around. Linus swung his club and connected with the ribs of one of the men. The man dropped his sword. Linus struck again and nailed the man to the deck. He didn't get back up.

The other pirate bore down on Aldan with a dagger in each hand. Aldan darted to one side, but the tip of one blade burned across his left bicep. The long scratch stung like fire, but he couldn't let the wound slow him down. Linus stumbled backward, knocked against Aldan, and they sprawled in a tangle of limbs.

"Get up. Get up!" Aldan scrambled away, grasping his sword in a white-knuckled hold, and dodged another strike from the man who'd cut him. Both the stranger and Aldan slipped in a pool of blood and fell. Aldan's knee connected with the wood, and he yelped.

Linus was on his feet and extended his hand. "Are you hurt?"

Aldan waved him away. "Don't worry about me. Watch your back!" Aldan kicked out at his opponent and swept the man's legs out from under him. He drove his sword into the man's gut, and their struggle was at an end. Aldan crouched, knees bent, balancing on the balls of his feet. He pivoted in a cautious circle, searching for the next threat, ready for anything except —

Linus had climbed atop a barrel and grabbed a rope above his head.

Aldan blinked. "What are you doing?"

"Watch my back."

Linus unwound the rope that anchored the block and tackle for lifting cargo through the hatch. In a flash, he shoved the heavy wooden pulley away from his chest. It flew on its tether across the breadth of the ship, striking the back of Scar's head. The first mate collapsed in a boneless heap.

Aldan tore his gaze from Scar to keep a wary eye on the flight of the block and tackle. The rope spun about in a crazy arc, struck the main mast, and clipped a *Falcon* crewman. Linus hopped off his perch as if nothing had happened.

Moments later, a cheer swept from the bow through the crowd. The *Falcon's* captain was dead. The few sailors from the *Falcon* who remained alive beat a hasty retreat to their ship.

"Cut 'em loose!" Rozar shouted.

Every man on deck turned in Rozar's direction, and a few dared to protest. Captain Rozar stood his ground in spite of the apparent disagreement with his unusual command. Several crew members cast furtive glances around the assembled crowd.

Aldan suppressed a smirk. No doubt Scar's friends were thinking this would be a good time for the first mate to seize command of the *Cathartid*, but that wasn't going to happen now, thanks to Linus. Was Scar dead or just unconscious?

Either way, Linus bought us some time.

Rozar repeated the order. "Cut 'em loose, boys. No time to waste on the *Falcon*. Port Azor awaits." After a few moments, the men knuckled under, deferring to Rozar's confident air of absolute authority.

<hr>

Srilani prayed as she'd never prayed before. *Please, El, please let it be Father's ship trying to rescue us. Save us from these pirates.*

A man's agonized scream pierced the air, ending in a gurgle. Maelan's fingers tightened on Srilani's. Her younger sister's skin had a green tinge under the tan, and beads of sweat glistened on her brow. Srilani drew Maelan into her lap as if she were Audrilan's age.

Maelan's green eyes were wide, rimmed with fear. "What's happening?" she whispered.

"I don't know, sweetheart." Srilani glanced at René's taut expression. Clearly, René understood all the things left unsaid, all that was at stake.

Srilani checked on the witch. Mirza seemed engrossed in listening to the conflict raging on the main deck.

Srilani leaned toward the others. "Listen to me," she whispered. "Keep your identities secret. If you're asked, use different names. We are still brother and sisters, but my name is . . . Ana." She touched René's knee. "René, do you mind? If you took Jessi's name, it would keep things simple."

"That's fine."

Bless Ana and Jessi. Their maids' names would be easy to remember.

Srilani pointed to her brother. "You could be—"

"I'll be Olson," he said.

Srilani patted his shoulder. "Good."

Maelan pointed to herself. "My name is Patience."

Jamson snorted, but Srilani quelled him with a look. "Remember to use those names when we talk from now on. Better yet, don't use names at all unless you have to. The less we speak in front of them, the better. Play dumb if they speak to you in Norlan."

She put out her fist, and Jamson covered her hand with his. Maelan followed his example, and René placed her hand on top. "No matter what happens, we can rely on El to see us through this."

A triumphant chorus of Norlan voices rose to a deafening shout as if to mock her words.

⋏⋏

Chaos reigned on deck as Sol's golden rays turned scarlet. Aldan's sword dangled in his hand, too heavy to lift, as if lead weights were attached to it. He forced himself to move. This was their only chance to obtain weapons and valuables under the cover of the disorder.

Sam sauntered across the deck to stand beside Aldan and Linus. He pulled up the hem of his shirt for a moment, then let it fall. Somehow, he'd managed to hide a sword in a scabbard down the leg of his trousers.

For the first time all day, Aldan smiled. "Be careful how you walk."

Sam winked. "Always."

"Help me lift this guy over the side," Aldan said. He gestured to the closest corpse, a pirate from the *Falcon*. Aldan bent down and ripped the golden hoops out of the sailor's ears. "Sorry," he whispered.

Sam rolled his eyes and grabbed the corpse's feet. "Better him than you."

"But—" Aldan palmed the loot into Linus's hand.

"Don't bother to argue. Lift."

They heaved the body over the railing and watched as it splashed into the waves. Several yards out, the dorsal fin of a shark cut a path toward the *Cathartid*. Then another appeared. And another. The entire crew worked to clear the deck of the dead, and Aldan averted his eyes from the feeding frenzy in the ship's wake.

"You'd better hide the loot now, while you have the chance," Aldan said. He held out his hands to Sam and Linus. "Hand me Rozar's weapons."

Aldan clutched the collection of weapons to his chest and picked his way through the debris, gore, and confusion until he found Rozar.

"Ah, Aldan. Good show. I saw you take the man in the striped trousers." Rozar's dark eyes glittered as he bared his teeth in a feral smile. "Did better than Scar. Don't think he'll be waking up anytime soon."

Aldan's mouth went dry. "He's dead?"

"No. But he's got a knot the size of an alligator egg on his head. He'll come around eventually." Rozar gestured at Aldan's wounded arm. "Don't wait too long to bind that up. Now, take the weapons below, clean them, and return them to the locker. After that, take care of our guests."

⋀⋀

A firm knock broke the silence in the cabin, and Mirza woke from her doze with a start.

"Come," the witch said in a shrill tone.

The slave, the one Rozar had called Aldan, pushed open the door. He carried a heavy tray laden with food and water. He carefully set it down.

Mirza's face turned purple with pent-up rage. "You locked me in, you bilge rat! You'll pay for that. Serve me first, you son of a sea serpent." Her insulting harangue continued but Aldan, who looked like he might be twenty or twenty-one years old, paid no attention to her vitriol.

His appearance had suffered terribly during his absence. A long smear of drying blood ran down one side of his tattered trousers, and he wore a makeshift bandage tied around his upper arm. His cheek sported a deep purple bruise. Large patches of sweat stained his tunic.

Aldan ladled soup into a bowl without haste and handed the bowl to Mirza.

Her wrinkled lips latched onto the bowl's rim, and she slurped noisily. She emptied the bowl in seconds and held it out for more. "What happened?"

"The *Falcon* attacked," Aldan said. "They came aboard and we fought." He handed a cup of cool water to Srilani and another to René.

"And?"

"Their captain's dead."

"Ha!" Mirza smirked. "Thought he'd steal our prizes, no doubt."

Srilani studied the young man between sips of water. Aldan's clothes fit poorly over his tall, wiry frame. His trousers were too short and so were his shirtsleeves. Fetter marks ringed his ankles, ridges of scar tissue, lighter than the deeply tanned skin beyond.

Aldan handed Srilani a steaming bowl of soup, took her cup, and refilled it with water. His dark brown eyes met hers and held.

"Thank you." She spoke in Marstan.

"You are welcome."

His Marstan was far better than Mirza's and lacked the Norlan accent of the captain's.

Curious. He'd probably been taken from Southern Marst, going by his speech and his name. There was something about his name. Her eyes dropped to his wrists. They, too, bore manacle marks. Would she have scars like that?

Aldan proceeded to dish food out for everyone.

"Fetch the screen and the chamber pot from my quarters," Mirza said in her raucous voice. "Bring more water in a bucket. Be quick about it."

Srilani's estimation of Aldan rose when he continued what he was doing and ignored the vile, bullying hag as if she'd said nothing. After he finished serving the food, he made several trips to bring the necessary items plus the cots Rozar had ordered earlier. Aldan left the door ajar while he was present, but every time he left, he latched the door from the outside.

Too soon, their meal was over. Aldan cleared the dishes and left the cabin. His presence had alleviated the oppressive atmosphere in the cabin.

Srilani and René encouraged the twins to sleep. Mirza dozed without any effort, upright in her chair. How could anyone rest that way?

The throbbing pain in her temple kept Srilani awake. How differently Third Day had turned out than what she'd imagined. She should be eating and dancing with Greyson at the Solstice Festival.

Srilani turned on her side to face René. Her sister's eyes were open. "What happened while I was unconscious?" Srilani whispered. "How did we get on Captain Rozar's ship? I don't remember anything that happened after breakfast."

René reached out from under her blanket and grasped one of Srilani's hands. "Mother and Father took a turn in the *Skylark*, and we went hunting for shells. General Bertson and Captain Corson were with us. But when we got close to the rock wall, Rozar's men surprised us. They killed two of the men and stabbed Bertson. You tried to help him, but one of the pirates knocked you out with a club. They rolled us up in the blankets, and made us drink something that tasted awful. That's all I remember."

Srilani swallowed. "Did Bertson die? What happened to Captain Corson?"

"Bertson was still moving the last time I saw him, but he couldn't help us." René averted her eyes in horror. "There was so much blood. Corson was right behind me when we reached the hidden bay. I don't know what happened to him."

Srilani's fist clenched on the blanket. "We must escape. We must save the twins. I would rather die than become a slave or Dzor's concubine."

CHAPTER SEVEN

Aldan returned the food tray to the galley, and Biscuits ordered him to wash the pots and dirty dishes. The day was never going to end. Most of the ship's company slept off the effects of extra grog and an eventful day, even though the darkness was still young.

Biscuits filled the time with gossip, but Aldan didn't bother to listen until the subject turned to the captives.

"They say they're all from one family. I only saw them for a second, but the older girls are—" The cook whistled softly and drew curves in the air with his hands. "Beautiful."

Biscuits handed Aldan another pot to scrub. "The men said they had an escort of guards. Did you know the oldest girl fought back?"

"No."

Biscuits shook his head. "I ask you, what's a girl know about fighting? You expect teeth and fingernails, but a sword?"

Aldan finished rinsing the pot. "Where did she get the weapon?"

"She took it from one of her dead guards. What a woman!" Biscuits paused as if to savor the idea of an attractive, sword-wielding female. He chuckled. "She injured Fratz, and then the stupid fool hit her with his club. He'll never live it down." He picked up a towel to wipe out the pot.

Aldan nodded. "Rozar was very angry."

Biscuits laughed, his belly jiggling with mirth. "I don't feel sorry for that idiot. He deserves all the grief he gets."

Aldan sloshed water around in a bowl. Had the girl been trained to fight or had she just been trying to defend herself and the others? If the captives had guards, they had to be a wealthy merchant's or baron's children.

Biscuits interrupted his thoughts. "Scar finally woke up for a few minutes. Madder than a kraken too. He missed the end of the action."

"I heard." Aldan shifted his feet and lowered his eyes. "What happened to him?"

"Got banged on the back of the head."

Biscuits bent down to stash some dishes under the tiny counter. He straightened and his gaze fell to Aldan's arm. "That bandage won't do, you great silly loon. Stop what you're doing and let me bind it up."

Aldan gritted his teeth through the painful session that followed. Biscuits, though well-intentioned, was a clumsy physician and jarred the wound several times as he cleaned and dressed it.

The job done, Biscuits slapped Aldan's back. "Gods, clam-head. You can't ignore a scratch like that. Your arm will fall off." The cook retrieved a basket from a high shelf, uncovered it, and took out two loaves. He shoved them into Aldan's hands. "Take these and share them with your mates."

"Thanks."

"I don't understand how Rozar expects you to survive on air and water. Get out of here before I think of something else for you to do."

Aldan took the bread below, but Sam and Linus were fast asleep. He climbed into his hammock, and something sharp poked him in the back. His hand closed around Sam's newly-acquired sword in its scabbard. They definitely needed a better place to hide their equipment. He shoved the weapon aside, wrapped the bread in a corner of his blanket, settled back, and let the ocean of sleep sweep him away.

A few hours later, Linus's quiet movements roused Aldan. Sam stirred in the rack below. Linus lit their small lamp and dipped his head in greeting, a tall silhouette in the dim light.

"I have food to share," Aldan said.

"Why didn't you wake me? I'm hungry." Sam lifted a hand, and Aldan gave him half a loaf. He gave the other half to Linus.

Aldan tore off a chunk of the second loaf. "Biscuits says the captives are from one family."

"Rozar sure knows how to pick 'em," Sam said. His tone was entirely too cheerful. "So he still plans to give them to King Dzor, eh?"

The bread turned bitter in Aldan's mouth, and he swallowed it with difficulty. "How'd you guess?"

Sam shrugged and bit off another hunk of his loaf.

Aldan turned to Linus. "Have you been up on deck?"

Linus nodded.

"How's the weather?"

"Red morning. A storm's coming."

"Oh, come on," Sam said with a groan. "We've got repairs to make, and now we have to deal with the weather? Yesterday was perfect. How could we have a storm today?"

Linus shrugged. "Waves from the south. The wind changed. It feels like a storm."

"Great." Sam stood and stretched his arms above his head with another groan. "Just once, O Great Sage, would it hurt if you were wrong about the weather?"

Aldan took another, closer look at Linus's solemn face. "You think it's a serious storm?"

"Yes."

Sam frowned at Linus. "I've gotta see this for myself." He extinguished the lamp, plunging them into darkness.

The sails luffed and undulated overhead, propelling the *Cathartid* north at a decent clip. Sol lurked beneath the horizon, and the rim of the world glowed a sullen red. The clear canopy of stars faded before the impending dawn. To the southeast, a smudgy gray line loomed. Only the sky to the northwest was clear.

Aldan turned in a slow circle. His brothers, as he called them, stood with him beside the main mast, looking across the Great Gulf. Twelve years at sea hadn't given Aldan the weather sense Linus possessed, but he didn't need Linus's uncanny knack of getting it right to predict this day's weather. The only question that remained was how large and fierce the storm would become.

The freckles above Sam's bushy beard stood out against the unusual pallor of his ruddy skin. He stared north, arms crossed over his broad chest, his golden-brown eyes clouded with concern. "How far do you think we are from Port Azor?"

Aldan, too, gazed in the direction of the Norlan coastline, at least two days away with favorable winds. "Too far," he said.

⋈

Familiar seafaring noises woke Srilani. The ship's bell rang five times, footsteps thumped overhead, wind rattled rigging and snapped sails, and water swooshed past the hull. Her cabin was pitch black with a sliver of light to mark the threshold. Soon it would be time to join Father and the ship's captain to inspect the crew and cargo. Not her favorite activity, but a welcome break from the rigid palace schedule.

She drew in a deep breath, savoring the scent of aged oak beams and —

Ugh.

The unmistakable tang of bloodshed, the stench of dirty bodies, and other revolting odors assaulted her. Srilani buried her nose in the crook of her arm, stifling a groan. They were on the *Cathartid* instead of one of Father's merchant ships.

Srilani's headache returned as she sifted through her few memories of the day before. How had the pirates chosen the one day when she and her siblings would be in that particular bay and without adequate protection?

Could it be coincidence?

She circled around the question. There was no such thing as coincidence. Who would betray them like this? A traitor or someone with a personal vendetta?

True, they had enemies as all royal families did. Who could have arranged such a cunning strike, though, eliminating four heirs in one swift blow? King Dzor, judging by all she'd ever heard of him, was a feckless fool. He didn't seem bright enough to make this happen.

Srilani snorted. Elison would tell her not to underestimate a fool because all fools were dangerous.

She sighed and turned onto her stomach. Something hard and knobby pressed into her sternum, and Srilani slipped her hand through her tunic's hidden slit. Her fingers closed around the hilt of her dagger. Father insisted they each carry a weapon at all times. How could she have forgotten her dagger?

"Thank you, Father," she whispered.

René's soft voice came from her left. "What did you say?"

"I have my dagger. Do you?"

"Yes. I didn't mention it because I thought you knew."

Srilani rolled to face in René's direction. "I wasn't thinking straight yesterday."

René's hand closed over hers. "How's your head?"

"It hurts."

"You need to rest," René said, her voice a perfect blend of nurture and no-nonsense. "Try to sleep."

Unlikely. Srilani shut her eyes and attempted to clear her mind, but another possibility presented itself.

Could Habidan, Queen Yolani's husband, have orchestrated their abduction? He preferred to be called *Lord* Habidan of Southern Marst, stopping short of claiming to be king. Father refused to recognize Habidan as Lord anything, even though he was the baron of a minor estate.

Rumors abounded that Habidan controlled the gangs of robbers who preyed on travelers along the River Marst. He traded on his wife's position and undermined her authority. Habidan was no fool and extremely dangerous.

Srilani's aching head throbbed.

"They must have forgotten to search us," Srilani whispered. "I can't believe it. How could they forget something so basic?"

"Sleep." René sounded exactly like a healer. She ought to. She'd already spent a couple of years learning to mix herbs and nurse the sick.

"What good will daggers do? It's not like we can fight off the entire crew."

René sighed. "You're not listening to me. You have a head injury. You need to rest."

"I'll try." Srilani's fingers crept up to her breastbone. Grandmother's necklace. She still had it on.

Would they ever see Kaeson again?

If not, poor, sweet Audrilan would be queen. If something happened to Father before she turned seventeen, a regent would be appointed. Would Audrilan survive that long? Was she in danger too?

Srilani moved her head into a more comfortable position. She could rule out the Separatists. They favored a strong monarchy from the royal lineage. All they wanted was to sever relations with the Southern kingdom. So Audrilan was safe from them.

A soft knock on the door interrupted the relentless stream of thoughts swirling in her mind. Another moment passed before the latch snicked out of its bracket. Aldan entered the cabin holding a fresh lamp aloft.

He threaded his way between the closely-spaced cots and replaced the burnt-out lantern. He looked down at Srilani and bowed ever so slightly.

"I'll be back soon," he said in a low voice. He left, pulling the door closed.

"He seems sympathetic," René said.

"Don't let your guard down."

"I'm not."

Mirza snorted in her sleep, and they froze. The old hag didn't wake.

"How does she sleep sitting up like that?"

Srilani shrugged. Her eyes followed the lantern's motion. "Something's different this morning. Can you tell?"

"What do you mean?"

"The ship rolls from side-to-side every once in a while."

René paused. "I don't feel it."

Maelan woke and sat up. She scrambled off her cot and tucked herself in beside Srilani, facing René. "I'm so scared," she whispered.

René smoothed Maelan's hair to one side. "We are too, darling."

"How are we going to get away?" Maelan's voice trembled, but the way she lifted her chin suggested a grim determination to do whatever was necessary.

Srilani hugged her younger sister. "You are as brave as always, I see. Do you have your dagger too?"

Maelan nodded. "I was keeping it a secret. Jamson — I mean . . . Olson has his too."

"That's good," Srilani said. "They won't help much against this crew, but it's nice to know you have some protection."

"I'll kill myself before—"

Srilani interrupted. "Agreed. But let's pray it won't come to that." The idea of Maelan harming herself was too horrible to speak aloud. "El protect us from such an end."

Maelan pressed her fingers to her forehead. "I have such a headache," she said.

"So do I."

Maelan wiggled around to look at Srilani's forehead. "No wonder."

René propped herself up on one arm and studied Srilani's bruise. "Your bump is the color of a plum. Do you feel sick at your stomach?"

"Somewhat, but I think that may be due to the ship's motion. The ocean seems rougher this morning."

On cue, the ship shimmied and pitched. The lamp swung about, throwing weird light patterns around the cabin. Mirza's chair lurched to the side, and she woke with a curse. "Azor's teeth! What's going on?"

Her screech woke Jamson.

"Get up, you sluggards," Mirza said in a harsh croak. "We're all going for a walk on deck." She creaked off the chair, stalked to the door, and pounded on it, shouting at the top of her lungs.

Srilani waited for Maelan to rise and then struggled out of her cot. They lined up near the door. Srilani raised a hand to her tangled hair and glanced at the creased material of her linen tunic and trousers. She wrinkled her nose. Ana would faint dead away to see her looking like this.

Moments later, Aldan swung the door open. For long moments, Mirza shrilled reproaches at the young man. He waited, without any change of expression, until she cut herself short.

"Get out of the way, you." Mirza pushed past him and entered the corridor. She looked over her shoulder at Srilani and switched to Marstan. "Well? Are you ready?"

"Yes."

A crafty smile curved Mirza's lips, and she wagged a bony finger in the air. "I doubt it, my fine lady, but you'd best follow me. And don't try nothing funny."

CHAPTER EIGHT

Srilani signaled Jamson to follow the witch. He took point, as she'd intended, and Maelan followed her twin. René left the cabin next. Her siblings didn't need an explanation of the silent instructions. They'd spent enough time training with the Palace Guard, at their father's insistence, to understand they were now on the defensive. *Another point in Father's favor.*

Srilani took the rear guard position, and Aldan fell in behind her. He passed them when they reached the hatch and shimmied up the ladder first.

Mirza stood at the ladder's foot. She poked Jamson's shoulder. "Get going, boy."

Jamson needed no help getting to the deck. The sea was his passion, and Father indulged him with frequent outings on the *Skylark* and their merchant ships. Maelan swarmed up the ladder with nearly as much skill as her brother. René, however, had no head for heights.

Srilani spoke to her in an urgent undertone. "Focus on the sky through the hatch. Don't look down. Take one rung at a time."

Aldan grasped René's elbow as soon as she was within reach. His voice sounded kind. "Almost there."

René disappeared from view, and Aldan extended a lean brown hand to Srilani. His calloused fingers were warm, his grip strong. He released her the moment she was steady.

Aldan made no move to help Mirza. The hag climbed with amazing nimbleness for someone of her advanced age. She turned on Aldan, probably to issue another insult, but her words were lost in the ear-splitting noise that erupted around them. The Norlan pirates yelled, whistled, and stamped their feet.

"Oh." René's cheeks lost all color, and her lids squeezed shut. Jamson and Maelan pressed close to René's side.

Srilani straightened her shoulders and schooled her face to an indifferent mask. Their jeers, crude gestures, and insults needed no translation. She couldn't keep her cheeks from burning with shame, but she refused to cower before these ruffians.

Captain Rozar shouted orders and threats. He motioned to a disfigured man — perhaps his first mate — who sprang into action.

The ugly brute roared, his voice rising above the tumult. "Quiet, you lot, or you'll feel the sting of my whip!" He wielded his scourge like a maniac, lashing out at the most vociferous men. At last, the crew subsided into surly obedience.

These unruly men were nothing like the sailors aboard Father's ships. The pirates were barefoot and wore no tunics, clad only in ragged breeches, hairy chests glistening with sweat. Bushy beards adorned most of the men, and every crewman bore the tattoo of Azor on his right cheek. Each one carried an assortment of weapons and bristled with menace. Even without proper tunics, they looked strangely uniform.

Srilani didn't dare look at the crew leering down at them. One false move seemed likely to incite another riot. She forced herself to focus on the captain. He smiled at her, his enjoyment of the situation obvious. Aldan stood a few feet away. Surely he was watching her too. She lifted her chin. *Let them look.*

Captain Rozar's smile grew, and he strolled over to stand in front of her. He bowed to her and murmured, "My lady."

She stared through him.

He stepped closer and pushed her hair back from her forehead. She froze at his touch, forgetting to breathe.

He doesn't exist. I am a statue. I feel nothing.

Rozar slid one arm behind her back, drawing her close, and the scent of his cologne filled her nostrils. A pity it didn't mask his body odor. She pushed against the rich, red brocade of his vest but he held her fast. The hairs on the back of her neck stood on end, and she suppressed a shudder. *I am a statue.*

"Ahh." Rozar's voice dropped to a low caress. "My pet . . . King Dzor admires spirit in a woman as much as I do." He bent his head so his cheek pressed against her ear, and inhaled. "Mmm. *I love playing with fire."* Hot, moist breath, reeking of garlic, gusted over her skin. "If not for your enormous value as an untouched virgin, I'd tame you myself."

He doesn't exist.

Rozar chuckled as if he could read her mind. His eyes wandered down to her curves and back to her face. His gaze sharpened. "What's this?" He shook his head. "Keeping secrets, my lady?"

Srilani's heart stuttered in her chest. Had he detected her weapon?

His fingertips trailed beneath her tunic's neckline, followed it around to her nape, and extracted the chain of Grandmother's necklace. He lifted it over her head. The aquamarine pendant in its silver frame winked and sparkled as it spun around.

"I'm afraid this won't do, Sweetness. I'll just put this trinket in a safe place." Rozar tucked the jewel into his coat's inside pocket.

She'd worn her Grandmother's necklace every day since Father had fastened it on her. Rozar might as well have torn a strip of her skin away. Srilani pressed her lips together and blinked back tears. A lump formed in her throat. *I won't cry. I will not cry.* She concentrated on breathing at a normal rate.

Rozar's eyes never wavered from her face, and he missed nothing of her struggle. He still held her in a tight embrace, his arm like an iron band behind her. His hand rose to stroke the loose tendrils near her right temple. "Has anyone ever told you that your eyes glow when you're angry?"

A wind gust rattled the rigging overhead. The *Cathartid* hit a swell, spraying sea foam across the deck. Rozar tapped Srilani's cheek and released her, turning his attention to the ship.

She stiffened her knees. Now wasn't the moment to fall apart.

Rozar addressed his slave. "Aldan, take our prizes for a stroll. Feed them. And lend the ladies a comb from my sea chest. We want them to look their best."

He spun around and switched to Norlan. "Mirza! A storm is coming. The men require an incantation for safety. Make it quick."

Srilani turned her head to look at Aldan. His expression was impossible to read, his dark brown eyes inscrutable. He extended his sinewy arm, and she placed her fingers on his tattered sleeve.

⋀

Aldan pushed the sandstone forward and back on the planks, removing the last remains of the *Falcon* fight with elbow grease and seawater. No matter how calloused his fingers, scrubbing the deck never got easier. Linus and Sam pushed their stones in rhythm with his. Sam marked time by singing a long, involved ballad. His deep voice was a thing of unexpected beauty in this desolate place.

Sol hid behind a thick blanket of swirling clouds and made time difficult to track. The ship's bell rang once, heralding afternoon's arrival. Cool wind from the south-southeast brought a welcome respite from the midsummer heat.

Scar brushed past them. From the back of his bald head, his bruise glared at them like a malevolent purple eye. He joined Captain Rozar at the helm, and Aldan raised his eyes from the planks to watch. The captain and his first mate stood shoulder to shoulder, faces turned skyward, taking in the status of wind and sail. Rozar's raven hair had escaped its usual tidy queue and flew outward in writhing tentacles.

Aldan nudged Sam and signaled him to lower his voice. Sam's song trailed off, and they strained to hear Rozar's voice.

"Prepare to heave to. Reef the sails and set the storm sails," Rozar said. "We'll run in front of the storm to The Hole."

Scar's gruff voice was hard to understand. "Why not Port Azor?"

"Too exposed." Rozar turned to his first mate. "Mark my words, the port's the last place to be during a hurricane. You remember what happened to all them ships five summers back?"

Scar nodded. "Oh, aye."

Rozar adjusted the ship's course. "Set 'em to work, Scar."

Aldan lowered his eyes to his work, and Sam started a new verse of his chantey. Scar ignored the brothers as he directed the crew. Aldan took a second to flex his fingers.

Linus spoke in a low voice. "Does your arm hurt?"

"Like a whip lash." Aldan grabbed his block of stone and matched Sam's beat. "So we're not going to Port Azor."

"Indeed."

"Rozar thinks he can beat the storm."

Sam's song cut off, and he glanced upward at the menacing sky. "From the look of things, we'd better hope he's right."

Aldan nodded. "Wonder how the captives are?"

"My guess is they're seasick by now," Sam said. "Pitiful landlubbers."

"Have a heart. You were a landlubber once." Aldan bore down on his sandstone. "Besides, you should have seen them climb the ladder. Only the second girl had a problem."

Sam's mouth turned down. "Rozar was mad to bring them on deck. Almost had a mutiny right then."

"Wasn't Rozar's idea," Aldan said. "Mirza brought them."

Sam took up his chantey in the middle of the chorus, but Rozar put an end to it soon after. "Aldan. All of you. Help Biscuits feed the crew. After that, man the pumps."

Sam let out a groan, and Aldan clapped him on the shoulder with a grin. "You knew it was only a matter of time."

"Yeah, but now it's here."

"At least we'll get to eat."

An hour later, Aldan pushed open the door to the captives' cabin. The little compartment reeked of vomit, but the youngest girl was the only one down. The older sisters and the brother were gathered around her cot. Aldan set the tray he carried beside the door and took a step toward them. "Is she sick?"

Rozar would mount his head on the bowsprit if something happened to one of the prizes.

The oldest girl straightened. "She's seasick." Her eyes fell to the tray and came back to his face. "You brought water?"

"Yes. And some biscuits. It's not much—"

"Thank you."

They stared at one another. What could he say? He backed away.

"Please. Wait."

He hesitated, hand on the latch.

"The sea seems very rough," she said. "What's happening?"

"There's a storm approaching."

"A bad storm?"

He dipped his chin. If he were in their place, he'd want to know the truth. "A hurricane."

The boy straightened up. "A hurricane?" His face showed no dismay at the prediction, only a kind of wild excitement. An excitement his sisters didn't seem to share. The oldest girl frowned at her brother, and he subsided.

"What does the captain plan to do?" she said.

Aldan shrugged his uninjured shoulder. "We're sailing downwind ahead of the storm."

"To Port Azor?"

Aldan shook his head. "Not right away."

The older girls shared a look of concern.

"Don't worry," he said. "Captain Rozar knows what he's about. We're headed to a safer place."

He hoped.

⁂

Aldan took Sam's place at the pump. Pumping bilge water out was the toughest sort of physical effort and required no particular expertise. That explained why Sam, Linus, and the cook were assigned to take turns with him. Rozar and Scar only trusted the deck hands to handle ropes and sails during hard weather.

"Azor's teeth." Sam wrung his hands together and studied his palms. "I hope we get to Rozar's special cove before he says we will. I can't take much more of this. My hands are blistered."

Aldan's callused palms stung and ached too. "Wrap your hands with strips off the old sails to protect them. Sit down, eat, and try to sleep. Like Linus."

Sam glanced at Linus, propped up against the far wall, sound asleep in spite of the howling fury outside. He shook his head. "There's no way I can rest with this going on."

Biscuits, too, lolled against the hull, snoring loudly enough to shake the timbers. An advantage of sharing pump duty with Biscuits was that the cook never went without a meal. Who cared if the fare was stale bread and water? Sam took a piece of hardtack and shoved it into his mouth.

Even here in the deepest recesses of the ship, the hissing rain and howling wind were audible. Aldan struggled to stay upright, balancing through the highs and lows of the pitching keel as the ship fought the waves.

Sam swallowed the last of his food. "My turn to check the weather."

Aldan watched him depart. They'd taken turns going topside to keep an eye on the storm's progress. Before the rain arrived, they'd been able to stay relatively dry in the lee of the poop deck. By late afternoon, the rain had poured over the *Cathartid* by the barrel-full and there'd been no hope of staying dry. By evening, the sky had changed from somber gray to a surly malachite green. The temperature had dropped to a frigid low, and hail had crashed down like a smith's hammer, punishing the deck and sailors without mercy. Just before dark, a huge water spout had plowed a furrow in the ocean's surface several leagues behind the ship. Thankfully, it had vanished in the distance.

Sam returned, dripping wet and shivering. He tapped the cook's knee several times before Biscuits stopped snoring and cracked open one eye.

"What do you want?"

"Captain wants you topside."

"Figures. This was too good to last." Biscuits blew out his lips and heaved to his feet. "Well, boys, keep her dry."

Sam took the cook's spot against the hull, folded his arms, and closed his eyes. Aldan worked in silence. Maybe Sam could grab some sleep after all.

The ship shook from the gale's force and shimmied from side to side, up and down through the waves. The wind shrieked a continuous stream of malicious intent. The silence, when it came, was sudden and shocking.

Linus and Sam bolted upright, eyes wide. The *Cathartid* bobbed about in a weird arc until she slid to a standstill.

Aldan abandoned the pump and moved closer to Sam and Linus. Without a word, the brothers scrambled up the ladders and passageways until they reached the deck. Linus froze at the top of the hatch, and Aldan pushed him from behind.

The sails and rigging hung limp. Brilliant, silver moonlight limned the crewmen who stood staring into the clear night sky like figures carved from ice.

Sam drew in a long, wondering breath. "You can see the moon and the stars," he whispered. "There's a hole in the clouds."

Aldan blinked at the lunar glow. He tore his gaze away to scan the horizon. The storm's center measured three, maybe four leagues across. In the distance, lightning crackled from cloud to cloud, but here there was only this ominous stillness.

Captain Rozar was the first to shake off the fascination of the storm's eye. He snapped out orders in a voice that promised retribution for anyone who didn't jump to obey.

The brothers ducked down the hatchway. Aldan took his place at the pump again, and Linus and Sam slumped back where they'd been.

After a few minutes, Sam spoke. "The clouds behind us looked nasty."

Linus crossed his arms and nodded. "Indeed."

"It's hard to believe anything could be worse than what we've already been through," Sam said. "But I think worse is coming our way."

"Indeed."

Sam glared at Linus. "Stop agreeing with me."

"As you wish." Linus closed his eyes and leaned back. "You're wrong about everything so don't worry about the storm."

"Oh, shut up."

CHAPTER NINE

Srilani lay as still as possible on the cot. *Be one with the ship. Ride it out.* Her stomach heaved, threatening to push all its contents up and out.

Jamson alone remained unaffected by the raging storm. He showed no signs of seasickness. Steady as a rock, he sat beside Maelan, holding her hand. Maelan's seasickness had struck first, but her sisters soon followed her into the bottomless well of misery. René's steady moaning echoed the thrum of the wind in the rigging.

Srilani had never been on the losing end of a voyage on the Great Gulf. When the sea was choppy, she'd be on deck, reveling in the motion of the waves. *Stupid, scummy, low-down pirate ship.*

René moaned nearby. "Mmm."

Srilani took a chance and turned her head. The pain in her temple had faded, but there was no reason to risk setting it off again. René flung her forearm over her eyes, and her other hand clutched her blanket as the ship executed a devilish twisting maneuver.

Srilani spoke through tight lips. "It's getting worse."

"We're on the dirty side of the storm now," Jamson said.

"Mmm," René said.

Srilani shut her eyes. "I just hope the captain knows what he's doing."

Nobody replied. She shouldn't have said that aloud. Would a life of enslavement be worse than drowning at sea? Faced with imminent death, life seemed too precious to waste — no matter what came later.

She tried to picture what was happening on deck. Was the *Cathartid* strong enough to survive? The men were strong — no doubt — but were they seasoned enough? And Rozar? Could he keep his bearings in this maelstrom?

The furious screeching of the storm increased to a yet unheard pitch, like a thousand furies going to battle against them. Srilani's stomach lurched again. Could a person die of seasickness? If so, death was taking too long.

Aldan took his place at the pump and flexed his fingers before he seized the handle. How much longer could he and his brothers go on? They'd each taken so many turns, he'd lost track. The *Cathartid* was hemorrhaging seawater. Even though they'd been pumping water out continuously, she carried much more in her bilge than normal. If they didn't keep working, she'd sink for sure.

For several minutes, Aldan pushed with all his might. Then a terrific cacophony of splitting wood thundered through the ship's frame, and the world tilted. The lamp crashed to the floor and flashed out. Aldan hurtled through the darkness. He fell end over end and landed on top of Sam. Men screamed. Cargo rumbled across the hold overhead. Linus yelled in his ear.

Sam wheezed under Aldan's weight. "Gods! The ship's smashed."

Another more terrifying sound overpowered the rest — gushing water.

Aldan struggled to rise. The ship's hull seemed to be under his feet. He bumped into Linus or Sam, and an elbow landed in his gut. "We've got to get out of here!"

"Where's the hatch?" Aldan felt around for anything familiar. Cold saltwater poured past his ankles and sprayed him in the face. His foot struck a coil of rope, and his hand knocked against someone's chin. Linus yipped.

Aldan sucked in a deep breath. "Hold onto me! I think the ladder is to our left."

Sam slipped in the rushing water and roared an oath. Aldan grabbed at the air several times before he located his friend's arm. Sam grasped Aldan's shirt to hoist himself up. The water cascaded around them, filling every crevice. The water whirled around their knees with unbelievable force, and it was rising fast. How long did they have before they were overwhelmed?

"Over here!" Linus tugged Aldan more to the left. "I found the ladder."

Linus clambered up ahead of Aldan and Sam, reaching back to seize Aldan's collar and pull him up through the hatchway. Water streamed through the opening. They both helped Sam negotiate the crooked ladder and, as one, heaved Sam onto the hold's deck. The brothers fumbled their way from the hold to the third deck.

A single lantern still burned in the crew's berthing area. Sea chests and other gear jumbled about in great disorder like fish on a deck. A massive reddish-black rock jutted through the hull, gristly as a shark's tooth embedded in flesh. The ocean's blood pulsed and jetted through the opening, seeking the lowest levels first and sealing the ship's doom.

The mortal wound in the *Cathartid's* side mesmerized them for precious seconds. Another colossal wave crashed over the deck above. The *Cathartid's* wound gaped wider, and the wood pushed down against the reef's sharp edges. Like a fillet knife, the ridge sliced deeper into the skin of the craft.

"Go." Aldan pushed Linus onward. "Keep moving."

⋈

Srilani woke in mid-air. Her elbow struck the floor and her arm went numb with pain. The cot that had dumped her onto the planks, hurtled toward her. She shielded her face with her hands and braced for the impact.

The cot rolled over her, clipping her shoulder. Her headache returned full-force.

"We hit something!" Jamson shouted. "We hit something!"

"Did we run aground?" Srilani asked, too stunned to move. *Please, El . . .*

The noise of the storm continued, but the *Cathartid* listed to the starboard side, flopping up and down like a bobber on a string. An ominous vibration rattled through the framework, and the ship lurched downward with a sickening crunch. Everyone shrieked like a chorus of startled birds.

Srilani rose to a sitting position and cradled her elbow, her breath coming in short bursts. Were they about to drown?

"The ship's run aground," Jamson said.

Maelan's voice quavered. "Are we going to die?"

"Stop it," René said. She crawled over and pulled Maelan close. "Let's think about what we should do instead of just being scared."

Srilani held up a hand. "Shh. Everyone. Listen."

The hiss of rushing water echoed beneath their feet. The hull was breached, and the ocean was pouring into the ship's interior.

Terror shook Srilani. "The ship's taking on water."

"We've got to get out of here," Maelan said.

Father's voice was as clear in Srilani's ear as if he stood beside her. *When you're presented with a crisis, act. Don't freeze because of fear. Act.*

Srilani forced herself off the floor and staggered to the cabin door. She rattled the door back and forth with all her strength. Its frame was askew, but the latch —

Was she only imagining a slight movement, a little give? *El, don't let us die like this.*

She rained blows on the thick door, and Jamson joined her. Together, they yelled and pounded on the rough wood. She stopped.

"It's no use," she said. "They can't hear us over the storm."

Jamson frowned. "Or there's nobody else aboard."

She rattled the door again and ran her fingertips around the edges, feeling for any weakness.

"We've got to open this door," Jamson said.

"We need tools."

Both of them turned to look. The search took half a minute, and the sound of rushing water continued.

"There's nothing," Jamson said.

"We can't beat the door down."

"Could we make a tool?" Maelan's question seemed so logical. She left René's arms and swayed to her feet to stand beside Jamson.

The twins' hazel eyes were intent, their brows pulled down in identical expressions of concentration.

Srilani blinked hard. *They're so brave.* She didn't have the heart to discourage them.

"What about your cot?" Jamson bent down and checked the frame of Srilani's cot. "See, it breaks down for storage."

Jamson pulled the makeshift bed apart and set out two long poles and four shorter ones, all made from stout pieces of wood. He brought out his dagger. "How fast do you think I can make a lever?"

Three agonizing minutes later, Jamson set his knife aside and held up a slender wedge of wood. "Let's see if I can raise the door up using this."

He worked the wedge under the crooked door and wiggled it around. The edge of the door grated upwards against the frame, and the latch outside thunked down into its groove.

"Ahh! That's not what I was trying to do." Jamson pulled the wedge out, and the door fell, one corner resting in a divot in the floorboards. "Wait. Let me raise it up just a bit, and you try to dislodge the latch with my dagger."

Srilani picked up the dagger. Jamson jammed his wedge beneath the door's bottom edge again. Srilani inserted the blade through the slim space he created between the door and the frame, but the opening wasn't wide enough for the blade to reach the latch on the other side.

"I'm sorry, Jamson."

"We've got to make this work," he said through his teeth. "If we don't—" He swallowed. "If we don't get out, we'll die."

"Let's try again."

They struggled with the door awhile longer without success. At last, Srilani withdrew the knife and held it out to her brother. "We need help from the outside. We'll have to wait until someone comes to check on us."

Jamson took the dagger and slumped to the floor by the door. "If someone does come, I say we use our weapons."

Srilani nodded. "I agree. We should protect ourselves." She unsheathed her dagger and sat on the deck next to him.

Overhead, their lantern flickered.

Dimmed.

Flared.

Died.

El, please let someone come.

Aldan poked his head above the deck. The storm soaked him to the skin and plastered his hair to his skull. The salty water stung his eyes, and he blinked several times to clear his vision.

Linus stood behind him on the ladder and crowded his back. "Wait, Linus. Let me see what's going on." Aldan craned his head from side to side, squinting through the driving rain. The deck was deserted.

A yell — more like a scream — reached his ears. He swung around. A figure in a long robe disappeared over the ship's railing. He rubbed his eyes. Had that been Mirza?

"What's happening?" Sam shouted his question from below.

"I don't know. I can't see anyone."

"What?"

"There's nobody up here, and I just saw someone jump overboard."

Linus shoved him hard, and Aldan reluctantly climbed out into the full brunt of the weather. He stayed on his hands and knees.

Linus knelt beside him. "Where'd they go?"

"I don't know!" The howling wind whipped his words away.

Aldan's head swam with a dizzying sense of vertigo, as if he were floating outside of his body, looking down at the scene from the clouds above. There he was. Beside Linus. Angry waves licked at the wreck of the *Cathartid* like sea devils tasting their prey. A heartbeat passed, and he was back where he belonged, the awful truth clear.

"They left us to die."

CHAPTER TEN

The swirling wind threw mist across Aldan's face. Saltwater burned his eyes like briny tears, and he scrubbed the moisture from his face with shaky hands. The furies howled their victory to the sky. They beat at him with fresh torrents of rain.

"Everybody's gone?" Sam's head and shoulders appeared in the opening. "Let me see." He pulled himself onto the slanted deck, bending low to battle the elements.

A wave washed over the railing and soaked them. The wind tore at their clothing. Aldan stepped over a fallen spar and pushed himself up against what was left of the main mast. He squinted around. Linus and Sam followed his example.

"The longboats are missing!"

"Everybody's gone," Sam said, as if repeating the words would help him understand.

"We're not dead yet." Aldan shook with cold. "We'll just have to find another way."

Sam shook his head in a futile effort to sling the water out of his face. "I can't think with my head under water."

"Me either," Aldan said. "Can we go back down or is the water still rising inside the ship?"

Sam descended the ladder. After a few moments, he reappeared at the top of the hatchway. "We can go below."

Aldan and Linus scrambled to get off the deck. They reached the second level, gasping and blowing as if they'd been running a race. The ship no longer moved except for the vibration of the waves against her hull.

Aldan met Linus's eyes. "We're going to have to wait this out."

"As if we have a choice," Sam said, his voice bitter.

"Stop." Aldan rounded on Sam. "Let's take time to think. We need a plan."

"How long do we have before the storm tears the ship apart and we all drown?"

"Shut up, Sam." Aldan's eyes adjusted to the gloom. Lanterns. *We need lanterns.*

His head jerked around. His stomach dipped. No light shone under the captives' cabin door near the end of the corridor. "The captives—"

"What about them?"

Heat ignited in Aldan's veins. "Come on, Sam. Don't you care at all?"

"I've got more on my mind than your precious prizes."

Aldan flexed his fingers. "They're not my prizes."

Linus touched Aldan's arm. "Rozar wouldn't leave them behind."

"You're right." Aldan rubbed his neck, trying to soothe the aching tension. "Of course Rozar would take his most valuable cargo."

"Too bad he couldn't be bothered to take us," Sam said. He seemed subdued.

Aldan put a hand on Sam's shoulder. "Yeah, it's too bad, but—" He swallowed. "They'll most likely capsize and drown or be swept out to sea." He tried to suppress the image of his charges at the hurricane's mercy. "And we've got no boat. We should wait until the storm quits. Worst case — if she sinks before it passes — we'll lash ourselves to the spar that fell by the main mast and hope for the best."

Aldan lowered himself to the decking, away from the precipitation falling through the hatch. He stretched his body on the worn planks. Pain and fatigue throbbed in every muscle and joint. They'd crammed three days of hard labor into one with little rest or food.

After a moment, Linus joined him.

Sam, a dark gray shadow, watched them settle down. "How can you think of sleeping?"

"Do you have a better idea?" Aldan waited for a response, but Sam sat down and put his head in his hands.

"I didn't think so," Aldan said. "Look. So far, she's holding together. Let's rest. We'll leave during the storm only if we must."

Sam snorted, but then he lay down too.

The storm's constant din created a melancholy rhythm. The minutes dragged. Linus's breathing evened out, and the corner of Aldan's mouth twitched. Linus could sleep through the end of the world.

"Hey, Aldan . . ." Sam's voice was gruff.

"Hmm?"

"I'm sorry about the captives."

Aldan's heart twisted in his chest. "I know you are."

Aldan wiped the sleep from his eyes. Milky light leaked through the hatchway. A light breeze cooled the dim corridor. The planks beneath his body were dark with dampness, and he shivered. Gulls cried in the distance. Gulls meant —

Land!

He rose on his elbow. The *Cathartid* seemed both familiar and foreign. She lay at an odd angle, lifeless and hollow, like a killer whale carcass he'd seen once on the coast of Norland.

Sam was snoring, but Linus was awake, staring into the morning light.

"Do you hear the gulls?" Aldan asked.

"Yes."

Aldan got to his feet and reached to lend Linus a hand. "Let's have a look around."

"Sam. Shake a leg."

Sam's snores continued. A furrow ran between his brows, and deep lines of exhaustion showed through his reddish-brown whiskers. The thick beard and wild red curls standing out in every direction completed the impression of a dangerous animal who shouldn't be disturbed.

Aldan nudged Sam's butt. "Get up, you big layabout."

Sam grunted and shifted to his front. Aldan put his foot between Sam's shoulders and pushed down. Sam came up swinging, and Aldan danced back.

"Whoa — it's just me."

Sam grunted. He rubbed his hands over his face and head, creating even more disorder.

"Storm's gone." Aldan mounted the first rung of the lopsided ladder. "Come on. Get moving."

He sprinted up the ladder, through the hatch, and onto the deck above. The Great Gulf was calm, and a thin layer of clouds diffused the morning light. He picked a path through the debris and climbed the tilted deck. Rigging hung in tatters like a spent spider web. Only shreds of the storm sails remained.

Linus joined him at the railing, suspended in the air above the waves. Even through the silt in the turquoise water, the dark reef stood out against the white sand on the ocean floor. The *Cathartid's* hull was embedded on the reef. Linus pointed to the sky on the northern horizon. "See?"

Seagulls rode the morning thermals as if the storm had never happened.

"Wonder how close we came to The Hole where Rozar was headed," Aldan said. "The mast must have broken when we slammed into the rocks."

Sam stumbled up the deck, yawning. "Can you see the shore?"

"No."

As one, they looked down at the waves washing over the reef below.

"It can't be too deep if we're caught on a reef," Sam said. He turned to watch the birds wheeling about on the horizon. "Azor's teeth. We're so close. I swear I can hear the surf."

"Yeah."

"Look there." Sam gestured to the north. "Are those breakers? There must be another line of coral closer in."

"I see it." Aldan's fingers tightened on the rail. So close, but so far. "I can't believe we're still alive, but we're dead if we don't get off this wreck." Aldan shoved away from the railing and took a hard look around. "Do you think we could hold onto a plank and float to shore?"

His friends said nothing. Linus looked terror-stricken, and Sam's face lost most of its color. He couldn't blame them for their lack of enthusiasm since none of them could swim.

He tried for an encouraging tone. "Let's scrounge around and see if there's something to eat or drink."

Aldan and Linus discovered a flint in the galley. Sam brought in two lanterns he'd found. They filled the lamps with oil, and Sam left to scavenge in the crew's quarters. Linus stayed in the galley to inventory everything edible. Aldan assigned himself the job of searching through Rozar's private stash.

Rozar had planned to resupply the *Cathartid* in Port Azor. Then came the opportunity to take the captives, and he'd stretched the ship's stores to stay out of port longer. There would be precious little left.

He entered the captain's cabin and hung his lantern on the hook inside the door. He turned and recoiled.

Rozar sprawled across the floor with an axe buried in his chest. His eyes, wide open, stared at the rafters as if frozen with shock. Dried blood surrounded his body.

The coppery stench overwhelmed Aldan's nose, and bile rose in his throat. He backed out of the cabin until his back bumped into the exterior of the captives' cabin. He bent, put his hands on his knees, and fought the urge to vomit. One long breath. Another.

Rozar was dead. *Murdered.*

Aldan stared at the corpse through the open doorway. When had Rozar been killed? An hour before the crew abandoned ship? Two?

Violent thumping shook the wall at his back. Aldan's entire body tensed. He spun around, crouching, pulse pounding.

"Help!" The stout door muffled the cry. More blows sounded on the door. "Is anyone there? Help!"

Aldan's eyes widened. The captives were still alive. Aldan lifted the bar from its rest and pushed the door open. Their cabin was dark, but the light shining from Rozar's cabin glinted across something silvery. Aldan stopped short. The oldest girl advanced, pointing the tip of a dagger at his gut.

Srilani followed the slave named Aldan as he backed away. He raised his hands.

"I have no weapon," he said. "I mean no harm." He took another backward step.

"Don't move."

He stopped and raised his hands higher. "You can put your weapons away."

"No . . . I don't think so. Not yet." She adjusted her grip on the dagger. He seemed genuinely sincere, and it seemed like a poor way to treat him after his care for them when they came aboard. But she couldn't afford to make a mistake. "Are you alone?"

"At the moment."

René, Jamson, and Maelan left the cabin and stood in a semi-circle beside her, daggers drawn.

"How many other pirates are there?" Srilani asked.

He shook his head. "I'm not a pirate. I'm a slave — or at least I was a slave."

"How's that?"

"Captain Rozar's dead. The crew abandoned ship and left us."

"The crew's gone?" The boy and his twin asked the question in unison.

Srilani shook her head. "Let me ask the questions, please."

"They took the longboats and deserted us. I can't believe they left you—" He paused. "Never mind. They must have been too frightened to think straight."

Srilani lowered her blade a couple of inches. If what he said was true, they were safe from the pirates. "Who else is left?"

"My two friends. They were Rozar's slaves too."

She stared at Aldan. He seemed sympathetic, as René had said before, but did she dare trust him and his fellow slaves? The lives of her brother and sisters hung in the balance.

Aldan's eyes looked straight into hers as he spoke. "I promise . . . all I want is to be free. My brother slaves and I just want to get off this wreck and live a free life."

His expression seemed sincere, and something about his words rang true. She'd spent her entire life around men — her teachers, her mentors, the officers — and few could meet her gaze with this kind of unflinching openness.

He shrugged. "Would you like to come with us?"

She raised her brows. Did she have any choice but to accept? She relaxed her stance, stepping back and tucking her dagger into her belt. "Lower your weapons," she said.

He let his hands fall to his sides and waited.

She hesitated. How much did she dare tell him? Better to stick as close to the truth as possible without revealing everything. "My name is Srilani." His face showed no recognition of her name, but he bowed as he'd done in previous encounters. Such a curious show of courtesy, so out of place on this wreck.

Srilani swept her hand to the side. "This is René and Maelan and Jamson."

Again, there was no sign that Aldan recognized their names. Good. He acknowledged the introductions to her siblings with another bow. Perhaps he'd learned the gesture from Rozar who'd struck her as a man with a checkered background.

"Would you like to come with us?" Aldan repeated.

She folded her arms. "How do you plan to get ashore?"

"We don't know yet." He shrugged. "My brothers and I are trying to figure out what's on hand."

She took a deep breath and let it out. "Why don't you introduce us to your brothers?"

⋀

Rozar's cabin was in the stern, and his door was the last one. Aldan led the others past the hatchway toward the galley, leaving the lantern in the captain's cabin. He'd return to take stock of Rozar's possessions as soon as he'd given his brothers the news that Rozar was dead and the captives were alive.

"Linus, see who I've found."

Linus straightened, eyes wary, and he came to stand in the entryway to the galley. Framed there, his height seemed pronounced. "They're alive."

"Yes. Where's Sam?"

"Crew quarters," Linus replied. He stared at the siblings, and they stared back.

Quick, hard steps echoed on the ladder leading below, and Sam appeared behind them. He cleared the ladder's top rung and approached like a charging bull. His big fists opened and closed, and he glowered at the newcomers. "What are they doing here? There's no way we can take them with us—"

The oldest girl closed the distance with him in less than a second, grabbed a fistful of his hair, and thrust her blade under his chin. The flashing edge pressed against his jugular. Her brother drew his weapon, too, holding it at the ready. Aldan froze in place. She'd moved so fast.

She lifted her chin to meet Sam's eyes and bit off her words, using Norlan. "You do not have a choice." She gave Sam's hair another tug. "Aldan. Tell your friend we're coming with you."

Sam's freckles stood out against his tan, and his eyes turned to Aldan in a silent plea for help.

Aldan suppressed the urge to smile — Sam always spoke first and thought later. "I asked them to come with us." He paused, looking between the two. "Srilani," he said, testing her name for the first time. "The man you're threatening is Samazor. We call him Sam."

Srilani glared up at Sam, daring him to move. He didn't even breathe as long moments passed. She released him, lowered her weapon, and stepped back. "Forgive me," she said in a husky voice. "I have a quick temper."

Sam rubbed his neck and gave a shaky laugh. "You have a quick blade," he said in Marstan. He kept his eyes on Srilani. "I take back what I said. Maybe it'll be easier if you're with us."

CHAPTER ELEVEN

Srilani tried to relax her tense muscles and keep her face from showing just how much the encounter with Sam had rattled her.

"You know Norlan," Aldan said. His statement sounded like an accusation.

"Yes and no," she said. "I speak Norlan, but not well enough to sound like a native. Go too fast, and I don't understand all of the words."

"What about them?" Aldan indicated Jamson and the others.

"About the same."

René shook her head. "You're definitely better at Norlan than I am, Srilani."

"From now on, we need to practice all the time," Srilani said. "If we get off this wreck, we'll be in Norland."

Sam turned to Aldan and raised an eyebrow. "Aren't you going to introduce us?"

"You've met Srilani. This is René. The twins are Jamson and Maelan."

"*Maelan* and Jamson," the youngest sister said, crossing her arms. "I'm older."

Jamson shoved his dagger into his belt and frowned. "By five minutes."

"Where did you get the weapons?" Sam said.

Aldan smiled. "They had the weapons when they were brought aboard. Nobody thought to search them."

"All of them?" Sam looked alarmed by the idea and none too happy. "They're better armed than we are." He shook his head. "And our weapons are buried somewhere in the hold."

Aldan's smile grew. "We'll get some weapons from Rozar's locker." He hesitated. "There's also an axe, but it's buried in Rozar's chest."

"What?" Linus and Sam gawked at him.

"Someone killed him with an axe."

"He's dead?" Sam sounded stunned. "Really dead? How many times has he escaped without a scratch?" Sam chuckled, and then slapped his thigh and roared with laughter. "Ah! That's too rich! Why couldn't I have been there to see it happen?" He laughed again and wiped his eyes. "Why couldn't I have *done* that?"

"You're blood-thirsty today." Aldan folded his arms. "Listen, you can have the axe. All you have to do is retrieve it."

Sam's laughter cut off, and he grimaced. "That's just nasty. Thanks for small favors, Brother."

The give-and-take between the "brothers" indicated a high level of camaraderie built over a long period. Sam was a few years older than Aldan and more physically imposing, but he seemed to defer to Aldan's opinion, as did Linus.

"We need a plan," Srilani said.

Sam crossed his arms. "Good luck with that. No boats. Hardly any food. We're low on fresh water, and none of us can swim."

Srilani gave him a cold look. The last thing they needed was a negative attitude. "We'll have to solve those problems. Won't we?" She shifted her attention to Aldan and waited.

Aldan cleared his throat. "Sam, what did you find in the crew quarters?"

"The deck is underwater on one end, but there's plenty of things that stayed dry," Sam reported. "Hammocks, blankets, ropes. Water skins. A few coins."

Srilani bit her lip. Their first priority had to be a way to get ashore. "You say we're pretty close to land. Could we reach the shore on a raft?"

Jamson's face lit with enthusiasm, and Linus looked interested. Sam looked over at Aldan, cautious hope in his expression.

Aldan hesitated. "Maybe. There's another line of reefs between us and the shore."

Jamson spoke before Srilani could answer. "We'd have to build it with a sail and a rudder to make it over the reef. I've helped build a raft before. We can do it if we have the right tools."

"Plenty of wood and rope." Linus remarked.

"There's sailcloth in the hold, if we can get to it," Sam said. "The hold is mostly underwater, but there are lots of things floating on top."

Srilani stored the information away — Sam could be positive if he had a goal in mind. Linus was a young man of action. Aldan was their leader. "Are there any tools? We can't build anything without tools."

"We'll have to check the carpenter's closet. I'll do that right now." Sam turned to leave.

"Let me help," Jamson said. He followed Sam through the galley and out of sight.

Srilani clasped her hands together. Should she let Jamson go off with that great brute?

"Don't worry."

"What?" Srilani turned to Aldan.

"Your brother is safe with Sam. I should be the one who's worried." Aldan's smile was gentle. "Sam doesn't have a weapon."

She didn't return his smile. Easy for him to joke — Sam was three times Jamson's size.

Aldan's smile faded. "We have to trust each other."

Srilani's eyes narrowed. "Sam hasn't earned my trust yet."

"Give him a chance."

"I'll try to keep an open mind." She took a deep breath and let her hands fall to her sides. "I'm going on deck to see what we're up against."

"I want to come too," Maelan said.

René shook her head. "No ladders for me, thanks. I'll help Linus."

Srilani took hold of the ladder and paused. Leaving René alone with a male, no matter how harmless he seemed, went against the most basic palace rules. Srilani pushed the thought away and started climbing. The palace's rules wouldn't work across the Great Gulf. Not if they wanted to survive.

Aldan re-entered Rozar's cabin. The blood scent, like rusted metal and sweat, burned his nostrils. He pinched his nose, but his imagination supplied the taste of rot on his tongue. *Gah.*

Aldan skirted the edge of the ruined rug and opened the stern porthole for fresh air, the same porthole where he'd stood and watched Rozar drink toasts with the man in the green tunic. Before their prolonged voyage. Before they'd taken the captives. Before the storm and the wreck.

The cool breeze diluted the rank air of the cabin. Aldan looked down at the sea, much closer now that the stern dipped at such a strange angle.

Rozar's sea chest was locked, of course. Aldan held his breath and bent over Rozar's wretched body. Where was Rozar's key pouch? There. Inside his shirt. Aldan lifted the pouch by its string, opened its mouth, and shook the key into his palm.

"I'll help you search the cabin."

Aldan jerked upright and dropped the key.

"Sorry." Srilani stood in the doorway.

"I didn't hear you." Aldan took another breath through his mouth and lifted the key from Rozar's shoulder where it had landed.

She put a hand over her mouth and nose. "We've got to dispose of his body before it gets worse."

"Right." He looked past her shoulder. "Where's your youngest sister?"

"Helping René and Linus."

"Good." He waved his hand toward Rozar's corpse. "She doesn't need to see . . . this."

He walked to the chest and inserted the key. The well-oiled lock clicked open, its action smooth. Srilani joined him as he lifted the lid. Her face gave no clues to her thoughts. She didn't seem bothered by anything but the smell.

The chest was full. Weapons of all sorts formed the top layer. Rozar had collected several fine swords, daggers, and maces. Beneath those were other things he'd kept under lock and key for one reason or another, but it wasn't the chest of gold, silver, and jewels most people would expect.

"He kept his most treasured things in here, but his fortune is stashed some place in Norland. Nobody knows where," Aldan said, and he shrugged. "I guess these things are ours now."

Srilani's troubled gaze met his. "What if . . . what if some of the crew survived? Wouldn't they come back for this?" She blinked. "For us?"

"If they survived and were close by? Yes."

Srilani stood aside as Aldan helped himself to a sword and a dagger and strapped them around his waist. She watched him pick through Rozar's coffer, setting aside selected items atop the blanket on Rozar's bunk. Aldan looked like a slave, but he was proving to be a thinking man, carefully selecting items according to usefulness — clothes, a bit of gold, two bottles of wine, and Rozar's looking glass. At the end, he bent over to search the farthest corner.

"This is yours," he said.

She caught her breath. Her grandmother's necklace dangled from his long fingers. The aquamarine caught the light from the porthole and flickered like blue fire.

He picked up her nerveless hand and put the necklace into her palm, closing her fingers around it. The stone was cool and smooth. She tried to speak but no sound came out. She'd thought never to see it again. Yet here it was, back in her possession. Could that mean there was hope that somehow they would see home again? Her hands shook too much to work the necklace's clasp.

"Here. Let me."

She handed him the necklace and turned, holding her braid out of the way while he made quick work of the clasp. "Thank you," she whispered.

"You're welcome."

They both looked over the chest's contents again. He put his hand on the lid. "I think we're done here."

"Wait." She reached into the box and retrieved a scroll bound with a leather strap. It couldn't be. She held the vellum close to her face, squinting at a mark on the outside corner. "Where did Rozar get this?"

"King Dzor gave that map to Rozar the last time they met. Rozar was in love with that map."

Her heart beat hard. "Let's take it up where there's better light. I need a closer look."

Aldan let the lid slam shut. He pulled the corners of the blanket together and slung the makeshift pack over his shoulder. "Lead the way."

Aldan followed Srilani to the top deck and took the opportunity to study the young lady. Her long, blonde braid swayed between her hips as she ascended the ladder. Every movement she made had an unconscious dignity. Her back was straight, and she held her head high. The crown of her head reached his chin, but her intensity gave her added height. And she was brave. Very brave. She'd proven that several times already. Toughness had been instilled in her by someone.

He knelt beside her as she spread the map open on the planks. She examined both sides of the vellum, running her fingers over the markings on one edge. "This map was created in Northern Marst."

"How do you know?"

"See this symbol?" She pointed to a curious mark in one corner. "This map maker only started drawing official maps three years ago. And see here? This is the king's seal."

She rose high on her knees and searched the horizon. The sea breeze molded the linen tunic to her form, and Aldan averted his gaze.

She sank down. "Hold this corner."

Aldan took it from her and watched her dagger trace along a jagged pattern drawn parallel to a coast. There were many labels inscribed on the chart, but he couldn't read them. The map showed the sea, obviously, because a school of fish sported among wavy lines.

"There are two places where coral is a problem for ships in the Great Gulf. Here. And here." Her knife point touched on the jagged patterns shown in two places. "This is north. The wind was blowing from the southeast the day we were taken. Captain Rozar had no reason to take us south, and he even mentioned King Dzor's court, so that rules out the coral reefs down here." Again, she pointed with her weapon. "We must be somewhere along this line."

Aldan studied the reef and the coast on the map. "How far offshore do you think we are?"

"In a ship with a steady wind from the south? Less than an hour."

Aldan's eyes left the map to consider the girl beside him. She seemed so certain. *What kind of girl reads maps and fights pirates?* She knew about sailing too.

"Who are you?" he asked. "How can you be so sure?"

She went still. Her pure blue eyes flashed up to his before she lowered them to the map.

"I am the daughter of a merchant. That's all you need to know." She snatched the map from beneath his fingers and rolled it up. "We'll need this for our journey."

CHAPTER TWELVE

The rest of that day and the next were filled with hard work and difficult decisions. The group spent most of their time constructing the raft, but the rest of their efforts went into gathering the necessities for an expedition into unknown territory. Their packs, made from repurposed hammocks, had to hold cooking utensils, blankets, water skins, rope, and any usable food that remained, but only as much as they could reasonably carry.

Srilani sat beside Aldan at the railing in the late afternoon of the second day, fishing to feed the group. Old leather boots encased her feet, and rough brown trousers clung to her legs. Sweat trickled down the neck of her borrowed man's shirt. What she wouldn't give for a real bath.

"We're making good progress," he said. "But we've got to get away or we'll run out of drinking water."

She wiped her forehead. "The heat makes us thirstier." They had one partial barrel of fresh water left, and "fresh water" was a misnomer since it was months old. "We need to leave with the tide tomorrow. Or the next day at the latest."

"I agree. Linus needs to work on the block and tackle so we can offload the raft and supplies."

"Why Linus?"

"He's the expert with the rigging. Sam and I will help, of course." He pointed to the mess of ropes and pulleys above their heads and scattered on the deck. "The storm didn't do us any favors. We'll work on that when it's cooler, after we eat."

She cleared her throat. "I have something to discuss with you and your brothers too. When it's cooler and we're not so busy."

Aldan lifted his eyebrows but said nothing. Thankfully, he'd refrained from asking personal questions since she'd snapped at him the day before. But that didn't mean he wasn't trying to put two and two together.

If Rozar had known their true identities, he'd taken that knowledge to his watery grave. She stayed on guard against betraying their secret. Aldan's mind was keen, like a snare trapping every detail that came his way. What if he saw too much? What if he somehow divined who they were?

"I've caught another one." Aldan rose to his feet and concentrated on keeping his catch on the hook.

She watched him land the fish on the deck, add it to the rest of their string, and sit to prepare his next cast. Their new friend was too thin for his height, but with enough nutritious food, he'd be her father's size or larger. He seemed wise beyond his years and lack of education. They'd studied the map twice, and even though he couldn't read, he remembered every town and village she mentioned. Intelligence looked out at her whenever his dark eyes met hers.

Behind them, Jamson said something and Sam laughed. At least one of them got along with Sam. Her shoulders slumped. To be honest, she was the only one who couldn't seem to get along with Aldan's best friend. She had no trouble working with Aldan and Linus. Why then did Sam present such a problem?

A fish struck her hook, yanking her pole toward the water.

"That's a big one," Aldan said.

"He's strong!" The fish thrashed at the end of the line, and she held on with all her strength. "I don't think I can haul him in."

Aldan stood and took the cane from her hands. "Take my line, Srilani. That fish wants to have you for supper."

⁂

Aldan savored the wahoo's meat. The fish tasted marvelous, all the better because it had put up a terrific fight. The meal seemed festive, the group upbeat. The raft was complete except for the rudder and sail. The mast and rudder were ready to install as soon as the raft hit the water.

After the meal was over, Aldan commandeered his brothers and Jamson to get the problems with the block and tackle solved. As Sol descended in the west and the air cooled, the men worked together to salvage materials from the wreck and get things in working order.

Linus and Jamson continued to refine the system of ropes and pulleys to lower the raft over the side while Sam and Aldan wrestled the precious water barrel to the upper deck. At last, Aldan sat with Sam to rest, their backs against the main mast.

Every few minutes, Aldan pressed the looking glass to his eye and scanned the horizon from the west through the north to the east.

"Looking for anything in particular?" Sam's voice sounded sleepy.

"The pirates."

Sam straightened. "Do you think they survived?"

"I can't say they didn't."

"Too right," Sam said. "Can I have a look?"

Aldan handed over the glass. "Do you think we're ready to leave?"

"I do."

"Then let's try to get the raft over the side tomorrow so we can leave at high tide the next morning."

Sam raised the glass and did a thorough sweep of the horizon. "Sounds good," he said. "Will the dagger lady approve?"

"You should call her Srilani."

Sam made a rude sound. "Will Lady Srilani approve?"

"It was her idea."

Sam lowered the glass. "Figures."

"What's that mean?"

"Never mind. Here comes Her Worship now."

※

After they'd finished eating, Srilani and Maelan helped René put the last touches on the sail. Srilani punched holes through the sailcloth's tough weave with a whale bone awl.

"It's a good thing you only need me to punch holes," Srilani said. "Remember my last sewing project?"

René laughed. "What a disaster. Mother finally gave up trying to teach you how to sew."

"I was too busy with my other lessons anyway."

"Wish she would have given up on me too," Maelan said. "I can't stand stitchery."

"But you're good at it. Truly, Srilani was a hopeless case."

"She's good at everything else," Maelan said with a sniff. "Sewing is the only thing Srilani's not good at."

"René wasn't insulting me, Maelan." Srilani smiled and shook her head. "And stop exaggerating my abilities, or my head will swell."

She finished making the last hole and handed Maelan the awl. "We each have our talents, like your special talent for finding useful things. Because of you, we each have a change of clothes and a pair of boots. Not that I like wearing pirate's clothes, but still . . . you did well."

Maelan's face glowed at the praise. Srilani rose to her feet.

René searched her face. "Where are you going?"

"To bargain with the brothers."

"Then I'm coming with you."

"Me too," Maelan said.

Aldan and Sam came to their feet as the sisters approached. Sam held the looking glass, and Srilani used that as her opening.

"See anything?"

"Not one thing," he said.

"I've been thinking about when we leave," she said.

"Aldan told me." Sam's voice was clipped. "Tomorrow or the next day."

"Do you agree?"

He shrugged. "I don't want to miss the boat."

"That's not what I asked."

He crossed his arms over his chest. "We don't have much choice, do we?"

This was going to be harder than she'd thought. She glanced at Aldan.

His expressionless face revealed nothing of his thoughts. She tried another tack. "What do you think we should do after we leave the wreck?"

Sam smoothed his beard for a few seconds. "We should try to get as far as we can over water before heading to shore."

Srilani's brows rose. "We don't want to be swept out to sea when the tide goes out."

"So you just want to go straight in to shore?"

"I didn't say that. But we definitely should cross the reef when the tide is with us."

Aldan held up a hand. "You're both right. We can cover much more distance over water in a shorter time. After we've gone as far west as we can go — right along the coast — we should cross the reef and go ashore. *Before* the tide changes."

Srilani waited for Sam to protest, but he nodded. Now was the moment for her to broach the more difficult topic, but Sam spoke before she could form any words.

"Where do you plan to go when we reach land?" Sam's question was obviously meant for Aldan, not for the rest of them.

"What if—" Srilani bit her lip and met their interested gazes. "What if you helped us get back to our home?" She rushed to make her case. "So far, we've been a good crew together. Three girls and a boy from Northern Marst won't get far in Norland without protection."

Linus and Jamson had joined the group in time to hear her question, and all eyes went to Sam's flinty expression.

"What's in it for us?"

"That's a fair question." Srilani resisted the urge to wipe her palms on her tunic. She took a deep breath. "Our father is wealthy enough to reward you handsomely for our return. More, in fact, than we would bring if we were sold in Port Azor. You would also be far away from Norland, so nobody could claim you as runaway slaves."

René stood at her elbow, lending her silent support. How much did they need to know?

"With your reward, you could buy a ship or some land or set up a business in Kaeson." She looked around the circle and back at Sam. "You and your brothers could form a partnership or something. Who knows?"

Sam rolled the looking glass between his hands. "So we'd travel with you and protect you and take you back to your father. He would reward us. Is that the deal?"

"Yes."

"What sort of guarantee do I have that your father will pay up?"

Aldan made a sound of protest, but Srilani ignored him. This was between Sam and herself. She took a steadying breath. He had to say yes. They needed Sam's help — he was the strongest and the most physically imposing of the three. Without his agreement, she couldn't count on Aldan and Linus.

"If my father doesn't agree to reward you—" She swallowed her distaste. "All you have to do is say that I've given myself to you. He'll disown me, and you'll be free to keep me or sell me as a slave."

Her sisters gasped, and Jamson looked as if he'd turned to stone. Sam jerked as if she'd slapped him.

"Srilani!" René sounded horrified. "You cannot! No! You mustn't even consider it."

René rounded on Sam, getting as close to his face as she could by standing on her toes. "If you ever — ever! — think of telling such a huge lie about Srilani, I'll kill you. Do you hear me?"

Srilani's heart melted at her sister's unexpected show of spirit.

"Whoa, woman." Sam raised his hands in surrender. "I didn't know she was going to say that."

"Don't even think about it." René gave a contemptuous sniff and turned her shoulder to him. "If you must have a guarantee, I will have to do."

Srilani gaped at René. Her sister, the little dove, had sprung to her defense like a hawk.

Aldan broke into the discussion, his words calm and measured. "I would like to go to Kaeson, since you asked. And I don't think we need any guarantee of a reward."

"You're hasty," Sam said, but his statement sounded half-hearted.

"No, I'm not. We'll leave this life behind us and get a fresh start far away from here. I couldn't ask for more. So reward or not, I'm in."

Srilani looked from one brother to the next. "What about Linus?"

"He goes where I go," Aldan said. "Sam?"

"I'm in," he said. "I was only trying to be careful."

Aldan snorted. "Try harder."

CHAPTER THIRTEEN

One day and part of another sped by before they were ready to depart. Lowering the raft over the side of the ship had been a monumental effort, taking well over half of the previous day. Installing the rudder and sail stole the rest of the day.

Unfortunately, today's waves were choppier. Getting the supplies over the side and lashing them down took longer than they'd planned, and they'd missed the tide.

Aldan stood on the raft and waited to receive Maelan. Sam dangled her over the *Cathartid's* railing. She grabbed the rope ladder that hung over the rail and clambered down to Aldan with the agility of a monkey. He caught her by the waist and set her on her feet.

"Sit by Linus."

Jamson was already aboard, and Maelan joined her twin at Linus's feet. Jamson threw his arm over her shoulder. They grinned and turned to watch their sisters descend.

René peered over the side and hesitated.

"Come on, René!" Maelan shouted. "You can do it!"

Jamson added his voice to Maelan's, and Aldan tried to look encouraging.

René's fear of heights wasn't helping. Her knuckles were white where she gripped the rail.

The raft crashed into the *Cathartid's* hull and drifted back with a slosh. Like a fretful colt, the raft curveted about on the waves, uncooperative and unpredictable. The apparent danger silenced the twins. At last, Linus steadied the raft and maneuvered it into position.

Sam joined René. "I'll hold onto you as you climb over the railing," he said. "I won't let you go until you're ready."

She nodded, but her gaze didn't leave the scene below. She pulled up one side of her tunic and slung a leg over the side.

Sam gripped her by the elbow, and put one hand on her waist. "That's it, sweet lady. Now, find the rung with your foot."

He grasped her forearms, and she swung her other leg over the rail. "That's good. I've still got you. Now find the rung with your other foot." He waited. "That's it. No, don't look down. René, look at me."

Aldan held his breath, willing her to look away from the frothing water. Her eyes were wide and unblinking.

Sam's voice grew insistent. "René, look at me."

She blinked and raised her eyes to meet his.

"Good." He smiled. "You're very brave. Are you ready?"

René nodded. She stared up into his face as he coaxed her through her descent. Sam's expression caught and held Aldan's attention. *So he does care.*

As soon as René came within reach, Aldan plucked her off the ladder and set her down.

Srilani was next. She'd been standing at Sam's elbow while he helped René, her brows furrowed with worry. As soon as René was safely on board, Srilani's inscrutable mask was back in place.

She couldn't be as calm as she looked.

Sam extended his hand to her but she waved him away.

"I've got this," she said.

He stepped aside. Srilani worked her way over the railing and found the first rung with her foot. She stared straight ahead as she climbed down. One step. Another. Hand on the first rung. The next. Sam leaned over the rail to watch.

Another wave drove the raft into the *Cathartid's* hull with a loud thump. The raft rebounded half a dozen feet, leaving a wide gap of open water. The impact unbalanced Aldan, and he fell to his knees.

"Wait! Stay there!" he shouted. "I can't help you yet."

Linus strained to guide the raft back into position, but the stubborn raft balked. He forced it closer.

Srilani descended a few more rungs and waited for the raft's return.

"Almost there!" Aldan called.

A gust of wind flipped the ladder, putting Srilani's back against the ship's hull. The ladder twisted back around like a snake, and she lost her grip, plunging into the gap between ship and raft.

The twins shrieked, and René rose to her feet. Aldan gasped and threw himself down on the deck to reach for her. She disappeared under the raft. Had she hit the reef?

Even the wind seemed to hold its breath as they searched the water, trying to look everywhere at once.

René pointed to the far side of the raft. "There she is!"

Aldan stared as Srilani surfaced several feet away and flung water out of her face. She kicked out, strong and sure, and swam back to the raft with graceful strokes. He reached out and grabbed her arms, heaving her up with all his might. They landed in a heap and fetched up against the side of a barrel.

"Oh." Srilani looked flustered, eyes wide, water drops clinging to her thick lashes like jewels. She struggled against his hold, and he let her go. "Sorry," she said. "The wind caught me by surprise."

Aldan sat up. "You can *swim*?"

The twins laughed behind them.

Her fingers reached up to adjust her necklace. "We can all swim," she said. "We learned from our mother."

He shook his head. "Sam claims that he can swim, but I don't know how and neither does Linus."

She stood and pulled her tunic away from her body, trying to squeeze it out. "I promise — we'll teach you at the earliest opportunity." Her voice sounded firm. "Every sailor should know how to swim."

"Most don't, you know."

"Strange, isn't it?" Srilani was all business as she turned away. "Linus, do you need help with the tiller?"

Sam came aboard without any problem. The wind that had troubled them for the last half hour became their ally once they cast off. Sam and Jamson raised the sail, and it billowed out with a pleasing snap in the steady sea breeze. The brothers turned to watch the *Cathartid* grow smaller in the distance.

Srilani's voice broke into Aldan's thoughts. "She was correctly named."

"Who?"

"The *Cathartid*."

"Oh?"

"Do you know what cathartids are?"

"No."

"They're birds of prey with long talons and sharp beaks. But they don't hunt like eagles or hawks. Cathartids pick the bones of the dead, feeding on their flesh."

"That fits," Sam said.

"The *Cathartid* is dead now," Aldan said. "She even looks like a pile of bones." He took the tiller from Linus. "Any last words, oh Wise One?"

Linus turned away from the wreck and sank down next to their supplies. "We are free."

CHAPTER FOURTEEN

Excerpt from *Histories of the Twin Kingdoms*

Written by the hand of Lady Elilan
As narrated by His Honor, Elison,
Judge and Counselor of Northern Marst

With a heavy heart, I record this account of the hurricane that occurred following the Summer Solstice. The hurricane caused terrible suffering and horror for the people of Northern Marst when it swept across the Great Gulf and the lands of Northern Marst and Norland. Many have fallen asleep, swept away into the ocean or drowned as they attempted to flee in front of the storm.

The hurricane was even more of a trial for His Majesty, King Terson, and his fair queen, Lady Kaelan, for the storm came only three days after the heir and his older sisters were abducted by Norlan pirates during the annual Solstice Festival.

Five days have passed since the festival that ended in such disaster, and I must record that we have counted three hundred forty-two subjects lost to the storm and many more left destitute and homeless.

The most notable and tragic loss for King Terson's court is the death of Barthson, Baron of Sea Watch and his most beautiful lady, Jocelan. The baron and his lady were away from their home on Sea Watch Island. As the storm approached, they attempted to return. Their boat capsized and all aboard were lost.

They are survived by one child, a daughter of nine years, Lady Angelan, who was at home in the cliffside fortification at the time of the storm. The new Baroness of Sea Watch is King Terson's ward. The young baroness and her nurse will be housed in Kaeson Palace until Lady Angelan's home and affairs are put in order.

The presence of Lady Angelan in the palace has been some comfort to Her Majesty, Lady Kaelan, who is bereft of all her children save Her Highness, Princess Audrilan.

In spite of her great personal distress, Lady Kaelan has been a true mother to her people. She is seen everywhere, providing comfort, support, and practical assistance. Many have been fed, clothed, and sheltered due to her efforts and the benevolence of the king.

Excerpt from *Histories of the Twin Kingdoms, The Revelations to Elison*

This is the account of the revelations of Elison, Judge and Counselor, which were revealed to him two days after the hurricane.

El sent me a vision. I saw the heir and his sisters hiding in the waves of the Great Gulf. The interpretation is clear — they are alive but not out of danger.

The Kingdom of Northern Marst, is in danger on two fronts: Southern Marst and Norland plot to destroy Kaeson's inheritance. El repeated His promise that our deliverance will come from a son of Mardan.

CHAPTER FIFTEEN

"The wind is on our side," Srilani said. She stood at Aldan's elbow as he worked the tiller.

"True, but it sure makes staying off the reef difficult."

They had covered a decent distance in the hours they'd been at sea. After losing sight of the *Cathartid*'s hulking form, the girls worked the sail while the brothers and Jamson manned the tiller in shifts. To ensure they would have food in the evening, they took turns fishing.

Srilani pushed loose strands of hair out of her face. "The tide should be coming in. May I borrow your looking glass?"

"Of course." Aldan retrieved the glass from his belt and handed it to her.

As the minutes passed, everyone scanned the sea for a wave big enough to take them over the reef line. In the days they'd spent making ready, the problem of safely crossing the second line of shallow reefs had been their chief worry.

Now wave after wave piled past them. When the waves reached the reef, most of them broke up on the hidden hazard and reformed on the other side.

Srilani studied the coast through the glass. "The shore looks deserted. I haven't seen any houses, boats, or people all day."

"Neither have I."

"There's a gigantic wave." Jamson jumped up, shading his eyes. "I'm sure it will get over the reef. Look!"

Srilani turned to follow his gaze. She swept the glass along the horizon, and found it, a far-off bulge on the water's surface. "I see it."

"What do you think?" Aldan asked.

"He's probably right. He spends all his spare time sailing. Do you want to look through the glass?"

"Sure. Sam, help Jamson steer. He may need your strength."

Jamson took the tiller, face shining with exhilaration.

Aldan watched the wave grow, stretch out, and pile up.

"I think he's right," Sam said after a moment.

After another few seconds, Aldan stowed the glass in his belt. "The wave will be here in less than two minutes. Everybody, hold onto something. We're going over the reef."

Srilani sat near her sisters and grabbed the ropes that secured the supplies. She checked that everybody was in position. Her sisters. Jamson. Linus. Sam. And Aldan. He took a seat in the space next to her. She studied him. Why had she let him take command? Why did she trust him?

The wave approached with majestic slowness. Inescapable power and energy flowed through the water ahead of it. Srilani met Aldan's gaze.

He raised his brows. "It's almost here. Are you scared?"

"Of course I'm scared."

"Your face doesn't show it."

"Don't believe everything you see." She gripped the ropes hard enough to leave creases in her palms.

The water thrummed under the raft as the wave approached, rumbling like distant thunder. Jamson turned the tiller, taking advantage of the water's momentum. At last, the wave reached them, lifting the raft up. And up. Aldan's hand covered hers, and he grinned. Her stomach did a little flip.

The rumble beneath them became a roar. The wave crested over the reef, and they plunged down into the water beyond. It was like flying. A laugh of pure joy bubbled up inside, and she let it out. They skidded across the surf, racing toward shore.

Linus dropped the sail, and Sam helped Jamson lift the rudder out of the water. As smoothly as a leaf on the wind, the craft rode onto the sandy beach and came to rest.

Aldan squeezed her hand and released it. "We made it." He laughed, white teeth flashing in his tanned face. "We made it!"

Everybody climbed off the raft, and the brothers pushed it farther out of the water.

René, looking happy for the first time in days, hugged Srilani. "Oh, it feels so good to be on land again. Remind me to never, ever get in a boat again."

Srilani hugged her back. "Right. I'm sure Father will go along with that. Now all we have to do is walk home so we can tell him."

René chuckled. "That's all? Then we should be there tomorrow, right?"

"If only that were true." Srilani sighed. *So much to do. So far to go.*

Aldan stood next to them, head down, hands loose at his sides. His posture caught Srilani's attention.

He took a few steps away from the water and fell to his knees. He plunged his hands into the sand and watched the particles flow through his fingers. Over and over, he cupped the sand in his hands and poured it out. Then he stretched out on the sand, flat on his back, and stared at the sky.

Sam and Linus grew serious. The twins stopped moving around to stare.

Sam crouched beside Aldan. "How long has it been? Twelve years?"

Aldan threw one arm over his eyes. "A few months more than that."

"Twelve years?" Srilani stepped closer. "As a slave?"

Sam spoke without taking his eyes from Aldan. "Aboard the ship."

Twelve years as Rozar's slave. Twelve years aboard ship.

"Are you saying it's been twelve years since you've been on dry land?"

Her question was directed to Aldan, but Sam answered for him. "Yes."

"But surely—" She paused as the horrible truth came clear. "Rozar never took you ashore?"

"Never."

She looked at Linus and back at Sam. "How long has it been for you and Linus?"

"Linus was captured when he was four. He's fourteen. I was sold into slavery the same year when I was thirteen. I'm twenty-three. So ten years."

The bitterness in Sam's voice burned her. Guilt rose up to shame her — she hadn't shown him enough respect.

Aldan pulled his arm from his dazed eyes to look at her. He tried to make a joke. "This isn't really the time for resting, is it?"

She attempted a smile in return. "No, I'm afraid not."

He sat up, and held out a hand to Linus who pulled him to his feet. He took a deep breath and let it out. "You know more about surviving on land than we do. What do we do first?"

The world was upside down. Aldan tilted his head and considered the Great Gulf, the ebb and flow of the surf, the sand beneath his feet. The ocean waves looked far different from the beach than from the *Cathartid's* deck.

Srilani paused at his side and looked over the water. She seemed lost in thought.

He cleared his throat. "What's next?"

Srilani blinked, and her normal air of authority snapped into place. What was it about her? She took charge of most situations as if command were as natural to her as breathing. She'd led them through choosing a site to spend the evening, setting up a fire ring, and unloading their supplies. René's idea to put their blankets and other equipment in empty water barrels had worked beautifully. The barrel with the rest of their water was woefully lightweight, but their spirits were high. Sam sang songs and told silly jokes. They'd laughed as they worked together. And laughed some more.

Srilani rubbed the back of her neck and turned to face the group. "Food," she said. "Let's gather any wood we can find and cook the fish." She pointed to the twins. "Maelan and Jamson, scout around and see if there's anything else that's edible in this area. Stay together and within shouting distance."

Maelan and Jamson nodded and took off.

"Linus and Sam, please arrange our packs on either side of the fire ring — women on one side and men on the other."

They kindled a fire and cleaned their catch as Sol's last rays lingered. Srilani put René in charge of showing the brothers how to cook their fish over the open fire.

Aldan sat on a gnarled piece of driftwood next to Jamson as they ate the meal. "Do you ever doubt that something is real?"

Jamson swallowed a bite of fish. "How do you mean?"

"Like you've discovered something so new and wonderful that you can't believe it's real."

Jamson licked his fingers and nodded. "That's how I felt the first time I rode a horse. It was like a miracle, sort of."

Freedom gave the food extra spice. Aldan savored every morsel and let his eyes wander to the darkening sky, the stars breaking through the film of the heavens, the fire licking at the wood, and the surf rolling onto the beach.

Had he ever done things like this before he was enslaved? Had he helped build a fire? Had he ever perched on a giant piece of driftwood to eat fish? Had he laughed and joked and sung songs, surrounded by friends or family? As always, his mind supplied no answers.

"This tastes wonderful," Sam said. He took another enthusiastic bite.

Aldan chuckled. "Always thinking of your stomach."

Sam spread his hands. "Look at me. I need lots of food."

"Finding food must be one of our biggest concerns," Aldan said. "I know how to fish, but where are we going to find enough food to feed Sam and the rest of us? We won't be near water all the time."

"We're going to follow the coast, aren't we?" Sam's questioning eyes swept the group.

"Actually, we don't know that," Srilani said. "We need fresh water. We'll die of thirst long before we die of starvation. Water takes first priority."

Aldan took a stick and drew a map in the sand. "This is Norland, all along here. This is the Great Gulf, and we're about here on the coast. Right?"

"That's right," she said.

He drew a star on the coastline. "This is Port Azor. There's a river somewhere close to us that flows from the north and enters the gulf." He drew a wavy line to represent the river. "One or two days away at the most. I hope."

Sam's brows knit together, and his voice rumbled like thunder from a distant storm. "You hope?"

Srilani stood and held out her hand. Aldan passed his drawing stick to her, and she added more detail to his sand map. "There's a reef that runs east to west, from here to here. The Hole, as Rozar called it, is over to the east. Obviously, we didn't reach it."

She checked Sam's expression. So far, he seemed open to what she had to say. Linus, too, seemed interested. "All we've seen today is wilderness and no river. The Trahn River would be impossible to miss, and we traveled a long distance to the west today."

Jamson cut in. "We were making good time for a raft. The wind was perfect."

"That doesn't reassure me," Sam said.

Srilani held the stick in front of her with both hands. "What do you mean?"

"How many days away is it?"

"I think we're within a day's walk of the river." She flexed the stick between her hands. "Maybe two."

Sam shifted and frowned. "Oh come on. We all know there's only enough water for half a day. You can't seriously intend to walk when we have a raft."

"No raft," Srilani said. "We'd have to cross back over the reef."

Jamson spread his hands. His expression was apologetic. "A proper boat could do it, but the raft? I wouldn't try it."

"But—"

"We can walk," Srilani said. "And we can do without water for a couple of days. In fact, once we run out of drinking water, it would be better if we don't eat either."

Sam's brow wrinkled. "Wonderful."

"We'll do what we have to," Aldan said. He turned to Srilani. "I think we need you more than you need us. We have a lot to learn and a long way to go."

She rolled the smooth stick between her palms and chose her words with care. "We all need each other. We need your protection, and you need us to teach you how to survive on land. Your part is as important as ours because you'll help us blend in."

Sam let out a huff and spoke in Norlan. "That won't be easy."

"Why?"

"Your accent is wrong, and you don't look right."

"What's wrong with the way we look?"

"Your clothes for one thing, but mainly your blonde hair and blue eyes. You and René definitely can't pass for Norlanders."

René's hand flew to her hair. "Oh dear."

Srilani froze. Hadn't Rozar gloated over their appearance? "That is a problem. We need to invent a story to explain our presence in Norland."

She added the drawing stick to the flames and watched it catch fire. "But what about the twins? Will their looks be a problem?"

Sam yawned and shook his head. "No. Greenish-brownish eyes are uncommon, but I've seen others like them. Their hair is straight and dark brown, and nobody will think anything of it."

Srilani let out a breath. If worse came to worst, Jamson and Maelan might make it home.

Sam raised his arms over his head in a huge stretch that emphasized his muscular chest. "Azor's teeth, I'm tired." He yawned again and stood up, turning to the side in another stretch. "Can't a man get a decent night's rest around here?"

After their grueling day, more conversation was pointless. She ignored Sam and spoke to Aldan. "Do you think we need to set watches tonight?"

"No. We all need to rest."

His face was in the shadows, and she couldn't read his expression. He'd supported her argument to stay on land. At least he was willing to listen, unlike Father.

Sleep was elusive. They could always cover their hair, but they couldn't change the color of their eyes. The unforeseen problem of their appearance haunted her. In the Twin Kingdoms, "the look of Mardan" was greatly prized, but here it might be their downfall.

A smattering of rain woke Aldan. The tiny shower subsided without waking the others. Aldan rolled to his side. The aches in his body brought the last few amazing days to mind — surviving the storm, building the raft, leaving the ship, and crossing the reef. His heart lifted. If he died trying to reach Kaeson, he'd be content to die a free man.

On the opposite side of the fire, the sisters huddled in their blankets. René and Srilani rested side-by-side. Their faces were remarkably similar. Most people would probably favor René because her face, and the rest of her, approached perfection. In his eyes both were beautiful, but Srilani had something — some indefinable something he couldn't pin down — that drew his attention back to her, time and time again.

Her brows puckered as she slept, as if she were trying to solve some puzzle. That intensity appealed to him. He noted the dagger she held in her right hand, and his mouth quirked. Of course Srilani would be on guard, and the gods help the fool who tried to harm her sisters or brother.

Her eyes opened and stared back at him for a few seconds. In one lithe movement, she rose to her feet and walked past him to the soft white beach beyond their camp.

He sat up and turned to watch.

Srilani sheathed her weapon and knelt in the sand, facing Sol as the great star rose in the east. She flattened her hands on the sand and pressed her forehead on top of them. He got up and knelt at a respectful distance. She prayed for several minutes before she lifted her head.

"You pray to Sol?"

She shook her head. "I pray to El, the maker of Sol."

"El." A ghost of a memory stirred in his mind but vanished as soon as he tried to hold onto it.

"Yes. I was praying for safe travel and deliverance."

"We need any help we can get," he said. Better to keep his skepticism to himself. No sense angering a god who might, or might not, be looking out for them.

She got to her feet and dusted the sand from her knees. "You don't believe."

He scrambled to his feet and fell into step beside her as she walked along the water's edge. "I don't know what I believe."

"You'll see," she said. "El will provide."

If you say so.

Her eyes scanned the gulf. "We are too visible here. Since we're not taking the raft, we should hide it. If any of the crew comes along here, we don't want to make it easy to find us."

A chill ran up his spine. "Let's wake the others and do that right away."

"Why don't you let my sisters and me pack the supplies and break camp? Linus, Sam, and Jamson can help you with the raft."

They stopped walking to turn back. "Srilani."

"Yes?"

He had her full attention and he couldn't think what he'd meant to say. "I'm glad you are here." He stopped. "No, I mean . . . not that you're here . . . but since you are—"

She nodded. "I know what you mean. I'm glad too."

CHAPTER SIXTEEN

Excerpts from *Histories of the Twin Kingdoms*

To Lady Kaelan, Queen Mother of Kaeson

Dearest Lady Kaelan,

I have heard the terrible news about the abduction of your children. My heart bleeds for you, my friend, since I know the pain of losing a child. Even after all these years, I mourn my son. Please know that I am praying to El every day, every hour, for your children's safety and eventual return to your arms.

Perhaps we can comfort one another. My daughter, Queen Yolani, has extended an invitation to you to visit us at Mardan's Palace. You are welcome to stay with us however long you wish.

I realize this invitation may be awkward to accept, given the strained relations that exist between our kingdoms; however, our people will surely understand that humanity must prevail over differences. You and I have always enjoyed our private correspondence, and I feel certain that we will gain strength from spending time together.

This note is carried by my personal steward, Leodan, who is loyal to me. Return your answer by his hand only. My daughter's husband will interfere if given any excuse, but he will not dare to object if I present your visit as an inevitable event. We will, of necessity, have to celebrate your visit with banquets and pomp, but we may spend the rest of our time in private conversation.

Please say you will come to us. Take a few days, if necessary, to consider your answer. I hope and pray that you will say yes.

Yours most sincerely,

Lady Raslan, Queen Mother of Kaedan

CHAPTER SEVENTEEN

Srilani's tongue stuck to the roof of her mouth, and thirst burned her throat. Swallowing provided no relief. Their drinking water had run out the night before. The ragged crew plodded along the beach in grim silence, in sharp contrast to yesterday's talkative group. Aldan had brimmed with questions for her.

"How old are you? And René? And the twins?"

"What's Kaeson like?"

"How long does it take to learn to read and write?"

He walked beside her now, probably as miserable as she, but he didn't seem unhappy or bitter.

Sol's cruel heat intensified the unpleasant odors of their surroundings, like a hot summer day on a wet dog's fur. Each scent was sharp and distinct, from the green tree oils to the rotting clumps of seaweed and even the dusty sand.

She checked over her shoulder. The twins trudged, shoulders slumped, on either side of Linus. Behind them, René stumbled. Sam caught her elbow and steadied her.

"Look out, Srilani." Aldan's voice was low and urgent. "Watch your step."

In the same instant, a pungent stench alerted her, and she instinctively danced back. A black, thick-bodied snake raised up in their path. Its mouth opened wide, startling white in contrast to its scales, and displayed a set of sharp fangs. Her hand flew to the sword she'd acquired from the ship, drawing it and holding it ready with both hands.

"Get back," she said. "It's venomous."

He backed away.

The viper wasn't appeased by their retreat. It undulated forward and feinted at Srilani, snapping its jaws an inch from her right boot. She leapt back, sword poised.

Jamson called to them. "What's wrong?"

The snake recoiled, slithered forward in an arc, and reared for another strike.

"Stay back!" Srilani shouted. The serpent struck at her again, but she swept the sword down and across with great force, severing its head from its body. Footsteps thudded in the sand behind her. The decapitated serpent writhed for several seconds before it flopped to a standstill.

"What was that?" Sam asked in a husky voice.

Jamson's shout was gleeful. "You killed a cottonmouth!"

Srilani fought a manic urge to giggle at the contrast between the two. Sam was ghost white, but Jamson was flushed with excitement. She looked around the circle. René hugged her arms with trembling hands. Linus and Maelan were wide-eyed.

Aldan stared at the dead snake. "What does 'venomous' mean?"

"Its bite can hurt you," Jamson said. "Sometimes people die from cottonmouth bites."

Srilani wiped her blade with a palm frond. "Thanks for the warning, Aldan. I wasn't paying close enough attention."

Aldan frowned. "You nearly stepped on its back."

Jamson snagged the snake's body from the sand, holding it aloft with an admiring whistle. "More than three feet long." He grinned at the brothers. "Ever eaten snake before?"

Maelan rolled her eyes. "I don't care if we eat at all. I just want something to drink."

Srilani sheathed her sword and adjusted her pack. "Let's keep going."

⋈

How far was that river? The question plagued Aldan. What if they didn't find water soon enough? He tried to distract himself by working on the problem Sam had raised the night before last — how to explain the presence of René and Srilani. Only one solution presented itself, and try as he might, Aldan couldn't think of another one.

Srilani glanced his way. "What's on your mind?"

When he didn't answer, she encouraged him. "Out with it. Have I offended you?"

"No. No, it's not that." He smiled and ducked his head. "It's more that I think I'll offend you." For certain, she wouldn't like his idea.

She lifted her brows, waiting. "Just say it straight out."

"Promise not to get angry. Keep in mind that it's just a possible solution to the problem we talked about."

"Go ahead. I'll try not to get angry."

He looked away, down the beach, and hunted for the right words. "Have you seen Norlan women before?"

"Only Mirza."

He grimaced. "Mirza doesn't count. I'm not sure she was even human. She was nothing like you."

Srilani chuckled. "Thanks. I think."

"Norlan women wear head coverings. I've seen them on other ships. When Rozar pulled into port, I saw women on the wharves. All of the women wore black head coverings."

Srilani's face lit with a rare smile. "That's promising. A head covering would make it much easier to blend in. Why did you think that would offend me?"

Aldan cleared his throat and let his head fall back to gaze up at the sky. Then he looked at her to gauge her reaction. "That's not the worst part. I think that I should . . . that it would be best if I claim you as my property. As my woman. René could belong to Sam."

Her smile vanished, and her face lost any hint of warmth.

He rushed on. "Please believe me, I wouldn't take advantage of you. But we need a story. The only believable explanation for you, a blue-eyed woman, is that you were brought here from somewhere else to be sold in the slave market." Other faces from the past flashed through his mind. "Rozar did it often enough. You and your sister weren't our first blue-eyed captives."

"That's—" Srilani forgot to speak in Norlan. "That's outrageous. Repulsive."

She sped over the rocky sand, head down, and Aldan took long steps to keep up.

"You promised not to get angry," he said.

"I said I would *try* not to get angry." She walked faster.

"I don't agree with slavery," he said. "You should know that. *Why was she being so unreasonable?* He tried to keep his voice calm. "If you and your sister seemed to belong to us, then your presence wouldn't cause so much comment. The less talk, the better." He reached out and brushed her arm, but Srilani shook off his touch and whirled to face him.

"*Some* stupid people might believe that you could afford me, but nobody — nobody! — would believe Samazor could afford to buy René." She ticked off her points on the fingers of one hand. "Rozar said we were valuable. He was going to offer us to King Dzor. We were his only real cargo, so we had to bring enough to pay for the crew and supplies."

She spun on her heel and stalked ahead. He strode after her, but now he was fighting his own temper.

Srilani's face was flushed, and her voice trembled. "René is one of the most beautiful women El ever created. She's worth a fortune, and you know it."

The silence thickened as they tramped on, and Aldan yielded to the contrary impulse to pour oil on the fire. "You're selling yourself short," he said. "You're valuable too."

Srilani lost her temper entirely. "Do *not* joke about this! We are what we are, and nobody would believe that *you* could buy us."

Aldan's face went hot. "Just forget I said anything. You have a point, and I'm sorry I brought it up. Forget it."

⋀

Srilani worried her lip. *Stupid, stupid, stupid. Why did I say that?*

Her anger was slow to fade, but remorse seeped in and took its place.

Aldan hadn't spoken to her for a full hour. She'd done exactly what she said she wouldn't. He'd been thinking about their problem, and she'd snapped his head off with the same precision she'd applied to the snake.

"Aldan."

"Hmm?"

"I'm sorry for losing my temper." She swallowed. Apologies were so hard. "You're right, of course. The only reason René and I would be here is if we were brought to Norland as slaves."

"You're right too. You're worth a fortune — far more than any sailor could afford."

"I sounded really . . . conceited." Heat crept into her cheeks at the crass evaluation of her own worth.

"No." Aldan shook his head. "Not conceited, just—"

"Conceited," she said. "If you and Sam *looked* like wealthy men, your idea might work."

"Too bad."

"Yes it is, isn't it?" She sighed. "I suppose we'll have to stay out of sight. That's easy to do in this wild place. But soon we're going to meet other people, and when we do, they might talk to others about us."

"They *will* talk," he said. "You and René are remarkable, and so are the twins. Because they're twins."

"Regardless of how likely the story is, I guess we'll have to use it and hope for the best."

As they walked on, Srilani's mind wouldn't be still. She went over and over their situation, all the potential problems and pitfalls they might encounter. She wasn't aware of speaking out loud until it was too late. "Making the twins less obvious is the most important thing."

Aldan slowed his pace. "Why is it most important?"

"What?"

"You said, 'Making the twins less obvious is most important.'"

Her skin prickled. The surf hissed a warning, but it was too late to take back her words. Aldan's razor-sharp mind had dissected everything they'd discussed and found the most telling part. She looked over her shoulder to make sure they couldn't be overheard. How much should she tell him?

Aldan's chin lifted in a challenge. "What did you mean?"

"Jamson is my father's heir. He's the most valuable to you."

"Only boys get to inherit?"

Srilani shook her head. "No, but—"

"Your father doesn't have other sons?"

"No."

Aldan held back the limb of a scrubby bush for her to pass. "You're the oldest. Wouldn't you inherit if Jamson doesn't make it back to Kaeson?"

"Yes, but—"

"What? Why is it most important that Jamson makes it back?"

"Because . . ." Srilani shook her head.

"What would happen if none of you returned?"

"Our baby sister would inherit."

He stopped talking, but his silence wasn't reassuring. Her pulse beat hard, faster than their footsteps and the pounding surf. The inevitable question hung between them even before he stepped in front of her. His body formed a wall and forced her to stop.

"What secret are you holding back? You haven't explained why Jamson is so important. You're older. You're wiser. I don't understand."

Curse my reckless tongue. Srilani whispered, "Can you keep a secret?"

"Yes."

How could she tell this man a secret that could change history? He was a slave — or he had been. What would he care if a kingdom's future was at stake?

"Water!" Maelan's shout shattered the silence. "I hear running water!"

⋀

Aldan dunked himself for the third time in the river's smooth current. He couldn't remember ever feeling so clean. The pleasure of the moment couldn't drown out the nagging question of Srilani's secret. He sloshed out of the water, dried off, and put his clothes on. There had to be a way to get her alone long enough for her to tell him what she'd been about to say.

Every time he came close, she found something else that needed her attention — assigning who should fish and who should set up camp. Building a fire. Cooking. Filling water skins. The woman was avoiding him, plain and simple.

Finally everyone was asleep except for Srilani, René, and him. Aldan watched Srilani across the campfire as she held an intense, whispered conversation with René.

Captain Rozar had been jubilant when he'd captured the four children. He'd planned to give the older sisters to King Dzor. Srilani hadn't made idle boasts about their high value.

What made them so much more valuable than other beautiful, blonde virgins with blue eyes? Why did Srilani believe her brother's survival was so much more important than her own? And René's and Maelan's? How could she believe that?

When Rozar had stroked Srilani's face, he'd looked almost sick with the longing to "tame" her. Yet he'd shown real restraint, and Aldan still marveled that the captain hadn't taken advantage of her. Only extreme motivation could explain Rozar's unusual self-control.

Baron's children? Would a baron's daughters be valuable enough to prompt King Dzor to reward Rozar with an estate and a title?

Aldan's eyes narrowed. The intensity of his scrutiny drew Srilani's attention. She lifted her chin and gave him a haughty glare.

There was that look again. The one that spoke plainly of a life of privilege and birth. All of the siblings seemed to expect a certain level of deference, accepting courtesies as their due.

She turned her head away, and Aldan closed his eyes, pretending to sleep. Srilani had claimed first watch.

An idea formed in the back of Aldan's mind. Like a wisp of cloud on the far horizon, the idea took shape, darkening in color and growing larger. Aldan examined his hypothesis from every angle as it pushed forward into his consciousness.

Could it be true? The idea was too incredible, and he tried to dismiss it.

The sisters talked in sibilant whispers for several minutes, their voices too low to distinguish one word from another. They were arguing. He chanced another peek in their direction. They were too focused on their discussion to pay any attention to him.

Srilani broke off what she was saying, stood up, and stalked off to the edge of the firelight.

Aldan waited. And listened. When he was certain René was asleep, he rose and joined Srilani, crouching beside her beneath the trees. "So when are you going to tell me who you are?"

He studied her profile in the moonlight. She didn't answer, and she didn't look at him. The crashing surf punctuated her silence and in that moment, he knew. He knew!

"I can't hear you." He leaned toward her and cupped his ear. "What did you say? You know . . . if you don't tell me, I'll be forced to guess."

He smiled in the darkness, and he couldn't keep the smugness out of his voice. "Tell me if I'm wrong, Princess Srilani."

CHAPTER EIGHTEEN

Aldan's smile grew as the seconds passed. She would have corrected him already if he'd guessed wrong.

Srilani turned in his direction and huffed. "How did you guess?"

"It's the way you stare when you're displeased with me. Like you're thinking of ways for me to die."

She groaned softly. "My wretched temper."

"You didn't think anything of it when I bowed to you on the ship. Neither did your brother or sisters. You take charge like Captain Rozar, except that you're better at command than he ever was. You're good with a knife." He spread his hands. "What girl needs to know how to handle a dagger unless she might have to fight? You *did* fight the day you were taken. I've never heard of a girl captive fighting back."

Aldan rubbed the stubble on his chin, thinking over their time together. "Plus Rozar was so pleased. In all the time I was his slave, I'd never seen him act like that. Like he'd found an entire chest of gold."

"Are you going to sell us out?" Her question was low, and her hand inched toward her scabbard.

He grabbed her hand, gripping her fingers tightly. "No, Srilani. I would never do that."

"What about your friends?"

She meant Sam. Her hand squirmed in his, but he held it tighter.

"They are my brothers. Sam, Linus, and I have been slaves together most of our lives. Sam's father sold him to Rozar to pay off debts."

She stopped struggling.

"Linus was taken when he was four years old, and his mother was killed trying to save him. We hate slavery, and there's no way we would sell you out."

He released her hand and leaned back against a tree trunk. For a long time, they gazed out to sea, watching the white lines of surf crawl onto the beach.

Aldan stretched his arms so he wouldn't doze off. "I'm so glad we found the river today. I'd forgotten how wonderful fresh water tasted."

She covered a yawn and flexed her neck from side to side. "Too bad it's so deep and wide. We'll have to follow it north until we can find a place to cross."

She didn't elaborate. He guessed that she didn't want to talk. Instead, he listened to the strange new sounds of the insects and rustling leaves. Maybe he'd blocked out his memories of childhood on land as a defense against the intense grief of being taken by Captain Rozar.

"I'm glad you know our secret." Srilani's low confession interrupted his thoughts. "But I'm not comfortable yet with your brothers knowing."

"They have to know the truth, Srilani. You can trust them with your life."

"You think so?" She sighed. "René was trying to convince me to tell you the truth just awhile ago."

"You should listen to your sister."

She stood and dusted herself off. "Are you taking the next watch?"

"Yes."

"Then I need to sleep. We'll tell your brothers in the morning. May El bless you."

Now, how am I supposed to respond to that? "Umm, thanks. Good night, Princess."

※

"Would you care for some wine, Srilani?"

Srilani's body jerked. She turned. Greyson sat beside her, holding a flagon of wine ready, poised over her goblet. They sat on the dais in the Great Hall, surrounded by the usual chatter of a Third Day banquet. Except it couldn't be an ordinary Third Day banquet. She wore a formal gown of North Marstan sapphire instead of white. Why was she wearing her court dress?

"Srilani?"

His blue eyes, the "eyes of Mardan," rested on her face. Affection and male appreciation glinted in their depths.

Warmth bloomed in her cheeks and around her heart. She nodded. "Yes," she whispered.

He smiled down at her, and she couldn't suppress a smile in return.

He lifted his goblet when he finished pouring, and she followed his lead, breathless and flustered. The noise in the Great Hall diminished because the nobles and the officers were interested in everything the First Princess did or said. Something about this moment was significant.

"May El bless you, Srilani."

"May El bless you, Greyson."

She took a sip, watching him watch her. He set his cup down and pushed back his chair. All conversation ceased. Srilani held her breath as Greyson knelt at her feet. A peculiar heat bathed her skin, and her heart slammed against her ribs.

She set her goblet down and turned to face him. At that moment, a heavy gold chain appeared in her lap as if by magic. Where had she seen this necklace before? The links were about an inch in diameter, heavy, and made for a man. She lifted the chain, turning it round and round in her hands. Candlelight played across its surfaces.

Greyson's attention focused on the chain, and she couldn't escape the impression that he was disappointed or angry or sad. She'd done this to him, but she couldn't undo what was done. She stood, facing him, and lifted the golden strand of links over his head, settling them on his shoulders. She smoothed the chain into place across his chest, tears springing into her eyes. *Why are we so unhappy?*

Srilani jolted awake when an insect bit her cheek. Her hand came away from her face, sticky with tears and a dark smear of blood. She stared blankly at her fingers in the dim light. Did Greyson think of her? Did he think she was dead? Did he miss her? Reality took a long time to return, and the sorrow of the dream took even longer to seep away.

Srilani huddled into her blanket, facing the embers' dull glow. The dream had chilled her, and she shivered in spite of the summer night's heat. Muffled footsteps approached. Aldan was back, and he bent over René.

"Your turn," he whispered.

"Thank you," she said.

Srilani's mood lightened as she remembered the heated discussion between René and Sam after the evening meal.

"I will so take a watch," René had insisted, pushing back her long braid and setting her feet apart. "I'm only a year younger than Srilani, and I'm older than Linus. Just because you're bigger and stronger than I am doesn't mean you're better at watching, Sam-a-zor. My eyes are every bit as good as yours."

Srilani couldn't believe René's willingness to stand up to the big redhead. Her sister avoided interaction with men because they acted so admiringly. So adoringly. But René inspired that response in men. They showered her with compliments. They wanted to talk to her. They showed off in front of her, and their behavior embarrassed her. Yet she seemed comfortable enough with Sam. Comfortable enough to go toe to toe, if necessary.

"Besides, I bet I can scream louder than you."

The twins had giggled, and Sam had given up the argument with a grumble.

René left the clearing and headed for the beach. Aldan bedded down on the opposite side of the fire. His easy acceptance of their abilities stood in sharp contrast to Sam's lower expectations.

She stared into the fire as Aldan fell asleep. It was pointless to try for sleep after the dream about Greyson.

Srilani didn't wake until Sol's light was pushing against her eyelids.

"You never sleep this late," René said. "Do you feel well?"

Srilani sat up. Aldan and Linus watched as René put her wrist against Srilani's forehead.

"You feel warm."

"It's just because I've been asleep. I'm fine." *What a lie.* More like she'd been beaten with a stick. She sat still as René's gentle fingers pushed back her hair to examine her temple.

"Your bruise is almost gone and your eyes are clear, but you don't look rested."

If you only knew. "Don't worry about it." Srilani made herself get up, shake out her blanket, and fold it. "I'll be back in a few minutes."

She escaped the camp and took a short walk. She took a couple of extra minutes to finger comb her hair and braid it. The hopeless tangles made her long for her maid. If she ever saw Ana again, she would be the best mistress anyone could ever have.

Sam and the twins had caught several fish while she slept. Aldan was stoking the fire, but when he saw her, he threw down his stick and strode to her side.

"Are you ready to give them the news?"

She nodded. "You tell them."

"That might be better." He lifted his voice. "Sam. Linus. There's something you need to know."

Both men stopped what they were doing to give Aldan their full attention.

"Captain Rozar had a secret, and nobody knew it except his captives."

René and the twins shared startled looks.

"Remember how we thought Rozar might have taken the children of a baron? Well, he did more than that. These are the children of the King of Northern Marst, and Jamson is his heir."

Linus nodded as if being introduced to royalty was nothing new.

Sam chuckled. "I can't say I'm surprised. Srilani has to be the most high-handed woman I've ever seen." He turned to her. "I mean, you really like things your way. Same for your sister."

René gave an outraged gasp.

Sam swept a bow to Srilani. "So, Your Highness, welcome to the land of my birth."

"Forgive us for keeping it a secret until now," she said.

He shrugged. "You were smart to keep it a secret. I would have done the same thing, but don't worry. We know how to keep a secret, don't we Linus?"

Linus stood straight and tall, placed his right fist over his heart, and bowed. "Indeed."

⋀⋀

"I think we need to rest for a day," Aldan said.

Srilani opened her mouth to speak, but Aldan held up his hand. "Wait. Think about it. We've spent the last several days surviving a hurricane, building a raft, getting to land, and finding the river. We're all exhausted."

"Now you're talking." Sam leaned up against a tree, watching the group finish the last of their breakfast. "I wouldn't mind fishing some more. We could find more berries too. I really liked those."

Aldan sat on a large rock near Sam and folded his arms over his chest. "Tomorrow we can set out early and follow the river north until we find a place narrow enough to cross."

"Srilani, please let us wait a day," Maelan said. "I'm so tired."

"We should rest." Jamson sat next to Aldan. "Just for today."

Srilani paused to think. "I agree," she said. "As long as we set out early tomorrow. And as long as we're ready to leave in a hurry." She turned to Jamson. "Remember Father's rules when we go out with the Palace Guard? Those rules should apply — two people on watch at all times during the day in one hour shifts so they stay alert."

Sam nudged Aldan. "Told you she was high-handed."

The twins hurried to put their packs in order while Linus gathered all the scraps from the meal.

"Who do you think should take the first watch, Princess René?" Sam's voice was a taunt.

"I will, Samazor. That way you can watch your fishing line."

"I'll watch with you, René" Srilani said.

René shook her head. "No, you won't. You're going to rest. You look like you didn't sleep at all last night."

"Let me stand guard with you," Linus said.

Aldan prepared to intervene in case Srilani argued, but she didn't protest. The morning eased by, and when Aldan returned from his turn fishing at noon, she was sound asleep on her pallet. René sat nearby, mending a hole in Jamson's original pair of trousers.

"It's lucky Maelan found these needles in the crews' quarters," she said.

"Mmm." Aldan didn't hear René's words. Instead, he crouched to examine Srilani. "Do you think she's ill?"

"I think she didn't rest well."

Aldan scratched his chin. "That makes sense. I heard her talking in her sleep."

The twins rushed into the clearing, breathless and pale.

"There's a—"

" — longboat!"

"It's full of—"

" — pirates!"

"I saw that ugly one—"

" — the one you call Scar."

Srilani jerked awake.

Aldan had to ward her off with a hand on her shoulder to avoid a collision. "You heard what they said?"

"Yes." She sounded out of breath, like she'd been running. Her face was flushed and lined with sleep.

"Get your bearings. I'll take a look." He gave her shoulder a squeeze, then turned to the twins. "Show me."

They raced back the way they'd come. He ran after them, and they crouched together at the edge of the trees.

Scar! Rozar's first mate, at least, was unmistakable. And there were five others from the ship. All of the pirates' attention was on their battle against the current at the mouth of the river. The river pushed them away from shore and toward the Great Gulf. What if they turned back to the east and beached near the campsite?

"Jamson, go tell Sam and Linus to stay out of sight. Maelan, come with me. We need to get away from here."

Jamson bounded off, and Aldan grabbed Maelan's hand, pulling her with him. To her credit, she kept up with his long strides. When they reached the campsite, Srilani was stuffing her blanket into her makeshift pack. Moments later, Jamson, Linus, and Sam crashed through the underbrush and stumbled into the clearing.

Srilani stopped what she was doing. "Well? Are they coming here?"

"Maybe," Aldan said. "They're busy fighting the river's current. They might give up and land nearby."

René gasped. Sam and Linus looked hunted.

"Or they might be swept out into the Gulf," Jamson said.

"Not likely," Sam said. "They know what they're doing."

"I agree with Sam," Aldan said. "If they can't cross the mouth of the river, they'll land on this side to get some rest. Then they'll try again."

"We need to hide any evidence that we were here," Srilani said. "Everybody, make sure you have all your gear together. Grab some brush and palm fronds to cover up where we slept. When you're ready, line up by this rock with Jamson at the front." She stooped and removed a couple of rocks from the fire ring.

A moment passed. Then they broke into a frenzy of work. The campsite was restored to its natural state in less than five minutes, and they were lined up with their packs, ready to set off. All except Srilani.

"What do you think you're doing?" Aldan demanded.

She turned to face him, chin lifted and voice determined. "I'll keep an eye on the pirates. Once I'm satisfied that it's safe, I will catch up with the rest of you. Jamson will take point and be in command while I'm not with you."

Everything inside Aldan rebelled against leaving Srilani behind. He stepped out of line and dropped his pack to the ground with a thump. "I'm staying with you. I'm not leaving you on your own."

CHAPTER NINETEEN

Srilani's nails pressed into the soft flesh of her palms. She had no time to stand here arguing, but Aldan looked as immovable as a boulder. "You must go with the others," she said. "You don't know anything about tracking, and you'll just get in my way."

He crossed his arms and shook his head. "I'm supposed to keep you safe. That was our deal. Sam and Linus can take care of your family, but I'm staying with you."

She bit her lip. What would Father do? What would he want her to do in this situation? She shook her head. He would tell her to send a man to take care of it. Father wouldn't listen to her ideas or allow her to make this kind of decision. Why was she tormenting herself? The moments were flying past, and Jamson's safety was paramount.

"Suit yourself, but stay out of my way." She brushed past Aldan. What if this was the last time she ever saw her family? Her throat tightened, and she struggled to sound normal. "Jamson, head north and stay close to the river. René and Maelan, help Jamson count steps. When you've traveled about five miles, take cover and wait for us. If we don't reach you by nightfall, stay hidden."

She hugged René. Hard. As they parted, René's troubled eyes met hers. Her sister — her best friend — understood the stakes. René gave her an encouraging nod, but her lips were quivering.

Srilani pulled Maelan close and kissed her forehead. Jamson endured her embrace with good grace. She stepped back, keeping a firm hold on his shoulders as she frowned at him. "No fire. If you see other people or if you have to leave the river, leave me a sign pointing out your direction. Just like you learned from the Palace Guard."

Srilani released her brother and glanced at Sam and Linus. The young men seemed stunned by the sudden turn of events, and Linus's anxious eyes were focused on Aldan. How could she leave her siblings under the doubtful protection of Aldan's brothers?

"You don't have to worry, Srilani," Jamson said, bringing her attention back to him. "I know what to do."

Her brother's misplaced confidence wasn't reassuring, but she had to get them away from here. "Wait for us for one day and then head for home. Don't turn back." She swallowed her fears and pointed upriver. "Go. May El bless you."

⋀

Aldan watched as Jamson set out, followed by Maelan, Sam, and Linus. A hollow spot opened inside his chest as his brothers left him behind. Linus looked back over his shoulder. Aldan lifted a hand in farewell. René took her customary place as rear guard. Within moments, the group was lost from sight. He picked up his pack and turned to Srilani. "What's your plan?"

Her eyes brimmed with disapproval. "We're going to find out what kind of trouble we're in. Please, show me where you saw the pirates."

Her chilly politeness was a rebuke, but he shrugged it off. She couldn't have everything her way.

"Over here." He led her to the beach, and from behind the trees they peered at the water. He pulled out his glass and surveyed the ocean, but there was no sign of Scar and his companions. His heart skipped a few beats. What if they couldn't figure out where the pirates were?

Srilani was close beside him, shading her eyes. "Look to the east. My greatest fear is that they'll land on our side of the river. If they land on the other side, we shouldn't have to worry."

He trained the glass on the space to the east of their location. The beach was empty. Thankfully. He moved the glass to take in the horizon, slowly working in a complete semi-circle and ending at the beach on the far side of the river.

"I don't see them anywhere," he said. "How did they vanish so quickly? How could ten minutes make such a difference?"

She dropped her hand to her side. "I don't think they made it to the other side of the river's mouth, but I have two ideas. First, the current might have pushed them out over the horizon, so that we can't see them even though they're not far away. Or second, like you said before, they gave up trying to cross the river mouth and decided to land back to the east and give it another try when they're rested."

"Or third," he said, "they're going to land back there and follow in our footsteps. They'd be right behind us."

She nodded. "That would be the worst scenario, but we need to know for sure. After we find them, we can decide what to do next. Let's go to the east, keeping the shore in view. We'll walk until Sol is halfway down the sky. If we don't see them, we'll return here, stay the night, and find the others tomorrow."

Aldan put his glass away. "That sounds reasonable. We can keep watch on the water the entire time."

The heat was unbearable, and so were the mosquitoes. He looked down at the crown of Srilani's straw hat as she walked in front of him. "It's a good thing you're not dressed in white anymore."

"Yes. Brown doesn't stand out as much, does it?"

The hours crawled by, and the time came to turn around. They stopped to rest. Srilani's expression was grim.

"What are you thinking?"

She sighed and fanned her face with her hat. "I'm thinking . . . I don't know. I'm not satisfied that we've walked far enough. I think we need to walk farther, but if we don't turn back soon . . ." Her voice drifted off.

He wiped the beads of sweat from his forehead and finished for her. "If we don't turn back soon, we'll fall far behind the others. But I think we need to keep walking. It's possible that they pulled ahead of us and made landfall. We need to know."

He closed his eyes, drowsy from the heat of the day, and pushed himself to think. The heavy, humid air pressed down on him. *It's so quiet here.* The birds, the frogs, the bugs — all the animals had gone silent. The hairs on the back of his neck stood at attention.

"It's too quiet."

"Yes." Her whisper was even quieter than his.

He didn't hear her leave. He turned in a circle and strained his ears, trying to hear her progress. A light gust of wind from the gulf rustled the leaves around him, but nothing else stirred. Where had she gone? His chest was tight, and blood thrummed in his ears.

Slowly, he lowered himself to the ground to wait for her return. If he moved, he might alert the pirates. Or she might not find him again.

Please, El —

Am I praying?

What was she doing? Would he hear if she called for help? Memories from the *Cathartid* fed his imagination during the long afternoon that followed. The only thing Scar loved as much as gold was torture, to draw it out, as if screams for mercy were wine, to be sipped and savored until at last — mercifully — they were used up. There had been that one lady aboard ship —

Aldan pushed to his feet, turning in a circle. Where could he go? What could he do? He ground his teeth together. What if Scar captured Srilani? She'd been away so long. *Please, El, keep her safe.*

Sol fell farther in the sky, and the shadows grew longer. Aldan sat under the fronds, as useless as a fouled anchor. The faint patter of footsteps alerted him. Srilani picked her way through the brush in the dim light of evening. She drew close and looked down at him. "The pirates are about a quarter of a mile from here."

In an instant, he had her wrapped close, holding her tightly against his chest in a bear hug, lifting her off her feet. He buried his face in her hair. "Don't you ever go off on your own like that again." His words sounded harsh. He swallowed and tried again. "Do you hear me?"

"Let me go." She tried to pull free, but he tightened his grip.

"What if they'd seen you?" He set her on her feet, holding her at arm's length. "What if you'd needed help? You could've been killed. Or worse."

She stopped struggling and held herself stiffly, eyes wary. "Let. Me. Go."

"Promise me you won't do that again. Promise."

"They didn't see me."

"You risked too much." He rested his forehead against hers, and his voice fell to a hoarse whisper. "Please, promise not to do that again."

She turned her face away. "I promise."

He released her, and she scrambled backward. She picked up her hat from where it had fallen and shoved it onto her head. He tried to see her expression, but she turned from him, the straw brim hiding her face.

He'd scared her.

I'm no better than the pirates.

"We need to move closer to keep watch," she said, her voice tight. "They're trying to set up a camp, gathering firewood."

"You think they're planning to stay overnight?"

"That's what I heard Scar say."

Aldan made a noise of protest. "You were close enough to hear them speak? What if they'd caught you?"

"They didn't."

"Srilani. You can't do everything by yourself. You need us, and we need you. Let me . . . let us help you." He put his hands on her shoulders and gently turned her about. Her eyes glinted. "If it's so important to get your brother home, you're going to have to accept this — *you're* the one we can't afford to lose."

A stubborn look settled on her face. "If I don't bring my brother home, I might as well not go back. My life would be over."

"Why? You said you're the First Princess. I thought that meant you're the next in line for the throne. They'd kill you?"

"No, you don't understand." She shrugged off his hands and looked around the tiny clearing where they stood. "If I returned without Jamson, I would become queen when my father is gone. But I would live under a cloud of suspicion. The barons and the Palace Guard wouldn't trust me. I would have the throne, but without trust, my reign would always be a struggle."

Aldan snorted. "That's not logical. Just because Jamson is the heir doesn't mean he's the only one who could rule the people. You can't guarantee his survival. If you keep taking chances — if you're captured or killed — the odds of Jamson getting back home aren't good." He walked away a few steps and then returned. "Don't do that again. At least, don't do it alone. You promised."

She seemed absorbed in observing the action of the surf instead of listening to him.

"A king or queen can rule by force, by using fear and manipulation." Her voice was pensive. "Or a ruler can reign through the will of the people, at their pleasure. My teacher used to tell me that inheriting the throne is only the first step to a successful reign." She turned and gave him a rueful smile. "Sorry to go on like this, but you must see why I'm willing to take the risk."

"I know about taking risks. I do. But you underestimate yourself, and I think your people would gladly accept you as their ruler. You are the reason we're here, alive, heading for Northern Marst. *You*. I don't believe that your life would be over if something happened to Jamson."

"But—"

"No. I won't argue about this." Politeness wasn't working. "I'm committed to getting Jamson back so he can be the next great king, but we need you much more than you're willing to admit. Accept it. We need you, and you need us."

Her eyes turned a frosty blue, and her lips thinned to a stern line. *That look again.* A silent dare. But she was the first to blink. She looked down at her feet and nodded. Once.

It was enough, and he allowed himself a smile.

"I don't mean this as an insult, but Sam's right . . . you're high-handed and you really do like things your way." He chuckled when her chin rose, and the frost in her eyes turned to solid ice. "That's another thing you'll have to accept — Sam's right, more often than not."

He took her elbow and urged her to start walking. "I wouldn't worry about being high-handed, though. People want their commanders to be sure of themselves."

Srilani was burning up, but not because of the hot summer evening. Truth was hard to hear, and Aldan's comments seared into her conscience. Because he was right. And Sam was right about her arrogance. And she was . . . wrong.

No use lying to herself. So what if she was responsible for keeping Jamson alive? That didn't mean her wishes should always come first.

Aldan was right about something else too. She was the key to Jamson's survival. René was a distant second choice for the role of guardian due to their father's rigid training standards for his First Princess. Her sisters hadn't been held to the same standards, and they didn't have nearly the same level of expertise she possessed.

She'd been so stupid to go off alone. What if the pirates had captured her? She shuddered. Hadn't she heard the stories?

Now, as they waited at a relatively safe distance from the pirates, she studied her companion in the dim light of the fading sunset. Aldan was perched on a downed tree next to her. He had the sailor's habit of watching the horizon. His darkly tanned hands rested on his knees. The manacle marks stood out on his wrists.

What was his life like aboard Rozar's ship? His face was smooth and solemn now, but lines fanned out beside his eyes, signs that he'd squinted against the sun for years. Lines framed his mouth too. Were they formed by pain or by laughter? How much had he suffered? He looked older than his years, but in this quiet moment, she caught a glimpse of how he must have looked when he was a young boy.

As if he sensed her scrutiny, Aldan glanced at her. His tentative smile was sweet, and the lines at the corners of his eyes crinkled, softening her heart. Her lips curved in response. Shyness gripped her throat, and she had to swallow. She couldn't hold his gaze. What was wrong with her?

"Do you suppose Sam's complaining about being hungry?" Aldan's quiet voice was wry.

She smiled and dared to look up. "I'm sure of it. I'm just as sure that my brother has built a fire to cook the fish they caught today."

"But you said no fire."

"See? I don't always get things my way."

Her smile broadened when Aldan smothered a laugh. "Ah, Srilani. I'm sorry I said that to you."

"No, it's all right. Few people tell me when I'm wrong. Naturally, I hate to hear it, but my teacher says the things we don't want to hear are often the things we most need to hear."

"He sounds wise. What's his name?"

She started a brief description of Elison but cut off what she was saying. Every moment was darker than the one before. She owed Aldan an apology before they moved closer to the pirate's camp.

"I know I was unpleasant when you insisted on staying with me, and I'm sorry for that." Hopefully, the creeping darkness covered her blush. "Two are better than one, and I'm glad you're here to help me." She stood up. "So . . . thank you."

His dark eyes seemed warmer as they rested on her face. The blush burned her cheeks like a wildfire.

"Did it hurt to say that?"

"A little."

"All you need is practice." His mouth quirked up on one side. "You can practice on me."

Srilani gave an exasperated huff. "What? Saying sorry or saying thank you?"

He chuckled. "Both, Srilani. Both."

CHAPTER TWENTY

Excerpts from *Histories of the Twin Kingdoms*

To Lady Raslan, Queen Mother of Kaedan

> Dearest Lady Raslan,
>
> Thank you for your kind invitation to visit Mardan's Palace. You cannot know the comfort I've experienced through your thoughtfulness and prayers.
>
> My husband and his council have approved my request to sojourn with you, provided I travel with an escort from our proud Palace Guard. I plan to arrive on the seventh day of this week for an extended visit, and I eagerly anticipate my stay with you.
>
> Please make suitable arrangements for housing two squads of men and stabling their mounts.
>
> Yours most gratefully,
> Lady Kaelan, Queen Mother of Kaeson

CHAPTER TWENTY-ONE

"I think we've gone too far, and we need to go back," Sam said. The sun scorched the back of his neck, and his shadow was as tall as a tree. Linus stood at his side as they faced the siblings.

René put her hands on her hips and squinted at him. "Believe me, we only walked five miles. Maelan and I helped each other count steps. This is the spot where Srilani will be expecting to find us."

Sam shook his head. "It feels too far."

"You're thinking like a sailor, Sam," Jamson said. "Distances at sea and distances on land feel different. Srilani said to stay here for the night and to wait another day. Changing the plan is a beginner's mistake."

"Please don't fight." Maelan perched on top of a rock and pulled her knees up to her chin. "I'm going to follow Srilani's plan, even if I have to stay here in the dark all by myself."

Jamson nodded, folded his arms, and looked up at Sam. "I can't tell you what to do, but my sisters and I are staying here. If we try to move now, we're asking for trouble."

"Do you always do what Srilani says?"

"Almost always."

With a long-suffering sigh, Sam dropped his pack by a fallen log, sat down, and pushed his long hair out of his face. "No fire. No fish. I guess we're going hungry today."

Jamson glanced at René and Maelan. "I said I almost always do what Srilani says. If we set a watch and walk the perimeter, I think we'd be safe to cook fish."

"But Srilani said not to have a fire," Maelan protested.

Jamson shrugged. "I'm not going hungry, and I'm not eating raw fish. We'll put out the fire when we're done instead of keeping it lit during the night."

Sam straightened up. "Hear, hear! Spoken like a man, my friend. So what do you say to that, René?"

She raised one slender brow as she set down her bag. "I think it's a reasonable solution, as long as we put out the fire immediately after the fish are cooked. But nothing's final until Jamson has searched the area. You should go with him. Linus, Maelan, and I will guard our supplies."

"Standing watch again, René?"

"Naturally."

⋀⋀

The ashes of their fire sent up tendrils of gray smoke, and the smell of cooked fish hung in the air. Sam put his hand on his abdomen and sighed. When had his stomach ever been so full? The fish had practically thrown themselves onto the bank in their hurry to be eaten.

Linus had eaten sparingly, as usual. He sat hunched over, pushing more sand over the ashes, dark eyes shuttered, deep in thought. Most likely, he was worried sick about Aldan. Well, he should be. Aldan was with Srilani, and she was just this side of crazy.

Jamson and Maelan entered the sheltered clearing. Their time on watch was over. René rose to her feet. So she'd decided to take another watch. Her pretty mouth had a white rim around it, and her shoulders looked tense.

Sam pushed himself up.

"Linus, you stay with Jamson and Maelan and get some rest," he said. René's wide-eyed gaze flew to his face. "I'll take this watch with you."

"Why?"

"Linus is good at night watches — he sees better in the dark than I do."

Not that I need to explain myself to you. He frowned. *Not that I'm going to say that to your face.*

They took up positions outside the campsite. He studied her outline through the cover of the trees along the dark river. She drooped in the shadows where her brother and sister couldn't see her. In their presence, she'd done a fair imitation of her older sister's confident attitude. Could Srilani be putting on an act too?

No. Srilani was every bit as arrogant and crazy as she seemed.

He crouched, making himself uncomfortable on purpose to stay alert. Every few minutes, he shifted to another awkward position to keep his legs from falling asleep. Falling asleep on watch could have dire consequences, even if he wasn't on the ship anymore.

A movement among the trees upriver caught his attention. He strained to see through the gathering dusk. There. A man. Coming their way. Sam snapped his fingers. Quicker than thought, René was beside him. Her face was as white as the feathers on an albatross. What would Aldan do if he were here?

The man wore the clothes and boots of a farmer. Sam's heartbeat slowed to a more normal rate. "He's not a pirate, René. Stay calm, and go tell the others to stay out of sight until I give you a sign."

Her head jerked down, and she ran into the vegetation on the far side of the path.

Sam called out to the stranger. "Hello, friend. Where are you bound?"

The man called back. "I smelled smoke from a fire and came to investigate."

The gray-haired farmer seemed spry for his age and covered the distance quickly. "You're on my land," he said. "Where did you come from?"

The old Norlan customs from childhood took over as if he'd never been away. Sam inclined his head to the older man. "I am Sam. My intentions are peaceful, Uncle."

The man stopped in front of him. His rolled-back sleeves revealed forearms corded with muscle. His hands, hanging loose at his sides, were calloused by years of hard work, and his face was leathery from the sun.

"Greetings, Sam. I am Nik." The man looked around. "I saw a woman with you. Where is your lady?"

Sam resisted the impulse to correct Nik's impression and stuck with the story they'd concocted. "She has gone to get the others."

"Others?"

"Yes. My lady has a brother and sister with her. We also have another friend with us."

The man shifted his weight from foot to foot. "I'm glad you've arrived. And your lady, especially. I'm desperately in need of some help since the storm."

The others had to be watching by now. Sam turned to the wall of bushes and trees and snapped his fingers. One by one, René and the others came into view, ranging themselves behind him. He pulled René forward.

"Uncle, this is René." Sam looked down at René's startled face. "This is Nik. He needs our help."

Sam bent down and spoke in Marstan. "He looks harmless, and we need a friend."

René curtsied to the old man and said in softly accented Norlan. "Uncle, we will be honored to help." She gestured to the twins. "These are my brother, Jam . . . Jamson, and my sister, Maelan. And this is our friend, Linus."

Nik's brows knit together as he studied René. He tore his gaze from her face to glance at Linus and the twins, and then he stared at her again.

"Sam is Norlan, but you are not." Nik gestured to Sam. "Are you this man's woman?"

She wound her fingers between Sam's and pressed herself against his arm. She laid her bright head on his shoulder. "Yes, Uncle."

Her touch did funny things to Sam's lungs.

"Are you his slave?"

She hesitated, and Nik's eyes narrowed. He took a step back.

"No. I'm not his slave." She looked up into Sam's eyes. "Sam is my protector."

Nik's expression turned skeptical, and he took another step back and then two more, as though he might turn tail and run away.

"Where did you come from?" Nik's voice rose a notch. He looked straight at Sam. "Are you a pirate?"

"No."

"I have nothing!" Nik's hand came away from his body, lifting to show empty palms. "I have no gold or silver."

"Wait," she said.

Nik was poised to flee. René squeezed Sam's hand before she pulled free and stepped in front of him. What was she up to?

She put out her hands toward Nik in a silent plea. "Please. Sam isn't a pirate. He and Linus rescued us from pirates. Don't go. We need your help just as much as you say you need ours."

Nik stopped his retreat to consider her, and she pressed her advantage.

"Please, Uncle. Help us."

Nik's face softened.

Good girl.

At last, Nik inclined his head, and his voice was husky. "Of course I will help you. My home is your home. If you will come with me, I will give you shelter. And I do need your help."

Sam released the breath he didn't know he'd been holding and patted René's shoulder. Her hair tickled his nose as he whispered in her ear. "Thank you."

⋀

Nik and Linus waited on the path several yards away, out of earshot, while everyone else packed their gear.

René took a stout branch and bent it over a rock to break off one end.

"We can't leave here," Jamson said. "Srilani expects us to be here when she comes."

"We must." René set the larger piece of wood on the ground, put the smaller piece at an angle near the top, and then hunted for another branch. She arranged a third piece of wood near the large branch and stepped back.

She slung her pack over her shoulder. "I think Srilani will find this marker."

The branches formed an arrow, plain as day. Pointing up the path they would take.

"She'll find it," Maelan agreed. "She's been on more field exercises with Father than any of us. Don't worry, René. I think she'll forgive us for going with Nik."

Jamson's mouth turned down. "I wish I hadn't lit the fire."

"Too late now," Maelan said, tossing her head. "You were fine with lighting the fire when you were hungry. I said we shouldn't light a fire. Remember?"

He kicked a rock off the path and picked up his pack. "Fine. Let's go. But I don't like it. What if they don't find the marker?"

René turned on her brother. "Jamson, why don't you put yourself in charge of leaving signs for Srilani? That will give you something to do besides complain. Everyone else thinks we should go with Nik."

Sam chuckled to himself. René had a temper under all that sweetness, and she could give as good as she got. Good thing she'd agreed with him. Teasing René was amusing, but fighting with her was not.

It made sense to have a native Norlander for an ally. Nik's need for their help put him in their debt, and they were going to need all the help they could get.

CHAPTER TWENTY-TWO

René's stomach clenched. *Poor woman.* The elderly Norlander, Drajna, was in a feverish, thrashing delirium. Nik had made a pallet for his wife and placed a bucket of clean water with a ladle near her pillow.

René struggled to control her trembling hands as she prodded her patient's right calf. It was red and purple in the lantern's light. Swollen and hot to the touch. Drajna was in desperate straits.

"Has she been like this ever since she was injured?"

Nik shook his head, and leaned over to stroke his wife's face. "No. At first, she was conscious. The pain was terrible for a few days, and then, yesterday, she fell asleep. I thought that was a good thing, but I can't wake her." Unshed tears made his dark eyes seem larger as he faced René.

Be strong. René forced sympathetic tears back by an act of will. The woman needed help, not tears. "She's had nothing to drink since yesterday?"

Nik's mouth clamped together, forming deep grooves from his nose to his chin. He opened his mouth to speak, but no words came out. He tried again and then shook his head.

Giving him time to gather his composure, René picked up Drajna's wrist. The woman's pulse was weak and too fast, her lips parched and peeling. She looked dead already.

"I've tried to care for her," her husband managed to say at last. "But I don't know the right thing to do. I think her leg is broken because she couldn't put any weight on it. The rafter fell on her during the storm."

Everyone turned to look at the gaping hole in the roof of the stone millhouse. Chickens roosted in the rafters. The top of the chimney was visible against the night sky. Thatch covered the floor at their feet, moldy and dank.

Drajna was a good housekeeper from the look of things. Order reigned everywhere else in Nik's home, but the fallen section of roof had wrecked one half of their abode. Both Drajna and the house smelled sour, more like a barn than a home.

"You're right about her leg. It's definitely broken." René met his anxious gaze and tried for an encouraging expression. "I'm not a healer, but I have some training. If you will allow my brother and sister to help me, I think we can set the bone."

"Of course. Of course. Thank the gods you're here!"

René cut him off. "Don't. Don't thank any other god than El." Her voice was sharp, and he stopped short. "Please, Nik. Only El hears our prayers. Do not anger him by praising other gods."

Sam's brows rose, and even Linus looked surprised by her sharpness. Nik, however, seemed to take her request in stride. "I will do as you say. I don't know a thing about nursing. She's always been the one to take care of me and our children. She's never been sick a day in her life."

René nodded. Hadn't Mother always told her that women were the strong ones?

"We're going to need more wood so we can heat water for cleaning. Is the hearth safe to use?"

Nik studied the mess and the fireplace. "If we can clear away the thatching and sweep the hearth, I think we can safely light the fire. If Sam and . . . Linus . . . can help me with clearing away the worst of the debris, I'll build a fire."

"Before that, please fetch me a straight piece of wood about this long." She held her hands apart to show him what she wanted. "And some bandages or material that we can tear into strips."

Sam's muscles corded up and relaxed as he brought down the axe with a resounding thump on the rafters attached to the fallen crossbeam. He grimaced as the impact sent ripples of fatigue up his arms and into his shoulders. But the labor soothed him too. Linus wielded another axe at the opposite end, and the large beam was almost ready to move. Nik would want to re-use the beam, and the shattered rafters could be used as firewood.

The light from several lamps revealed their progress as they restored order to the interior of the millhouse. They would have to stop soon and rest after working late into the night on top of their long, tension-filled day.

The royal children worked like deck hands too, putting their backs into the tasks at hand. Maelan helped René make a clean pallet for Drajna behind a screen, and Jamson assisted Nik with shoveling thatch into a wheelbarrow.

René's soft hands and royal upbringing had led Sam to believe she'd never set foot in a kitchen, but she was competent with every task, from heating water on the hearth to making some sort of broth using dried herbs from the root cellar. Well, he'd been wrong before. She'd shown amazing knowledge and skill in nursing Drajna too.

Jamson shoveled with unnecessary vigor, making an unholy racket as he dumped another load of thatch. So Jamson was still upset. Too bad. The prince was angry with René for supporting the snap decision to abandon Srilani's plan and go with Nik. Jamson had brought it on himself. Besides, they were only a quarter of a mile from their abandoned hiding place.

The rafter split apart under their blows. Sam took up one end and Linus grabbed the other to take it outside. Exiting the house, they had to pause to let their eyes adjust. The moon was waning, but the stars seemed brighter.

"Over here," Linus said.

Sam paused. "Wait another moment. I can't see yet." Linus waited until he was ready, and they took the beam over to the side of the barn about a stone's throw from the house.

Sam let Linus make the rest of the trips outside with the smaller timbers. Might as well take advantage of his brother's excellent night vision. Jamson and Nik needed help clearing the rest of the debris covering the place they would bed down for the night.

Over an hour later, they were ready to set out their pallets. Nik rested his shovel against the wall. "I'm going out to the barn to take care of the animals."

"Do you need help?" Sam asked.

"No. You stay here and get some rest. I'll be back soon."

Nik took one of the lanterns from its hook and left by the millhouse's back door.

"Where's Linus?" Maelan asked.

Sam's head snapped up, and his heart stuttered in his chest. He threw down his blanket and hurried out of the house.

The moon had traveled a significant distance across the sky. Slowly — too slowly — his eyes adjusted to the night. He slapped his thigh with an open palm and bent to brace his hands on his knees. He sucked in a deep breath for calm. Why had he even bothered to rush out here? Of course Linus was gone.

Just to be sure, Sam walked around the property's perimeter inside the tree line. Impotent rage warred with desolation. That boy! Sam's pounded his fist into his palm. What if something happened to Linus? How would he ever face Aldan again if Linus got lost, never to be seen again?

⋈

Sam entered the millhouse, closed the door, and leaned against it. "Linus is gone."

"What?" Jamson's shout startled the chickens, and they ran for cover.

"Linus isn't here." Sam crossed his arms. Why? Why hadn't he kept a better eye on Linus?

"But how could he go without saying anything?" Maelan's voice was plaintive.

"I think he actually did say something, Maelan." Sam shrugged. "Only I didn't understand what he meant."

"What did he say?" René asked.

"He asked me about an hour ago if I thought we should go find Aldan. I said, 'No.' Linus didn't argue with me, so I thought it was settled. Guess I was wrong."

Jamson started stuffing his blanket back in his pack. "We need to find him before he gets too far away."

Sam shook his head. "No. We need to stay put." If they only knew how much he wanted to agree with Jamson. "Linus has probably been gone for half an hour or more. Has anyone seen him more recently than that?"

Nobody moved except Jamson. He was on the floor, pulling his boots back onto his feet.

"That's what I thought. So no, we shouldn't try to go after him. Linus sees better in the dark than most people, and he's really good at hiding. If we tried to catch up with him, we wouldn't find him as long as he didn't want to be found."

"But—"

"But what? Look, Jamson. Are you going to go after him alone? Because I'm not going with you. René isn't going with you." He paused to meet her eyes. "Am I right?"

René nodded. "I have to stay with Drajna."

"And Maelan," Sam looked down at Jamson's twin. Her face wore the same mutinous expression as Jamson's. "You wouldn't leave your sister here, all alone with me and Nik, would you?"

Her eyes fell, and she shrugged one shoulder.

"Say it, Maelan."

"I'll stay here with René."

"Thank you." Sam picked up his blanket and shook it out. "I promised to look after all of you. The only way that's going to happen is if we all stay together. Don't even think about going off on your own, Jamson. Would you leave your sisters with two men you don't know well?"

Jamson thrust his jaw forward. "You would choose us over Linus? You're going to let him go off alone? What if something happens to him?"

"Linus chose to go off against my advice. I'll feel terrible if something happens to him, but I made a promise I intend to keep. Linus is my brother, and he knows I won't break my word to Aldan. We're staying here."

Sam stretched his length out on top of his blanket, put his arms behind his head, and stared at the stars through the hole in the roof. René's movements drew his attention. She turned down the lamp and sat on the low stool beside her patient. Their eyes met.

"What are we going to tell Nik about Linus?" she asked.

Good question.

"We will tell Nik the truth — we don't know where Linus went, but we expect him to return."

CHAPTER TWENTY-THREE

Four of the pirates were asleep. Their pitiful fire smoked and flickered, throwing shadows onto Scar's face. A chill washed over Aldan. Why couldn't Scar have been one of those who didn't survive the storm? There he sat, as mean and ugly as ever. The first mate inspired fear with a single glance from his wicked eyes. Rozar had chosen his right-hand man well.

Or maybe not. Had Scar killed Rozar?

Srilani alternated between sleep and nodding off. Every now and then a gust of wind caused the pirates' fire to flare and spark, giving Aldan a glimpse of her features, highlighting the length of her eyelashes against her cheeks, the vulnerable curve of her lips. How could she even think of coming here alone? She was intrepid for sure, but she needed protection. She'd fooled everyone with her strong, confident approach to their situation.

I've got you figured out. Don't I? You're not as strong as you want everyone to believe, are you? Can you forgive me for treating you so roughly?

She slumped to the side, losing her fight with sleep. He slid closer, and her head came to rest on his shoulder. A grin of anticipation tugged at his lips. She'd hate it when she woke and found herself like this.

A noise drew his attention back to the fire. The pirate who'd been sitting across from Scar was walking straight for them. Aldan slid a hand over Srilani's mouth. "Shh. We've got company."

She nodded, and he took his hand away. The pirate stomped into the vegetation to their left. As one, they sank back into the shadows. The pirate threw some food scraps into the vegetation. Srilani shrank into Aldan's arms with a shudder.

The burly fellow left without glancing in their direction.

Aldan breathed a sigh. "That was too close."

She nodded and sat up. "Don't let me doze off again."

They stared into the pirates' campsite. Once they were sure they could leave unnoticed, they would slip away to a safer distance. Scar lay down to sleep, but he kept tossing and turning, prolonging their stay.

The night stretched out in front of them, an eternity of dark hours. How were the others faring? How would they do without a fire? Or had they built a fire against Srilani's advice? *El, please keep them safe.*

⋏⋏

The screeching night sounds accompanied Srilani's wretched thoughts. Hundreds of frogs and peepers created a mad symphony of racket around them. Aldan didn't try to communicate in the darkness, showing a true skill for staying awake. There was nothing to see. The pirates had chosen to rest, not even setting a watch. *Typical.* Or more likely, they were too exhausted from rowing against the current.

Aldan might not have any problem staying awake, but she was struggling. Scar couldn't seem to settle, and so they were stuck here until he did. If her eyelids closed for longer than necessary, she jerked herself to stiff attention. She pinched herself and dug her fingernails into the tender underside of her arm. She held one arm above her head until it became too painful. Then, the other arm. Anything to stay awake.

What was happening at home? Had her parents given them up for dead? Had Kaeson suffered much damage from the storm? Maybe her father was sending out his ships to search the Great Gulf for Rozar's ship. Or sending a search team to travel along the coast. What would she do if she were in his place?

Aldan shifted his weight, bumping her shoulder. He was a rock. If she'd known, if she'd guessed how useful he would prove to be, she wouldn't have been so silly about opposing his interference. Thinking back to the scare a couple of hours ago, she gave thanks to El for providing Aldan to help. *I'm such a fool.* Why on earth had she objected to having him along?

Gah. She had to stop thinking about Aldan. She had no right to think about him or admire him. Her father had made his approval of Greyson clear before they were taken from the beach. If they reached home — *when* they reached home — her father would expect her to accept Greyson.

If Greyson was still interested. Why couldn't she remember the details of his face anymore? He was impossibly handsome inside and out. He was so admirable and worthy. But an impression of a tall man with fair hair and blue eyes was as far as her mind would go. Would he be waiting for her if she returned?

Don't think if. *Think* when.

Would her untarnished reputation withstand this protracted absence from home in the company of men? Jamson was safe from these kinds of worries, but what about the rest of them? Would they be tainted by this experience? None of what had happened to them could have been avoided.

Fatigue pulled at her, and her head fell forward. Again. She opened her eyes as wide as they would go, willing herself to stay awake. How many centuries was this night going to last?

The sound of a twig snapping brought her head up with a jerk. The frogs' sudden silence was deafening, and Aldan's hand wrapped around hers, giving it a meaningful squeeze.

Scar lifted his head. He poked his nearest companion. With a gesture even a blind man could understand, Scar set the other man to watch over the group.

The first mate rose to a crouch. His watchful eyes were black holes, like the eye sockets of a skull, and they seemed to be focused right on her face. Srilani began to shake. What if Scar could see them? What if they were caught?

He was still staring their way.

How soon would Scar let her die? The tremors grew stronger.

Scar turned his head in the direction of the beach. Like a wraith, the big pirate disappeared from view.

Srilani forced herself to relax her grip on Aldan's fingers as she tried to breathe naturally. *Scar can't see us. All we need to do is remain still, and he won't see us. Hopefully.*

Aldan's hand was warm and steady. Another twig snapped, farther off. Was it Scar? Or something else?

The moon had finished its circuit two hours ago and only starlight remained. She willed the gray-blue of dawn to stay away. *El, hide us.* She shivered violently, and Aldan's arm slid around her waist. She shouldn't let Aldan get so close, but she didn't pull away.

⋀

Aldan drew Srilani close to his side. She was as stiff as a plank. Her hand was cold in his, and an occasional tremor passed through her frame. The night breeze coming off the ocean was cool but not that cool. Because of Scar? Was this the same brave girl who'd endured Rozar's attentions without a flinch? Several long minutes passed, and bit by bit, her posture yielded to the pressure of his arm until she was nestled against his ribs.

Aldan shook his head. Nothing about this situation was logical, but he couldn't afford to get distracted.

Scar had hidden himself, a hunter on the prowl — crafty, suspicious, and dangerous. Could he have sensed their presence? Was he playing some sick game with them? Surely not. If Scar had suspected they were hiding here, he would've attacked instead of going off into the trees.

They were trapped here with nowhere else to go. If they moved, Scar would see them. If they didn't move, dawn was coming, and the morning light would drive away the shadows where they hid. Even now, a pale mist was creeping into the sky.

What was Scar searching for, if not for them? What had made the cracking sound in the distance? The hairs on Aldan's arms stood up. What if some fearsome beast was nearby? They'd glimpsed a bear a day ago, and Jamson had said that noise was their best defense against bears.

Yet here they sat, as dumb as two clams, waiting to be discovered either by the pirates or by some unknown something.

Aldan frowned. He'd prefer to face a bear any day than to face Scar. Scar had always been the enemy, but all these years Aldan — and Sam and Linus — had been off limits. They'd been Rozar's possessions and relatively safe from the malicious attentions of the first mate. If Scar found them now, there was no telling what entertaining punishments the sadistic monster might devise.

The midnight-blue sky lightened, and the trees around them were painted in shades of gray. In the new light, the oversized form of Biscuits was easy to recognize. That was one less person to worry about — Biscuits couldn't fight his way out of a burlap sack. The pirates slept on, except for the one who watched the horizon, oblivious to their presence.

A yell echoed through the trees, and Aldan's whole body tensed. Srilani sat upright and whispered, "Linus?"

Oh yes. It was Linus. With Scar!

Aldan sprang up and pulled Srilani to her feet. The pirate on watch wrenched around, almost falling over, mouth agape, as they dashed from their hideaway. Srilani yanked her hand out of his hold. They pelted over and under bushes and trees. Norlan voices shouted behind them.

Aldan reached for a weapon — any weapon. His fingers wrapped around the hilt of his sword, sliding it free of its scabbard. Srilani's sword was in her right hand and her dagger was in her left. She ran at his side, her expression hard and set, straining forward like a wolf pursuing its prey.

Scar shouted for his crew, and Aldan found an extra measure of speed, leaving Srilani to catch up. He raced flat out, faster than ever before as he followed the sound of Scar's voice.

Finally! Two figures, silhouetted ahead, struggled for dominance. Linus, though taller than Scar, was no match for his opponent's bulging muscles. Scar grabbed Linus from behind, wrapping one arm tightly around his neck and the other around his chest, securing his arms.

Aldan burst into the clearing with a hoarse shout. "Linus! Get clear!"

The pirate turned his head to locate his new adversary, and Aldan launched himself at Scar. But Scar, like quicksilver, stepped clear of Aldan's blade. He threw Linus aside, and Linus tumbled at Srilani's feet.

Aldan's knees bent, and he balanced himself on the balls of his feet, holding himself ready for Scar's next move.

Scar paced back and forth in front of him, a crooked smile making the namesake scar on his face pucker. He laughed. "Ah, I knew you couldn't be too far from your trusty shadow, Aldan." He spread his hands out to his side, and his dagger glinted in Sol's sullen light "But bringing the lady . . . I didn't expect that. Now I have a prize to work for, and I'll even let you watch how we use her before I kill you."

Aldan's stomach churned, and he gritted his teeth. *Never look away.* Scar wanted to see him react, but an emotional response would tip the odds in Scar's favor. A flurry of footsteps, breaking branches, and curses marked the arrival of four other men into the small space, but Aldan ignored them.

On his right, Srilani went into action. The clang and hiss of her blade filled his ears. Linus let out a war whoop at his left.

Time took on the consistency of tree sap, sticky and slow. Scar's eyes narrowed, and Aldan read his intent a moment before he struck. He parried Scar's attempt at a direct attack and twisted away, bringing his own sword down in a slicing arc and connecting with Scar's exposed calf. Aldan danced away, keeping his guard up.

Scar hissed like an enormous snake. Blood beaded up on his leg, but the injury didn't slow him down. Scar's blade menaced Aldan again and again, and every time Aldan blocked a strike, a painful jolt traveled up his arm.

Somehow, Srilani was holding off two pirates by herself. Linus had his back. Together, they formed a defensive unit. Linus's axe connected with the head of a pirate. It sounded wet and hollow, like he'd split open a coconut. The man fell under the feet of another pirate, causing that man to fall as well. Scar didn't miss a beat, but Aldan had to sidestep the tangle of arms and legs at his feet.

Their huddle was forced apart, and Scar's mouth widened into a grim smile, teeth bared. Aldan's lips pulled back in a snarl, and he took the offensive. A fresh wave of energy ripped through his body, and he pressed Scar back.

A scream of pain echoed in the clearing, and one of Srilani's adversaries stumbled back, clutching his arm. He bumped into Scar, jarring Scar's sword arm. With a curse, the first mate shoved the wounded man out of the way, but Aldan took advantage of the distraction. He drew back and plunged his sword between Scar's ribs. He pushed hard and deep. The blade vibrated in his hand as it scraped against bone.

Aldan braced his free hand against Scar's shoulder for leverage to withdraw the sword. Scar's dark eyes met Aldan's, and Aldan could smell the man's fear as the blade came free.

Scar stared down at the mortal wound in his side. Emotions scrolled across his face as he looked back at Aldan. He seemed stupefied, then incredulous, and finally accusing. He clutched his side with his free hand and collapsed. His hand fell, and a trickle of blood appeared at the corner of his mouth.

Aldan reached down, yanked the sword out of Scar's unresisting grasp, and stepped back. He looked about. The wounded pirate who'd given Aldan his opportunity was unarmed and preoccupied, staring at Scar. Another pirate, with Linus's axe still embedded in his skull, was sprawled on the sand. Srilani was missing, and Linus, deprived of his axe, was fending off a fourth man with a forked branch. Aldan rushed over to help his brother, and it was no contest. The pirate broke away and ran for his life, followed closely by the injured man.

Linus bent over, hands on his knees.

Aldan gave his arm a shake. "Where's Srilani?"

Linus pointed in the direction of the pirates' campsite. "Fratz took her through there."

Fratz. The pirate who had nearly killed Srilani on the first day. Aldan couldn't hear over the booming in his ears. He tore through the trees, ignoring the scratchy limbs brushing his face and arms.

By the time Aldan reached the beach, the pirates ahead of him were helping Biscuits push the longboat across the sand. Fratz was frogmarching Srilani in the direction of the boat with her arm twisted behind her back. The boat slithered into the surf, and Biscuits and his helpers piled into the craft.

Srilani fought harder when they entered the water. She reached her foot back and tripped Fratz, and they both fell into the surf. She rolled over twice. Staggering to her feet, she faced her captor. Fratz stood up. He stalked toward her.

Aldan's lungs heaved like a bellows as he stretched out his legs. Spurts of sand flew up under his boots. Almost there. Almost there.

Fratz jumped at Srilani, and in a move too quick for Aldan to follow, she caused Fratz to drop, face first, into the surf at her ankles.

She took several steps back and turned on Aldan as he splashed toward her, dropping into a fighting stance, fists clenched.

He slowed to a walk, and when she didn't relax, he stopped. "Srilani, it's me. You're safe."

Her hands came up to her pale cheeks, and she looked down at Fratz. Her voice quavered. "Is he dead?"

A pool of blood was blooming around Fratz's body. Aldan slogged to her side, took her shoulders, and guided her away from the pirate.

"Quite dead." He gave her a gentle push. "Go sit on the beach. I'll be with you in a moment."

Her unquestioning obedience was the proof — Srilani wasn't herself. Aldan waited until she made it to dry land before he bent to turn the corpse over and retrieve her dagger.

A voice reached him over the sounds of the waves. It was Biscuits. "What a woman!"

Aldan straightened, and his eyes narrowed on his sometimes friend. The portly cook was handling an oar, trying to coordinate his strokes with those of the pirate who had escaped. The pirate Srilani had injured reclined in the bow of the longboat.

Biscuits waved, as if they were on the best of terms. "Farewell, Aldan! Farewell!"

CHAPTER TWENTY-FOUR

René rubbed her eyes with the palms of her hands. "Maelan, I can't keep my eyes open another moment. Could you please watch Drajna while I take a nap?"

"Of course I can watch her. I tried to get you to rest after breakfast. You're pushing yourself too hard."

René abandoned the low stool beside Drajna's makeshift pallet, and Maelan took her place. René handed her sister a rag and pointed to the pan of water nearby. "Keep bathing her wrists, face, and neck. She's more feverish than before."

"Don't worry. I know what to do. Besides, I can't see that anything has changed since we first saw her."

René shook her head. So much misplaced confidence. "I wish that were true. But listen to her breathing. What do you hear?"

Maelan leaned over, putting her ear close to Drajna's nose and examining the rise and fall of the older woman's chest. "She sounds like she can't catch her breath."

"And here." René took Maelan's fingers to position them on Drajna's pulse. "Can you feel her pulse?"

A crease appeared between Maelan's brows. "It's too fast, right?" She laid Drajna's hand on top of the blanket. "What do you want me to watch for?"

Her sister had taken on a new air of maturity, but was she ready for the task?

"Let me know if you notice any changes. Just try to keep her as cool and comfortable as you can." Was she doing the right thing? What if Drajna died while Maelan was on duty? "And don't blame yourself if anything happens. Drajna may not make it through another night."

"What was that?" A deep voice echoed in her ears.

When had Sam returned?

"Do you think she's going to die?" His question was sharp. He loomed at her side like an angry bear.

She stiffened her spine and tried to sound calm. "I'm afraid so. She's getting worse, and I don't know anything else to do for her."

"Have you told Nik what you think?"

"No," René admitted. "But he must suspect she isn't getting better."

"Isn't there . . . I don't know . . . a sacrifice or an incantation you can do? I don't believe in those things, but . . ." Sam shrugged. "We should do anything we can think of."

"I won't sacrifice to Azor, if that's what you're suggesting." René's hands gripped the folds of her tunic. "I'm a healer-in-training, not a witch like Mirza."

"I know." Sam met her eyes squarely. His gentle expression didn't match his wild appearance. "Don't take my suggestion as an insult. I'm trying to be helpful." He looked away and stroked his beard. "I suppose the best thing you can do for Drajna is to get some rest." He paused. "Nik needs to know the truth. I'll talk to him for you."

"Thank you." Her throat closed up, and she squeezed her eyes shut against the ready tears. When she opened them again, the door was closing behind Sam.

"Sam isn't so bad, is he?" Maelan's voice interrupted René's thoughts.

"No. Not so bad."

⋀⋀

"René. Wake up. Oh, hurry. Wake up!" Maelan's hands clutched René's arm, shaking it back and forth.

"What — ?"

"Drajna. Something's happening, and I don't know what to do."

René sprang to her feet and fought to stay upright. Her knees were made of water. Maelan continued to shake her arm like a dog with a bone. "You're not helping, Maelan. Let go of me."

Maelan released her and whirled back to their patient. "Look. She's shaking."

Drajna's entire body convulsed. Her eyes were wide, staring blindly, and her mouth gaped open like a skeleton.

René shooed her sister away. "Run. Get the others."

She crouched beside the pallet. Drajna's tremors abated. An eternity of moments passed before the door slapped against the wall. Nik flung himself to his knees beside Drajna, taking her hands in his.

"Drajna! Drajna, don't die." Nik's voice was choked, desperate.

His wife's face was waxy, and she lay as still as a stone effigy.

Jamson, following Sam into the house, came to stand across from Nik. He turned to René. "Is she going to die? You've got to do something."

René spread her hands out and let them fall to her sides. "What do you want me to do, Jamson? What would you suggest?"

He hauled in a huge gulp of air and swallowed. "Why don't you do what Lady Elilan does?"

"I've already done what she trained me to do."

"No. I mean do what she does with the oil and everything."

"Yes." Maelan clasped her hands together. "Please, René. You know Elilan would sing 'The Song of Blessing.'"

"But I'm not a healer. I know the words, but what good will it do to copy her?"

Nik's gaze swung back and forth between the siblings, and René avoided his hopeful expression.

But her brother wasn't giving up. "We know you're not a healer like Lady Elilan, but even if Drajna dies, she'll die in peace."

"Please, lady," Nik put in. "Give Drajna a blessing. All the gods have abandoned us and left us to die. Perhaps your god will listen."

René bit her lip. Who could say no? And what harm would it do? She nodded. "I need some oil in a cup."

Nik scrambled to his feet and hurried to the larder. He returned with a cup of oil which he handed to René with a small bow.

She brought the cup to her nose, closed her eyes, and took a delicate sniff. The oil smelled fresh. She opened her eyes and nodded. "This will do," she said. She tried to remember Elilan's exact procedure.

"Everyone, gather around Drajna's bed. Nik, sit by her head. Maelan and Jamson, you're fine where you are." Sam stood near the door, and she waved him over. "Sam. You must take part in the blessing. Stand next to me."

Sam pushed himself away from the wall and crossed to her side. He straightened his shoulders. "What do you want me to do?"

René knelt at Drajna's feet and pushed the covering up to reveal Drajna's wounded leg. Nik gasped. The leg was so swollen that it looked like it belonged to someone twice Drajna's size.

Slowly, Sam lowered himself at René's side.

"When your turn comes, put your hand on Drajna's uninjured knee," she told him. "Nik, you will place your hands on her shoulders. Maelan and Jamson, take her hands. I will get you started."

René dipped her fingers into the oil and dribbled it onto Drajna's misshapen flesh. Leaning forward, she smoothed the ointment over the heated skin. She repeated the procedure twice more before setting the cup aside.

"Repeat what I say, one at a time, beginning with Jamson." Her brother nodded, and she took a moment to translate into Norlan.

"El, Most High, Creator of All, bless Drajna."

First, Jamson spoke the blessing, then Nik timidly intoned the words. When Maelan spoke, her young voice resonated with hopefulness. "El, Most High, Creator of All, bless Drajna."

Sam's chin lowered to his chest. He shifted his weight, coughed, and wiped his hands on his trousers. René held her breath. Would Sam speak the blessing? He'd never shown the least sign of belief — in any god.

Sam's lips parted. He placed one long-fingered hand on Drajna's knee, and repeated the blessing in a low voice.

Butterflies fluttered in René's stomach, and she averted her eyes from the large man at her side. René beat a soft rhythm with her hands. She turned the words into a chant. Jamson and Maelan joined in immediately, followed by Nik and Sam. Five times. Six. Nineteen. Twenty. With each iteration, Sam's voice grew stronger. René made a circling motion for them to continue. She caught Maelan's eye, and her sister nodded.

René lifted her hands in supplication and began "The Song of Blessing." Her eyes drifted shut, and the notes soared, echoing against the stone and wood. This was the right thing to do. The chant was in Norlan and the song was in Marstan, but the meaning of the song was what mattered. The worship transcended mere words, and the blessing would help Nik and Drajna, no matter what language she used.

The third time through, Nik's voice dropped out of the chant. Perhaps he was too choked up to continue. René carried on with the psalm. Sam captured one of her hands, and she faltered. His calloused fingers were warm. Her eyes opened, and she had a hard time finishing the verse. The last words drifted away, and everyone was quiet. Sam placed her hand on Drajna's injured leg where the oil still glistened.

"Look," he whispered. She tried to pull her hand away, but he pressed her hand down. "Look what you did, René." His voice was hoarse, accusing.

Drajna's knees matched. The redness and swelling were gone. Sam released René, stood abruptly, and moved away from the group.

Nik's cheeks were bathed in tears. He rocked back and forth on his haunches. "Thank you. Thank you."

René's eyes fell to her patient's face. Drajna's lips were no longer tinged with blue. They were a normal shade of dusky rose. Her cheeks were pink instead of waxy white. René lifted Drajna's wrist. A steady pulse beat beneath her fingertips. René's heart galloped far faster than Drajna's, threatening to escape from her ribcage. What did this mean? Had El answered her prayer?

The twins wore identical expressions of wonder.

"You did it, René," Maelan said.

"I did nothing. Nothing!"

"But Drajna's better," Jamson said.

"I only sang 'The Song of Blessing.'" René looked back at Drajna's legs and pulled the covers over her feet. "If Drajna is better, then El blessed her. I had nothing to do with it."

"What are you?" Sam's face was pale and beaded with sweat. He stared at René as if he'd never seen her before.

"What do you mean? You were here. You saw what happened." She took a step toward him, and he backed away.

"You said you're not a witch. You said you couldn't do incantations. What are you?"

She pressed her hands to her waist and swallowed back the hurt. Was he *afraid* of her? "I . . . I'm just a girl." But her voice sounded uncertain even to her ears. She took another step, and he made a sign of warding with his hands.

"Don't come any closer!"

At that moment, the door of the millhouse creaked open, spilling sunlight onto the hard oak floor and framing three tall silhouettes.

Maelan was the first to recognize them. "Srilani!" she squealed. "You found us!"

CHAPTER TWENTY-FIVE

Aldan blinked. The dim millhouse interior contrasted sharply with the late afternoon sunshine and blinded him. He froze in his tracks after stepping over the threshold. The scene inside didn't add up. Everyone was inside with the older couple Linus had described. An older woman on a pallet slept through all the noise of their arrival, including the shouts of the twins. The woman's husband was crying.

"Srilani! You found us!" Maelan sprinted across the room to grab Srilani and kiss her. Jamson lined up behind Maelan to hug Srilani. The twins acted happy, so the woman on the floor couldn't be dead.

Maelan kissed Srilani several times and then turned to slide her arms around Aldan's middle. Reflexively, his arms came around the younger girl. She gave him a tight squeeze, chattering like a sparrow. "I'm so glad you're back, Aldan. We were worried about you. Did you find the pirates? Why do you have blood on your sleeve?"

René was slower to cross the room. She was pale and her hands were shaking. Aldan searched for Sam and found him standing apart from the group with the oddest expression on his face. What ailed him?

Maelan didn't wait for Aldan's answers to her questions. She left him to hug Linus. "Linus, you came back. I was so mad at you for leaving without saying farewell."

Linus accepted her embrace and mussed her hair with one hand on the back of her head.

"You shouldn't have done that," she said, pulling back. "What happened while you were gone?"

"Give them a moment to catch their breath, Maelan," René said. "You all look exhausted. Come. Sit on this bench, and we'll get something for you to eat and drink. Maelan and Jamson, leave them alone for now and help me." René brushed past Sam, who stepped out of her way without a word.

Sam's glittering eyes settled on Linus, and his fists clenched. "You and I have some unfinished business, Linus."

Aldan moved between Sam and Linus. "Later," he said.

Sam didn't look away from Linus.

"We'll take it outside later," Aldan promised. "But first introduce us to your new friends. Then tell me what's going on here."

Sam nodded, and his fists relaxed. He waved one hand toward Nik, who wiped the moisture from his face with one grubby sleeve.

"Nik." He gestured to Aldan. "This is my brother, Aldan. We were separated, but as you see, Linus found him and brought him here."

Nik left his wife's side to meet Aldan in the center of the room. "So you're the reason Linus left us."

"Yes, Uncle."

"And is she your lady?" Nik's shrewd eyes rested on Srilani for a moment.

Aldan glanced over at Srilani to gauge her reaction to the question. She looked much the worse for wear. The skirmish in the woods and her struggle in the surf with Fratz had taken their toll on her clothes. And they'd weathered a brief rainstorm on the trail. Long strands of dark blonde hair had escaped from her braid and there were purple smudges under her eyes. She sat, staring back at him from the bench. One shoulder came up in a half shrug as if to say, "Do what you think best."

"Srilani is not my slave."

Nik crossed his arms, waiting for more.

What to say? "We escaped from pirates, and I am her protector."

"Hmm." Nik studied him a moment longer. "I would hear your story. But for now, it can wait." Nik approached Srilani and bowed. "Welcome to our home, Daughter. These others are your sisters and brother?"

"Yes, Uncle." Srilani's accent was nearly flawless. "May El bless you for your care of my family."

Nik bowed again, more deeply this time.

"Your god . . . El . . . has already blessed me beyond what I can ever repay, Lady. All that I have is yours." A film of moisture made his eyes shine. "Your sister saved my Drajna."

René dropped a plate onto the table with a clatter, and Sam made a rough sound in his throat. She clutched the other plates to her chest as she turned to Nik.

"I — Nik, I didn't save Drajna. El healed her."

Her words seemed to ignite Sam's temper. He stomped to the corner of the room, grabbed his fishing pole, and slammed out of the millhouse.

Jamson turned to Aldan. "What's wrong with him?"

"I think he's being stupid," Maelan said.

"Maelan." René set the plates down. "That is quite enough."

"It's true, though." Maelan poured water into a cup for Linus, set it on the table, and addressed Aldan. "Are you going to go talk to him?"

Aldan shook his head and sat next to Srilani at the table. "When Sam's in this kind of mood, it's better to let him cool down and think it through. Tell us what's happened since we left."

Jamson and Maelan eagerly took up the tale of their adventures.

"Well done, René," Srilani said. "So you're truly a healer." She frowned. "You don't seem pleased."

"The healing upset Sam. Instead of being excited about Drajna's recovery, he accused me of being a witch. Like Mirza, I suppose."

"What nonsense," Aldan said, frowning. "I've never known him to be so—"

"Stupid," Maelan said.

René frowned, but Aldan chuckled. "Stupid. That's the word. Tell us the rest of what happened while we were apart."

When they finished, Srilani's eyes were drooping. Aldan nudged her elbow.

"Take a nap," he said. "We'll be back before dark."

Srilani's eyes flew open. "Where are you going?"

"Linus and I are going to talk to Sam."

Aldan and Linus found Sam in the shade of a sycamore tree with his line in the water of the Trahn River.

Sam glared at Linus. He put aside his pole with exaggerated care, rose to his feet, and placed his fists on his hips. "So. You just decided to leave in the middle of the night without telling me. Is that the way it is? You're such a graybeard you can do whatever you want?" Sam crossed his formidable arms across his chest. When he inhaled a deep breath, his chest expanded to an alarming size. "I owe you a thrashing."

Linus planted his feet shoulder-width apart and let his hands hang at his sides. He shrugged. "Now or later. Your choice."

"Nobody's going to thrash anybody," Aldan said.

"Don't count on it."

Linus stepped closer. "Indeed."

"Sam," Aldan tried again. "Linus shouldn't have left the way he did. But on the other hand, it's a good thing he did or Srilani and I wouldn't be here." He looked back and forth between his brothers and sighed. "Sit down."

They didn't move.

"Please, sit down. At least let us tell you the story. Then you'll know why you shouldn't be fighting each other."

Sam broke eye contact with Linus. "Make it good."

Half an hour later, Sam was laughing.

"Scar's dead? And she finished off Fratz?" He let go of his fishing pole long enough to lift both fists in the air. "Yes! The world is a better place this day." A tug on the line forced him to pay attention to his business, and he pulled in another fish to add to his stringer.

"That woman is dangerous, Aldan," Sam said. "I'm serious. Don't ever turn your back on her."

Aldan snorted. "I would fight beside Srilani any day. She had my back today. And Linus too. That's the truth."

Sam raised an eyebrow as he looked past Aldan at Linus. "Maybe that's true." He grinned. "But I still owe him a thrashing."

Linus smiled, showing his teeth. "Now or later. Your choice."

"Ha! Later, then."

Aldan allowed long minutes to flow by accompanied by the sound of the river. "So you think Srilani is dangerous, do you?"

"Absolutely."

"Do you think René is dangerous?"

Sam cast his line with unnecessary force, lost his bait, and cursed. He busied himself putting more bait on the hook, his expression hidden.

Aldan flexed his fingers. "You listen to me. René is the gentlest person I know. She's innocent, too, and kind and generous."

A muscle worked in Sam's cheek, but he didn't say anything.

"I wish I had been here this afternoon to see what happened to Drajna," Aldan said. "But I know this — you couldn't choose a less likely person to compare to Mirza. You may think you owe Linus a thrashing, but you definitely owe René an apology."

Sam threw out his line, leaned back against the tree, and sighed. "I know." He paused. "The real problem is that I finally believe in this mysterious El they talk about. Before I met René and her family, the idea of an all-powerful, Creator god was nonsense. But when René healed Drajna, I was convinced El exists, and now I know He's watching me. It was easier to blame René for making me uncomfortable."

Aldan shook his head. "Not your best moment." He stood up, stripped off his shirt and trousers, and waded into the river. "But if you don't apologize to René, I'll owe you a thrashing."

"I'd like to see you try."

Linus stood and followed Aldan's example. He turned back to Sam. "Aldan would win."

"Oh really? How's that?"

"I would help him."

CHAPTER TWENTY-SIX

Srilani examined her hands in the late afternoon light streaming through the millhouse roof. The grooves in her skin were brown, a mixture of dirt and dried blood. She'd washed her hands twice, but the blood was a stain that seemed more than skin deep. Or was it her imagination? Were her hands clean or dirty? She folded her fingers together to control an attack of tremors.

Nik left Drajna's side, bowed to Srilani and René, and bundled the twins off to help with evening chores. A short hour later, the older girls were awakened by a new voice.

"Soshi? Nik?"

Every one of Srilani's muscles protested as she sat up, but she forced herself to follow René across the room.

René reached Drajna's bedside and crouched beside her with a disarming smile. "Let me get you a drink," she offered.

"Who are you? Where's Soshi?" The woman's eyes passed over the interior of the millhouse, paused on Srilani, and returned to René's face. "Why are you here? Where's Nik?"

"My name is René and this is my sister, Srilani. Nik has gone into the forest to set some traps. I'm sorry, but I don't know Soshi." She poured a measure of water into a cup. "Here, Aunt. Drink this."

Drajna sipped the water, but her brow furrowed. René took the cup away and sat on the stool. Drajna's fingers plucked at her covers, and she stared at the hole in the roof.

"What happened? Why am I down here like this?"

René tried to explain, but her Norlan kept getting in the way. Srilani took over.

"Do you remember the storm that damaged your roof?"

Drajna hesitated before she nodded.

"A beam from the roof fell on you, and your leg was broken. You became sick and nearly died."

Drajna drew up her legs, bending her knees with ease. "But I feel fine."

"El healed you," René said. "Let's have a look at your leg."

Drajna sat up, threw off her covers, and pinched her nose. "I smell terrible."

"You've been asleep for four days," Srilani said.

Drajna's head jerked up. "Four days! That's impossible."

"It's been a week since the storm, Aunt."

"A week?" Drajna put her hand to her head. "Ow. My head hurts."

René stood up. "You need food. Srilani will bathe you while I cook some eggs."

Drajna allowed Srilani to help her clean up and change clothes. By the time the eggs were ready, Drajna was able to stand and walk on her own, but she was weak from lack of food and water. She studied the sisters over her plate of food. "You are both so beautiful." She shrugged. "But your clothes are horrible."

Srilani surveyed her travel-stained tunic, holding it away from her skin. What would Ana say if she could see this outfit? Srilani ran a hand over her tangle of hair. What indeed?

"Soshi, my daughter, is a large woman now, but I still have some of her clothes from before she married and had all those children. Perhaps there's something in my storage chest you can use."

Srilani grinned at René. Clothes. How wonderful would that be?

"Thank you, Aunt," Srilani said. "If we could bathe and wash our hair, we would be the happiest girls in Norland."

"Then I'll tell you where to find my favorite place to wash."

Nik entered the house carrying a brace of rabbits. On his heels came Maelan and Jamson. As soon as he saw Drajna, he handed the rabbits to

Jamson and hurried to pull Drajna from her seat and into his embrace. Nik held Drajna close and kissed her fervently, murmuring to her between kisses.

Srilani blushed at the raw emotion of their affectionate display. She turned to the twins. "What did you do while we slept?"

"We chased the chickens into the coop," Jamson said.

"And hunted for eggs in the barn," Maelan added as she set a basket of eggs on the table. "We found another horse too. It isn't Nik's, but we put it in the barn so Nik can return it to its owner."

René's face brightened. "You brought milk and eggs." She smiled. "Excellent. I thought Nik's cow was still lost."

Jamson nodded and flopped on the bench. "The cow's gone, but two of the goats are still giving milk."

Maelan peeked at the older couple who still held each other. "Is Drajna completely healed?"

"Yes," René said. "I can hardly believe it."

Maelan sat on the bench next to Jamson. "Wait until Lady Elilan hears about the healing."

"It's not something to boast about."

"If you don't tell Elilan, I will," Maelan shot back. "It's not something to be ashamed of."

René gave a bitter snort. "Tell that to Sam."

Drajna interrupted them. "Who are these young people?"

Nik introduced the twins to his wife. Drajna smiled at Maelan, but her smile faded when she saw Jamson.

⋈

"No, no, and no. The pirate men may not sleep in my house. Or the boy, either." Drajna's voice was flat. Final. Over Nik's protests, she continued to refuse. "They look like pirates. Let them sleep in the loft of the barn."

After Drajna's ruling, conversation during the evening meal died. Srilani sighed. Nik's catch and René's scrambled eggs were simple fare. At least they were all together under one roof, eating at a table, using dishes instead of their fingers. Two days ago, she'd worried about letting Jamson out of her sight. She glanced at Aldan. After the last two days, the brothers could be trusted to take care of Jamson.

Nik pushed his plate away. "Sam and Aldan, I would ask a favor from you."

Aldan leaned forward. "What do you need, Uncle?"

"Drajna's leg is healed, but she's still weak. I'm worried about my daughter, Soshi, and her family. I want to find out if they are well. I also want to invite Soshi to come back with me to help her mother."

"What do you need from us?"

Nik tapped his fingers on the table and drew a deep breath. "Could you stay here for a few days while I travel there and back?"

Drajna started to protest, but Nik cut her off. "These men are not pirates, Wife. I trust them to look after you and protect our home while I am away." He wore an anxious expression as he turned back to the brothers. "You will stay, won't you?"

Aldan spread his hands out, palms up. "Uncle, of course we want to help you, but you are asking the wrong person. We have already committed to protect Srilani and the others. This is her decision to make."

Srilani straightened. Aldan intended to honor their agreement.

"Would this be agreeable to you, Srilani?" Aldan's eyes met hers and held.

He wanted her opinion. Warmth enveloped her heart. How many times had Father said, 'A strong man can take advice from a woman'? But Father rarely asked for her opinion or her permission.

Nik spoke before she could answer Aldan. "Dear Lady, my Drajna needs someone to care for her. And I'm not able to repair my roof and property without help. If you agree to stay with Drajna while I'm gone and if these men help me with the repairs, then I will do what I can to supply you for your travels."

She gripped her hands together beneath the table, weighing their options. Wasn't she the daughter of a merchant family? Supplies could make the difference between failure and success. Elison's training took over. *Drive a bargain with clear terms.*

"You are right to say that Drajna must take time to recover from her illness. Plainly, you need help with your roof." Srilani restated Nik's requirements and waited, letting the words sink in, asking a silent question. And Nik rose to the occasion.

"We will give you a horse to carry your bags. We will supply you with flour and dried herbs."

"Clothes too." Drajna smiled. "For the girls."

Srilani nodded. "Clothes would be most welcome. Thank you, Aunt. And one other thing." She pointed to the stone wall above the mantle. "We need the bow and the quiver of arrows. Also, we cannot stay beyond seven days from today."

"Seven days. Thank you, Lady. We have an agreement." Nik smiled. "The arrows were fletched by my brother. You won't be sorry when you go hunting."

CHAPTER TWENTY-SEVEN

Srilani splashed icy water onto René, and René splashed her back. Maelan dived beneath the moonlit water and broke the surface with a shriek a couple of seconds later. The hollowed-out place downstream of the mill was perfect for bathing, just as Drajna had promised. They took turns combing out each other's hair, and Srilani told her sisters about the fight with the pirates.

"You killed him?" René sat back, her mouth awry. "Oh, Srilani . . . I'm sorry that happened to you."

Srilani tried to brush it off. "He was going to drag me into the boat. They would have taken me prisoner. I had to defend myself."

"I know that you didn't have a choice. I'm only sorry you had to do it. How terrible for you."

Srilani examined her hands. Even though she'd washed them several times, the coppery tang of blood was in her nostrils again, and her stomach turned over.

Thankfully, Aldan had been there that morning to get her going again. "Srilani, they're gone," he'd said. "You're safe. Come. Let's get you cleaned up." He had pulled her to her feet and escorted her down the beach. When they'd been unable to see the pirates or the body anymore, he had helped her wash the blood away. Between them, Aldan and Linus had guided her to their old campsite, and from there Linus had brought them to the millhouse.

Would she be able to sleep tonight? She'd been too tired to dream during her short afternoon nap, but now, if she stayed still too long, the faces of the pirates plagued her.

Maelan broke into her unpleasant reverie. "I can't believe Drajna. She was so hardhearted about Aldan, Sam, and Linus. She doesn't even like Jamson." She pulled her spare tunic over her head and braided her hair. "I suppose we'll have to wear head coverings. It's too bad the men can't change their appearance so easily."

By the time they returned to the millhouse, the moon was high in the sky, and the men had retired to the barn.

Nik escorted his wife up the stairs to their bedroom in the loft underneath the eaves. The couple had been fortunate in the way the storm damaged their home, wrecking the roof above the main room and leaving most of the roof over the loft and larder untouched. The girls spread their pallets out, and Srilani stared through the hole in the roof at the blanket of stars above. No clouds threatened to drop rain on them.

Maelan tossed and turned, too excited by the day to settle down. She started listing things she missed about home, and finally, she whispered, "I miss Jamson and the brothers."

"Shh," René said. "Maelan, please be quiet."

Their little sister grumbled to herself and curled into a ball.

Srilani put an arm behind her head, trying to ease the ache in her muscles. If only it was as easy to calm her chaotic thoughts. Maelan was right about missing the men. Nik seemed like an honorable man, but she'd rather be across a campfire from Aldan and the others.

The night was as wretched as she had feared, so when Drajna crept down the stairs at the crack of dawn, Srilani was more than ready to distract herself with work. Nik and Drajna made the most of their temporary workforce. Drajna sat on the stool to conserve her strength and supervised the girls while they cooked and cleaned and worked in the garden, putting things to rights.

Nik took the men and Jamson out to gather palm fronds. They brought the horses back to the house time and time again, laden with stacks of fronds to patch the roof. Then they left to cut wood for new rafters.

The next morning, Nik departed before the rooster crowed.

Drajna turned out to be a stern mistress, pestering the men to be quick about it and to do it right. Once they had the rafters hammered into place, she was implacable about the thatch having to be just so. The men, inexperienced and slow as they were, could not please her.

René finally convinced Drajna to take a nap during the heat of the day and let the men go fishing so there would be enough to eat.

"She's like a female version of Scar," Sam said, keeping his voice low.

Linus adjusted his hat. "She doesn't have a whip."

"Yeah, well, she definitely wants to finish us off."

Aldan caught Srilani's eye, and she smothered a laugh. Sam wouldn't appreciate their ill-timed sense of humor. He followed his brothers to the door.

"Aldan. Wait a moment," she said

Aldan turned back to her, his hand on the door handle. "Yes?"

"You should all bathe in the river before you return."

His brows rose.

"Maelan gave me an idea to help you win Drajna's favor."

Aldan bought into her idea for shaving and shearing the brothers. He handled the straight edge and shears to remove Sam's thicket of a beard, leaving behind an authoritative mustache and goatee. Aldan handed the shears to René with a wicked sort of glee.

"Why don't you take over? Undoubtedly, you'll know how to cut the rest of Sam's hair while I take care of Linus."

René's mouth firmed into a straight line and her blue eyes glittered.

Sam, who had yet to apologize for his bad behavior two days ago, looked apprehensive.

"Before you start, we need to talk."

She shook her head. "Sit still and be quiet, if you know what's good for you."

Aldan's shoulders shook and the twins giggled. Maelan danced from one foot to the other as she watched René cut away at Sam's mane until it was closely cropped. Crisp waves of red hair molded themselves to his head.

Maelan clapped her hands. "Oh, Sam. You look so handsome."

Sam's face turned a deep shade of burgundy as he brushed loose hairs off his shoulders. René glared, and Maelan covered her mouth with her hands. René was nearly as flushed as he.

"I think we need more fish," he said. He stood and strode away without a backward glance.

René handed the shears to Srilani and went back into the millhouse.

Srilani tapped the shears against her palm and pinned Maelan with a pointed stare. "My dear, I've spoken to you about this before. A princess does not say the first thing that pops into her head. You've embarrassed both Sam and René. What if you made a personal remark like that at court?"

Maelan hung her head. "I know. But he looks so different. I was surprised."

"So was I," Aldan put in. He finished shaving Linus's face. "I don't know what we should do with your hair, Linus. I think it needs to be shorter, but your hair won't act the same as Sam's."

"What if—" Maelan stopped herself, looking up at Srilani as if for permission.

"You may make a suggestion. Just try not to embarrass Linus."

Linus spoke up. "Say what you think."

"What if Aldan shaved your head? Your dark skin is such a pretty color. I mean, not pretty like a girl, but—"

Jamson cut in. "Ah, Maelan. Stop. You talk too much."

"Shave it," Linus said. "My head feels hot."

"You'll have to learn to keep it shaved," Aldan warned him.

"I can live with that."

Linus's transformation was as startling as Sam's. Paradoxically, Linus seemed even taller without the bushy hair.

"That turned out well," Aldan said. "Good idea. So, Maelan, what should I do to change my appearance?"

She tilted her head to the side, taking her time. "You should wear a short, neat beard with a trimmed mustache. Grow your hair to shoulder length, straight down or pulled back."

"What do you think, Jamson?"

Jamson shrugged. "Many of our soldiers wear their hair that length."

"It doesn't seem fair that we've plucked Sam and Linus like chickens, and I don't have to change anything. What do you think, Srilani?"

Srilani shrugged one shoulder. "We'll have to wait and see how you look once it's grown out. Why is your hair so much shorter than theirs?"

"Rozar required me to keep my hair short and my face shaved. I think he wanted to remind the crew that I was his property. I don't know why he didn't restrict Sam and Linus about their hair, but he made all of us wear shirts, unlike the rest of the crew." He ran his fingers over the stubble on his chin. "I'm glad to have a choice."

CHAPTER TWENTY-EIGHT

Aldan tapped on the door to the millhouse and waited. The rooster's crowing split the morning air. That old rascal belonged in a stew pot for waking them before dawn. Sam approached from behind with a heavy tread, but Linus made no sound as he took his place at Aldan's elbow.

Maelan answered their knock, throwing the door wide. She held it open, looking out. "Where's Jamson?"

"He's taking care of the horses," Aldan said as he took a seat at the end of the table.

Maelan sat down close to Aldan. "How's the old mare he found?"

Before Aldan could answer, René called Maelan to help carry food.

She jumped to her feet, took the tray and plunked it down on the table, reclaiming her seat. She poked him in the ribs with her elbow. "Is something wrong with the horse?"

"I don't think so," Aldan said, inching away.

Drajna turned away from the hearth and pointed her ladle at Aldan. "Describe the horse to me."

"She's rust-colored with a white nose."

"Does she have a blaze between the eyes?"

"You mean the long white mark?"

Maelan came to his rescue. "She has a blaze and four stockings."

"Ah." Drajna turned back to the porridge she'd been stirring, lifted the pot off its hook, and hobbled to the table.

Ever since Drajna had seen the transformed version of Sam and Linus, she'd seemed confused about how to treat them. She dipped out a generous helping of porridge for Maelan and each brother, serving Aldan last.

"Thank you, Aunt," Aldan said in a meek voice.

She stared at him suspiciously. "Eat some eggs, young man." It was an order. "You need to eat more."

"Yes, Aunt." Aldan stuffed a spoonful of oatmeal into his mouth. If he laughed at her contradictions, she'd never forgive him.

René brought the skillet from the hearth and scraped some eggs onto a plate in front of Aldan. Her eyes glittered with mischief. "Your eggs, I believe." Aldan answered her smirk with one of his own.

René set the skillet in the middle of the table and nudged Drajna to take a seat. "You're trying to do too much, Aunt. You need to eat."

"Ha! Look who's talking." But Drajna sat down and lifted her spoon. After a few bites, she outlined the day of work ahead. The brothers ate quickly, knowing Drajna was about to shoo them outside to work.

She interrupted her planning. "I'm getting worried. The mare belongs to the baker in the village down the road. So why hasn't anyone come by the mill in the three days since the storm?"

"Nine days," Linus said.

"What?"

"Drajna, don't you remember?" René's words were gentle as she served herself. "This is the ninth day since the storm struck your home. The storm hit here the day after it grounded our ship."

"Nine days?" Drajna's voice quavered and she dropped her spoon into her bowl. "How could it be nine days ago?"

"You were sick, so sick you almost died. You were asleep for four days. Remember? Nik told you the whole story."

Drajna put her face in her hands. "I forgot," she mumbled. "How could I forget?" She raised her head. "That means nobody from the village has been here in over a week. A week! No ferries on the river. Nobody on horseback. No wagons. What can it mean?"

The door opened, and light poured into the room. Jamson held the heavy door for Srilani, who carried two buckets of milk. Her face was heated, mouth set in a straight line.

Sam smirked. "Where have *you* been?"

She put her burden down and wiped her forehead with her sleeve. "Milking the goats. What does it look like?"

"Like you've been wrestling with a sea serpent."

Aldan kicked Sam's shin under the table and tried to smooth things over. "You know how to milk goats?"

"I know how, but I can't claim to be good at it." She turned to Drajna. "I'm sorry, Aunt. There's not much milk. Your nanny goat with the brown spots kicked over her bucket twice." She stopped and peered into the older woman's face. "How do you feel? You don't look well."

Drajna's eyes dropped to her bowl, and she shook her head.

"What's wrong?" Srilani asked René.

"She's worried about the people in the nearest village because we've had no visitors."

Aldan stood up, clearing his place. "Is it possible that the villagers are too busy with repairs to come by the mill?"

Drajna picked up her spoon and sighed. "I hope that's the reason."

A clear vision of *Cathartid's* splintered mast and ravaged sails passed through Aldan's mind. Had the storm been as severe over land as it was at sea? Surely not.

Srilani and Jamson washed their hands and sat down to eat.

"Sam and Linus, finish up," Aldan said. "We need to start work before it gets any warmer."

Drajna put her spoon down and clapped her hands together. "You heard him. Get going. Handsome is as handsome does. Go!"

⋀

Aldan laughed after they were clear of the house. "Drajna thinks you're handsome."

Sam grumbled something unintelligible, and Aldan's mouth spread into a knowing grin.

Jamson came outside to offer his help, and Aldan put him to work with

Sam, tying palm fronds together in bundles. The morning coolness evaporated like water in a cauldron. The hours crawled past.

Jamson shielded his eyes and watched as Linus lashed a bundle to the horizontal ribbing of the roof. "Why can't I help Linus and Aldan?"

Sam snorted. "Do you really think we'd let you up there? Srilani would skin us alive."

"But I don't weigh as much as either one of them."

"Get used to disappointment."

Jamson's brows formed a V. "I climb the rigging on my father's ships. Why wouldn't I be able to climb on the roof? It's not even moving around."

Aldan descended the ladder. Time to intervene. He reached the ground and put his hands on his hips as he met Jamson's glare. "When you reach your home, you can climb around in the rigging of your father's ships as much as you like. But we're not taking any chances."

Jamson glared at him.

"Why don't you ask Srilani what she wants us to do, Jamson?"

He lifted one shoulder and looked away. Clearly, he knew what her answer would be.

"Look, you have a job to do. At least you're in the shade. We're melting in this heat. If you want to help Linus and me, then use that pole to lift the bundles up to us. Save me the trips on the ladder." He couldn't blame Jamson for feeling frustrated. Perhaps they were being too protective, but better to be too cautious than endanger Jamson's life.

Aldan joined Linus on the roof above the loft. The damage here was relatively minor.

"We need to dislodge that branch before we make repairs," he said.

They moved to the roof's ridge, looking out over the barn, the pastures, the garden plots, and the river as it snaked toward the Great Gulf.

"Weird." Linus pointed at the enormous tree branch sticking out of the thatch, like a spear from a target.

"The wind must have broken it off and pushed it through the roof."

A tiny grin formed on Linus's face. "What if it was part of our mast?"

"That would be very weird." Aldan grabbed the wood with both hands and gave it a tug. "Well, let's work it loose."

Linus balanced himself on the other side of the limb, and they labored to push it back and forth, extracting it inch by inch. All at once, it popped free. They released the limb, and it toppled over the back side of the millhouse into the river below. Linus crouched down, hugging the ridgepole, but Aldan lost his balance and fell to his knees.

With a loud crack, the weak area of the roof gave way, and Aldan flung out his arms, flailing to catch onto something — anything — as he plummeted through the thatch. His left hand clutched a rafter, and a massive jolt passed through his body, wrenching his shoulder. He lost his grip and continued to fall.

CHAPTER TWENTY-NINE

Srilani bent over the chest in Drajna's bedroom. Drajna sorted through its contents, occasionally handing a carefully folded garment to Srilani. They set aside a wedding dress, a baby's gown, and raw materials.

"Here we are," Drajna said. "Soshi was as slender as you before she had six children. So two dresses, one for you and your sister. And head coverings." She paused, mouth pursed. "Hmm. What to do for your Maelan? She's shorter, but she has the curves of an older girl. If I didn't know her age, I would guess she is fifteen."

"She takes after my father's family. René and I look like our mother."

"Ha. My Soshi is a larger version of myself. Her brothers—" She fell silent, and her mouth drooped.

"You have sons?"

"They are no longer my sons," Drajna said brusquely. "They are dead to me."

Srilani hesitated. "Is that why you don't like my brother and the men?"

Drajna shrugged one shoulder. She pulled more things out of the chest, stacking them to the side. The sounds of the men working and joking came to them clearly from above.

Srilani paused to listen. Linus's voice, rarely heard, sounded strong and confident.

She ran her fingers over the intricate carving on the front of the chest and turned her head to the side, studying the detail. "This is a beautiful chest. This spells your name?"

"Yes. My father built it for me. One of my uncles carved my name and the other symbols. This is my marriage chest. It's traditional for a girl to have one."

"Oh?"

"You don't know this?" Drajna clicked her tongue, shaking her head. "From the moment a girl is born, her family begins setting things aside, mostly fabric. So when the girl is married, she will have what she needs to clothe herself and her babies for several years."

"That's a wonderful tradition."

"Here." Drajna shook out a garment of deepest scarlet, a dress. In her other hand, she held up a black headdress with a matching scarlet trim. "For Maelan."

What would Mother say if she knew Maelan was going to wear a red dress?

"Thank you, Aunt. Maelan has never worn anything of such a beautiful color." Srilani took the dress and added it to her stack. There was no way to make Drajna understand why Maelan had never worn a dress the exact shade of a poppy flower. The high moral standard expected of a princess, the deadly consequences for failing to remain pure, the serious importance of appearances. Yet the three eldest daughters of King Terson were keeping company with Norlan men. What would happen when they arrived in Kaeson?

The noise of the roof work increased overhead, and they heard Aldan call, "Let's work it loose."

Bits of thatching rained down on Nik and Drajna's bed. Drajna hurried to a cabinet in the corner and extracted a sheet. "Take the corners. They're making a mess."

Srilani helped her shake the sheet out and throw it over the plump mattress. Drajna stepped back, hands on hips. "There. That will catch the dirt, dust, and dead bugs."

She turned back to the chest and replaced items one at a time. "I'm afraid I don't have anything else to offer you." Her voice sounded genuinely regretful.

"You've been generous, Aunt. Thank you."

Drajna looked sad. "The dresses need to be altered. I loved to stitch when I was younger, but I'm not much good for sewing these days. My hands hurt so much." She held her hands out, turning them over to show Srilani the swollen joints. "See?"

A storm of wood particles, accompanied by a loud grating sound, interrupted Drajna. A hole opened up overhead, and something large rolled down the slope of the ceiling, followed by a splash. The thatch quivered, and then Aldan's tall form crashed through the roof. For a moment, he clung one-handed to a rafter, but he lost his grip and landed with a *thump* on the bed below.

"Aldan!" Linus poked his head and shoulders through the gaping hole above.

Srilani, without knowing she'd moved, found herself at the side of the mattress. Aldan groaned. She placed her hand in the center of his chest. "Hold still."

He sputtered and coughed, gulping in air. He tried to grab his shoulder, groaned again and let his hand fall back at his side.

"I said to hold still." Srilani took his hand and gave it a gentle squeeze. "You're going to be all right." *I hope.*

"Is he hurt?" Linus asked.

"We don't know yet."

Drajna pointed a finger at Linus. "Get off the roof and tell the others."

She came to Srilani's side and peered down at Aldan. His eyes were squeezed shut, and his chest heaved like a bellows.

René and Maelan clattered into the bedroom and hurried to the bedside. Maelan covered her mouth with her hand, stifling a cry, but René's face looked calm.

"We should check for broken bones." René started her examination at his shins. "What hurts?"

Aldan grunted. "Shoulder."

"On his left side," Srilani said. She forced herself to release Aldan's hand.

Drajna moved around the end of the bed. She ran her hands over Aldan's shoulder. "His arm is out of the socket."

The brothers' footsteps pounded up the steps leading to the loft and they burst into the room. Even with short hair, Sam looked like a wild man. "What's wrong with Aldan?"

Aldan opened one eye to glare at Sam. "What isn't wrong with Aldan?"

"His shoulder is dislocated," René said.

"And he's bleeding on my bed," Drajna added, sounding indignant.

"What?" Sam's question was more of a shout, and everyone crowded forward, clamoring.

"Be quiet!" Srilani didn't shout, but her command cut through the commotion.

Drajna squawked. "He's bleeding on my bed. Get him off."

Sam looked ready to protest, but Srilani stopped him. No time to waste on useless arguments. "Sam and Linus, please lift his torso, and Jamson, lift his feet."

"Put him on the floor over there," Drajna said. "Take the sheet with him."

As soon as Aldan was relocated, Drajna knelt down beside him. "Why are you bleeding?"

He didn't seem to think the question was as silly as it sounded. "I feel a cut — on my back."

"Let's have a look," she said. With Sam's help, she rolled Aldan onto his right side long enough for everyone to glimpse the gash over his shoulder blade through the rip in his shirt. Drajna clucked her tongue. "You need stitches."

Srilani's stomach turned over as she met René's horrified expression.

"First things first. You." Drajna pointed at Jamson. "Go to the larder and bring back a bottle of cane spirits. Sam, you stay where you are. And Linus, over there." Drajna stationed them on either side of Aldan's head. She glanced at Srilani and René. "You know what comes next?"

Srilani nodded. Her throat tightened, and she couldn't swallow. Everyone waited in silence until Jamson returned with the cane spirits.

Drajna took the bottle from Jamson and held it to Aldan's lips while Sam and Linus supported him, trying not to jar his shoulder. "You must drink at least half of the bottle," Drajna said. "If you tense up while we try to set your shoulder, you'll injure yourself more."

"Hate cane spirits," Aldan gritted out between sips.

"Well, when you've done your duty, I'll take care of the rest," Sam said.

Drajna's retort was swift. "You'll do no such thing. The cane spirits are not to be wasted on the likes of you."

"And here I thought we were going to be friends."

"Hmf." Drajna tilted the bottle, prompting Aldan to drink. "A few more swallows, young man. Then your *friend* is going to hurt you."

Aldan drank until Drajna let him quit, and they lowered him back to the floor.

"Now we wait."

"For what?" Sam asked.

"For the spirits to take effect."

"And how am I going to hurt Aldan?"

"By popping his shoulder back into place, of course."

Sam's face turned a sick shade of green, and he seemed incapable of speech.

While they waited, Drajna retrieved a needle and some thread from her corner cabinet and wordlessly handed them to Srilani.

Srilani's hands shook too badly to thread the string.

"Here," René said. "Let me thread it."

Aldan's head turned to the side, and he stared at Srilani. A slow, lopsided grin spread across his face. "You're pretty." His dark eyes glittered, and he added, "Why aren't you holding my hand? I liked it."

Unwelcome heat traveled up Srilani's neck.

"He's drunk," Sam said.

"Not." Aldan sounded put out. "Srilani *is* pretty. She's beautiful."

"Brother, you need to quit before you say something you'll regret."

Aldan's brows furrowed. "What?"

"Never mind." Srilani cleared her throat. "I think we don't have to wait any longer for the spirits to take effect. Do we, Drajna?"

"I think he's relaxed enough." Drajna turned to the twins. "You don't want to see this. Go to the barn and find something useful to do."

"We'll call you when Aldan is ready for visitors," René said.

As soon as the front door closed, everyone looked back at Sam.

"What do I do?"

"You have to push his arm back into place."

"How?"

Drajna made a huffing sound, and she shrugged. "I don't know, exactly. I've never done it or seen it done."

René shook her head. "Neither have I."

"Why don't you heal Aldan like you healed Drajna?" Sam's question sounded like a challenge.

"Because that's not how healers work," René said in a hard voice.

Srilani cut in. "I've seen shoulders put back in place. I don't think I'm strong enough to do it myself, but I can show Sam where to put his hands and what to do. First, we need to remove Aldan's shirt so we can see properly."

Drajna produced a pair of shears from her sewing supplies, and Srilani knelt down to cut Aldan's shirt away.

He blinked up at her like a child trying to stay awake, looking as sober as a judge as he studied her face. The cane spirits scented his breath. His words slurred together. "Are you going to sew me up?"

"Yes."

"Good. That's good." Aldan's eyes drifted shut. His eyelashes were ridiculously long, darkly feathered against his cheeks.

"Are you sleepy?"

"Yes."

Srilani peeled back the front of his shirt, averting her eyes from his chest. She sat back on her heels and addressed Sam. "Are you ready?"

He swallowed. "I guess I'll have to be."

"Here's what to do." Srilani placed Sam's hands where they needed to go and mimed the necessary actions. She positioned Linus to hold Aldan still and got out of their way.

"Linus, on one," Sam said, voice grim. "Three. Two. One!"

Aldan woke from his stupor with a blood-curdling yell. Then he passed out.

"That was horrible," Sam said. His hands shook as he wiped his brow.

"Indeed." Linus released Aldan's shoulders, wiping his palms down his trouser legs.

Without a word, Drajna handed Sam the bottle of cane spirits. The brothers stood and passed the bottle back and forth until Drajna took it away. "That's enough of that, silly boys," she scolded. "We're going to need the rest to help your friend."

"You did well," René said. "Do you want to stay and watch the rest?"

"No!"

At any other time, Sam's vehement answer would have been laughable, but René's manner was all business. "The cut won't wait," she told the men. "You need to leave now."

Drajna followed the men. When she reached the doorway, she looked back at the sisters. "You will work better without me. Remember to rinse the needle and thread and the wound with the cane spirits. The spirits chase away infection." She left the room and closed the door.

René handed Srilani the threaded needle. "I know you don't want to do this, but Drajna expects you to take care of Aldan's wound."

Srilani sighed. She looked down at Aldan's unconscious face. "Thank goodness for all those times I went on maneuvers with Father and the Palace Guard. Soldiers were always getting hurt, and I learned the treatments for most minor wounds. What if I hadn't known what to do for his shoulder?"

"Don't worry about that now. Let's turn him over so you can get started."

Srilani retrieved the bottle of cane spirits and saturated the needle and thread. *El, help me to do this right.* She handed the bottle to her sister who doused Aldan's shoulder with a generous splash of the pungent liquid.

She drew the edges of the wound together with her left hand, her pale fingers a vivid contrast to his brown skin. "Here goes." She gritted her teeth and inserted the needle. The copper tang of blood filled the air. She gagged, and her eyes watered.

"Try to imagine that his skin is cloth," René said. "You can do this."

Srilani drew in a long breath, careful to breathe through her mouth. Her stomach settled, and she opened her eyes. Drawing the thread through the skin was the worst. One stitch. Another. Breathe. More stitches, more breaths, and finally the ordeal was over.

René handed her Aldan's ruined shirt and the shears. "I knew you could do it."

Srilani focused on her patient. His skin was smeared with drying blood, but the stitches looked strong. "What a mess. Can you get the water pitcher and the basin from the nightstand for me?"

She used the shears to cut the shirt into strips. "We'll need to make a bandage and a sling. I don't know if this is going to be enough cloth."

"I'll ask Drajna if she has any scraps we can use." René set the pitcher and basin conveniently close at hand. "He needs another shirt. I'll get the spare from his bag."

"Wait—"

René was already gone.

Srilani poured water into the basin, dipped a rag, and wrung it out. Carefully, she wiped the blood from Aldan's shoulders, rinsing the rag with fresh water from the pitcher. His back had other scrapes from the fall and thin silver welts criss-crossed the skin, clear evidence of punishment and abuse with a lash. She swallowed the bitter tang of bile, trying not to picture how the scars came to be. She strove for a more clinical frame of mind.

Like her father, Aldan had little hair on his torso. He couldn't be a full-blooded, native Marstan because he had facial hair. Timdan, her father's steward, never had to shave.

She worked downward, washing and drying. His skin was like silk. Warm, brown silk. He shifted under her hands and grumbled incoherently. She jerked her fingers away as if she'd been singed. Her cheeks burned, and she glanced at his face. Had she awakened him?

Thankfully, he still slept. One especially black mark at the waistline of his trousers drew her attention. The mark came to a point and looked like part of a tattoo. What did the rest of the tattoo look like?

Curiosity was a living thing inside her, and she itched to pull the fabric down far enough to see. Aldan stirred again, and the small tattoo came into view. Interlocking peaks, side by side, formed an *M* with a bar beneath. The symbol wavered in front of her eyes and she forgot to breathe.

Mardan's mark.

Impossible. Aldan couldn't bear the crest — it was a closely guarded secret of Mardan's royal descendants and their personal servants. Her father didn't have any son but Jamson, and King Baydan's son had been assassinated with his father.

She bent closer. The tattoo was perfectly placed and well done — sharp edges, pointed tips, and strong lines. He had to be the heir. There was no other explanation.

We'll leave this life behind us and get a fresh start far away from here. I couldn't ask for more.

Her heart fell. If she told Aldan the truth, his dreams would come to nothing, and his life would be in danger. But if she kept the secret from him, he'd be free. Her father would reward him, and he could do or be whatever he pleased.

It wasn't as if Aldan's people were expecting their prince to return from the dead. He could live life the way he wanted, and he never had to know.

She sat back on her heels. His face was relaxed, eyes closed, breathing soft and even. He seemed so vulnerable. If only she'd never seen his mark. Did she have the right to withhold what she knew?

His sister and mother still lived, and he was heir to a kingdom. Aldan would probably love to know he had a family.

What kind of person was she anyway? What would El want her to do? There was no such thing as coincidence — El's purposes always prevailed. Did she believe that or not?

"What's wrong?"

Srilani jerked around, and the rag plopped onto the floor.

René stood near the door, Aldan's spare shirt draped over her arm. "You look like you're going to pass out. Are you ill? Is something else wrong with Aldan?"

Srilani pointed, unable to speak.

"What?"

"His back."

"Yes?"

"Look at his back." Srilani pointed to the mark. "What do you see?"

"A tattoo."

"What does it look like to you?"

"Sort of like two triangles."

Srilani shook her head. "Come here and look."

René closed the distance and crouched down. A moment passed, and then she gasped. "It looks like Mardan's mark."

"Like our tattoos, right?"

"I don't understand. How he can have Mardan's mark?" René frowned. "It's exactly like ours."

"Except that our tattoos are on the left and his is on the right."

René sat back on her heels, looking stunned. "Can this mean . . ."

Srilani nodded. "It can't mean anything else. Aldan is King Baydan's son."

They stared at one another, and René bit her lip. "What are you going to do?"

CHAPTER THIRTY

Sam sat beside Linus at the table, forehead on top of his folded arms, staring at the floor between his boots. Aldan's shout echoed in his ears, and the joint grated into place again under his hands. He shuddered. Linus shifted his weight, and Sam raised his head.

Drajna sat with her eyes closed in her rocking chair, gently pushing it to and fro with one foot. As if she sensed Sam's scrutiny, her eyes opened, and she stared back at him. She stopped rocking. "Young man, I can tell you're going to be useless for a while, but you can't just sit there like a bump on a log. Take your friend there — and the boy — and follow the road to Trahnville. Return the baker's mare to him. You'll get some fresh air, and I won't have to look at you."

Linus sprang up beside him and hurried to the door, but Sam was slower coming to his feet. "Where will we find the baker's shop?"

"It's easy," she said. "Just ask anyone you see. But if you're feeling shy, follow the smoke from the smith's forge as you get close to the village and turn right on the street near the square. Don't dawdle. Don't talk to any girls. Be back in time to eat supper, or you'll go hungry. Understand?"

Sam bit back a retort and nodded. He turned to follow Linus.

"Send Maelan to me before you leave."

He pushed Linus outside and shut the door before Drajna could think of any more orders.

Maelan rushed over as they entered the shadowy interior of the barn. "How is Aldan?" She looked from Sam to Linus and back.

"We don't know," Sam said. "Drajna wants you back at the house. You'll know about Aldan before we do."

"What are you going to do?"

Sam gestured to Jamson and Linus. "We're taking the mare to the town."

"But—"

"You're staying here."

Maelan frowned as she watched her brother pluck a halter from a peg on the wall.

"Let me help you coax Stockings out of the paddock," she insisted. "I want to say farewell to her. She likes me best, you know."

Sam didn't contradict her. What he knew about horses would fit inside a thimble, but Maelan had a way with animals.

She held out her hand, and Jamson put the halter into it. In a matter of minutes, she led the mare to the gate of the paddock, ready for the trip to town. Maelan rubbed Stocking's velvety muzzle and stepped back. "Take care, Stockings. I hope the baker is kind to you."

"Linus, walk Maelan back to the house."

Maelan's face fell, and Sam suppressed a smile. He'd been right to be suspicious. Drajna wouldn't give Maelan an opportunity to follow them.

※

The road to town was long and winding. Many wagons had passed here, making permanent twin tracks that followed the path of the river. Sam trudged beside Linus, each in their own path, immersed in their thoughts. Jamson followed Sam, leading the mare. Thankfully, the dense trees on either side shaded them from Sol's heat.

As they rounded the next bend, Linus pointed to the right. Far off the path, deep in the forest, a cart sprawled against the trunk of a tree. Above it, there was a hole in the canopy of branches.

Sam's brows lifted. The wagon seemed to have fallen out of the sky. The small wagon could not have fit through the thick grove of trees between its present location and the road. Sam's gaze swept the rest of the terrain around the road. Nothing else seemed out of place.

The next bend revealed more man-made objects — a chair sitting in the middle of the road, a blanket flapping listlessly from the branch of a tree, a cup hiding near the verge of the road. The farther they walked, the more misplaced items came to view. Sam's stomach drew into a knot. He'd been missing the midday meal, but now, his appetite was gone. His steps slowed, and Linus stopped altogether, causing the mare to jerk up her head and paw the ground.

"Here now, Stockings. Stay calm." Jamson's voice was low and soothing. He put a hand on the mare's neck. "Why did we stop?"

Sam didn't answer him directly. "Linus, would you mind waiting here with Jamson?"

Linus shook his head. A dreadful knowledge lurked in his dark eyes.

"Something terrible has happened, hasn't it?" Jamson's voice was a thread of sound.

"Stay with me, little brother," Linus said. "You and I will let the horse rest."

Jamson hesitated. "Sure."

Sam stiffened his resolve and left them behind. The road rose, gently ascending a hill. It bent around the hillside and again in the opposite direction. The river hissed over rocks, unseen at the base of the hill. Sam crested the hill and a valley spread before him. Untended fields stretched toward the ruins of a town. Sam bent to brace his hands on his knees, sucking the air into his starved lungs. What had Drajna said this morning?

Nobody from the village has been here in over a week.

He straightened and studied the scene. Not one building, home, or fence was left standing in the village. Foundations were all that remained, as if a giant hand had swept the town away. The village well, a hole in the center of town, was visible even at this distance. Beyond the village, a herd of deer grazed in the middle of a field. Large, black birds hopped about among the rubble and several more floated in lazy circles high in the air.

Sam forced himself to descend the hill into the village. What had Trahnville been like before it was leveled? How many people had died here? He picked his way to the well and turned in a circle. Here and there, among the wreckage, were glimpses of life before the storm. A table, miraculously complete with a tablecloth and dishes, stood in the middle of an empty lot. A child's doll leaned against a stone foundation, sightless eyes watching the main road from a water-stained face.

An ornate chest rested, upright, at the edge of the square. He lifted the lid and peered inside at a large quantity of cloth. He lifted out a bundle of black cloth and folded it over his arm. The chest's exterior was battered and had suffered from exposure to the elements, but the interior was entirely untouched and dry. The cloth smelled of dye. Sam closed the lid. Hugging the cloth to his chest, he returned to his friends.

CHAPTER THIRTY-ONE

Aldan took the water cup from René. The movement jarred his injured shoulder, and pain radiated down his arm and back. René sat on the bench across from him, studying his face.

"How do you feel this morning?"

"About as you'd expect." He set the cup on the table and tried to settle his arm in a more comfortable position.

"Do you feel like eating breakfast? It's almost ready."

"Yes, thank you." The main room was empty except for them. "Where is everyone?"

"Sam and Linus are in the barn. The twins are trying to milk the goats." She glanced at the ceiling for a moment. "Srilani is still with Drajna."

"Did she stay with her all night?"

René nodded and rose to stir the porridge. "Poor Drajna. Such hard news to receive while Nik is away and she's surrounded by strangers." She shook her head. "Sam was in shock too, I think."

"Sam acts tough, but he has a good heart."

René focused on her cooking, her face hidden by her hair. "I wouldn't know about that."

Aldan studied the knuckles on his right hand. Apparently, he still owed Sam a thrashing. "You'll have to take my word for it, I guess." He hesitated a moment. "Srilani hasn't spoken to me since she stitched me together. Is she avoiding me?"

René shrugged. "You'll have to ask her."

The door to the outside opened, admitting Sam and the rest of the group. Breakfast passed in subdued silence. The cane spirits clouded Aldan's memories of the previous day, but he remembered Sam's account of the total destruction in Trahnville and Drajna's reaction to the news.

She'd collapsed on the floor, wailing her heart out over the loss of family, friends, and acquaintances. Srilani had enfolded Drajna in her arms, comforting her and sharing her tears. All the women, including Maelan, had retreated to the loft for more than an hour. Srilani had remained there to keep a vigil over Drajna.

As if he'd summoned her with his thoughts, the door at the head of the stairs opened. Srilani descended, her face pinched from lack of sleep, her eyes red-rimmed and puffy. René met her sister near the hearth. Together, they fixed a tray of food and exchanged whispers. Srilani disappeared into the loft again, and René returned to her seat.

"When do you suppose Nik will be back?" Sam's rumbling voice pulled Aldan's attention back to his companions.

"It's only the third day since he left," Aldan said. "We gave him seven days."

"I know, but what if he's not back on schedule?"

"We can't leave Drajna now," René protested, glaring at Sam. "If Nik's late, we'll just have to stay until he returns."

Sam's gaze swung around to her. "I wasn't suggesting that we leave her alone. Is that what you think I meant?"

René put her nose in the air, averting her eyes. "I can't read your mind. Who knows what you meant?"

Sam studied her profile for a moment and slowly pushed his bowl away. He stood up, walked around the table, and put a hand under René's elbow, prompting her to stand too.

"I think it's time we had a talk, Princess." His voice was soft with a hint of steel. She didn't protest as he led her to the millhouse door, opened it, and propelled her outside. Over his shoulder he said, "We'll be back in a few minutes." The door thumped closed behind them.

"Srilani would not approve," Maelan said, but she shared a meaningful look with Jamson, and he grinned. Linus's dark eyes twinkled too, as if he shared their joke.

Aldan smiled at their obvious rapport. "He'd better be apologizing to René for being so unreasonable the last few days."

"Weeks," Maelan said under her breath. "You mean weeks."

Linus leaned over and whispered to her loudly enough for everyone to hear. "Sam is never reasonable."

Maelan turned her giggles into an unconvincing fit of coughing. Linus's dry humor cleared the air, and Aldan didn't correct their assassination of Sam's character.

※

René was acutely aware of Sam's fingers under her elbow as they left the millhouse. His touch erased all the things she'd been saving up to say since he'd as good as called her a witch. She'd rehearsed a hundred little speeches to put him in his place, to cut him like he'd cut her.

Not that she would ever have the nerve to utter any of those witty phrases.

Sam had demolished the mistaken ideas she had about herself, that she was even-tempered and peaceable. He had proved — more than once already — that she could lose her temper quite like anyone else.

He guided her to a giant oak that stood guard between the barn and the house. One of its massive limbs, as big around as a normal tree, had broken off during the storm and formed a natural bench.

"Have a seat," he said. "Please."

The *please* was clearly an afterthought. She sat. Maybe it was better to keep silent after all.

Sam crouched on his heels in front of her and looked straight into her face. His eyes were precisely the color of honey. "Tell me, do you really think I'm mean enough to leave Drajna here alone when she's just lost everyone she knows?"

When he put it like that . . . She shook her head.

"You know, I don't think this is about Drajna at all." He braced his hands on his knees. "I think this is about how I reacted when you healed her."

"But I didn't—"

He held up one hand. "I know. You didn't heal Drajna. El healed her. But you have to admit that it was you who used the oil, that you were the one who sang the song."

The healing must have seemed like witchcraft to someone who'd only ever been exposed to the dark arts. Mirza had been around Sam for at least ten years, doing her conjurings and incantations. "I can see how it would look to you. It hurt my feelings that you could believe I was like her." She wrinkled her nose. "Mirza was . . . disgusting."

Sam snorted. "Mirza was worse than disgusting. I'm sorry for what I said and the way I acted. I was a real clam-head."

"No. Your reaction was understandable, and I—"

"Do *not* make excuses for me, Princess."

René put her hands on her hips. "Do *not* call me Princess." She smiled. "That's my sister."

"Ha!"

She'd surprised him. Good. Her smile widened. "Call me René."

"Do you forgive me for being a clam-head, René?"

"If you'll forgive me for believing the worst about you."

"We're both guilty of that." His golden-brown eyes met hers as he grew serious. "This journey is going to be difficult enough without stupid arguments."

Her smile faded. "Yes."

"There's something else . . ."

She hesitated. "Please, won't you sit beside me? You look uncomfortable."

The log shifted under his weight. He leaned forward, hands between his knees, and looked down at the carpet of sticks and leaves at their feet. She had a clear view of his coppery hair. He seemed to be working up to something, so she composed herself to wait.

Finally, he turned his head to speak to her. "We were lucky to run into Nik and Drajna first. Next time, we won't get off so easily."

She gripped her hands together. "What do you mean?"

"When we met Nik, you played along and convinced him that you belonged to me. But I don't think he actually believed it. He needed our help too much to ask a lot of questions. "

She focused on her fingers, unable to meet his gaze.

"Next time we meet someone — starting with Nik's daughter — we need to be more convincing. Mostly, that will be up to you and your sisters. You'll need to act the way slaves are expected to act."

"I can do that, I think," she said softly. "We all can."

"I'm not actually worried about you or Maelan. Not too much. But your sister . . ."

"Srilani will do what she must."

"Well, I'm not so sure. Your sister and I don't exactly get along, but she listens to you." He scooped up a branch and drew patterns on the ground. "When we're around strangers, Srilani can't be in charge. If Aldan touches her in public, she can't pull away. The same applies to me and you."

René swallowed. A slave had no boundaries. No rights. Of course a master could touch his slave anytime he wished.

"She can't talk back or argue," he said. "Most of all, both of you must look at the ground and hide your eyes. *Never* look directly at a man. Can you tell your sisters these things?"

She shrugged one shoulder. "Of course."

Sam tossed the stick aside and grabbed her hand. His fingers were terribly, cruelly strong, and her response was immediate. She yanked out of his grip, stumbled to her feet, and beat a hasty retreat.

He rose too. "That's what I thought." Deep lines bracketed his mouth. "Do you see what I'm talking about?"

Oh. She bit her lip and scuffed her toe in the leaves. He had even warned her. Was he angry?

As if he could read her mind, he shook his head. "You've got to trust me. Let's try again." He snagged her hand and drew her closer.

This time she followed his lead until she stood by his side.

"Remember to keep your eyes down." His hand still engulfed hers.

Her mouth was dry as she looked away. A long moment passed, and she could hardly breathe.

"René, you are entirely too beautiful for your own good." He cleared his throat, and his next words were a low rasp. "I will try to keep you safe. May El bless us all."

CHAPTER THIRTY-TWO

Srilani opened her eyes wide. Had someone spoken to her?

Mid-morning sun streamed through the hole in the ceiling above the bed, bathing the room in golden light. The remains of their breakfast were piled atop the marriage chest. She turned her head. Drajna slept, but she was far from peaceful. The older woman's lips were forming words, but they were unintelligible — like the gibberish of a child.

Yesterday's events rolled over Srilani like a dark cloud, and she relived the intense, gut-wrenching fear of Aldan's accident. What if he had died? What if she'd harmed him when she was trying to help? How could she face him again after touching him as she had?

Heat flooded her cheeks, and she closed her eyes to block the memory. The image of the tattoo on his lower back taunted her. How could she admit what she'd seen? Or its meaning?

Srilani swung her legs out of the bed and stepped away. She pushed open the shutters of the window facing east. Kneeling there, she tried to pray — for her parents, Nik's return, their journey back to Kaeson, Aldan, for wisdom and honor.

"Please, El, please . . ."

Her prayers seemed frantic. Where was the calm, trusting communion with El? Where was the peace? She labored to pray for a while longer but finally gave it up. Surely El could work out what she meant to say.

She opened her eyes and noticed the black cloth Sam had brought back. Perhaps René could show her how to sew something. She could spend her time being productive. Leaving the loft's door open, she descended the stairs. René was alone.

"If you're wondering, I sent Aldan away to rest," René said. "He thinks you're avoiding him." She sat in Drajna's rocking chair, working on some mending. "Did you get any rest?"

"Not much. Drajna was very restless."

"Come here and let me braid your hair. You'll feel better."

Srilani tried to inspect her hair with one hand. "Does it look that bad?" She sank down in front of René and smoothed the fabric over her knees.

René set to work. "What are you going to do with the cloth?"

"I need something to keep my hands busy, and I thought you could show me what to do."

René chuckled. "Not a chance. Remember the last time you tried to sew? I won't let you massacre good material like that again. Leave the sewing to me."

Srilani's hands plucked at the cloth, worrying it between her fingers. "What can I do then? You're the one with all the domestic talents." Her mouth pulled down at the corners. "Father saw to that."

"Yes, you mastered archery, and I learned to stitch. However, you did well yesterday — Aldan will have a pretty scar, thanks to you."

Srilani shuddered. "Don't remind me."

"You're forgetting that you'll have to remove the stitches in a few days."

Srilani moaned, and René patted her shoulder. "Maybe Sam or Linus will be willing to take them out."

"Not likely." Srilani waited until her sister finished braiding and scrambled to her feet. "Here's the fabric you don't want me to ruin."

"What are you going to do about Aldan?" René asked. Her eyes were warm with sympathy. "You have to tell him soon."

"I know." Srilani brushed imaginary dust from her sleeve. "We've trusted Aldan with our secrets, and he can trust us with his, of course. I just think he needs to wait before he tells his friends."

René shook her head. "You know he won't agree to that. Sam and Linus are his brothers."

Srilani put a hand to her temple. "I have to think. To be honest, I'm reluctant to face Aldan again after . . . touching him like that."

Her sister's mouth curved into a knowing smile. "You're not used to nursing. The awkwardness will pass. Why don't you take a walk down by the river and clear your head?"

Srilani followed the path through the kitchen garden. Maelan wandered among the vegetables, showing Linus how to tell the difference between the desirable plants and the weeds. Beyond them, Sam and Jamson were preparing more bundles for the roof. Every day that passed here in this quiet place made the twins more comfortable with their surroundings. Left to themselves, would they choose to return to their places in the palace? To the rigorous schedule of training, the rules and restrictions?

The breeze lifted the tendrils around her face, and she stopped at the riverbank, closing her eyes and opening her ears to the quiet sounds all around her. Given the choice — without the honor and duty she'd learned at her father's knee — would she choose to return home? Certainly, she missed her parents and her baby sister, but would she stay or would she go back?

And what of Lieutenant Greyson? Would she miss him enough to return? If she had the choice? She prayed for him, but she couldn't even remember his voice or his face.

She moved upriver and tried to redirect her treacherous thoughts by playing the childhood game of spotting fish in the water. She should have brought the fishing pole. The eddy created by the small dam Nik's family had built was full of dark shapes, lurking in the shade of willows and reeds.

Just as the millhouse disappeared from view, she found Aldan, asleep under a large tree.

René had sent her here on purpose. When had her sister become so cunning?

His eyes opened, and she couldn't turn back.

Aldan struggled to rise. The sling on his left arm made it difficult. Srilani's footsteps must have awakened him, but he didn't care. She was the one he needed to talk to.

"Don't get up," Srilani said. "You need to rest. I'll just leave so you can go back to sleep." She seemed poised to go back the way she'd come.

"No." Aldan stretched out his good hand and gestured to the place beside him. "Stay here with me. I want to talk to you."

She hesitated.

"Please. Don't go." He shrugged and grimaced. "Ouch."

She bit her lip and stepped closer. "Be careful of your shoulder."

"Come on. Sit and let me tell you about the crazy dreams I just had."

She sat on the grass a few feet away and pulled her knees up under her chin. "How do you feel?"

He flashed her an easy smile. "I feel like I've taken a beating aboard ship."

"That's horrible."

"You asked."

She averted her eyes, fastening them on the opposite shore. He'd expected a comeback, but she said nothing.

"Why so shy, Srilani?"

Her lashes flickered once, but otherwise her expression didn't change. He settled his back against the trunk of the tree. Was she shy? Or was she haughty, as Sam thought? He was beneath her notice, of course, but he'd hoped . . .

What? That they were friends?

His shoulders ached, and his head pounded. At the best of times, Srilani was difficult to read, and today definitely wasn't one of his best days.

After a long moment, she sighed and rested her cheek on her knees, facing him but with her eyes closed. "Tell me about your dream." Her voice sounded infinitely tired.

"I can tell you later," he offered.

"No. I want to hear about it, and we may not have another opportunity."

While he gathered his thoughts, he stole a moment to memorize her features. She was like a living statue — strong, beautiful, and cool on the surface, but a fire burned inside her. Her heat might repel some people, but he was attracted to it. With an effort, he tore his gaze away and watched the other riverbank.

"There were three short dreams," he began. "I've never had dreams like these — so colorful, so bright, unlike anything I've experienced before. I was terrified, and I wanted to run and hide. I couldn't move, and I couldn't look away."

Aldan shook his head. Some of the emotion of the dreams returned. "In the first dream, I was in an incredibly large room. There were tall, stone pillars — like masts on a ship — all around the room, but at one end, there was a chair made of stone on a platform. I couldn't see who might be sitting there because I was behind the chair, but I saw a woman with dark hair kneeling in front of the platform. She was crying with her face in her hands. I wanted to help her, but the dream ended and another one began."

"What colors did you see?"

"What?"

"You said the colors were bright in the dreams."

"The stone walls, the chair, and the pillars were white. Her dress was green."

Srilani gave a little nod, keeping her head on her knees, eyes closed.

"The next dream had green too. Men were building a bridge over a river, a giant bridge of white stones. The river was very wide. Some of the workers wore green uniforms."

Aldan picked up a twig and twirled it between his fingers. "That dream was short, but I can see every part of the bridge. I could draw it or carve it out of wood. The dreams are in my mind, and it's hard to believe I'll ever forget any part of them."

"What about the third dream?"

"It was stranger than the others, if that's possible." He shifted position. "I wasn't human in this dream. I was me, but I was an animal. I don't know what kind, but there were others with me, and I know I was their leader. We ran through the forest. There were many trees like those we saw on the way to Nik's house. We were racing up a mountain and ready to fight. I felt . . .

fierce. Like I used to feel when our ship was attacked."

"What colors?"

"The forest was dark green, of course. We . . . I . . . had dark fur. It doesn't make any sense, does it?"

Srilani's eyes opened, looking straight into his. "Did you know the others who were with you?"

Aldan's stomach did a flip. How had she known to ask that question? "Yes. My brothers were with me, and Jamson. And you. You were there too."

Srilani laughed weakly, and her voice wobbled. "Those *were* crazy dreams." She tried for humor again. "Jamson would like to be an animal. No . . . that's stupid. You know what I mean. He would enjoy being some kind of animal for a day."

Aldan tilted his head and examined her face, but Srilani wiped a sleeve across her brow. There was a fine tremor in her fingers. She laughed again, more brightly. "We should be fishing. That way we can rest and work at the same time." She got up and used her sternest voice. "Stay here."

With more haste than grace, she left the sanctuary of the willow's shade and rushed into the house. She retrieved the fishing poles from the corner of the main room, sent a meaningful frown in René's direction, and stalked outside to find Sam. He seemed surprised by her sudden appearance but readily accepted his new task, taking Jamson with him. That left Maelan with Linus, but no matter. They seemed only too happy to continue their work in the garden. Good. She had a few choice words for dearest René.

The main room was deserted when she returned. René had escaped to Drajna's room, and the door to the loft was closed. With exaggerated care, Srilani took René's place in the rocking chair and let her head drop against the headrest.

Crazy dreams.

No, Aldan's dreams weren't crazy. Visions from El were never crazy. They were vivid, full of symbols, and always came true. But they were never crazy.

CHAPTER THIRTY-THREE

Aldan sprawled on top of a crate in the barn, watching his brothers and Jamson work with the livestock. His right shoulder was almost pain-free now, but the stitches itched. Every attempt to take some of the work had been rejected.

Sam's coppery hair blazed in the early morning light coming through the barn door. Sol's rays poked through the boards and slats of the walls. Dust moats glimmered, and the hay glowed like burnished gold as Sam sweated over the horse's stall.

Linus and Jamson struggled manfully to milk the goat. Their efforts had turned into a competition, and Linus, only a year or so older than Jamson, was enjoying more success.

"This goat doesn't like me," Jamson complained, stepping back to let Linus take his place. "She keeps trying to bite me."

"You're not patient enough," Linus said. He smoothed his hand over the goat's back, murmuring to the sturdy creature in low tones. "You make her nervous."

Sam paused in his work and leaned on the handle of his pitchfork. "That's Aldan's problem with Srilani. He makes her nervous."

"Srilani's never nervous," Jamson said, "but I can tell she has something on her mind."

Sam scoffed. "Ha! She hasn't spoken to him in three days."

Aldan propped himself up with his good arm. "She's avoiding me for sure. She won't even look in my direction. Is this how she acts when she's angry?"

Sam set to work again, and Linus and Jamson became absorbed with the goat. Aldan sighed. He could never get any answers. What had happened after he was injured? There was a conspiracy of silence.

Sam stared outside for a moment and murmured, "Speak of the . . . Here she comes."

A long shadow appeared on the barn floor, and Srilani stopped in the doorway. She had Nik's bow in her hand. Had she heard them talking?

"Drajna is up now," she announced. "René insisted that I leave the house."

"Could you help us with this goat, Srilani?" Jamson's question was plaintive. "We've only managed to get half a pail. And she's nipped me twice already."

"Then stay away from her head," Srilani advised. "Let me see what you're doing." She strolled over to Jamson's side and observed Linus as he tried to milk the goat.

Jamson glanced at the bow in her hand. "Why do you have the bow? Target practice?"

"Actually, I think everyone's getting tired of eating only fish. I don't mean any offense, Sam, but since we know there are deer in the woods, I thought I would go hunting today." She set aside the weapon and crouched beside the goat's hind quarters. "Linus, position your hands like this. Watch." Two alternating streams of milk hit the inside wall of the pail. After a few moments, she stopped. "There. Like that."

Linus took his turn, and the goat's milk flowed smoothly. She smiled across the animal's back at him. "You're doing really well. When you're finished, Maelan wants you to help her in the garden."

Even from across the barn, Aldan could see Linus's eyes light up.

"Sam, for today would you stay at the millhouse and keep watch over everyone?"

Sam kept his attention on his efforts, but he nodded.

Aldan sat up. What was she up to? Would she speak to him or not? If she didn't, he'd just have to speak to her first. Enough was enough. He stood up and straightened his shoulders.

"Jamson, I'll need your help if I make a kill, so you're coming with me." She stooped to retrieve her bow and faced the door. "Aldan." Slowly she turned about and looked straight at him. "Will you come with us, please?"

Aldan followed Jamson through the shady woods. He tried to place his feet exactly in Jamson's footprints, avoiding branches and twigs. Srilani was as silent as a spirit, winding through the trees ahead.

Srilani held up one hand for them to halt and signaled them to look ahead. Light filtered through the underbrush, and Aldan spotted a herd of deer. As yet, the deer were not aware of their presence.

Slowly, Srilani nocked an arrow and pulled back on the string. Aldan held his breath. The arrow leapt from the bow as if it were a living thing. The silence was shattered by the stampede of terrified creatures racing away.

Srilani lowered her bow and strode out of sight.

"She got one," Jamson said over his shoulder. He followed Srilani into the trees. Aldan forced his shoulders to relax. He reached a small clearing in time to see Srilani remove her arrow from a young buck.

"Nicely done, Sri," Jamson said. "Right in the heart."

She placed a hand on the stag's shoulder and bowed her head for a few moments. Her gaze lifted to Aldan. She beckoned him over.

"We're going to dress the deer. Watch and learn."

Aldan moved closer. Srilani and Jamson worked as a team, efficiently removing the animal's internal organs and narrating the procedure for his benefit. He swallowed. Hard.

She glanced up at his face. "Are you going to be sick?"

"No. But this is much worse than cleaning fish."

"This isn't my favorite part, either. The only thing I like about hunting is the hunt, and eating good meat afterward. But this part must be done too. Fortunately, he's not too large, so we can carry him over to the river. You've healed enough to help with your left hand."

They managed the short hike without any problem. "You have more to learn, Aldan. It's a shame you are injured, or I would let you do some of this. Next time, perhaps, you can give it a try."

Why was she being so particular to teach him every detail?

Srilani focused on the task of dressing the deer. Why was it more difficult to stitch up Aldan's back than to dissect this buck? Srilani continued to wield her knife, forcing her mind to find the words to start. How was she going to get through this conversation? Her throat constricted, and she sucked in a deep breath. Better to get it out in the open.

"Jamson, go wash your hands and come right back. I have something to tell you." Her brother walked down the bank to the river's edge.

"Srilani."

Her hands paused. "Yes?"

Aldan crouched at her side. "Did I offend you?"

"I'm not offended." *What to tell him?* "I am embarrassed."

"I embarrassed you? I'm sorry, I didn't mean to—"

"It's not your fault. The circumstances embarrassed me." Her eyes met his for a moment and swiftly dropped to her work. "I feel awkward because I—" Her cheeks burned, and she ducked her head. "Touching the skin of your back is not something I would normally do. René says I'm just not used to being a nurse."

"You're shy because you had to touch me." He sounded bewildered. "Is that all?"

She bit her lip and shook her head. "I've been keeping a secret from you."

How could she tell him something that was going to change his entire future? Aldan might be happy to learn he was a long-lost prince. Wouldn't most men? But Aldan seemed to want freedom above all else. Freedom to live his life, go where he wanted, be what he wanted, dream his own dreams, be his own man.

Her life was proof that a royal child had no freedom. No matter how she felt or thought, she couldn't keep the truth of Aldan's identity to herself. El's will was clear.

Aldan chuckled. "What could be so bad? You look like someone died. What secret could be bigger than the one you've already told me?" His face was bright with amusement. "Are you actually a queen instead of a princess?"

Jamson arrived in time to hear her say, "The secret is bigger than that."

"What secret?" Jamson asked.

She stood and met Jamson's eyes. "You'll know in a minute." Aldan's brows lifted, and she forged ahead. "Aldan, the tattoo on your lower back..."

"What about it?" He unfolded his long legs and rose to his feet. "I don't think about it because it's so difficult for me to see." He shrugged. "Besides, Rozar insisted that I wear a shirt. Sam and Linus too."

So Rozar probably knew what the mark meant, and he went to the trouble of keeping the mark hidden. She turned away, stepping down to the riverbank. Rozar must have learned the secret from someone very close to the throne. She plunged her hands into the chilly current, washing her knife.

"Srilani, what were you going to tell me?" Jamson sounded impatient.

She shook her head sharply and focused on her brother. "I'm not going to look, but I'm going to give you directions."

Srilani turned her back, keeping her eyes on the river. "Aldan, please show Jamson your tattoo."

The silence stretched out so long she almost turned around. When Jamson finally spoke, his voice trembled. "His mark looks just like mine. How can that be? What does it mean?"

She took her time ascending the bank and looked from the boy to the man. "I'm not a queen, Aldan, but you were born to be a king. You are King Baydan's son. On the same night your father was murdered, you disappeared and everyone assumed you were dead too. It's been twelve years, so I didn't connect your name to the story until I saw Mardan's mark. Your visions provided the final proof."

⋀⋀

The world tilted under Aldan's feet, and he rocked back on his heels. "There's no way that can be true."

Jamson stared at his sister. "How could you keep something like that to yourself for three days?" He clapped his hands together. "This is great news!"

Aldan stared at Jamson. "Great news?" He threw the question at Jamson like a challenge. "First of all, I don't believe it. Second, I don't know a single thing about being a king or a prince or whatever." He switched his focus to Srilani. "Why would you ever say such a thing?"

"I assure you it's true."

"Don't say that!" Aldan's heartbeat pounded in his ears. His words were rough in his throat. "It can't be true. I'm a slave! I've always been a slave, and even if I'm a free man now, I don't know how to be anything but a slave. Don't be ridiculous. I can't be a king."

"But . . ." Jamson opened his mouth, but he couldn't seem to put any words together.

"Do you accuse me of being a liar?" Srilani's face was chiseled from alabaster, hard and cold. "I do not lie."

Her words brought Aldan up short. The silence threatened to last for the rest of eternity as he struggled to think. Srilani had secrets, but she didn't tell lies. Jamson had believed her outrageous statements immediately. He shook his head, trying to clear the fog. How could her words be true?

Her face softened, and she stepped closer. "Why would I make that up? You've seen your tattoo. See my brother's. Jamson." She twirled her finger in a circle. "Show him. The only difference is which side the mark is on."

The twin peaks on Jamson's lower back floated in front of Aldan's vision.

Jamson lowered his tunic and grinned. "Told you. My mark is on the left because I'm from the northern kingdom, and yours is on the right because you're from the south."

"You haven't always been a slave," Srilani said. "You were raised in Mardan's Palace until you were stolen. That's why you seem to know certain things instinctively."

"Like what?"

"You know things about horses that Linus and Sam don't. You speak Marstan without a Norlan accent. I'm sure we'll discover other things too. The mark is probably the reason Rozar made you and your brothers wear shirts all the time. Because he knew. Somehow, he knew what the mark meant, and he didn't want you to stand out."

What she said made sense, especially after the captain's hints about being paid to enslave him."

Her eyes were serious. "Aldan, I agree that you're not ready to be a king yet, but we can teach you the things you must know. It's your choice. You could decide to walk away from your past entirely."

"Are you crazy?" Jamson threw his arms in the air as he turned on his older sister. "How could he walk away from being king?"

She shrugged. "Aldan could decide it's not what he wants. He could decide he'd rather live life on his own instead of risking death trying to take back his throne."

"What do you mean? Of course he can get his throne back," Jamson said. But to Aldan's ears, the young prince no longer sounded as confident.

"Do you think all Aldan has to do is show up and his sister will step down and hand him the crown? Lord Habidan would love that. He's filled the court with his cronies, displacing most of the old families. And don't forget that General Zordan is Habidan's brother. Which one of those closest to the throne betrayed King Baydan, I wonder."

"I have a sister?" The question fell into the brief span when Srilani paused for breath.

She nodded. "Yes, and your mother is still alive too. Your older sister, First Princess Yolani, became queen in your place when your father was killed and you were taken. She appointed her husband, Lord Habidan, to be Judge and Counselor since the old prophet, Jeridan, died a few years before your father."

I have a sister and a mother. Why don't I remember them? The dream featuring the sorrowful dark-haired woman replayed in his memory. Did his dreams hold the keys to the past or to the future?

Aldan put his fists on his hips. "Why have you told me about my identity if you don't think it matters?"

Srilani's solemn, blue eyes met his directly, and she pressed her hands together. "I didn't say it doesn't matter. I said you have a choice." She extended her left hand to the side, palm up. "On one hand, you could simply walk away with your friends. We would keep your secret if you asked. You would be free to live your life." She extended her other hand. "On the other hand, you could stay with us and learn all you can and then . . . we'll see what happens."

She began to pace, talking it through. "When we reach our home, we will ask our father to support your cause. He may not agree to support you for his own reasons. He might agree to support you because he sees an advantage in having a friend on the Southern throne."

Jamson stepped into Srilani's path. "Oh, come on, Sri. You know Father would support Aldan."

"I know nothing of the kind, Jamson." She stepped around her brother and continued her journey. "I hope he would help, but Father does what he wants regardless of what I say. Your opinions and wishes matter far more than mine."

Jamson sighed, but he didn't contradict her.

Aldan watched Srilani as she paced, lost in her thoughts. No doubt she believed her feelings were hidden, but her matter-of-fact words revealed a soul-deep hurt. What had her father done to earn her bitterness and distrust? Could this explain part of the mystery of Srilani?

She halted in front of Aldan, looking up into his face. "Once your identity is revealed, you will be in danger. Whether my father supports your claim or not, you will have to win your throne back. You don't know who betrayed you, and even if your sister is willing to abdicate, Habidan loves his position of power and won't give it up without a fight."

CHAPTER THIRTY-FOUR

Aldan breathed in the sultry night air as he trudged to the barn beside Sam. Linus and Jamson straggled along behind them. The earthy odor of the livestock enveloped them as they stopped just inside the door. Aldan's eyes adjusted slowly to the gloom.

"Wish we could use a lantern in here," Sam said.

"You say that every night. You'll miss the roof over our heads when we're on the road."

"*If* we ever leave."

Sam's mood was as dark as the barn's interior. Aldan shook his head and bit back a retort. Today had been Nik's last day, according to their bargain, but they'd already agreed to stay with Drajna. "Nik will come soon," Aldan said instead. "If not, I'll go and find him."

Linus and Jamson caught up with them.

"No, you'll stay here." Sam's voice resembled a growl. He navigated his way to the ladder leading to his usual berth in the hayloft. "I'll go find Nik. There's no way I'm staying here to deal with Her Highness by myself."

Jamson and Linus snickered, and Aldan couldn't resist. "Which Highness are you talking about?"

A snort was Sam's only answer, and Aldan laughed with the others. He felt his way over to the crates he'd adopted as his bed after the accident.

Jamson called out to Aldan. "So you're thinking we need to search for Nik?"

Aldan breathed in through his nose and let it out. "Let's give him another day before we decide. Besides, Srilani may want to make the search with me."

"Then I'm coming with you." Jamson's voice cracked, but he forged ahead. "I have to do a better job of taking care of her reputation."

Sam's voice came from his lofty perch. "How does that work? You'd leave René and Maelan here with me while you protect Srilani from Aldan the Evil?"

Jamson's retort was swift. "You'll be here with René, Drajna, Maelan, and Linus. It's not the same."

"What if I decided to leave without you, knocked Linus out, and took the girls away?"

"I know you wouldn't do that. I trust you." A hard note entered Aldan had never heard before Jamson's voice. "But if you did take my sisters, I would find you and kill you."

Sam chuckled. "You don't have to worry about me. I've been wondering if you were even aware of the dangers for them. I'm very concerned about keeping your sisters safe as we travel through Norland. How well do you fight?"

"You might be surprised. We should start drilling together every day. My sisters too. I've missed practicing."

"I think that's a good idea," Aldan said. "Drilling with a weapon will help my shoulder get stronger, and we can keep each other sharp." Aldan shifted his weight, trying to find a more comfortable position. He settled back and closed his eyes. Clever of Jamson to work Srilani's idea into the conversation.

"Count me in," Sam said. "I'd love to spar with Srilani."

"I'm sure she'll give you the opportunity," Jamson said.

A huge grin broke across Aldan's face in the darkness. After witnessing Srilani's prowess with sword, dagger, and bow, he could hardly wait to watch her drill with Sam. He tried to let go of his busy thoughts, welcoming sleep.

"I hear something," Linus said from his spot near Aldan's position. Linus moved without a sound to the gaping barn door.

Sleep forgotten, Aldan swung his legs over the edge of the crates. He joined Linus and looked out over the fields. The crescent moon cast sufficient light to see there was nobody between where they stood and the millhouse.

Jamson squeezed between them, and Sam slid down the ladder and landed with a soft thump. In moments, they all stood in the gap.

"What do you think it was?" Jamson asked.

"Mama!" The unfamiliar cry of a small child was as clear as a bell. Aldan's head jerked in the direction of the voice, but the fields were empty.

"Wait here for me," Aldan said. He ran down the path to the house, fumbled with the latch on the big door, and pushed it wide.

"Someone's coming," he said, pitching his voice low.

Moments later, Srilani appeared at his side, dagger drawn. She paused on the threshold, her shoulder pressed close to his. Her hair in its braid glowed like silver in the moonlight, and Aldan breathed in the clean scent of it.

"I don't see anything," she whispered.

"We heard a child yell." Aldan pointed. "It came from that direction."

Faintly, other sounds reached them — children giggling, a man's voice, and squeaking wheels. René came up behind them. "What is it?"

"People, including children," Srilani said.

Aldan touched her arm. "Cover your hair," he said. "Get yourself ready, and Sam and I will go see who it is."

She opened her mouth to speak, but he held up his good hand. "I'll send Jamson and Linus here. Help me remove this sling, please." He turned his back and bent awkwardly so she could reach the knot. Her cool fingers brushed his neck beneath his hair, and the sling came away in her hand. She retreated into the house. Aldan stuck his head through the doorway and whispered, "Set a lantern in the window when you're ready to be seen."

⁂

Srilani shook Maelan. "Someone's coming, dear. Get ready. You know what to do."

Maelan raised her head from her pallet, but it flopped down again.

"Get up. Now." Srilani let the lantern's light shine into Maelan's eyes. "Maelan. Darling girl. Sit up and grab my hand." She raised her sister to her feet, struggling to hold her upright. "Here's your Norlan dress."

Srilani fumbled with Maelan's veil, pulling it into position like they'd practiced. "Stay here."

"You're using Marstan," René said.

Srilani switched to Norlan. "Stay here," she repeated. "I can't believe I forgot something as critical as which language to use."

"I'm sure you won't do it again," René said with a reassuring smile.

Srilani returned her attention to Maelan. "Tell me your story." They'd practiced that too.

"My name is Mae. My twin brother and I belong to Samazor. He is a kind master. His woman is our sister, René."

"Fine. Have I put this on straight?" Srilani tugged at her head covering. René came over to help. They took turns making adjustments until they were satisfied. Srilani set the lantern in the front window at the same moment a soft knock sounded on the door.

"Maelan, that's Jamson and Linus. Please let them inside. René, do you want to wake Drajna or shall I?"

For answer, René climbed the stairs. As soon as Jamson entered the house, Maelan pulled him close. She transferred her attention to his companion. "Linus. I'm so glad you're here."

"You look different."

"Do I look like a Norlander?"

He shrugged. "Maybe."

Srilani didn't stay to listen to Maelan's chatter. Instead, she stepped out of the house, pulling the door closed behind her. The stars in the black velvet sky shimmered, and the moon seemed unusually close. Aldan and Sam stood on a rise to the east, silhouetted against the eastern horizon. Aldan turned back to look at the house, and her heart squeezed.

The men walked out of sight. Her fingers clenched and unclenched, and she forced herself to relax and breathe normally. Long, long minutes passed. What kept them?

Aldan, Sam, and a third man crested the hill, followed by a wagon overflowing with people. A team of four oxen strained against their yokes. In addition, there were a couple of horses, loaded down with large packs.

Srilani's bones melted, and her heart lifted. Nik was back. With lighter steps she reentered the house. She walked directly to Drajna who sat in her trusty rocker. Taking her hands, Srilani leaned over so she was at eye-level. "Nik is here, Aunt. And your daughter and her family. You're going to be cooking for a real crowd now."

Drajna laughed with tears in her eyes. Her voice quavered. "You have been a gift, Daughter. And I won't forget your god, the mighty El."

Srilani nodded and turned away, meeting René's gaze. "Let's go." On the way out of the house, she stopped in front of Linus, Maelan, and Jamson to whisper, "Keep your stories straight."

The arrival of Soshi and her family signaled the end of the group's sojourn with Nik and Drajna. The next day, Aldan sorted through the rubble at his feet. He worked in the town square around the gaping hole in the ground — all that was left of Trahnville's well. The deceased citizens would haunt his dreams, but as Nik had pointed out, they no longer needed their possessions. Aldan searched for valuables to sell and barter for provisions. With Nik's advice, they'd selected the city of Minazor as the best place to raise traveling funds.

Nearby, Srilani stood and rubbed the small of her back with one hand. In the other, she held a silver goblet. Aldan picked his way to her side while Soshi inspected the piece.

Nik's daughter took her time, turning the item round several times. "This is a traditional gift for a young couple when they are wed, but this one is new. See? It has the artist's mark, but there's no engraving. Usually, the smith engraves the family symbol in the side. You will find a buyer for it because it's good work." She handed the cup to Srilani. "Don't take less than twenty pieces of silver for it."

Srilani held out the goblet to Aldan, and he stowed the piece in his pack.

Nik, Soshi, and her five oldest children stayed with them until early afternoon, helping the group hunt through the wreckage for things to sell. Nik spent the entire time between Aldan and Sam, discussing important things they needed to know, such as how to make payment to the priests.

Finally Aldan raised his voice. "We need to stop searching and start our journey. We've found as much as we can carry."

A collective sigh went up, and the group gathered near the well. Sam and Aldan traded last minute words with their host and watched as Soshi hugged each sister in turn.

Soshi stood in front of Srilani and René. "You have my undying gratitude for your service to my parents. And you too, Mae. My mother has told me of how you saved her life and of your tender care afterward. I hope I will have a chance to repay the good you've done for me."

"El brought us here, Soshi," Srilani said. "Thank Him. You have done enough by helping us on our way."

Nik stood beside his daughter, surrounded by his grandchildren. "Aldan, Sam . . . if you ever have an opportunity to return, you are assured of a welcome here. And your ladies and brothers too. Keep your women away from the priests and the temple guardians." He hesitated. "May El bless you."

Aldan inclined his head. "May El bless you, Uncle, and all of your family."

Srilani adjusted her head covering for the hundredth time, and René glared at her. "Ignore the veil, Srilani. Make like it's your hair. If you continue to mess with it, you will accidentally brush it back and your disguise will be useless."

"I hate it. The cursed thing is hot, and it cuts into my side vision."

"Remember when we had to practice wearing grandmother's crown? Keep your hands at your side."

"Walk tall," Srilani said, trying to mimic her grandmother's voice. "Do not touch the crown." She would always miss Grandmother. "You're right, of course. I'll get used to it."

She looked straight ahead at Aldan's shoulders. Why couldn't she put him out of her mind for even a couple of minutes? This morning, he hadn't complained once as she had removed his stitches.

"Does it hurt now, as I pull the threads out?" Srilani drew her hands back from his warm skin.

"No, it doesn't hurt. It pulls, but don't worry. I'll be happy to get rid of the itching. "

Soshi praised the results. "He's good as new. You made nice, even stitches. You should see my second son's knee. His stitches came out puckered and crooked. Of course, he wiggled and screamed the whole time."

"They got me drunk on cane spirits," Aldan said. "When they put my shoulder back in the socket, I passed out entirely. I didn't feel a thing while Srilani did her work."

Aldan had been a much better patient than she ever was. As if he sensed her scrutiny, he stopped and turned in his tracks to address her. "This is far enough, don't you think?"

What? Oh. "Yes." Far enough, but not far enough. She took in their surroundings. He'd chosen well. But he wasn't only talking about the place they would camp for the night. Her eyes returned to his face. How could he be so calm about telling his friends such a huge secret? She squared her shoulders and nodded. "Yes, this is far enough."

CHAPTER THIRTY-FIVE

Aldan set his pack at his feet and straightened his shoulders. Tall weeds lined the wagon trail they had been following. The surrounding wilderness, undisturbed for a couple of weeks, was already reclaiming the road, trying to cut Nik's mill and the remains of Trahnville off from the rest of Norland. His own path forward was obscured by uncertainties, but he could walk any path with his brothers at his side. He faced Sam and Linus. "There's something you need to know."

"Sounds serious," Sam said.

"I have news — unbelievable news. And it involves a secret."

Linus lifted his face like a hound testing the air, and Sam's gaze swept over the siblings who wore similar, watchful expressions. "Why do I get the impression Linus and I are the last to know?"

Aldan grimaced. Sam seemed to be spoiling for a fight. "Because you *are* the last to know. Srilani and René discovered it together when I was injured."

Sam dropped his pack and crossed his arms over his chest. He scowled. "And what did Her Majesty and Her Highness discover?"

Aldan shook his head — this wasn't the time to call Sam out on his negative attitude. "Do you remember the mark on my back?"

"Sure, I remember." Sam leaned forward. "And what do they say about your tattoo?"

"It's called the Mark of Mardan." The ancient king's name was awkward on his tongue. "Only royal children have the mark."

Linus's mouth lifted on one side as he stared at Aldan. "You're a prince?"

Aldan nodded.

"Let me get this straight," Sam said, and his voice had an ugly edge. "By some amazing coincidence, Her Worship sees your mark and instantly recognizes you as a prince?"

Aldan drew in a sharp breath. "It wasn't like that."

"Oh really? What was it like?"

Aldan tried to decipher the expression on Sam's face. He hadn't bargained on this sharp skepticism. "Srilani saw the mark when she stitched up my shoulder. She showed it to René and Jamson. They all agree on its meaning."

Linus spoke again. "You were taken by Rozar."

"I believe that's what happened even though I don't remember it."

"So . . . what? Are you their long-lost brother or something?" Sam's gaze veered to Srilani, and his lips twisted into a sneer. "That's going to be awkward."

"Shut up, Sam," Aldan said. An angry tide of heat rose in his face. "Why don't you just shut up and let me explain?"

"Fine. I'm all ears."

Aldan turned to Jamson. "Do you mind showing your mark? I think they need to see what we're talking about."

Jamson's eyes glittered, and his mouth was set. In that moment, the family resemblance between Jamson and his eldest sister was clear. Jamson's chin lifted. "Let me do the talking," he said. He put his hands on his hips.

"The first king — King Mardan — had twin sons named Kaedan and Kaeson. They were identical twins, and their parents were afraid their sons' identities would get switched. So the twins were separated for the first few days until the king's advisors had the idea of putting a tattoo on each child. A week after they were born, the marks were put on the babies. Kaedan, the older twin, had the mark on his right side, and Kaeson, his younger brother, on the left. Only the servants closest to the king and queen knew about the tattoos. The royal children have been marked ever since."

Jamson turned about and raised his tunic to show his tattoo. "I am the heir to Northern Marst, the realm of Kaeson, so my mark is on the left. Aldan is the missing heir of Southern Marst, the realm of Kaedan, the older brother."

Aldan mimicked Jamson and quickly showed his mark to Sam and Linus. He slapped down his shirt and turned back. Linus wore a mild, accepting expression, but Sam —

"Why didn't you tell us this several days ago?" Sam asked. "What possible difference does it make? So what if you *are* supposed to be the king? Someone else is ruling Southern Marst now. You can't just show up and say, 'Hey, I'm your king. Look. I have this secret mark on my backside.'"

Aldan stepped right up to Sam, nose-to-nose with his best friend. Sam could have used more sarcasm, but he would have needed a wagon to carry it in. "I didn't tell you a few days ago because Srilani asked me not to. She had this strange idea that you would react poorly. I told her that my brothers would back me up, no matter what." He retreated a couple of steps, looking between Sam and Linus. "I was only half right."

Aldan bit back other hasty words crowding to get out. A heavy silence filled the clearing as he reached for his bag. Pointedly ignoring Sam, he turned to Jamson. "I'll take first watch. You want to go second?"

Srilani pushed her hair back from her face, raking her fingers through the clean, wet strands. The river trickled over the rocks nearby, music to her ears as she sat on the rocks with her sisters. She pulled Rozar's comb through the entire length again. The evening breeze provided heavenly relief from the heat of the day and the confinement of the veil.

"That was awful," René said. "That's the first time I've seen Aldan lose his temper."

"I was afraid they were going to start fighting," Maelan said in a small voice. "I didn't know Sam was so mean."

Srilani handed the comb to Maelan and pulled her knees up under her chin. "He's not really mean." She paused. How could she defend one of her least favorite people? "I think Aldan caught Sam completely by surprise, and Sam spoke without thinking."

"But he didn't have to be so disrespectful to you," Maelan said. "He should pay for that."

Srilani couldn't remember encountering outright rudeness from anyone before Sam. Judge Elison's teachings made more sense now. "You can't force people to respect you. Respect is something that's earned. Apparently, I haven't earned it from Sam yet."

Srilani tugged gently on a strand of Maelan's straight, mink-colored hair. Her sister was growing up so fast, and she deserved to hear the truth. "Sam's right, you know. It's not as if Aldan has an army to help him take back his throne."

"I don't care. Aldan will make a good king." Maelan waved the comb in the air. "He's smart and kind. He's brave. He's tall and handsome."

"Like that matters," Srilani said, trying to keep her voice casual.

René laughed softly. "Aldan's not perfect like Greyson, but the way he looks won't hurt."

Srilani redirected the conversation — it was getting out of hand. "Weren't we talking about Sam? I know his biggest problem is with me, and I'll be polite — even if it kills me. You will be polite too. Do you understand what I'm saying, Maelan?"

"Ugh." Maelan attacked her hair with the comb. "That would be easier to do if I hadn't heard him say those things."

"Forget what he said. It won't help Aldan if we alienate Sam." Her mouth pulled down at the corners. "I hope there's actually a way to win him over. He truly dislikes me."

"Think about it from Sam's point of view," René said. "We've been acquainted for what, two weeks?"

"Only two weeks?" Maelan asked. "It seems much longer."

"Well, I'm counting from the day Aldan released us. I guess we met Aldan three days before that." René took the comb from Maelan. "Anyway, we haven't known them that long, but Aldan has spent a fair amount of that time with Srilani for one reason and another." She touched Srilani's arm. "And then — out of the blue — you're the one who sees the mark and mysteriously understands what it means. No wonder Sam is suspicious and resentful."

Srilani bit her lip. Had she come between Aldan and his brother? What would happen to them if Sam decided to leave the group? Or worse, would he betray them when they reached Minazor?

※

Aldan checked his steps as they rounded a bend in the road. Sol was high overhead, and they were weary from walking, mile after mile. Headed in the opposite direction, a man trudged beside his team of horses, hauling a wagon overflowing with burlap bags. A young man rode on the seat of the wagon holding the reins.

Aldan checked over his shoulder. The short riding lessons for Sam and Linus were at an end, and Stockings, led by Jamson, was again loaded with their wares. The sisters were behind him, and his brothers brought up the rear. "Make way," he ordered. At once, his group moved off to the side of the road, and the sisters took shelter behind the horse and the men.

Just as the wagon pulled even with them, the equipage slowed and stopped. "What news, friends?"

Aldan stepped forward and nodded to the man in the road. "A fair day and easy travel."

"That is good news."

Aldan took his cue from the man's greeting. "Where are you bound, friend?"

"Trahnville, and then to Nik's mill."

"Ah. My friend, I have sad news." Aldan looked full into the lined and weathered face of the older man, and then, up at his companion. "I'm sorry to tell you that Trahnville is no more. The terrible storm destroyed the town, and there are no survivors."

The man gaped at him, the color draining from his face. "None?"

"Not one. However, Nik is well. And his good wife, Drajna."

The man grasped the bridge of his nose with a shaking hand, seemingly unable to speak. The younger man secured the reins and jumped to the ground. He hurried forward to put his arm around the older man's shoulders. "Father, sit for a moment. Over here." The son led his father to the verge and sat beside him.

"My father grew up in Trahnville until he inherited our farm from his cousin," the son said. "He knew most of the people who lived there."

"He needs some water and a blanket." René's voice came from directly behind Aldan. "He could die from the shock."

Aldan spun around. She shouldn't have put herself forward in front of these strangers. But who could blame her?

"Immediately," she said. "There's a blanket on the seat of the wagon. And a water skin."

Aldan nodded and followed her directions. He handed the water skin to the son and wrapped the colorful wool rug around the farmer's shoulders. René returned to her place beside her sisters, but both men were staring after her.

Aldan inserted himself between them and the group. "Where is your farm?"

The young man blinked, and the father lost interest in René. "Near Minazor."

"And how did Minazor fare against the storm?"

"We had plenty of wind and rain, but we didn't suffer any real damage. We had just harvested the wheat and put it into the barns. As you can see, it was a good crop this year."

"You must be the first to the mill. We haven't seen anyone else for the last day or two."

The older man lifted his head. "We were hoping to be among the first."

"Father, how do you feel?"

"Very, very tired, but I'll be fine."

"Let's switch places. It's my turn to walk."

Aldan helped the son lift the man to his feet, each taking a side, and they supported him to the wagon. The father looked down once he'd gained the seat, and his eyes passed over the silent group waiting for the wagon to pass. His gaze rested on the sisters for several long moments.

"Friend — a word of advice," he said, his voice low and gravelly. "Keep your women away from the priests — especially the one named Lector — and beware of the temple guardians."

Srilani kept her eyes lowered as the overloaded wagon rolled away. Their first encounter with strangers hadn't gone according to plan.

Sam turned on René as soon as the wagon was far enough away. "What were you thinking, René?" He towered over her, and his lips were pulled tight against his teeth. "What possessed you to bring yourself to their attention? They saw your face clearly, and they're going to talk."

René said nothing, but her cheeks paled as she absorbed his fierce words. Srilani, standing at her side, said nothing. If only she could defend René's actions, but Sam was right — René's compassionate actions had put them at risk.

"Fortunately," Aldan said, "we have a few days before it matters." His voice sounded so reasonable. "They have another day before they reach Nik's mill, and I assume they'll stay a few days." He addressed René's bent head. "However, if something like that comes up again, pass your message through Sam or Linus."

René nodded, and Srilani reached for her hand and gave it a squeeze.

Aldan focused on Srilani. "Why don't you take point with me? You promised to answer my questions."

Sam stiffened, and Srilani met the big man's golden-brown eyes directly. "Would you like to join us?" Sam declined, so she tried again. "Then perhaps you'd like to learn more about caring for horses from Jamson and Maelan." She didn't wait for an answer. So far, he'd rebuffed every one of her overtures. All she could do was keep trying.

Aldan started right in with his questions, beginning with everything she knew about his family history and branching out to the southern royal court. His mind absorbed every detail. Every few minutes, she asked him to recall what she had told him and he recited the information with amazing accuracy. "Tonight we will get out Rozar's map and find the places we've discussed," she said.

"I was hoping we could practice drills."

"We'll drill first, while the light is still good. Thankfully, Drajna was very generous with her gifts so we don't need to hunt. Not yet."

Aldan lowered his voice. "Thanks for trying to reach Sam. He can be unreasonable when he gets an idea stuck in his head."

"I hadn't noticed."

Aldan laughed for the first time in a couple of days, and an answering smile tugged at Srilani's lips. Her smile faded. This wasn't a laughing matter. "Sam is your best friend — your brother. He's important to our success on this journey. He seems to hate me, and I don't know how to win him over."

"Don't try. That's my advice."

Srilani checked Aldan's face. Was he serious?

"No, really," Aldan said. "Just give him time. Sam will change his mind about you. He thinks you're a spoiled princess—"

"I am. I'm a princess, at least. And I think he's right about the spoiled part too." She gestured to their surroundings. "Being here without money, servants, guards, or parents has made me see how . . . arrogant I had become."

Aldan didn't reply right away, and when he did, he spoke slowly. "It's easy to see that you're used to command and that you expect to be obeyed. But I don't see that as a bad thing. Most of your decisions have been good ones, and none of them have been easy to make."

"Most of my decisions were made with your help," she pointed out. "We decided to build the raft, sail to shore, and we decided how to proceed together. You were as big a part of those decisions as I was, so don't give me more credit than I deserve."

"The point is, you've done your part. You've done the dirty work without acting like someone else should be doing it for you."

She brushed his remark aside. "I've done what's necessary, but I think you've given me an idea."

"Oh?"

"You and I have been making the big decisions, and the decision to hold back the information about your mark was wrong." She swallowed the pride that was choking her. "I was wrong, even though I was right about Sam's reaction. Perhaps if we'd told him immediately, he wouldn't have reacted that way." She drew a deep breath and let it out all at once. "I think Sam needs to have a say in the decisions from now on."

Aldan rubbed the stubble on his chin and stared at the road ahead. She looked up at his thoughtful face, waiting to see what he would say. His dark brown eyes switched to her face, and something fluttered in her stomach. He smiled at her, touching her elbow without a word. She averted her eyes, and his hand fell to his side. *El, help me!*

⋀

Aldan wiped the sweat from his brow and sat beside Linus on a rock close to their campsite. They'd worn each other out in their practice match, and the cool evening provided welcome relief.

Maelan perched next to Linus, settling back to watch Sam and Srilani. "Come on, Sam, show us what you've got," Jamson said. He grinned and flourished his stick sword toward Srilani, beckoning her forward.

Aldan leaned forward and covered his smile with one hand, trying to look thoughtful.

Jamson was acting as sword master. Srilani had deferred to her brother, and when he'd protested, she had insisted it was good practice for when he went to live in the barracks. So Jamson demonstrated each form and called out the moves to the group.

Since this was their second night of drills, Jamson had reviewed the lessons from the day before and added more to the routine. Then, he'd asked René to go through a practice round with him to show the moves in action. René looked dainty and feminine, but she parried her brother's attacks and survived without a scratch. Next Jamson paired Aldan and Linus for a practice match. He made them stop and start over several times, critiquing their opening moves.

"Most fights don't last very long, right?"

Aldan and Linus nodded. Aldan's mind went back to the last battle aboard the *Cathartid* — each skirmish had passed in a matter of seconds.

"Your opening move may be your last if you make a mistake. Again."

Aldan had managed to strike a killing blow on Linus, and their match had ended.

Now Srilani retrieved her stick and walked into the circle of stones to face Sam. Her blonde hair was tightly bound with a leather cord, and she'd discarded the bulky dress and head covering she'd been wearing over her original white trousers and tunic. She moved with economy and purpose, and the air seemed to ripple away from her in waves. Aldan blinked. She was like a force of nature — so intense and focused.

Sam bowed low with a flourish of his sword. "I've been looking forward to this, Your Majesty. I'm not sure it's fair for Jamson to do this to you."

"Why is that?"

He shrugged, his grin a sharp contrast to Srilani's lack of expression. "You're a woman. I'm a man."

"Not all of your enemies will be men."

"Then I have less to worry about, don't I?"

Each of them sidestepped a few paces, and Sam went on the offensive. His direct approach met nothing but air as Srilani neatly moved out of reach. He tried again and again to land a blow, but each time she eluded him.

"You think you're so smart," he said.

She parried a blow. "The question is . . . can you learn from a woman or will your manhood get in the way?"

His grin vanished, but her expression never wavered. Their exchange morphed as she went on the offensive. After a few moments, she added, "I have nothing against you, Sam, except your attitude." She thrust at him, and he leapt back to avoid her stick. "Your attitude stinks."

He tried to regain his previous momentum, but she proved ready for his every move.

"Funny. I don't like your attitude, either," he said through bared teeth. "In fact, I don't like anything about you."

Aldan's fingers curled into fists at Sam's words, but she shrugged one shoulder. "You're breaking my heart."

She sounded amused.

Sam fought hard, but it was obvious Srilani was in control, testing his defenses, her feints and thrusts measured and calculated. She was toying with him, like a cat with a mouse and then she wasn't playing anymore.

She pressed him, moving faster and still faster. Sweat stood out on Sam's brow as he tried to defend himself. She struck at will, sharp taps landing on his sides, legs, and arms. But no killing thrust. Just blow after blow as Sam's face turned scarlet.

"Enough!" Sam bellowed. He flung his stick into the woods and stalked away. But then he returned, his anger a physical presence, and Aldan tensed. Srilani stood her ground, feet planted, the stick sword dangling at her side.

"You're my worst nightmare," he railed at her. "A siren, leading us to our doom. A she-devil."

"You're probably right. And yet . . ." Her tone was mild, almost reflective.

"What?" He shoved his face close to hers.

She looked up into his face, her eyes glittering. "And yet I think you have the makings of an extraordinary leader. If — and only if — you decide to learn from us."

Sam's head jerked back. He stared at her for a moment, snorted, and spun away. This time, he continued walking, vanishing into the thick woods.

CHAPTER THIRTY-SIX

Aldan left the group outside Minazor's city walls on the morning of the fourth day. He entered the gates and made his way to the temple at the city's center. Yes, they'd been warned to stay away from Azor's priests, but Nik had instructed him in the necessary ritual of visiting the head priest before setting up shop. At least this way the women could remain out of sight.

The Minazor temple crouched by itself, a dark gray one-story structure topped by a dome. A muscular fellow in black armor with a prominent tattoo of Azor on his right cheek met him on the front steps and waved him inside. "I am Lector. Follow me."

The entryway was actually a series of doors in a long tunnel leading to the center of the temple. Even though the morning heat burned outside, the coolness of the interior chilled the sweat on his arms and face.

His escort led him through oak doors, iron gates, a portcullis, and finally another set of ornately carved oak doors — each manned by a couple of "priests" dressed in black leather armor, daggers, axes, and swords. All of the temple guardians were physically imposing men. Like land-dwelling pirates. Who knew if they actually had religious duties?

"Wait here," Lector said.

Aldan clamped his teeth together, fighting the urge to shiver. The unspoken message was clear — the only way to see Sol again was to satisfy the priests of Azor.

The guard walked around the perimeter of the large circular room and knocked on an unmarked door on the far side.

Aldan's attention fixed on the enormous, dark green sculpture of Azor that dominated the simulated swamp in the center of the room. The creature's elongated snout was open in a snarl, displaying sharp ivory teeth. Its eyes of gold and onyx glimmered in the light streaming from windows set high beneath the dome overhead. Azor's low body was partially submerged in a pool of water set into the floor, and his tail was frozen in a menacing curl beside the length of his body.

"Come." Lector beckoned him from the far side of the pond.

Aldan forced his feet to move, retracing the man's steps around the swamp. They crossed the threshold of a small room devoid of windows. A couple of lanterns illuminated the waxy features of an elder priest seated behind a desk covered in parchments.

"Welcome to Minazor," the priest said. "My name is Telek. Who are you and what is your purpose in coming to my city?"

Aldan bowed. "My name is Aldan, and I've come to Minazor in hopes of selling my wares."

Telek set his elbows on the desk, steepling his fingers. "Are you alone?"

"No, Your Worship. I have two business partners and a few servants with me."

"How long do you plan to stay?"

"One day, perhaps two if business is slow."

"And what have you brought me?"

Aldan swallowed and pulled out the small pouch René had created for this purpose. He bowed again and extended it to the priest.

"Let's see what we have here," Telek said, taking the pouch and untying the string. He poured four of Rozar's gold coins into his palm and pondered them. His dark eyes came up and examined Aldan's face. "This is enough for a day of commerce. If you wish to stay another day, you must match this amount tomorrow morning." He flicked his chubby, white fingers toward Aldan's burly escort. "Lector, my captain, will direct you where to set up your stall. He will visit you late in the day to collect the temple tax on your sales."

He was dismissed. Aldan bowed once more. "Thank you, Your Worship."

Gratefully, Aldan lifted his face to Sol's bright rays as they left the hulking edifice. He followed Lector through Minazor's square and down a short alley that opened into a long row of stalls, teaming with vendors of all kinds. At length, they reached an empty stall set between a merchant hawking produce and another displaying textiles.

"This is where you will be today. Do not leave before I return to collect the tax," Lector said. His biceps bulged as he folded his arms over his armored chest and looked Aldan up and down. "For your sake, I hope you have something worth buying." He turned on his heel and stalked away.

Srilani wiped the sweat from her face with a scrap of fabric and shifted to escape the afternoon light burning through a rip in the ragged awning overhead. The sisters sat on their packs in the small space behind the heavy, woven curtain at the rear of their assigned market stall. What she wouldn't give for a breath of fresh air. The curtain hid them from view, but it also cut off any hint of breeze.

In fact, the entire market consisted of nothing more elaborate than wooden frames with heavy fabric partitions, roofs, and awnings. Srilani strained her ears, trying to decipher the action in the front part of their allotted space.

Sam could have been a vendor all his life, going by his natural grasp of the patter. His voice resonated with confidence as he cajoled a potential buyer. "Ah, sweet lady, you know this serving dish is just what you were looking for to put food on your table. Observe the craftsmanship of this fine piece. Here, hold it. See how heavy it is? And what a bargain. If you buy it today, I will throw in this little glass pitcher. See how it catches the light?"

People responded well to Aldan's quiet charm and warmth too. The rift between Sam and Aldan hadn't healed, and tensions had run high the entire distance to Minazor. At least for today, they seemed to be working well together to sell their goods.

Sol's rays beat down on Minazor's merchants, and dust swirled in the streets. The shouts of the vendors were just as unremitting as the heat and dust. Somewhere nearby, a trio of street musicians beat out a raucous sailor's ditty in a minor key.

"That terrible music is really getting to me," Maelan said, pressing her fingers to her temples. "Someone, please have mercy on us all and take his flute away."

René patted her shoulder. "He's not nearly as talented as Linus, is he?"

"No, he's not." Maelan perked up. "Weren't you surprised when Linus brought out his flute and started to play? He says he'll teach me how."

Linus's music was about the only good thing to come out of the last few days on the road. Sam's cheerful songs had been noticeably absent.

"This reminds me of being locked up on the ship," René said, keeping her voice low. "Except for the children."

Whole families were in town for market day, and children were everywhere. In the next stall, a baby had set up a squall a few times during the long hours of the morning. From the sounds of things, several younger children were passing the time there.

"And the animals," Maelan added. "The sounds remind me of the market at Kaeson."

"Mae . . ." Srilani said in a warning tone, deliberately drawing out her shortened name. "Guard your tongue."

Maelan's face fell. "Oh. Sorry."

"I'm sorry too. You've done so well up to now, but we simply don't know who might overhear a casual remark. Just be careful."

A moment later, Linus entered the little chamber. He carried a pitcher in one hand and a bowl of fruit in the other.

Srilani gasped. "Thank you. You've chosen the perfect time." She stood to dig her cup out of her pack.

Maelan was quicker than she, holding out her cup for a serving of fresh water. "Thank you, Linus," she said, raising bright hazel eyes to his face. "Where have you been?"

"To the well and to a fruit seller," he said, turning to fill René's cup. Srilani took a piece of fruit and bit into it. The sweet nectar bathed her parched throat, and her lashes fluttered down as she sighed. How she missed eating fruit every day.

"And Jamson?" Maelan asked.

"He's taking care of the horse."

Srilani's eyes snapped open as her heart started to pound. "Is Jamson by himself?"

Linus shook his head. "He's at the front, waiting for me. We've been together all day."

"Stay as close to the stand as you can."

"That's what Aldan told us," Linus said. "We had to go to the square for the water, but otherwise we stayed close."

"Thank you." She held out her cup. "How are they doing with our wares?"

"Over half the things are gone."

"We still need to buy the supplies we discussed. Do you think you can manage that with Jamson to help?"

Linus nodded. "We know where to find things now."

"The merchants expect you to bargain, so don't pay the first price they tell you. How are you at counting?"

"Sam taught me."

"That's fine, then. I've heard him dealing with the buyers, and he knows what he's doing. Check with your brothers to make sure they agree."

He nodded and left.

"That's the most I've ever heard him say at one time," René said with a smile.

"Linus can talk," Maelan said in a defensive voice. "He just doesn't do it very often."

"I wasn't criticizing him."

"Well, it sounds like you think he's stupid or something."

René's back stiffened. "Now who's being critical?"

Srilani broke in. "Don't pick a fight, Mae. René and I know Linus takes time to choose his words wisely." She gave her sister a hard look. "You should be more like him in that way."

Maelan's eyes filled with quick tears, but she turned to René. "I'm sorry."

"I'm sorry too."

The out-of-tune flute wailed even louder, and the infant in the next stall wailed again. None of them spoke until Linus and Jamson returned with their first batch of supplies. Then it was all business as they distributed the weight among the packs. The younger men returned twice more as the strip of Sol's light crossed the floor.

The small band finally stopped playing in the late afternoon, and the shouts of the vendors took on a strange urgency. The children next door started a rowdy game of keep away that threatened to explode into all-out war. Srilani double-checked all of the packs, redistributing several items, more for a way to stay busy than any real need.

"I'll warn them." Aldan's voice came clearly through the curtains, and then he stepped through the flap.

Srilani whirled around to face him. "Warn us about what?"

"Lector, the priest from this morning, is approaching. It would be better if you didn't talk or move around until he's gone."

She nodded, and he disappeared to the front area again. She sat between her sisters and offered a hand to each. Maelan squeezed her fingers and tucked her head against Srilani's shoulder. René's fingers trembled in her grasp. Soon they were all holding their breath as Aldan spoke to the mysterious Lector. He demanded to inspect their money box, and peppered the men with questions about their day in the market.

The little girl in the next stall shrilled at her brothers, complaining and threatening to tell on them. Her yells drowned out the men's voices. Something hit the base of the curtain wall, and a rag doll slid to a stop at Srilani's feet. She released René's hand and hurriedly bent to push the doll back under the wall just in time to come face to face with its owner.

CHAPTER THIRTY-SEVEN

Aldan pretended not to notice Lector's arrival at their stall. He continued rearranging the remaining goods to display to advantage. Sam stood at the rear with his back to the curtain, arms crossed, face set, and eyes watchful.

"I have returned for the temple tax," Lector said, planting himself at the front of the stall. He had two henchmen with him. Together, they cast a large shadow across Aldan's face.

Aldan raised his head slowly, placing the object in his hands down with care. "Ah, good, you are here. We were hoping to complete our business with you."

"How have you fared today?"

Nik had coached him about what to expect from the priests. "Well enough, I trust. A profitable undertaking for the temple. Please step this way."

Aldan led Lector to the box they were using as a till and flipped back the lid. He took care to keep out of Lector's way, stepping back and trying to appear relaxed. Lector stacked the coins inside the box in order of value.

Aldan glanced at the other men. They were nearly as large as Lector, wearing black leather armor and helmets, and sporting several weapons apiece. Their attention was focused on Lector and the money. He met Sam's solemn gaze briefly before he looked back at Lector.

The priest finished stacking, and removed half of each stack, dumping the tax money into a leather pouch hanging from his belt. "A good day indeed for the temple. Do you intend to work here tomorrow?"

"No, we must be on our way."

Lector tilted his head to the side, assessing Aldan's expression. "Are you sure I can't persuade you to stay another day?"

Was that a threat or a simple question? Better to take it at face value until he knew better. "I'm flattered, but we are for Port Azor. We'd like to meet a certain ship — the *Cardinal* — whenever she comes into port. Since the storm, we're anxious to see if she made it back. We need to replenish our stock." Aldan gestured to Sam. "My partner's the cousin of the captain, and sometimes he'll give us the first look at his take."

"Plan to return, then."

Aldan nodded. "Of course." He shrugged. "However, it's best not to wear out our welcome. People get jealous."

Lector snapped his fingers, and his men straightened. As they turned to leave, a girl's voice, as shrill as a plover's call, exclaimed, "The lady has blue eyes!"

Her voice came from behind Sam, and Sam gave a start. Aldan used every ounce of his will to keep from flinching as Lector turned back.

"What's this?" Lector's smile was anything but reassuring as his gaze locked onto Aldan's face. "This morning you only mentioned servants. I'm sure I remember correctly."

"Servants only, my lord."

"You won't mind if I see them for myself, will you? Selling slaves secretly without paying the temple is a mistake, you know."

Aldan's heart stopped beating for a moment and then jumped about in his chest like a deer bounding for cover. "I have no slaves for sale, my lord."

The flap behind Sam was thrust aside, and Maelan stalked out. She put her hand on Sam's arm, going up on her tiptoes. "Master, you promised," she whined. "You promised you would get me some food this afternoon. I'm so hungry."

Sam's brows met in an awful frown as he shook off her grasp. "Mae. Be silent! Can't you see we have important business here?"

Maelan twisted about as if in surprise, her hazel gaze flicking up toward Lector's face. She raised a hand to her mouth and backed away with a startled,

"Oh." She whisked behind Sam as if she were hiding behind a tree.

"I told you to stay put." Sam's growl was a deep rumble. "Get back there."

Lector held out his hand, his voice a purr. "Not so fast. Come here, girl."

"See what you've done?" Sam glared down at her. "You've offended the priest. Be sure I'll deal with you later."

Lector crooked a finger at Maelan. "I said, come here."

"Yes, my lord." Maelan's voice was as meek as a kitten's. She came forward slowly, head drooping and eyes downcast. She stopped before she reached the priest.

"What have we here?" Lector placed his fingers under Maelan's chin and raised her face for inspection. "Open your eyes, wench."

Obediently, trembling visibly, Maelan opened her eyes. "She's a pretty thing, but . . . not what I thought to see." He pinched her cheek and gave her a shove toward Sam. "Teach her to hold her tongue."

Maelan ran behind the curtain, and the priest seemed amused. He strolled idly about the stall, picking items up and putting them down.

"Tell me, how many servants did you bring with you?"

"Only my woman," Aldan said and forced a chuckle. "My partner has *three*, his woman and her sister and brother."

Lector's brows rose in apparent surprise, and Sam feigned a sheepish smile. "I had a lucky streak in Port Azor, and so I bought all three together."

The priest nodded as though he understood, and then he just stood there. Why wouldn't he leave? Again, the priest tilted his head to the side. "Besides the girl, where are your servants? And your third partner?"

"Buying supplies, my lord."

"The women too?" Lector's voice sounded skeptical.

Aldan shrugged. "Of course."

Lector's voice grew hard. "Still, I'll just have a look."

Sam moved aside as Lector strode to the back of the stall, and Aldan swallowed. His palm itched to retrieve the dagger from his boot. If it came to a fight, could they defeat Lector and his men before the rest of the guards in the marketplace heard the ruckus and came running?

The air was too heavy to breathe.

Lector yanked aside the flap to the back section, and Mae, who was sitting atop her pack, shrank back from the priest with a tiny scream. She was alone. Where were Srilani and René? They'd disappeared into thin air. Even their packs were gone.

Lector dropped the flap into place and turned to address Aldan directly. "Don't leave before I've met your other partner and all of your servants." He spread his hands and smiled. "In view of our profitable day together, you must allow me to guarantee your safety."

He sauntered to the front of the stall and clapped one of his men on the shoulder. "Bolz will stay here to make sure nobody bothers you."

Truly, there was no way to refuse. They were trapped. After Lector departed to collect more taxes, Sam and Aldan stared at Bolz, and Bolz stared back.

⋏⋏

Srilani's pack thumped against the small of her back, making it seem doubly heavy. René kept pace behind her as they jogged down the alley behind the market stalls. Finally they reached a gap between the stalls that led to the street. They ducked into the space and looked out into the marketplace.

Srilani sighed and allowed her pack to slide to the ground at her feet.

"Can you see our stall from here?" René whispered.

Srilani shook her head. "It's too far away."

René tugged at her arm. "Did we do the right thing?"

"I don't know."

"At least Sam seemed to catch on quickly," René said. "He went right along with her."

"I'll give him credit for that. He had his chance to give us away entirely, and he didn't take it." Srilani sucked in a breath. "I wish we'd been able to hear the rest." They'd gotten away — for the moment — but what now?

"I'm sure Aldan and Sam will do their best to keep Maelan safe."

Srilani couldn't speak. Her veins filled with ice water, and she shuddered. Had they allowed Maelan to sacrifice herself for them?

Quicker than thought, Maelan had pushed the little girl who'd given them away back into her space and grabbed René's arm.

"Go out the back," she'd whispered. "If he sees you, we're all dead." Her bright eyes almost glowed as she turned to Srilani. "You too. He won't care about me."

Before either of them could understand Maelan's intentions, she'd flung herself through the gap like an actress walking onstage. Had there been another way? Srilani put a trembling hand to her temple. What should they do next?

⋏⋏

Bolz seemed content to pass the time by watching the scene outside. After all, where could they go? Aldan's mind raced. They had to get Maelan away before Lector returned. They all had to get away. Bolz narrowed his eyes at a rowdy group of young men who passed. Aldan took the opportunity to brush past Sam and whisper, "I'll distract him, and you take him out."

Sam's only answer was a single nod.

Aldan opened the till box and noisily divided the money into three stacks. The pleasant sound of chinking coins drew the guard's attention like a moth to a flame. Aldan scooped up two-thirds of the money, put it in a small sack, and handed it to Sam. He deposited the rest in the money pouch at his waist and addressed Bolz. "Tell Lector that I'll be back."

Aldan lifted the flap at the back and ducked into the private area.

"Wait!" Bolz exclaimed.

Aldan cautioned Maelan to be silent with a finger to his lips. He pulled up the rear edge of the stall and paused, deliberately waiting for the moment Bolz came through the curtain.

The sound of running feet penetrated the thick fabric. "Stay!"

Bolz managed the one word before an unseen force threw him through the curtain to the floor at Aldan's feet, unconscious. Maelan gave a squeak of dismay and flung herself at Aldan. Automatically, his arms closed around her, and he gave her a hug.

Sam's grim face peered into the space. "Tie him up," he said. "I'll keep watch."

Aldan used the belt from Bolz's waist to bind the man's hands behind his back. He cut a strip of the awning to form a gag. "That should keep him for a while."

Aldan guided Maelan to Sam's side. "Any sign of Lector?"

"Over that way," Sam said with a lift of his chin. "You need to get her out of here and find the other girls."

"Me? You're the one who needs to go. I got you into this — I'm the one who should take the risks."

"I decide which risks I'm willing to take. They need you more than they need me." Sam hesitated. "And you need them. How else are you going to take back what's yours?"

Maelan's eyes traveled from Aldan's face to Sam's and back. She bit her lip.

Aldan's brows rose, and he snorted. "Oh, so now you're on their side? That argument won't cut it, Brother. A couple of days ago, you said it was impossible. Don't expect me to believe you've suddenly changed your mind. You're not getting rid of me that easily." He poked Sam in the chest. "You're bigger. You're stronger. You're a native. You're the one they need the most."

"They don't even like me."

"So? Srilani told me they couldn't make it without you. You. Not me."

Maelan spoke up, sounding shy. "It's true, Sam. Srilani did say that."

Sam's laugh sounded derisive, but he sobered quickly when Maelan glowered at him and stamped her foot. "I mean it, Sam," she said, fists on hips.

Aldan gave Sam a push. "Get going. I'll wait until you're out of sight and head in the opposite direction. Gather the rest of the group and take them out the northern gate as quickly as possible. Hide. Tie up Linus if you have to, but whatever you do, get away and don't let him come back to get me. I'll catch up as quickly as I can."

"I don't want to leave you behind," Sam said, shaking his head. "Besides, why should you trust me? I've been a pain in the butt for days and given you nothing but grief."

Aldan faced Sam squarely. "You've been a pain in the butt your entire life, but I still trust you."

The expression on Sam's face altered in some indefinable way. "If something happens to you, I'll never forgive myself."

Aldan pressed his advantage. "The sooner you get going, the sooner we'll be back together." He extended his arm, and Sam took hold of it with a pressure that bordered on pain.

"You can trust me to fulfill our promises to Srilani. Or die trying," Sam said, releasing his hold. "Take care, Brother." He grabbed Maelan's hand and strode away.

The marketplace swallowed them without a trace. Aldan closed his eyes for a second. *El, if you're listening, guard my brothers and bring us together again.*

He retrieved his pack and glanced one last time around the little stall. It was probably a good thing they couldn't take the rest of the merchandise with them. But the marriage cup Srilani found in Trahnville caught his attention. He picked it up and rolled it between his palms. He hesitated for a moment, then slipped the cup into the opening of his pack.

As he passed into the street, he caught sight of Lector exiting from a nearby stall. One second too late, Aldan ducked into the nearest vendor's tent.

"Wait!" Lector yelled. "In the name of Azor, halt!"

Aldan tore through the vendor's area, upsetting a cart of produce and toppling a couple of chicken crates. He bounded into the private area beyond. An old woman gaped at him as he staggered over her mats and into the back wall. He yanked the dagger from his boot top and slashed at the awning. The material ripped easily. He slipped through the opening into another private area. This stall was unoccupied, and he sped through the curtain and into the next street.

Shouts and the sound of many feet followed him as he searched for a path, a hiding place, anywhere to get away.

CHAPTER THIRTY-EIGHT

"Get behind me, Mae," Sam said under his breath. "You have to act like a servant. Keep close and don't look at anyone. Do you understand?"

She nodded, released his hand, and stepped back a pace.

"You're being very brave. Speak up if I start to lose you or if you see your sisters or Linus and Jamson."

She nodded again. He set off, making a path through the crowd with his wide shoulders. How had they come to this? Everything had been going so well. Even as his eyes swept the crowd for familiar faces, his mind focused on Aldan's face at that moment of separation.

Sam swallowed the bitter taste in his mouth. Why? Why had he been so horrible to Aldan?

Guards were everywhere in the marketplace. Most were on foot, but there were a few guardians on horseback. They must be serious about collecting their tax. He still couldn't believe Lector had taken half their money. Just like that. How could the people afford to eat at that rate? Had it been that bad when he was a boy, before his father sold him to Rozar? Sam pushed the thought away — it did no good to think about his childhood. Sam's gaze sharpened, and he slowed.

Maelan bumped into his back. "Oh. I'm sorry. What's the matter?" A moment passed. "Master?"

"Isn't that our horse?"

She peeked around his side, going up on her toes. "Yes."

They hurried to Stockings. The mare was hitched to a post, but Linus and Jamson weren't immediately visible.

"I hope this means they're nearby," Sam muttered. Trying to appear casual, he searched the closest stalls while Maelan went to the mare's head and checked her over.

"Master."

Sam spun about. Maelan pointed across the way to a gap between the stalls. His heart thumped hard, and his breathing turned raspy. Linus had his back turned to them, and all of his attention was focused on the tiny passageway.

"Stay here."

"Yes, Master." Nobody overhearing her would suspect she wasn't a servant girl — she really was a natural actress. He waited for a wagon to pass, but as soon as the way was clear, he made his way to Linus's side.

There, squashed into the gap, were Srilani, René, and Jamson. Srilani released her brother's shoulders and met Sam's eyes. René, too, stared up at him. They seemed more vulnerable now than ever before, and he rushed to reassure them. "Your sister is with me."

René pressed her palms together and brought them to her forehead. "Thank you," she whispered.

Srilani grasped the nearest post, knuckles white. "Where's Aldan?"

"Aldan sent me to find all of you and take you out of the city."

"He's not with you." Her voice was a breath of sound, and her face lost all color. The sound of shouting echoed down the street, and she seemed to sway. "He's drawing them away from us?"

Sam's stomach turned over as the disturbance grew. "I'm afraid so."

Linus turned to leave, and Sam grabbed hold of his arm. Linus's sinewy arm was as tight as a ship's line in a high wind.

"Stay. Aldan told me to tie you up, if necessary. We're going to stick together this time." Linus tried to pull away, and Sam's grip tightened. "We have to follow the plan, Linus. Otherwise, he won't be able to find us."

Srilani put a hand on Linus's other arm, and she added her arguments to his, even though her voice sounded shaky. "Linus, if you go off on your own, you'll do more harm than good. Follow Aldan's plan."

Linus groaned, and all the fight seeped away.

"Let's go," Sam said.

They rejoined Maelan, and Linus took Stocking's reins from her hand. Two mounted guardians swept past them, yelling at pedestrians to make way. After that, the marketplace fell into a state of pandemonium. People were either packing their wares and calling their children or running toward the source of the excitement. More guardians ran past them.

They joined the stream of people forming at the northern gate. The guardians there were waving most people through, but others they pulled to the side. Sam reached into his purse, grabbed a couple of the largest coins, and handed the purse to Srilani. "Hide this. You and your sisters line up behind me and keep your eyes on the ground. Jamson, take that side, and Linus, take the other with the horse."

The group of people directly in front of them was motioned to the side amid a clamor of protests, and Sam rolled his shoulders and lifted his chin. He stepped up to the guard he'd decided was actually in charge and held out his closed fist. The guardian, who was almost as large as Sam, looked him up and down. The man extended his hand and Sam placed the coins on his palm. The money disappeared so quickly that Sam blinked.

"Fare well on your journey," the guard said, waving them on.

They crowded through the narrow gate and passed out of Minazor.

"Well done," Srilani said. "What now?"

"Let's stay on the road until we can't see the walls anymore. Then we'll find a place to hide and wait."

⟁

Using the temple as his reference point, Aldan zigzagged through the marketplace, causing as much mayhem as possible. He took precious seconds to open an enclosure of sheep and goats, stampeding them into the streets. He ran into the path of a wagon, waving his arms and shouting. The team of horses shied away from him and upset their load. Barrels of cane spirits flew in all directions.

Aldan ran pell-mell for several blocks, but even with all the obstacles he'd thrown up, he could hear his pursuers catching up and closing in from more than one direction. If only he could discover some hiding spot and wait for night to fall.

He reached the outer city wall at the same time a contingent of guards reached it one street away. He spun around, heading back the way he'd come, and tried to jump over a stack of pallets. His toe caught in the top of the pile, and he crashed full length on the far side.

A new sound was added to the shouts and curses of the men — the baying of hounds — and even though he'd never heard the noise before, his blood turned into icy slush. Rozar's crew had told wild stories about war hounds — the cries of the beasts, their powerful jaws and agility, their uncanny ability to hunt using scent alone. Aldan scrambled to his knees and found his feet, reenergized by primal terror.

His sides heaved with the effort to draw in precious oxygen, and his palms stung from skidding across the paving stones. Moving forward was the only option. Otherwise, they'd trap him in this canyon of walls. The war hounds' barks echoed from all directions. He ducked behind some barrels to catch his breath and think.

If he stayed here, they would find him. The hounds would sniff him out, no matter how well he hid himself. He needed to be outside the walls, but passing through the city gates was out of the question. Had the others escaped?

He studied the building across the way. It wasn't actually a single building, but a collection of houses built atop one another in a haphazard fashion. The structure stretched in a long line and curved toward the center of town. How did people reach the layers above street level? An arched door several yards away caught his eye. He raced across the alley, launching himself at the door and yanking it open.

Sol's late afternoon light poured into the alleyway from the street beyond. Aldan quickly pulled the door closed behind him and studied his options. This building faced another. Colorful awnings stretched between the buildings along with rope lines for hanging laundry. Children played nearby, oblivious to the hue and cry that haunted Aldan.

Multiple ladders and stairways led from the street to the apartments above. After a cursory look at the arrangement of houses, Aldan pushed away from the arched doorway, crossed the street to the next set of houses, and mounted some stairs. He trotted up the steps and forced himself to walk calmly along a landing. Most of the people in the street and on the landings were women going about their business.

He didn't make eye contact or speak to anyone. *I belong here. You don't notice me.*

Aldan took a series of stairs and ladders until he found an access to the rooftops. From this vantage point, the entire city of Minazor stretched out beneath his feet, a maze of red tiles. And there to his left was where the hounds searched.

He was alone for now, but it wouldn't last.

Srilani walked between Maelan and Jamson. She suppressed the desire to hold their hands as if they were three years old. The twins had proven their mettle, and they deserved to be treated as young adults.

Today they'd come close to disaster, but they weren't safe yet. Lector's reputation for ruthlessness had been confirmed by his actions. Setting a guard. Insisting on seeing the entire party together. Obviously, they'd had to run, but their flight was the most damning evidence of all.

And where was Aldan? Had he been captured? Was he safe? Was he alive? A deep pain like the shaft of an arrow had burrowed into her chest as soon as she'd realized he wasn't with Sam and Maelan. *El, please keep him safe.*

Sam pointed to the east. "What do you think of that hill over there?"

He was ahead of them, but he slowed until they caught up with him. "To the right and away from the road. With some luck, we can keep watch on the road from behind those rocks."

The hill could barely be called a hill, but its rocky top rose above the tree line enough to be seen from the road, so the road would be visible from its crest.

"If we stay on the far side without a fire, I think it's probably as good as we can hope for," Srilani said. "We might escape notice that far from the road."

"Maybe we can see Aldan once he reaches this stretch."

The shaft of pain thrust deeper into her chest. What if Aldan didn't make it out of Minazor?

Sam looked straight into her eyes for once, and his grim expression seemed to indicate he had the same fears. By mutual consent, they didn't voice the terrible possibility. He checked over his shoulder. "Nobody's in sight for the moment, and Sol's light will be gone within the hour. Let's go."

Aldan pressed his back against the wall next to the open doorway. He held his dagger in one hand and covered his nose and mouth with the other to stifle the sounds of his breathing. A guardian stood on the other side of the threshold, and the man's shadow, unnaturally tall and slender in the orange light of sunset, fell across the floor at Aldan's feet.

He glanced around the shabby room. A broken table sprawled in the corner. The building, so close to the city gates, had few inhabitants, and this house was abandoned. Two doorways led off the main room and the only window overlooked a three-story drop.

His pursuers seemed to be searching from house to house. He'd been fortunate to spot the guardian before the guardian spotted him. Aldan's grip on his dagger tightened. He'd have to strike first and strike hard when the man looked in here — he'd never let himself be taken captive again.

The war dogs bayed in the courtyard. With a scuff of boots, the shadow retreated. Aldan sagged against the wall and sucked air into his starving lungs. That was cutting it too close.

When he dared to look, the walkway was empty. He crossed to the window. The Southern Gate was across from the building, but he couldn't see it well enough from here.

Aldan left the door of the house open, the way he'd found it. With an eye on the courtyard below, he sheathed his dagger and crept up a ladder leading to the roof. He crouched low over the red tiles until he neared the edge. He set aside his pack and wormed his way to the edge of the roof on his belly.

The heat from the roof radiated into the marrow of his bones. He ignored the discomfort to get a good look at the wide street below.

A quartet of guardians was stationed at the Southern Gate. As he watched, a traveler came to the gate, seeking to leave the city. The guards questioned him closely before they opened the heavy doors for the man and his wagon to exit.

As the great doors closed, a couple of mounted guards rode into view. Immediately, the doors of the gate were re-opened, and they galloped through. The priests seemed to be sending horsemen out to search the countryside around Minazor. Hopefully, Sam and the others had found a good place to hide.

Smoke rose from courtyards all over the city. The scent of meat cooked in onions and spices tantalized his nose, and his mouth watered. He shook his head. This wasn't the time to think of trivial details like an empty stomach. Aldan rolled onto his back and threw one arm over his eyes. The tiles dug into his injured shoulder, but the pain served to focus his mind on the task at hand. He had no choice. He'd have to find a hole to hide in until the guardians gave up the search.

Looking to the east, he found the young moon was already on the rise as Sol set. In a matter of days, the moon would be full. At least he'd be able to see tonight. He'd have to be careful not to be seen, though.

Reluctantly, he rose, retrieved his pack, and headed off the roof. No guards or dogs remained in the courtyard three stories below, so he descended to the second level. In case anybody watched, he tried for a casual air as he sauntered along the landing, working his way toward the far end of the long set of houses away from the gate and the city wall.

At the extreme end, he reached a cross street and stopped. The landing ended abruptly in open air — perhaps there had been a ladder here previously. On his left, two elderly women were completing their meal preparations in the courtyard. The derelict house to his right wavered over the street below like an overhang on a cliff, ready to fall into the sea.

Aldan pushed open the door. Not a single stick of furniture. The dark shape of a rat slithered off a shelf set into the wall and skittered away. He entered the house and closed the door. Rats he could handle.

CHAPTER THIRTY-NINE

Aldan woke with a start and jerked upright. His sword, cool and dark gray, still lay across his knees. How could he have fallen asleep? His pack, acting as his chair, was hard and lumpy, and his neck had a crick in it. A horse's snort echoed directly beneath his feet, and he froze. The hairs on the back of his neck prickled. He jumped to his feet and hurried to stand on the far side of the door. Two moments later, it creaked open.

Someone paused in the doorway, shielded from view by the door. Then, a man stepped toward the pack on the floor by the wall and into a milky ray of light from the window. Bulky armor marked the stranger as a guardian.

Aldan brought the hilt of his sword down on the man's bare head, but the guardian only staggered, staying on his feet and swinging around in a furious counter-attack. Aldan dodged an elbow to the face and kicked out. The heel of his boot connected with the guard's knee, and the man grunted.

Undeterred, the guardian swung a massive fist into Aldan's jaw, knocking him against the wall near the door. His ears rang from the force of the blow. He threw himself out of the path of a second punishing punch, pushed off the wall, and thrust at the man with his sword. His opponent jumped back, giving Aldan just enough time to scurry out onto the landing.

With a curse, the guardian ran onto the landing too. Aldan ducked his head and ran full tilt into the man's chest, knocking him backward. The guard's arms flailed. He tried to catch onto the railing, but Aldan pushed with all his might, shoving the man back and back until there was only air and the street below. Aldan fell full-length onto the landing, and the guardian disappeared through the opening at the end. A yell echoed on the walls, followed by a nasty thud like a net of fish landing on a deck.

Aldan's stomach turned over, and he scrambled to the ledge, breathing hard. The man's body was sprawled on the deserted street below, his head bent at an unnatural angle. Aldan looked over his shoulder at the courtyard. Nobody was about, and more than likely, nobody would let their curiosity get the best of them. Still, if another guardian came across the body, there would be hell to pay.

He forced himself to descend the stairs. A large, dark horse was tied to a railing on the cross street, just under the leaning wall of Aldan's hiding place. He put his hand on the horse's neck, and it sniffed at his hair, blowing out a gentle breath. The animal seemed calm and unlikely to raise a fuss.

Aldan left the horse and dragged the dead man out of the street by his feet. There was no way he could carry him up the stairs, so he left the man to hurriedly search the row of houses on the first floor until he found one that was obviously unoccupied. He rushed back and pulled the body out of sight.

Aldan brushed the hair out of his eyes and fingered his tender jaw. The ringing in his ears had subsided, but his head throbbed. He drew in a deep breath and crouched near his late adversary. He'd done it now. Killing a guardian would be punishable by death for sure.

Come to think of it, how had the guardian known where to find him? Had he given himself away? Had one of the nearby residents tipped the guardian off?

Either way, he couldn't stay here.

His brows lifted as he stared at the body. Here was the means to disappear.

***

The scuff of a heavy tread sent pebbles flying past Srilani.

"Can't sleep?" Sam asked.

She raised her chin from her knees and shook her head. The air around her stirred as he lowered his bulk onto the ledge at her side.

"You need to try."

She snorted softly. "Like you care." She stared at the ribbon of road visible from their perch. The moon was getting ready to set. Did that mean it was two or three bells in the morning?

"Srilani, listen to me. You're wasting your time here. Staying up all night won't help Aldan. Besides, Linus is down there, hiding beside the road, and nobody can watch better than he can. Nobody."

"So why are you here?"

"I'm on watch over the camp. Remember?"

She shrugged. "You may as well rest and let me do it."

"No way. If you insist, we'll watch together." Sam's voice took on a stern note. "But when the moon's gone, you're going to try to sleep while Jamson takes his turn."

"Oh? How's that?" The question came out sounding aggressive and too harsh.

A powerful hand curled around her upper arm, pulling her around gently to face Sam. His face was level with hers, and the moonlight glinted off the planes of his face. "Don't push me, Princess. I'm trying to be reasonable, but you'll not enspell me like you've done with Aldan."

"I would never — I haven't *enspelled* Aldan," she ground out, yanking her arm from his hold. "I've told him the truth. Everything else, he's decided on his own."

"Uh-huh. I've seen the way you smile at him. You've used every woman's trick to bring him to your side. He's just too . . . inexperienced to see it."

"If I've smiled at him, it's because he's charming and funny, unlike some others I could name." Pointedly, she looked away from him and focused her attention on the road.

"I can be charming and funny."

She turned back to him. "Are you still here?"

"Ah, now," he said, shaking his head sorrowfully. "What would Aldan think about your attitude? What a grouch."

"Bully."

"Princess."

"Pirate."

He grinned, his white teeth gleaming in the darkness. "Get over it."

She stared. Why did she let him get under her skin? She couldn't seem to help rising to the bait whenever he set out to irritate her. Slowly, she extended her arm, as she would to a soldier. "I'll 'get over it' if you will."

He hesitated and then grasped her forearm. "Agreed."

They ended the salute, and Srilani resumed her original position, hands clasped and chin on her knees. The ledge where they sat, just beneath the brow of the hill, was long and perfectly situated to let them watch the road without being silhouetted against the sky.

"Can you keep it down?" René carefully descended to the ledge and sat next to Srilani. "Your voices might carry on the night air."

"I'm sorry if we woke you," Srilani said, keeping her voice low.

"It's all right. I couldn't sleep anyway. The moon's too bright, and I'm too upset about Aldan." She put her head on Srilani's shoulder. "So what were you arguing about this time?"

Sam cleared his throat. "We were agreeing to the terms of our new friendship. She's agreed that I'm a charming and funny pirate, and I've agreed that she's a grouchy princess. We both agreed to get over it."

René looked past Srilani at Sam. She put her head back onto Srilani's shoulder. "You need to agree about *something*. The last few days have been unbearable."

The wind shifted, blowing from the south, rustling leaves and branches. Sam's sigh seemed to belong to the night wind too. "Actually," he said, "I regret the way I've been acting. I hope you can forgive me — both of you — for the things I've said and done to offend you since we met."

Srilani shifted. "Why this sudden change of heart?" Could he possibly be sincere?

"I barely had a moment to set things straight with Aldan today, and then he was gone. Maybe I've lost my best friend and brother—" Sam's voice broke off. When he spoke again, his voice sounded raspy. "My life may have changed forever in just a few minutes. Life's too short to waste being at odds over stupid things."

Srilani's fingers knotted together. Did Sam believe Aldan wouldn't escape?

"I promised Aldan that I'd make good on our agreement with you or die trying. We have to work well together or we won't survive. And if we do get Aldan back, I've decided to support him, no matter what. He's the best person I've ever known. If he's some kind of prince, then he deserves to have a kingdom."

"Did you tell him that?"

Sam's head fell forward. "Yes, but he didn't believe me."

The night wind picked up speed, and the leaves of the trees below the ledge shimmered like a thousand silver ornaments. Srilani put an arm around René's shoulders and rested her head against her sister's hair. After a few minutes, René's breathing evened out as she fell soundly asleep. Srilani's eyelids were heavy too, but she refused to succumb.

Thunder rolled far to the south, and Srilani searched the horizon for storm clouds.

"I wonder if we're going to be caught in a rain storm," Sam said.

There were no clouds and no lightning. The thunder grew louder and her eyes widened. "Sam, that's not thunder — it's horses. I think the guardians are riding out to search for us." She gave René a gentle shake. "René, wake up. We've got to go."

René sat up, blinking like an owl. "What—"

Srilani hopped up and left them behind, carefully climbing off the ledge. She hurried to where the twins slept, lost to the world and oblivious to the approaching danger.

"Guardians," she whispered, placing a hand on each dear face. "Don't speak. Maelan, keep Stockings quiet. Jamson, load the horse."

Maelan nodded. Jamson sat up and pulled his boots on. Maelan followed his example and without a word, they set to work. Srilani helped Jamson pack the few items that were out, and they took them to the glade where Stockings was hobbled. By the time Maelan had freed the horse's legs, they were joined by Sam and René.

"They've split up," Sam said. "Most of the guardians are headed down the road, but a couple of them are coming up the hill. We need to disappear."

"You take everyone into the ravine on the far side. I'll take rear guard," Srilani said. She strung her bow and adjusted her quiver. "The moon is almost gone. That should work in our favor."

Sam hesitated. "Aldan wouldn't like for me to leave you behind."

"Aldan isn't here," she said. "I won't tell if you won't. And I don't plan to take any shots unless I must."

Sam nodded. "Don't try to be a hero." He looked at René, Jamson, and Maelan. "Jamson, take point. Let's make this as quick and quiet as possible."

As soon as they were out of sight, Srilani scoured the campsite. Just as she turned to follow them, she spotted Jamson's water skin in the dirt. The blood drained out of her face. She scooped it up. Thank goodness she'd taken the time to check. In the fading light, she double-checked for any other signs they'd been here. Nothing.

Male voices reached the hilltop, and she hid in the woods near the head of the deer trail that led to the ravine. Another minute passed before two men entered the camp. One held a torch.

"Someone's been here recently," the torchbearer said. "There're tracks all over."

Srilani bit her lip. There'd been no time to be thorough, but if Father were here, he'd have said plenty about such an oversight. A beginner's mistake for sure.

The men searched the entire hilltop and the ledge. They didn't go as far as the glade where Stockings had been, so they missed the obvious signs she'd certainly left behind. But just as they turned to leave, the man with the torch paused near a bush beside the trail leading back to the road. "Looky here. See what I see?"

Srilani stared so hard that her eyes watered. She blinked. What had they found?

"Well, well. Lector was right, after all," the second man said. He plucked something off a limb. Srilani strained to see, but to no avail. The man stretched out his hands, holding whatever it was up to the torchlight.

"So he didn't send us out for no good reason. I wouldn't have seen it except it caught the light," the torchbearer said. "Did you ever see a woman with golden hair up close? I hear Dzor has twenty or more in his palace."

The other man shook his head. "Never seen one, but I'd love to get the reward for bringing one in."

The torchbearer glanced around the hilltop once more. "She can't be far off. Let's catch up with the others and bring them back. We can start the search from here."

"There's no way we can catch the others. They're halfway to Dullon Bridge by now. We ought to report back to Minazor and ask to see Lector."

"Right."

"Bring the strands of hair with you."

⁂

The moon's descent left them in deeper darkness, and Srilani cursed the fact that they'd have to move at a slower pace without the benefit of a torch or lantern.

"They must be sending guardians to search every side trail," Jamson said. "Of all the bad luck. Stray hairs."

"I remember now," René confessed. "We had to duck under the branches, and the bush snagged my hair. It hurt, but I didn't realize—"

"You couldn't know you'd done anything wrong," Srilani said. "We had no light to see stray hairs." She patted René's back. "Besides, the tracks were a dead giveaway."

Jamson shrugged. "The tracks couldn't be helped. At least the men didn't look any harder. Still, the hair will confirm Lector's suspicions, and we can be sure more men will come."

"We also know we can't pass Dullon Bridge," Sam said. "We'll need to find another way to get across."

Srilani nodded. "Dullon Bridge may be the only place to cross the Trahn River with a horse. They'll be certain to set up a checkpoint there."

"We can't leave Stockings behind," Maelan said.

Srilani's lips firmed. "I would prefer not to lose our packhorse, but get your mind around the possibility, Maelan. Nothing's more important than getting safely home, and if that means leaving the horse, we will. Don't worry about it until we have to make a decision."

"Whatever we do about the horse," René said, "the new group from Minazor will be all over this hill at the crack of dawn." She wrung her hands together. "And we know the first group is waiting ahead of us. That means we have precious little time to find a place to cross the river."

"René's right," Sam said. "They won't rest until they find us now that they have real evidence you actually exist. Srilani, do you still want to be rear guard?"

"Yes."

"Then I'll take point. I think we'll run into Linus on the way downhill."

The forest closed around them as they carefully picked their way down the trail to the Minazor road. As Sam predicted, Linus joined them near the base of the hill. He pulled Sam aside and talked rapidly with an occasional gesture toward Minazor. Srilani joined them in time to hear Linus say, " . . . leave a sign."

"Leave a sign?" she asked. "How can you leave a sign without giving us away?"

"They already know we're here somewhere," Sam said. "Right?"

She nodded.

"Linus thinks we can leave signs that only Aldan can understand, so he'll know how to find us."

"What signs could you possibly leave that only Aldan would understand? What would keep the guardians from being able to follow us?"

"Don't worry. We had a system aboard ship. We thought it up so the crew wouldn't be able to find our stashes of food. Of course, we used coal, but Linus can carve the symbols on trees, as large as he pleases, and all the guardians will know is that we're here somewhere."

A grim smile tugged at Srilani's lips. "And since they already know we're here, it won't matter." She spread her hands out, indicating the forest around them. "Carve away, Linus. I think the more symbols you carve, the better. It may confuse our pursuers."

He bowed, ever so slightly. "Indeed."

CHAPTER FORTY

Aldan spent the hours before dawn patrolling the streets of Minazor, learning the layout, and talking himself into putting the next step of his plan into action. The sky began to hint at Sol's return, lightening to blackish gray, as Aldan rode the black gelding to the Northern Gate. He patted the neck of his mount. Thankfully, the horse was well trained and responded to his prompts, however inexpert they were.

The helmet he'd found hanging on the saddle was too big, but it hid most of his face. Likewise, the armor hung loosely on his shoulders and chest, but at least it wasn't too small. Not one of the people he'd passed — citizen or guardian — had given him a second glance.

Aldan mimicked the mounted guardians he'd seen during the previous day and night. Evidently, a hierarchy existed among the guardians in which the guards on foot were beneath the notice of the ones on horseback. Time to put that theory to the test.

As he rode up the street toward the gate, the doors swung open to admit a long line of farmers driving carts and herding animals to market. Perfect.

He nudged the horse into a trot with his heels and pointed him straight toward the gate. The guards on duty halted the stream of traffic and stood at attention as he entered the tunnel under the city wall. He passed sour-faced vendors as he entered the early morning light on the far side of the gate. True to his role, he paid them no notice and concentrated on staying upright in the saddle.

The weight of the world dropped from his shoulders as he left the deep shadows of the city wall behind. The wind was at his back, and he soaked in the fresh air. The sparkling joy racing through his veins lasted only a couple of minutes.

How to find the group? Even now, they could be prisoners of the temple guards, on their way back to Minazor. Surely he'd have seen or heard something during the night if they'd been brought back to the city. If the guardians had found the group and captured them, he'd know soon enough, simply by meeting them on the road.

He kept his horse at a trot, scanning the roadside for any hint, any clue of his friends. How far could they have gone — on foot, not horseback — before they took cover? Had he already passed them by? Were they behind him instead of ahead?

The anchor mark on the tree was unmistakable. He slowed the horse to a walk and steered him to the right. His heart leapt. They'd been here. Linus or Sam had to have carved it there. Probably Linus because he was more adept with a knife. Aldan pushed on, holding the horse to a walk, searching for other signs as the sky brightened.

And there were many signs. A few were carved, but most of them were drawn in the dirt at the roadside or formed with rocks to save time. And to throw off their pursuers. Trust Linus to leave false trails — he had a suspicious mind. Good for him.

Leaving out the obviously misleading symbols, like arrows, Aldan paid attention to those they'd used aboard ship — the curl of a wave, the arc of a dolphin, teardrops, stars, coiled rope, lightning, anchors, and so on. Symbols continued as far as he could see down the road, but the message was clear. The rest were part of the deception.

Aldan dismounted and entered the woods to the left, leading the horse toward the Trahn River. The morning light wasn't much help in the thick growth of trees, but Aldan's decision to leave the road was confirmed by another carved symbol. He ran his fingers over the wave's curl embedded in the thick bark of an oak.

Without warning, a hand covered his mouth and an arm tightened across his throat. Immediately, Aldan dropped the reins to struggle against his captor. The horse snorted and backed away. Srilani rushed into his field of view, her arrow aimed at his chest, bowstring drawn tight. Aldan put his hands in the air and froze.

The arrow's tip was sharply in focus. Aldan tried to speak, but Linus's hand muffled the words. He didn't dare struggle or move.

"Wait. Don't shoot!" Sam's voice was low and urgent. "Srilani, don't shoot. It's Aldan."

The grip around his neck and mouth fell away, but she took several seconds to lower the bow and loosen the string. Her eyes were sunken and shadowed, and a terrible tension stretched her cheeks as she stared at him.

"Aldan?" She took a tentative step toward him and dropped the bow. "El, help me — I almost shot you." Her whole body trembled. "I thought you were a temple guardian."

He took hold of her shoulders. "My fault," he said. "I didn't consider how I looked in this armor."

She shuddered, and her hands came up to brace against his chest.

"You didn't hurt me," he said, but her eyes flooded with unshed tears. She blinked rapidly, and one tear escaped.

His voice stopped working properly. "No, Srilani, don't." He rubbed the tear away with his thumb. "Don't cry. I'm fine."

"I might have killed you." She pressed her lips together, obviously striving for calm, but more tears spilled over. She hid her face with her hands, and he put his arms around her, pulling her close.

Aldan met René's eyes over Srilani's head. She looked stunned by Srilani's behavior. Sam's brows rose into his hairline, and Linus — Well, who knew what Linus was thinking?

After a minute, Aldan bent to whisper in her ear. "Who are you, and where have you hidden Srilani?"

Her answering chuckle sounded weak, but she turned her head and wiped her face with the heels of her hands. "She'll be back in a minute." She sniffed and stepped out of his embrace. "I'm sorry."

Her eyes, rimmed with wet lashes, had turned the same brilliant blue as the water on the Citrus Coast. She smiled crookedly. "I'm glad you're back."

"So am I."

"What do you know?" Sam broke in. "The grouchy princess actually knows how to smile." He laughed and clapped Aldan on the shoulder. "Welcome back, Brother. You have no idea how worried we were."

"Oh, I think I do."

Sam grabbed him in a huge hug. Linus approached, and they pulled him into their huddle. The twins led the new horse closer, and the brothers broke apart.

Sam looked from Aldan to the gelding. "How did you acquire the horse and the armor?"

"Let's just say I won an argument," Aldan said with a grimace. "I'll tell you the story when we have more time, but now I'm wondering why we're here in the woods instead of on the road."

"The temple guards are waiting for us, so we have no choice but to cross the river," Sam said. "Let me show you what we've found."

The group halted near a deep gorge where the Trahn River roared past, throwing a cold spray thirty feet into the air. Frigid air swirled near the banks, and the fine mist gave Srilani goose bumps. What if she'd shot Aldan? She shivered again.

The banks on either side hung out over the river, like two sides of a tunnel with the top caved in. Somewhere far to the north, a flood had been released, and the gorge acted as a natural funnel, speeding the water on its way to the Great Gulf miles to the south. This was the narrowest part of the river in view, but its most attractive feature was the downed tree. The giant oak's trunk spanned the distance to the other side.

"So we can walk across here," Aldan said above the noise.

Sam nodded. "Yes, but we have a problem."

Maelan pushed forward until she stood at Sam's elbow facing Aldan. "Don't you see? We can't take Stockings across. Or the other horse." She looked up at Sam and then over at Srilani. "Why can't we stay on this side of the river and just keep out of sight? Maybe there's another place to cross in a couple of miles. We don't know — there may even be a shallow place that won't be so dangerous."

"That may be true, Maelan," Srilani said, "but we don't know for sure that there's another place to cross. Every minute we stay close to the road makes it more likely that we'll be discovered."

"But we can't carry everything. Besides, what will happen to the horses? They'll get killed by mountain lions or starve or get injured and die!"

"You're being overly dramatic, Maelan. The horses aren't worth the risk of losing our freedom or our lives."

Sam cleared his throat. "She has a point about the horses carrying the gear. It would be a shame to abandon the supplies that we can't carry."

Srilani opened her mouth and then snapped it shut. What he said was painfully true. "Do you have any suggestions?"

Sam's mouth twisted to the side. He crossed his arms and looked over the whole group and then at the horses. His eyes traveled back to Aldan and took on a distinct gleam. "What if I could hide the horses in plain sight?" He shrugged. "I'm just copying Aldan's idea. But this time *I'll* wear the armor. I can take the horses right across Dullon Bridge and through the checkpoint."

Jamson punched the air. "That's brilliant."

Aldan shook his head, but Sam ignored him. "I can meet up with you on the far side of Dullon Bridge. We get to keep the horses and the supplies and you'll have less to carry through the wilderness on the other side."

"I don't like it," Aldan said. "We're stronger together."

"But getting past the Trahn is only the first step." Sam turned to Srilani. "How long did you say the journey was from Dullon Bridge to the border?"

"Five or six weeks on foot — without delays. Two weeks on horseback."

He pounded his fist into his palm. "It would be better to keep the horses and try to get more. We've already agreed that we need these supplies — that's why we went to all the trouble of setting up shop in Minazor."

Aldan's head fell back as he sighed, and Sam pounced. "I can pass for a guardian. You know I'm right. That armor will fit me better than it fits you. Even Lector wouldn't recognize me if I looked the part."

Srilani held her tongue. This was between the brothers. If Sam managed to convince Aldan, then she would abide by their decision. What Sam said was true, and his plan was workable. They could make it to Northern Marst either way, although it would be easier with the horses and supplies.

Her conscience prodded her. *You're just glad it won't be Aldan.*

She swallowed. Was she a bad person for wanting Aldan to be safe? Even if his best friend was risking everything?

"I don't like it," Aldan said. "But if you're sure . . ."

"I'm sure."

"Then we better get ready." Aldan pulled off his helmet and turned to Jamson. "Help me with this armor, will you?"

"Wait." René's soft protest brought everyone up short. She stepped closer to Sam. "You won't make it through the checkpoint without a tattoo."

"I have to try," he said.

"Let me draw the mark on your cheek. I can use the ink Nik gave us for marking the map."

Sam's face flushed and he nodded. "Good idea."

Srilani opened her pack, withdrew the pot of ink she'd stored so carefully, and gave it to René. Linus and Maelan fashioned a crude paint brush from a reed and a hank of Stocking's mane.

Srilani rearranged the supplies on the horse, taking out the essential items they'd need for crossing the wilderness. She stole glances at René while she painted the mark on Sam's face. His eyes were trained on René's face as she worked. How long had René worn that particular expression when she looked at Sam?

Poor René.

ᛉ

Aldan walked around Sam, examining his friend's new appearance in every detail. "It's a convincing disguise," he said. "The mark is a crucial detail. It's a good thing René thought of it. You'll have to find a way to renew it while we're apart."

Sam looked away and cleared his throat. "She's pretty smart," he said in a gruff voice.

Aldan rocked back on his heels. "You're worried about René?"

"Yes."

"Well, don't be. You've got enough to worry about."

Sam snorted. "I'm sure you didn't worry about us while you were trapped in the city."

"*Try* not to worry. Promise you won't take unnecessary risks."

"I promise."

Their eyes met and held. "I hate this idea," Aldan said.

Sam chuckled, shaking his head. "So do I." He clapped Aldan on the shoulder. "Let's get started."

The others waited with the horses by the downed tree, and Aldan joined them. Sam took the reins for Stockings and the black horse from Jamson.

"Your horse has a name," Maelan said. "It's stitched on his saddle blanket."

"Oh? What should I call him?"

"He's named Victor."

"Then let's hope that's a good sign," Sam said. "I'll see you on the other side."

"Five days," Srilani said. "I think we can make it in five."

"Five days or ten. I'll wait." He raised his hand in farewell, turned, and walked away.

As soon as Sam was out of sight, Aldan turned to the group. "Who wants to be the first to cross?"

CHAPTER FORTY-ONE

Srilani held her breath as Linus took the first few steps across. The wet wood glinted black in the weak light that filtered through the canopy above.

The men had discussed their plan for a couple of minutes before Linus raised one bare foot onto the downed tree's trunk and heaved himself up. A rope encircled his waist and wound around the base of a nearby tree. Aldan took up the slack.

Over one arm, Linus carried his remaining coil of rope, and in the other hand, he carried an axe. This close to the river, the roar of the whitewater obscured most of the woodland noises. The distance to the other side seemed to stretch and grow longer, but Linus seemed utterly confident.

"Don't worry," Aldan said near her ear. "He's used to walking across the yards of a ship in motion."

She released the air from her lungs in a long sigh and turned to look up into his face. "I had forgotten."

He smiled at her. "What order do you want us to go across?"

She hesitated. "Jamson. Or Maelan. They can choose. And René next. It will give her confidence to see the others cross."

"I will go after you," he said. The firmness of his statement brooked no argument.

She nodded and returned her attention to Linus. He'd stopped midway over the crashing torrent to straddle the fallen tree. In front of him, a gnarled limb pointed to the sky like a crooked finger. Linus wielded his axe, hacking away until the limb toppled to the bottom of the gorge. Everyone watched the limb as it was swept downstream. Srilani shuddered. If Linus fell, he'd certainly drown.

Linus continued to lop off stray branches as he inched along. Many of the offshoots broke off in his hands, made brittle by exposure to the mist rising from the river. Srilani rubbed her arms, suppressing a shiver as the chill penetrated her clothing.

At last, Linus stood on the overhanging bank where the tree's top rested. He released the rope from his waist, and tied it off to a cypress tree. The rope ran parallel to the tree bridge, just right for a safety line. There was much more to Linus than met the eye — the tall, silent young man kept proving his inventiveness and shrewd intelligence.

Maelan jumped from one foot to the other, like a runner getting ready for a race. "I want to go next."

"Jamson should go first," René said, but Maelan shook her head.

"No. I'm ready to go now. If I wait, I'll just get nervous."

"Let her go," Jamson said. "I can wait."

Srilani nodded. That was Jamson — always looking out for his twin.

Maelan sat on a rock and pulled off her boots. She hopped up and shoved them in her pack.

"Here. Hand that to me," Aldan said. He made certain the pack was tightly closed. He approached the edge and flung her pack over the raging torrent. Linus caught it before it hit the ground. Setting it aside, he motioned to Aldan to throw across the pack he'd left behind. Linus caught the second bundle, set it aside, and picked up the coil of spare rope. He anchored it to the cypress tree and cast it to Aldan, just as if they did this every day.

"Hold your arms out to the side, Maelan," Aldan said. He passed the line around her middle and wrapped one end around the other several times as the first step to creating a harness. He instructed her to wrap the rope around the inside of one leg and then the other, mating the end to the beginning directly in front of her navel. "How does that feel?"

"Fine." Maelan's voice was thin, and her lips had lost their usual color.

"Look straight at Linus. Hold the safety line in your right hand. Loosely. It's only there to help you balance. If you slip and fall, Linus will reel you in like a fish."

She dipped her chin, and Aldan caught it, tilting it up until she met his eyes. "You're going to be fine. Linus can catch any fish."

She smiled crookedly. "I'm ready."

Aldan gave her a hand so she could mount the splintered base of the fallen tree. "Eyes on Linus, Maelan."

"I know."

She took hold of the balance line and traversed the distance without any more hesitation. When she reached Linus, he plucked her off the timber and put her down a few feet away from the edge. Quickly, he freed her from the harness, gathered it into a loop, and hurled it across.

Jamson was next, but he hardly waited for Aldan to finish his knots before speeding across the gorge.

"That boy!" René sounded horrified. "He didn't even hold onto the rope."

"He made it — that's all that's important," Srilani said. "Remember all the time he's spent aboard Father's ships. He's had plenty of practice dealing with heights." She patted René on the shoulder. "Your turn."

"I think I'm going to be sick."

"No, you're not." Srilani helped Aldan bind the cordage around René's slender frame. "Keep your eyes on the goal. You can do this." She took René's face in her hands, and communicated all the conviction she could muster. "This is easier than going over the ship's rail. I have complete faith in you."

René stared back at her, unblinking.

"Just think . . . in a few days, we'll put the Trahn River behind us and meet up with Sam. We'll be on the way home. But first you have to take these twenty steps."

Some of the color returned to René's face, and Srilani let her hands fall.

René turned to the makeshift bridge. Srilani and Aldan helped her climb onto the log. She took hold of the line and stepped out, looking straight ahead.

Everything went well until she reached the middle and her foot slipped on a patch of slimy moss. René shrieked and yanked on the safety line, upsetting her balance even more. The tree bridge bounced under her feet. Her other arm flailed about, and she shrieked again. Finally, she regained her balance and froze, arms outstretched.

Srilani swallowed hard. That was too close.

"You can do it, René!" Maelan's voice was barely audible from where Srilani stood. Jamson joined in, shouting encouragement.

After a breathless minute, René seemed to gather herself and each step she took was quicker than the last. She reached the end of the ramp and tumbled off, landing on her hands and knees. She scrambled to the end of the rope, wrapped her arms around the trunk of the cypress, and wretched. Maelan hurried to René's side and gave her sister a hug before reaching to untie the knots.

Srilani's stomach rolled over. Her turn. Telling René it was easy wasn't the same as doing it herself.

Aldan captured the rope and stood in front of her, blocking her view of the ravine. "Look at me."

She raised her eyes. He had to be the kindest person alive.

He smiled. "You'll do fine, Princess." His smile faded, and he cleared his throat. "Let's get this done so you can take your turn." His arms slid against her sides as he threaded the lifeline behind her and brought it forward. The backs of his hands brushed her waist as he worked, and her stomach fluttered. Warmth washed up to her cheeks as she passed the rope underneath her body as required and handed the rope back to him. She couldn't take her eyes off the smooth planes of his face, his serious expression, and firm lips as he made his knots.

When he finished, he met her gaze, and something gave way inside her. The collapse of her natural defenses was absolute, and she swayed toward him and ducked her face, resting her forehead on his chest. One of his hands came to rest on the nape of her neck, pushing aside her braid, while the other tightened on the rope at her waist, pulling her closer. "Be strong, Srilani," he said. "We'll get through this."

She sighed. In the last two days, her strength had deserted her. Aldan's support helped her discover new reserves. She straightened and stepped back, and his hands fell away.

"May El bless you, Aldan."

"And you," he said. "Now get going."

She approached the trunk, and Aldan made a step with his hands. She clambered up, making use of the balance line. From this perspective, the gorge below appeared far deeper and more threatening. The water roiled and frothed, splashing over the jagged rocks at the bottom. Unlike Jamson, she'd never been allowed to climb in the rigging of her family's ships. After this, she'd never dream of asking permission to try.

"Srilani! Eyes straight ahead!" Jamson's shout brought her up short. She'd failed to follow her own advice. She closed her eyes and willed the vertigo to pass. She fixed her eyes on her brother and took her first step.

Twenty steps seemed like a hundred, and the wood creaked and groaned at the middle of the river, at the point of René's near disaster. The bark was cold and slick under her bare feet, and the mist lowered the temperature even more. Her teeth chattered. Was it really that cold or had she lost her nerve?

Eager hands reached out to help her down. She continued to shiver, and when Aldan tossed her pack across, she dug out her blanket and wrapped it around her shoulders. Aldan's pack, too, landed with a thud, followed by the rope that had served as the safety rail.

Her head jerked up. Why hadn't she foreseen that he'd be crossing without it? He still had the harness, but somehow that wasn't reassuring. She pulled the blanket tighter, hugging it close, as Aldan vaulted onto the shattered tree trunk.

⁂

Aldan turned in a circle. They'd left nothing behind to mark their passage. Excellent. They were all safe, and he could breathe easy.

Like Linus, he'd been up in the rigging of the *Cathartid* nearly every day of his captivity. Balancing on this broad beam was no challenge at all.

He quickly knotted the rope about his waist and took a running leap to land squarely atop the decaying oak. He took a moment to center his weight. He fixed his eyes on Srilani's pale face. Today had been a nightmare for her.

But he'd had a glimpse of the vulnerable person behind the mask she kept between herself and the world. For a few moments, she'd trusted him enough to let him see the real Srilani. Even now, she didn't try to hide the fear on her face. Fear for him.

Halfway across, the wood crackled beneath his feet, and Aldan paused. He pushed at the bark experimentally with his toes, and several chips sloughed off, carried away by the turbulent air from the racing river. A couple more steps and the crackling sound intensified, changing to the creak of wood under duress. Aldan froze. He had no choice but to proceed.

Crack! Aldan's heart jumped into his throat, and he started running. Too late, Aldan lunged for the bank as the oak gave way under his feet. He plummeted straight down into the water, and it billowed over his head. Wood fell around him in huge chunks, shapes whipping past in a froth of bubbles. The current buffeted his body and spun him about. When he reached the end of the rope, it jerked him to a stop, forcing all the air from his lungs and burning his skin.

He grabbed the rope in a hopeless attempt to pull himself up. His harness tightened like a vice. His lungs were starved for air, and he fought the urge to breathe.

At last his head broke the surface. Then his torso. He dangled helplessly, gasping. Shouts echoed strangely, coming to his ears from all directions.

The river had carved into the limestone riverbank so that the banks resembled the inside of a clam's shell, smooth and concave. The ledge above cast a dark shadow. He looked up, but the ledge hid his friends from view. He sucked in a giant lungful of air and gave a shout.

The cacophony above stopped, and the echoes died away.

"I'm here!" Aldan shouted. "Can you hear me?"

Linus shouted back. "Yes!"

He grabbed onto the line to alleviate the pressure as the group raised him several feet. The rope twisted, spinning him in a slow circle. The ascent ground to a halt.

Aldan leaned his head far back to get a better perspective. The rope had rolled into a crevice in the lip of the cliff and was firmly wedged into the narrow crack. The harder they pulled, the more hopeless their efforts became.

"The rope is stuck." Jamson's voice sounded despairing.

"This isn't going to work!" Aldan yelled. "Linus!"

"Yes?"

"Tie knots in the other rope and let it down. I'll try to climb up."

"Give me a minute."

As if there were anything else he could do. His teeth chattered. He flexed his fingers. If they didn't hurry, his hands would be too numb for rope climbing.

"Aldan."

Aldan's head jerked to his left. Tremors shook his body. He opened his mouth to scream, but no sound escaped his lips. The scream simply lodged in his throat as he stared at the man in brilliant white.

A smile curved the corners of the man's mouth, and he spoke gently. "Don't be afraid. I mean you no harm." His voice was like a low rumble of thunder.

Aldan's gaze swept downward. He squeezed his eyes tightly shut and opened them wide. The man stood on thin air, and the river's mist billowed around him. The man was at least seven feet tall and heavily muscled. His skin, tunic, and armor glowed like a harvest moon on a cloudless night.

"My name is Joel. El has sent me to give you a message." Joel took a firm hold under Aldan's arms, lifting him up without any effort. The pressure of the ropes eased, and the pain of the rope burns vanished.

"El is with you." Joel's words reverberated in Aldan's bones. "El will restore you to your throne. As long as you uphold the name of El, He will support you. You will bring new unity to the Twin Kingdoms and honor to the name of El. His spirit will dwell in you and your days will be prolonged, filled with wisdom and power."

Aldan stared into Joel's radiant face, and the man smiled once more. They rose through the air until they were immediately below the ledge. Joel tilted his head to the side as Linus's knotted line came into view. "There's your rope. May El bless you."

Aldan grasped the rope and found a foothold on one of the knots. Joel released him and vanished.

Once they'd pulled him over the edge, Aldan's knees refused to cooperate, and he staggered about like a newborn fawn. Linus and Srilani leapt to hold him upright, and the others joined them, clinging together and laughing hysterically. Gradually, their giddy laughter subsided, and Aldan regained his balance.

He opened his mouth to tell them what he'd seen, but his voice refused to work. He started to shiver uncontrollably. Srilani drew the blanket from her shoulders and wrapped it around him. Blessed warmth from her body enveloped him and he pressed his nose into the blanket to catch her scent. The shaking subsided, bit by bit.

By mutual, unspoken consent, the group separated and moved away from the river's brink to set up camp. The men collapsed, spent from the physical exertion required by Aldan's rescue. Srilani, René, and Maelan quickly built up a fire and set to work on meal preparations.

Aldan reclined, breathing in the heady aroma of the stew as it simmered. He hadn't eaten anything since the previous day in Minazor, and his stomach complained loudly. Srilani approached, holding an orange, and he sat up. She took out her dagger and sliced the fruit into pieces, handing him one section at a time.

"Thank you," he said between bites. "I'll probably think of oranges every time I remember this little adventure."

She offered him the last piece, and he took it. He caught her hand and brought it to his lips. "Thank you, Srilani."

She hesitated, her fingers clinging to his. "You're welcome, Aldan." She retrieved her hand, turned away, and busied herself with other tasks.

Aldan lay down, covering his eyes with his arm, and slept. Darkness came early to the woods, and they ate the meal by fire light. Srilani brought him a bowl of stew and took the space by his side.

The meal passed in silence until Maelan set down her cup and leaned forward. "How did you get up the rope so fast?"

Aldan told them about Joel, and Maelan clasped her hands together. "An angel. I wish I could have seen him."

"I've never been more frightened in my whole life. You might change your mind if you ever see one for yourself."

Srilani looked thoughtful. "The histories of Mardan name Joel as the angel who visited King Mardan. He was terrified, according to the account I've read."

"I think it would be worth the terror to actually meet an angel," Jamson said.

"Joel was tall and strong," Aldan said, "but I was most frightened by his ability to appear and disappear and to stand on nothing at all."

Linus shook his head. "If an angel needs to talk to me, I hope he'll just give *you* the message and let you pass it on."

Aldan threw his head back and laughed. "I don't think you get to choose whether or not El sends his messenger to see you." He clapped Linus on the back. "Pray, my friend. Pray you never have to meet Joel."

Linus folded his arms across his chest. "Indeed."

CHAPTER FORTY-TWO

Sam made camp on a bluff overlooking the village of Gan, several leagues from where he'd left the group. The lights of the town glimmered invitingly. Perhaps he could have stayed at an inn, but better not to court unnecessary problems. A fire, though . . . Surely he was allowed a fire.

He was dressed like a temple guardian, after all, and it would be strange for one of Azor's priests, traveling alone, to sleep in the wild without a fire. Besides, the flames drove back the darkness and the solitude. Sam searched his memories back to his childhood. When had he ever been alone like this? This far from other humans, good or bad?

He remembered to string the packs containing food up in a tree with the ropes Linus had left. That boy and his ropes — forever unraveling the twines and tying knots to create useful items.

Sam lay down, armor and all, wrapped in the guardian's cloak. The sky above twinkled with lights. More than he could ever count. There was the Star of the North and the Crab constellation. The Dogs of War. The Three Sisters. For a moment, he missed the rise and fall of a ship's deck and the salty tang of brine.

No. He'd only known captivity and hardship aboard the *Cathartid*. But even here, thirty leagues from shore, the elements soothed him. Or was there more than the elements at work here? Was El here too?

Sam turned on his side, staring into the flames. Movement near his head drew his attention. A raccoon, one of the many creatures he'd learned about so far on this journey, sat on its haunches a couple yards away, as if it planned to camp here too. The animal raised its head, sniffing loudly. Sam watched as it climbed the tree where the food hung. It dangled from the limb by its hind feet, gazing down at the packs with glittering eyes. After many failed attempts to reach the food, it climbed down and shuffled away.

Thankfully, he'd followed the procedures René had taught him or he might have lost some of their hard-won supplies. He smiled grimly. *See, Srilani? I can learn from women. At least, I can learn from René.*

Why couldn't Srilani be more like René? Less intimidating. Less infuriating. Less —

He shrugged. Aldan seemed to appreciate the very qualities in Srilani that most irked him. René, though, was another matter. A little smile curled his lips as he considered René's last words to him under cover of painting his cheek.

"Be careful," she'd said, daubing at his right cheekbone.

"Always am," he said with a smirk.

René snorted. "Right. If you don't make it back in one piece, I'll . . ." She bit her lip, stopping the words, brush poised in the air.

"You'll what?" He touched her wrist. "What, René?"

She shook her head. "If you don't come back, I'll probably die of a broken heart."

That was plain enough. He closed his eyes and submitted to her touch, soaking in her presence, but when she was done, he opened them to address her. "Don't let me break your heart, Princess. You know, and I know, there's no future there. Your father probably has a long list of wealthy barons and sons of barons all picked out for you to choose from. I'm a *pirate*."

He lifted his hand, palm up. "Unlike Aldan, I don't have a single claim to wealth except the gold in my pouch. I have no great ancestors. I'm a Norlander. My name is Samazor. Azor, that god your family hates so much, is *in my name*." He let his hand fall.

"I don't care," she said. Her eyes, for once, were fierce.

"I care," he said quietly. "But I'm not going to do a thing about it. So don't let me break your heart."

She'd turned away from him but not before he glimpsed her tears.

He threw an arm over his eyes, blanking out the starlight. She wasn't the only one whose heart would break.

Aldan took a firmer grip on his makeshift cudgel, scanning the murky water. He slogged forward and blinked the sweat out of his eyes. He glanced at Srilani. She was soaked to the waist from stumbling through the swamp. Everyone was wet and bedraggled.

A gator shifted to watch her passage.

"Keep your eyes open." Jamson's voice rose. "I see at least four alligators."

"Srilani, to your right," Aldan said.

"I see him. Thanks."

Earlier in the day, the forest had given way to swamp, and pines vied with cypress trees for every spit of land. After studying the map, they'd decided this trip through the swamp was a necessity. Their other options were to cross back over the Trahn — a sure route to capture — or to travel an unknown number of leagues around the southern and western edges of the swamp, almost halfway to Port Azor. They'd never find Sam again.

"Watch out." Srilani pointed at the rippling surface between them.

A small, three-foot long alligator surfaced near Aldan's knees, and he swung the cudgel with enough force to crack its skull. He bashed it again for good measure.

Linus waded to his side, picked its glistening body up by the tail, and popped it into his net. He grinned, white teeth flashing. "Good for supper."

"Urgh." Maelan made a face. She opened her mouth to say something else but coughed instead. The youngest sister had complained of a sore throat since the day before, but here she was, as intrepid as ever, plowing ahead in spite of the coughing fits.

They spent another fifteen minutes in the water before they reached a long bar of land laden with every form of vegetation — giant cypress trees, oaks dripping with gray moss, vines with lively orange flowers, and a creeping carpet of waist-high grass littered with small, saw-edged palms.

Aldan didn't relax his vigilance. As incredible as it seemed, the strips of land were as dangerous as the water. Here, aggressive female alligators guarded their nests, even after their babies hatched. Not to mention the rattlesnakes and water moccasins, both of which they'd seen too many to count.

Srilani put away her club and strung her bow, and Aldan helped her adjust her pack.

Linus took point, as he'd done for the last two days, with Jamson and Maelan following directly in his tracks. Linus had displayed an uncanny ability to detect the creatures first, holding up his fist for the group to halt until he'd dealt with the problem or the creature made itself scarce.

Aldan waited for René and Srilani to precede him, keeping a wary eye behind and to the sides as they wound through the deep shadows of the overhanging trees.

They were all breathing hard from the effort of pushing through the water, but when Aldan could breathe normally, he resumed his line of questioning from earlier in the day. "How did your father's feud with King Dzor begin?"

"It actually began before my father was crowned." Srilani paused to let him walk with her, then started forward again. "My grandmother was queen, and King Dzor, a brash young man at the time, brought his army across the Rhynder River to capture our fortress at the Cauldron."

She ducked under a mossy limb. "If he'd managed to do that, he could have captured several of our towns and villages without too much opposition, plundering the barons' estates along the eastern border and pressing our people into slavery. That's the Norlan way."

"What happened?"

She shrugged. "The queen's spies brought word to her in time."

Jamson waved René forward and waited for them. "Are you talking about Dzor's attack?"

"Yes."

"Did you tell him about Bertson?"

"Not yet."

"I love that part," Jamson said. He looked around to make sure Aldan was paying attention. "General Bertson was a captain back then, and he led a small group of men into Dzor's camp and assassinated two of Dzor's generals." He swiped a grimy hand across his forehead, pushing his hair back. "But Dzor was so stupid—"

"Reckless," Srilani said.

"Reckless . . . stupidly brave . . . whatever."

"You really need to be more diplomatic, Jamson."

Jamson flashed a mischievous grin in Aldan's direction. "Dzor decided to go ahead with his stupid plans, in spite of the fact that he'd lost his officers and the heavy spring rains had started."

Srilani shook her head but didn't correct her brother.

"He lost about seven hundred men. Most drowned trying to ford the flooded river. The rest of the army panicked and ran away."

Jamson scrambled over a giant fallen tree and hurried ahead. Aldan assisted Srilani over the fallen tree, and she thanked him. She seemed to have grown accustomed to his help since he'd rejoined the group.

Alone again, Aldan and Srilani picked their way through the vegetation, stepping carefully around the knees of cypress trees jutting out of the ground in their path.

"Has Dzor ever tried to come back?"

"King Dzor seems content to harass our ships, grabbing what he can. Every so-called pirate from Norland is directly associated with the king." Her foot slipped on a patch of mud, and he kept her from falling with a hand at her waist.

She grabbed his arm for support. "Thank you."

Color rose up her neck and into her face, and she quickly released him. After another moment, she finished her answer. "The pirates serve as Dzor's unofficial navy. We've heard that he rewards the most successful commanders lavishly."

Aldan nodded. "That fits. Captain Rozar visited King Dzor's palace several times, and after the last visit, he bragged about the map he'd received as a gift."

"I still wonder how Dzor came to have it. Remember, I showed you the mapmaker's mark?"

"You suspect a traitor?"

Her face clouded up. "I can't seem to help myself. In the first place, I have trouble trusting people. This little adventure hasn't exactly helped."

"You trust me." It wasn't a question.

She stopped and looked him straight in the eyes. "I do trust you. You have no idea how much that means to me." Swiftly she turned and left him behind.

Aldan allowed himself one satisfied smile before he followed her.

⁜

The temple guardian priest's garb and fake tattoo had an almost magical effect on the travelers Sam met on the road from Gan to Orin. Every group moved to the side of the road, bowing low and avoiding eye contact until he was gone. He took his cue from their behavior, riding past them in stern silence.

Late in the afternoon of his second day on the road, he rounded a bend in the well-worn path and came face to face with another traveler. The man drove a small covered caravan drawn by a pair of oxen.

"Whoa there." The wiry little man with walnut skin pulled his team to a halt. From his seat, he bowed toward Sam.

Victor shied away from the wagon. Sam used every bit of his hard-earned skill to bring the horse back under control.

"Sorry, Your Honor," the man said. "I hope you'll forgive me for getting in your way."

Sam stared down at the man. What to say? "What is your name and where are you headed?"

"Triz the Tinker, Your Honor. I'm bound for Gan, Minazor, and Trahnville."

"Ah. Where have you been?"

"From Port Azor by Dullon Bridge."

"Oh?"

"The ferries were destroyed by the storm so there was no choice."

Surely there was no harm in trying to get more information. "It's been a long time since I crossed Dullon Bridge."

Triz removed his cap and scratched his head. "You won't recognize it. All those dratted soldiers of the king taking every spare space in town . . . and every spare woman too. Good thing you get to stay at the temple. It's crowded too. There are many, many temple guards in town. But you already know that, I expect."

Triz plunked the cap back on his straggling curls and spat over the far side of his wagon. "I'm glad to put Dullon Bridge behind me." He sighed. "I hope things will improve in Gan, but I doubt it."

"Why is that?"

"I could use a priest's guidance, if you're willing." Triz looked at him doubtfully. "I mean no disrespect."

Guilt squirmed in Sam's chest, but since Triz thought he was a priest, he had no option but to act as one. "Tell me of your trouble."

"'Tis a matter of dispute between that fat farmer, Olaz, and me. Every year I come this way. Olaz promises to buy so many of one thing or another if I bring it back from Port Azor when I visit. But when I get to Gan, he won't pay for all the things he promised to buy or, like last year, *nothing* of what he promised. I'm at the end of my wits. He's the only one who treats me this way." Triz fidgeted on his seat, removing his cap again to squint up at Sam. "He does me great damage, but what can I do?"

Sam averted his face, looking down at Victor's sweat-lathered neck, his mind racing to come up with a plausible answer.

"Here's what I say," Sam ventured. He looked back at Triz and used his most serious voice. "Don't take promises from Olaz anymore. Insist that he pay you everything in advance. And if he fails to purchase everything he ordered from you this trip, take the matter up with the temple priests. I'm certain they'll want to know of false promises and lost tribute money."

"Thank you, Guardian. You relieve my mind. I have no wish to displease the temple by making trouble."

Sam's voice dropped to a growl. "The temple is more likely to frown on lost tribute than on your fight to make Olaz pay up. If you doubt me, go to the head priest before you talk to Olaz. It is a serious offense to cheat the temple."

Triz nodded. "Don't I know it?" He looked up and down the road and lowered his voice. "I hear that many priests like you are searching for some fugitives because of unpaid tribute to Minazor's temple."

"True." Sam bit the word off and glared at the hapless tinker. It was time to end this discussion.

Triz took the hint and clucked to his team. He guided his wagon to the verge of the road. "Thank you for the advice, Your Honor. I'll not take any more of your time."

Sam waved the tinker's thanks aside and nudged Victor's flanks. Just how many priests and soldiers were looking for them now? He was still a full day and night from Dullon Bridge, and he needed to get there before Aldan and the others. He had to find them and warn them to stay away. Far away.

/\/\

Sam angled the blade of his dagger to get a better view of his right cheekbone. The horsetail paintbrush tickled as he dabbed at what remained of his Azor tattoo. After a few painstaking minutes, he rinsed the brush in the stream beside his campsite.

It would have to do. Hopefully, nobody would bother giving his face more than a cursory glance.

He checked the horses' hooves and made quick work of saddling Victor and distributing the packs on Stockings. Victor turned to nuzzle his cloak, and Sam smoothed his hand over the horse's withers.

"Good boy," Sam said. "Let's go."

They covered the distance to the wrecked ferry crossing quickly since the path angled downhill at a gentle slope. A group of about two dozen slaves lugged stout pillars to the riverside for the construction of a new dock. A task master with a long whip stood over them, shouting orders.

Victor jerked his head, and Sam loosened his too-tight hold on the reins. He patted the horse's neck. "Sorry." One of Victor's ears swiveled back, listening for Sam's voice. "Seeing the slaves upsets me. I didn't mean to take it out on you."

A fresh breeze swept down from the foothills to the north and ruffled the surface of the Trahn River. Gray clouds pushed the blue sky away, and Sam didn't need Linus to tell him rain was on the way. A long wharf came into view on the western side. It was lined with ramshackle warehouses all the way to the bridge. From the looks of things, the area had taken a beating from high water and wind. The dark smudge on the far side of the Trahn must be the overcrowded town of Dullon Bridge.

The wind strengthened each moment, and the brilliant morning light passed into shadow.

Sam stopped Victor and dismounted. He checked the tarp he'd tied over their belongings. A fat drop struck his cheek. Without thinking, he reached up and wiped it away. Ink smeared his fingertips. So much for the mark of Azor.

More drops fell. There was nothing for it but to wipe the rest of the tattoo away with the hem of the guardian's black cloak. He used his dagger as a mirror again and scrubbed at his cheek. As he pulled himself into the saddle, the heavens opened and soaked him thoroughly.

The eight soldiers guarding the bridge hardly spared him a moment of attention. They'd sought shelter from the deluge under the eaves of the nearest warehouse. The rain struck the boards of the bridge with such force, a mist of dancing drops sprang back around Victor's knees.

Sam's first impression of Dullon Bridge was gray — gray buildings and houses with gray people huddled in doorways waiting for the rain to abate. On the north side of the muddy main road, a temple squatted at the foot of the hills that formed a natural boundary for the town. To the south behind the warehouses, an imposing fort towered over the inns and storefronts in front of it.

The temple's front steps were ahead, and two guardians were posted there. Sam's mouth went dry, and he guided Victor and Stockings left, down a side street, toward the fort and away from the temple. No sense giving the guardians a closer look.

As soon as he found a westbound street, he guided Victor to the right again. The route brought him close to the fort. It seemed to be the only edifice — other than the temple — built entirely of river rock instead of wood. The stone construction extended to the stables that sprawled at the rear of the fortress, visible down an alley west of the barracks.

He urged the horses toward the western edge of town. He spotted a trio of guardians ahead. They were on foot, making quick dashes between eaves. One of the men caught his attention. Was that . . . Could it be?

Sam's gaze sharpened as the man lifted his head to find the next patch of shelter.

Lector.

CHAPTER FORTY-THREE

Srilani leaned over and placed her wrist across Maelan's forehead. Her sister's skin was hot, and her lips were pinched and blue. A fit of coughing shook Maelan's entire body, but she didn't wake.

"Can you do anything for her?" Srilani asked.

"I've done all I know to do," René said, squeezing her hands together. She straightened her shoulders. "At this point, we have to keep her warm and let her sleep. She's in El's hands."

"I can carry her," Aldan said from behind them.

Srilani stood and turned around. "Not for long. Maelan is the size of a small adult."

"I know." He shrugged, face somber. "But we have to keep moving. From what I remember of the map, I think we're past the worst of the swamp."

Srilani fingered her grandmother's pendant, trying to consider their problem clearly. Aldan had been a silent onlooker as they examined Maelan, but he'd communicated his sympathy and support without words. Throughout this ordeal, he had been her rock. Where would they be without him? And Linus? And Sam?

Yesterday's deluge had punished them. They'd constructed a small shelter from whatever they could find, but there was no hope of lighting a fire.

Everyone suffered, but Maelan started sneezing, her coughing grew worse, and she developed a fever. By morning, she was out of her head, mumbling in her sleep.

"I can take turns carrying her," Linus said.

Aldan nodded.

"I'll carry your packs," Jamson said. His voice cracked. "I can strap one pack on back and one on front."

Aldan squeezed his shoulder. "You're pretty strong. Think you could carry Maelan's pack instead? Your sisters can carry our packs."

"Of course."

Srilani gave her brother a quick hug. Poor Jamson. If Maelan didn't recover, he'd be utterly lost without her.

Srilani sighed. "If we all share the weight and take frequent breaks, I think we can go on." Her muscles shrieked in protest as she hefted Aldan's pack, but she blocked out the pain. He carefully scooped Maelan up, and they set out.

"Father?" Maelan's eyes opened, and she addressed Aldan in Marstan.

"How are you?" He used Marstan.

A crease appeared between Maelan's brows. "Will you ride with me today on the beach?"

"Umm." Aldan stared down at Maelan and then at Srilani who walked by his side.

"Maelan, you're sick," Srilani said. "We can ride on the beach when you're well again."

"Oh."

"Go to sleep."

Obediently Maelan shut her eyes and turned into Aldan's chest.

"Thank you," Srilani whispered.

"For what?"

"For . . . being here. For staying with us." Her eyes glanced off his. "For everything."

ᚥ

Didn't she trust him to see this through to the end? Aldan trudged beside Srilani. His lips tightened. Where else would he be? It all came down to trust.

"Talk to me," he said. "Maelan's heavier than she looks, and I need to be distracted."

Srilani pushed the traditional veil behind her head, and the gold of her hair glinted in the morning light. "What do you want to talk about?"

"Tell me why you and René don't look like the twins."

She hesitated, raising one hand to touch her braid.

"It goes back to Mardan, the first king. He's often called the Golden King by people who are fond of embellishing history." She pulled back a low-hanging branch so he could pass. "The chronicles say he had blond hair and blue eyes. After his first wife and daughter died, he married a native woman who bore the twins, Kaedan and Kaeson. But you already know that."

Aldan carefully crossed a small ditch. "That doesn't explain your coloring."

"Those same people call my coloring the look of Mardan. Most people in Norland and the Twin Kingdoms have dark hair, tanned skin, and brown eyes like yours, but for whatever reason, Mardan's coloring is passed to a few of his descendants."

She waved away a swarm of gnats. "Both my mother and father are directly descended from Mardan, many generations removed, and I think that's why René and I and our baby sister inherited the first king's coloring. Our mother has Mardan's coloring." She lowered her voice. "The twins' coloring is like Father's. I've often wondered if that's why they are his favorites."

Aldan bit back a protest. Surely a father wouldn't favor certain children based on appearance. But then again, how would *he* know?

Several moments passed before she spoke again. "It's considered some kind of honor to look this way — people even reach out and touch me as if I'm some sort of lucky amulet."

That explained several things he'd noticed about Srilani, especially her skeptical attitude.

"René and I receive lots of unwanted attention. Everything we do is watched and discussed. People flatter us and try to gain favor." She pulled her veil up to cover her head. "Or they stab us in the back."

Aldan switched off with Linus several times for the next few hours. When

Linus took his turn carrying Maelan, Jamson stayed by his side and Aldan took point, with Srilani and René to help.

"I don't get it," Aldan said.

"What?" Srilani's voice sounded tired.

"How does your father protect his border with Norland? It looks so long on the map." He put up his hand to call a halt. Using a long stick, he encouraged a snake to move off the deer path they followed. "Has King Dzor tried to invade since he was defeated during your grandmother's reign?"

"Norlan raiding parties frequently cross the Rhynder River at night to grab what they can take, especially women and children."

The snake slithered away, and Aldan glanced back at the sisters. "And?"

"And the barons chase them off. The barons are always vigilant, but my father has his hands full."

Aldan kept a wary eye on the path ahead as they progressed. "Doesn't your father ever retaliate?"

"No. He supports the barons in their efforts to defend themselves, but we need nothing from Norland." She paused. "Look around us. What would we do with this swamp?"

René cleared her throat. "Srilani, that's not really fair."

"You're right. There's obviously rich farmland around Minazor and all the way to Nik's mill. And there's more fertile land to the west."

Aldan stopped and looked over his shoulder to check on Linus. The sisters waited with him. "Isn't that sufficient reason to invade?" he asked.

Srilani shook her head. "We have enough. The Rhynder River forms a natural boundary. Why try to expand beyond it?" She spread her hands. "Besides, the Twin Kingdoms don't barter in slaves. That's forbidden in the laws of Mardan."

"Wait." He frowned down at her. "Slaves are forbidden by your laws? What about all the servants you talk about in Kaeson Palace?"

Her chin lifted. "They're not slaves. Our family pays each of our servants. We house and feed them. We care for them. And they are free to leave us at any time. Many of the families have served us for generations." She stooped and pulled several burs from the hem of her long dress.

When she straightened, her face was calm again. "The royal family and the people of Kaeson share a close relationship, much closer than masters and servants. In fact, our families have intermarried for over three hundred years."

Aldan smiled. "I can tell you love your people."

She smiled back, and he stared. Aldan tore his eyes away from Srilani. René's gaze flashed from one face to the other, and one corner of her mouth hitched up.

"Linus," he called. "You're starting to lag. Don't overdo it. It's probably time to hand Maelan to me."

Aldan gave his pack to Srilani and stepped in front of Linus whose head jerked up as if he were surprised. "Come on, Brother, you've gone far enough. René needs a break from hauling your pack."

"Actually, I think we all need a rest," Srilani said. "I don't want to complain, but we've been trading off for half a day, and I'm not sure I can go much further. I'm sure that's true for Jamson too."

Jamson's face took on a dogged expression. "I can keep going."

"No," Aldan said. "Your sister is right. We need to pace ourselves."

"But we'll be late meeting Sam."

Aldan shook his head. "We're already late, and there's no way we'll arrive today. Sam said he'd wait, and he will."

CHAPTER FORTY-FOUR

Sam poked the sullen fire. The wood was damp and he'd had to resort to burning strands from one of Linus's beloved ropes to get it started.

Dinner consisted of dried fruit and lumpy porridge.

If René and Srilani didn't show up soon, he would starve to death. Wouldn't Srilani think that was funny? At least this fire and food were an improvement over the rainy night he'd just spent with no light at all.

Where were they? *Please, El, help them find me.*

He stood up and walked the perimeter of his chosen space far to the southwest of Dullon Bridge. Here, he was hidden from view of the fortress and the town, behind a dense screen of trees. A large meadow sprawled beside the lake formed by some beavers on a tributary of the Trahn. He'd spent the entire day watching the busy creatures take down trees to add to their dam.

The rain had proven to be his ally yesterday. He'd managed to leave Dullon Bridge without being recognized by Lector and his men. However, there were possible benefits to returning. He could buy more oats for the horses and real food for himself. And gather information.

Had Triz the Tinker been right about the search? Were the priests still actively pursuing them? And why were there so many soldiers gathered? Triz had clearly thought the numbers were far above normal.

If the group didn't find him by late tomorrow, it might be worth the risk to enter the town during the evening in the guise of a traveler on foot. One thing was certain — he wouldn't go as a priest.

Sam adjusted his sword belt and checked the dagger in his boot top. He counted out a moderate amount of money and buried the rest. Wood stood ready for kindling when he returned, the provisions hung high in a tree, and the horses grazed on their pickets within reach of water. Victor and Stockings turned to watch as he left the meadow. Aldan would take a dim view of this visit to town, but he had to do something or he'd go crazy.

The soldiers at the western gate allowed him to enter with the injunction that the gates shut at midnight and reopened at first light. He received directions to a place that sold oats and an inn known for good cooking. The oats came first. He easily found the vendor beside the fortress stables. He bought as much as he could comfortably carry and made his way back to the main street to discover the inn.

Five bells rang out as Sam found a seat in the corner of the tavern. Quietly, he ate everything the host set before him and accepted the large tankard of cane spirits he was offered. He was early, but the room filled with soldiers and workers in the next hour. He finished his drink and asked for water, casually visiting with anyone who sat in his vicinity. At seven bells, the lanterns were lit, and the noise increased.

Sam bided his time after he paid his tab. Snippets of conversation reached him, and he listened carefully.

"New around here?" A young soldier, maybe his age or a year less, claimed a seat beside him at the long table.

"Passing through."

"Which way?"

"West."

"Wish I was going with you. Been here a month and nothing but drill, drill, drill." The young man's eyes had a faraway look. "I miss my girl."

"Lots of soldiers here," Sam said.

It wasn't a question, but the man nodded. "Yes, but not all the soldiers are being trained in Dullon Bridge. I hear there are many, many more in Port Azor and in several villages along the Rhynder road." He dunked his spoon into his bowl of stew. "Old Dzor's going to give Kaeson something to think about — that's the rumor. Wish he'd left me out of it, though. Grandfather will have to bring the harvest in without me. Guess my sisters can help him."

"That's tough."

"You don't know the half of it."

The tavern door banged open to admit a half-dozen temple guardians, and a collective groan rose from the other patrons. Lector led the group inside. Sam held his breath as the priest surveyed the room, but Lector's eyes passed right over the table where he sat.

The soldier beside him cursed and gulped the rest of his stew straight from the side of the bowl. He plunked the bowl on the wooden tabletop, threw down a couple of coins, and rose. "May as well leave now before it gets ugly. Whenever they come, there's always trouble."

Sam swung the bag of oats over his shoulder and followed the young man into the darkening streets.

Lector. This was an opportunity he couldn't pass up.

Sam said farewell to the soldier and circled back to stand in the shadows outside the tavern. He peered into the room through a window. Sam's collar tightened and he ran a finger around the edge. Lector sat at a table across the room, facing the corner where he had been moments before.

Several of the tavern's recent occupants milled about in the street, continuing their conversations. Sam leaned against the wall outside and listened with all his might.

"Minazor." Just the one word came through the hubbub. He sidled along the wall until he stood near the next window. "Better be ready to travel for a week or more. He's sending us out to search all the way to the border."

"Am I going with you?"

"Of course, else I wouldn't bring it up," the first man said.

"How many groups?"

"Six or seven. Leastwise, that's what Lector let on. Why'd he have to come around and stir things up? This was a good place to be until he showed up."

"Watch your tongue. He's got friends in high places."

"Don't want to talk about him, anyways. Let's get something else to drink."

Sam pushed away from the wall and shouldered the bag of feed. Dullon Bridge wasn't all that large — he could probably see most of it before they closed the gates for the night.

Night in the noisy, fetid swamp brought no real rest. Srilani's shoulders ached from the strain of carrying two packs through the swamp the day before and sleeping on a hastily constructed pallet to stay off the ground. The bug bites itched incessantly, and her feet hurt.

She handed Jamson her bow. "Please be careful out there."

"Don't worry. I will," Jamson said. "And I'll try to bring all the arrows back."

"Just bring yourself back."

Srilani gave him her quiver and settled next to Maelan's pallet. "If you don't take any game, we'll still have something to eat."

Aldan dropped the armload of branches he'd gathered and squatted next to her, putting his face level with hers. "Are you sure about this?" His voice was low.

"I'm sure." She gave him a tentative smile. His dark hair had grown since they'd met. He'd had no opportunity to shave recently, and stubble covered his cheeks. Her eyes dropped to her lap. "Jamson's a fair hunter, and I don't want to leave Maelan." She lifted one shoulder and let it fall. "As long as you're with him, I won't worry."

He shifted closer. "I'll take care of your brother."

She pleated the fabric across her knees and nodded. The silence stretched between them. He made a sound deep in his throat, rose to his full height, and followed Jamson.

What is wrong with me? Srilani turned to help René give Maelan a drink. Since when was she too shy to look a man in the eyes?

Linus retrieved his flute and played a soft tune, lulling Maelan to sleep.

"Thank El her fever broke last night," René said. "I'm so relieved."

"Yes." Srilani got up and began to pace.

"She needs to eat, though."

"Yes."

René joined Srilani and pulled her to a halt. "Is something wrong?"

"No." *If only you knew.*

"Are you worried about Jamson and Aldan?"

Srilani hesitated. "I'm more concerned about our lack of progress."

"Yesterday you said you thought we should stop to rest, and you were right. I'm still exhausted today." René gave her a penetrating look. "If you'll lie down for a while, then so will I."

René made it impossible to refuse. Srilani complied, and René pulled her pallet over so they were side by side in a patch of shade.

The song Linus played had a haunting beauty that matched their surroundings, and Srilani let herself float away. Light and shadow from the trees overhead dipped and swayed across her eyelids. *So beautiful.*

Strains of music filled the Great Hall and many people in their finest clothes danced under the arched ceiling. Candlelight shimmered on the lustrous material of her green dress, and she fingered the intricate lace at its neckline. A heavy gold ring shone on her left hand. It was set with an emerald that matched her dress. She turned the ring this way and that, delighting in the fiery depths of the stone.

"Srilani, will you dance with me?" Aldan put his hand under her elbow and escorted her off the dais.

When they reached the floor of the Great Hall, they took their places, side by side. Aldan wrapped his arm around her back, and her arm slid behind his waist. The muscles of his back were firm and warm through his tunic. He took her other hand in his and they joined the promenade around the perimeter of the room.

They followed the other couples round and round, but when the music ended, he led her behind a pillar and leaned into her for a kiss. His lips were gentle at first, but each kiss was more insistent than the last. After a couple of heady moments, she reached her arms around his neck and pushed up against him, returning the pressure, kiss for kiss.

"Srilani." Aldan's voice at her ear wrenched her out of the dream, and she stared dazedly into his eyes. Scorching heat flooded her face, and she covered her cheeks with her hands.

"We—" He stopped and looked at her closely. "Is something wrong?"

She shook her head. *Yes.* Her fingers crept to her lips. *Something is definitely wrong.*

"Are you awake yet?" He pressed his wrist to her forehead for a moment. "You look . . . strange . . . like you don't feel well."

Not well. Not at all.

He took her hand and helped her sit up. "We found Sam."

⋀

Aldan studied Srilani's flushed face and overly bright eyes. Maelan wasn't completely well yet, and it would be terrible for Srilani to fall sick too. "We brought Stockings back from Sam's camp for Maelan to ride," he said. Perhaps she was just having trouble waking up.

René reached down and took Srilani's other hand. "Come on, Dreamer, get up. We need to move camp."

Together, Aldan and René helped her to her feet. Srilani said a quick thanks without meeting his eyes and bent all her attention on folding blankets. Aldan's eyes narrowed. The last time she'd acted this way — at Nik's mill — she'd been trying to keep a secret. What was she hiding now?

"We found Sam about two miles that way," Jamson said, pointing to the north. "The location is much better — there's a meadow, a lake, and a stream. He says he's starving."

Aldan snorted. "Sam and his stomach. We better hurry before he wastes away."

René laughed, face alight, and shook her head. Her fatigue seemed to have vanished as she chivied everyone, including Srilani, to gather their belongings and move with all possible speed.

Stockings took all the toil out of transporting Maelan. Jamson rode behind his twin to hold her up, and within the hour, they entered the clearing where Sam waited with Victor.

Sam grabbed Linus into a bear hug, released him, and lifted Maelan off the horse's back, tsking and scolding. "What's this I hear about you sleeping all day, young lady? Did you miss me?"

"We all missed you," she said. "We were worried. How did you get past the guardians?"

"Wait a little while, Maelan," Aldan said. "Sam can tell us his story when we're ready to eat. Let's get you settled."

Sam handed Maelan to Aldan and turned to greet her older sisters.

"Grouchy princess," he said as he bowed to Srilani.

Srilani's lips lifted at the corners. "Pirate."

René surged forward to give Sam a quick, hard hug. Aldan couldn't fault the way Sam returned her embrace. At least he didn't prolong the contact.

René and Srilani pulled out supplies to prepare a meal from the provisions they'd purchased in Minazor, and Sam led the men, including Jamson, to a place where he could point out the features of Dullon Bridge.

Sam's information erased Aldan's smile. "Six or seven search parties?"

"Maybe more if they send out soldiers too," Sam said.

Aldan stared at Sam, taking in his new air of confidence and energy. He crossed his arms and frowned. "So you've turned into a spy, have you?"

Sam's jaw lifted and he, too, crossed his arms over his chest. "We needed the information, and the horses needed oats."

"You took a huge risk. What if you'd been captured?"

Sam shrugged. "I wasn't."

Aldan let his arms fall and took a few steps away. Sam's information was valuable, and Sam was the one best equipped to be alone in a Norlan town. He frowned.

"I knew you'd object," Sam said.

Aldan swung around to face him. "The only thing I object to is that you were in danger. But we needed to know. From what you say, any moment a bunch of guardians could ride down on us." Jamson's face paled, and he looked around the circle of faces.

Aldan gave himself a mental shake. There had to be *something* they could do to even the odds. "We need horses," he said.

"That would be a fine thing," Jamson scoffed.

"We can't make it to the western border fast enough any other way," Aldan said. "Maelan's getting better, but she's really weak. And what if someone else gets sick or injured?"

Linus tapped Aldan's shoulder to get his attention, and then he gestured toward the town. "Lots of horses right there."

Four pairs of eyes focused on the enormous stables behind the fortress.

After a long moment, Aldan said, "We need a diversion."

Sam's answering chuckle was low and menacing. "I have a few ideas about that."

CHAPTER FORTY-FIVE

Srilani fingered the hilt of her dagger as she listened to the brothers finalize their plans. Her other hand clasped her grandmother's pendant. The dim starlight couldn't hide the enthusiasm in their voices even though it made it difficult to read their faces. The brothers had cooked up this idea on their own, but they didn't have to persuade her to go along.

"We need to make our move before the moon comes up," Sam said. "Yesterday, it came up after eleven bells, just before I left through the western gate."

Aldan leaned into their circle of four. "Between ten and eleven bells then. Once things get started, Srilani and Linus can enter the stables. We'll join up there."

Overall, it was a good plan, even though it left Jamson exposed for a few hours. Maelan's persistent cough would give the game away, so she'd have to stay behind. René volunteered to stay with Maelan, and Jamson had reluctantly agreed to be their guard.

As if he'd read her mind, Aldan fixed his dark eyes on her face. "Don't worry, Srilani. We haven't forgotten our pact." His voice sounded grim. "If something happens to any one of us, the rest will take care of your family."

"Thank you," she said.

Aldan clapped his hands together. "Let's go over the plan again. Then we'll get into position."

Bells tolled desperately, sounding the alarm to the residents of Dullon Bridge.

Acrid smoke reached Srilani and Linus in their hiding place near the rear of the stables. She wrinkled her nose and searched the sky. A smudge of gray clouded the clear night. The eastern horizon glowed as the fires flared.

Oaths, orders, and curses accompanied the sounds of running feet. Sam and Aldan had agreed to start four fires along the wharf. Their plan relied on the assumption that every able-bodied man in Dullon Bridge would turn out to fight the blazes near the riverfront.

Srilani said a quick prayer for the regular citizens. Hopefully, they could put out the fire before it engulfed the entire town.

"This is it," Linus whispered.

"No, we need to wait."

She counted out five minutes. "Let's go," she said. Linus stayed behind her as they entered the building.

The interior of the stables was vast but even so, it was over capacity. Not only was every stall occupied, a herd of horses filled each of three paddocks adjacent to the back of the stables, outside the city walls. Had any of the caretakers or soldiers stayed behind?

"Looks like the tack is kept near each stall. That will make our task easier." She grabbed a torch and started down the line, examining the stalls' occupants. "This mare will do for René."

Linus led the horse out into the aisle and started getting her ready. Srilani continued to search. "Ah. This one for Aldan." She lodged the torch in a mount on the wall and coaxed a blood bay gelding out of a nearby stall. "Aren't you a beauty?" she crooned.

"What do you think you're doin'?"

Her head whipped around. An elderly groom stood at her side, hands on his hips and chin thrust forward. Without hesitation, she punched him in the stomach with her elbow, driving all the air from his lungs. He doubled over and hit the floor.

"Sorry," she said. "You're in the wrong place at the wrong time." The bay gelding retreated, but she took the chance he wouldn't go far and dropped the rope attached to his halter.

Taking a lead rein from a nail, she bound the groom's hands behind his back. He gasped like a fish trying to breathe out of water. She waved Linus over, and together they dragged the man into the bay's stall. She made a gag from one of the strips of material they'd brought with them for hobbles. Linus held the groom's head while she finished tying the gag.

"He's seen you," Linus said, slipping the dagger from his belt. "Are you sure we should leave him alive?"

The man struggled against his bonds, frantic to get out of reach, entirely helpless to defend himself.

"Put your knife away," she said. Linus looked perfectly capable of killing the man in cold blood. "He's only done his duty, and I won't kill needlessly."

Linus put the weapon back into its sheath and bent to check the man's restraints. He grabbed the back of the groom's head and put his face close to the man's ear. "El has spared your life today. Keep what you know to yourself."

Srilani's brows rose. Who knew what was going on in Linus's head?

They left the groom alone and returned to work. Srilani tethered Aldan's bay, ready for Linus, and chose four more steeds. She concentrated on the task of preparing the horses for travel. Halters, lead lines, and other miscellaneous equipment went into saddlebags, along with extra measures of oats. They led the horses out the way they'd entered and tied them to a paddock fence. Srilani blindfolded each horse to keep it calm.

The smoke burned her nostrils, and the horses in the paddocks milled about nervously.

"Linus, I have an idea."

Her silent partner leaned down.

"Help me remove some of the bars on this paddock. We'll drive the horses out. First the paddocks, and then as many as we can from the stables. They'll return eventually, but it may delay the search for us."

"Good." A mischievous grin split his face, startling in the darkness.

Once the bars on the split-rail fence were down, the horses spilled out of the paddocks, and most of them headed to the west.

"Be careful not to get trampled. We'll start at the central door and work our way to the walls. Open a stall, lead the horse outside, and remove the halter. They'll want to join the herd."

The moon hadn't risen into the sky yet, but it wouldn't be long. Aldan and Sam should have joined them by now.

"We've done enough," Aldan said. The fires now threatened the entire warehouse area along the wharf. Just as they'd predicted, soldiers, citizens, and guardians worked shoulder-to-shoulder to contain the blaze.

"That took longer than I thought it would," Sam said. "If we're not careful, Linus will come looking for us."

"If he leaves Srilani by herself, I'll have something to say about that."

Sam led the way west, past the temple, and left, toward the fortress. The entry of the fortress was wide open without any visible guards. They jogged around the corner and down the long side, but when they exited through the door to the paddocks, they both stopped short.

Six horses, saddled and ready, were tied off to a rail. There was no sign of Linus or Srilani.

Aldan's heart jumped into his throat. Many other horses wandered outside of the paddocks. Aldan ran to the stable door and looked inside. Linus came into view, leading a white horse. He nodded to them and led the horse outside. After a moment, he returned with a halter that he threw onto a pile in the corner.

"Where's Srilani?" Aldan said.

"I'm here." She, too, led a horse. "We're setting them free to cause delays. We could use some help."

By the time the third quarter moon was high above, the group had traveled several leagues at a ground-eating lope. Aldan led the horse meant for Maelan, and Srilani led Stockings. Sam rode double with Maelan on Victor, holding her in front of him since she was still too weak to ride on her own.

"We need to give the horses a break," Srilani said. "Besides, I think we're getting close to the next town."

The group dismounted and walked, all except for Maelan, who insisted she could stay on the horse by herself at a walking pace.

"I've told you my tale," Sam said, looking over his shoulder at Aldan. "What happened while we were separated? In fact, back up to Minazor. I still haven't heard the whole story of how you escaped."

Aldan recounted the night he spent alone in Minazor, downplaying the part where he'd killed the guardian.

"I'm sorry you went through that," Sam said when Aldan paused. "But thanks for the horse."

"Victor is a great horse, but I think I'm going to like the one Srilani chose for me better."

"Just as well," Sam said. "You're not getting Victor back. What happened next?"

"Tell Sam about Joel," Maelan said from her perch on Victor's back.

When he'd heard the part about the angel, Sam pulled Victor to a halt in the middle of the road and turned to stare at Aldan. "If someone else told me a story like that, I'd accuse him of being drunk." He shook his head. "Joel is *not* someone I want to meet."

Aldan laughed. "That's what Linus said."

Aldan studied his new mount in the moonlight. The horse's coat was dark, nearly as dark as Victor's. "You say he's red?"

Srilani looked his direction. "Dark red. Have you decided on a name for him yet?"

"I think I'll wait to see him in the daylight."

"Wise choice."

The group alternated riding and walking for another couple of hours. They were back in the saddle, now, and the moon had descended to the horizon. A bell in the distance tolled five times.

"If we can hear bells, then we're almost to the next town," Aldan said. "We need to get up into those hills before day breaks or we'll be seen."

Srilani didn't reply, but up ahead, Jamson pointed out a path leading into the foothills to the north. "That seems to be our best chance," he said. "We might not find another good place to get off this road in time."

Aldan tried to gauge Srilani's reaction. She seemed not to hear what was going on around her, exhausted almost to the point of falling out of her saddle. René was drooping too. It was time to make a decision.

"Lead the way, Jamson," he said. "Once we're hidden by the hills, we need to find a place to rest. We should stay within a league of the road to keep an eye on what's happening down here."

Srilani jerked, attempting to sit upright. "That's what I've been thinking too," she said. Her words were slurred and indistinct.

Another hour passed before they found a suitable spot in the foothills, high above the road and hidden from view. Aldan dismounted and with the reins looped over his arm, came around to help Srilani down. Her cream-colored mare, a cremello, had its head down, breathing heavily from the effort of the climb.

Srilani slid from the saddle, limp as a wet rag, and he caught her before she fell. She leaned against his side as he guided her to the large rock where René sat.

"Give me a minute," Srilani said.

"Rest."

"But—"

"Rest." He stooped to the level of her face. "Let us take care of the horses. When you feel ready, you can pull out your blankets and go to sleep."

She looked ready to argue. He put a finger to her lips. "Shh. We can disagree after you've rested."

René gave a weak chuckle. "Srilani, you can't do everything. Help me get Maelan settled, and after you and I have slept, we'll take a watch." She raised one brow in question. "Right, Aldan?"

"Absolutely."

CHAPTER FORTY-SIX

"What?" Srilani's eyes narrowed on Linus, and she set her bow down with exaggerated care. "You let them go?"

One of the chief advantages of traveling by night was avoiding the heat of Norland's late summer days. The empty, moonlit road stretched out ahead of the group, and the leagues melted away as they traveled west. Each dawn, they ascended the hills to the north of the road and chose a hiding place. Srilani elected to hunt during the cooler, early morning hours, and Jamson carried the results of her labor, a brace of rabbits.

"Why did you let them go?" she asked again.

Linus met her gaze without expression.

Jamson stepped in front of his friend. "It's not as if Linus could stop Aldan and Sam from going, Srilani."

"Why?" She looked at the sky as if the answers might dawn on her. She blinked several times and swallowed hard. Her gaze slowly descended to her sisters' anxious faces. "Why did they go to town?"

"The horses need oats, Sri," Maelan said. "You know it's difficult for them to get enough to eat up here. It's mostly pine needles and oak leaves."

René crossed her arms over her bosom. "You have to admit, Srilani, we could use some fresh provisions."

"But why didn't he . . . they . . . tell me? Why sneak away the minute Jamson and I left camp to hunt?" Srilani swallowed again, trying to modulate the note of hurt in her voice. "And what about the group of horsemen Linus spotted this morning? Aren't Aldan and Sam just a little concerned about running into Lector again?"

René blanched, and Maelan dropped her eyes, digging her toe into the thick carpet of leaves on the forest floor. "I don't know," Maelan muttered.

Srilani took a deep breath and let it out slowly. She turned away from the others and pinched the bridge of her nose. Tears pricked behind her eyelids. She let her hand fall, straightened her shoulders, and grabbed onto her dignity with both hands.

When she turned back, René and Maelan stood near the fire they'd built, watching her. Jamson seemed to have forgotten the rabbits hanging from the stick balanced over his shoulder. They'd taken sufficient meat for everyone to eat their fill.

What if Aldan and Sam didn't return? What if they were captured? They could be imprisoned, injured, or killed. Tears, so close to the surface these days, threatened again.

"I need a few minutes alone," she said and turned away. She walked up the hill a few yards to the spring trickling from the hillside, one of hundreds that dotted the area. She washed away traces of the hunt, splashed her face, combed out her hair, and braided it again.

Did Aldan let Sam talk him into the trip, or had it been his idea? They'd rushed off without a word to her.

Just like Father.

Father always knew best — to his way of thinking — and he saw nothing wrong with making major decisions for her life without asking what she thought or what she wanted. She was the first child, the unwanted girl her father was obligated to train as if she were a son, the secondary heir, the one who must be perfect and respectable and not put a step out of line. The child he'd forgotten the moment he'd laid eyes on Jamson nearly fourteen years ago.

Didn't Aldan want to know how she felt about things? Of course Sam wouldn't care, but Aldan? Didn't he respect her enough to ask what she thought? She should have a part in making decisions that would affect the entire group. Her brother. Her sisters. Her friends.

There was also the issue of trust. Hadn't she trusted both men to look after her sisters when she took Jamson hunting? Why couldn't Sam have taken Linus? Something close to a sob escaped her control, and she pressed her hands over her mouth.

They had approximately half a month of travel ahead before they reached the Rhynder River and the Cauldron fortress, as long as things went well. If they made it home, she'd return to her old life. Father would marry her off to some man with wealth, family connections, influence, and land. She'd be lucky if the husband he chose for her were someone she liked as much as Greyson. Her life's path would be decided for her. Aldan would go off to fight for his kingdom, get himself killed, and she'd never see or talk to him again.

⋀⋀

"We're being followed," Sam said.

"I know." Aldan looked over his shoulder. "He's huge. And persistent."

"Do you think he'll attack us?"

"Your guess is as good as mine."

Aldan took another opportunity to glance back past Stockings and the bags of supplies she carried. The slender, long-legged dog looked similar to the wolves in his vision, but bigger. Much bigger. Its pointed snout and gray, wiry fur weren't like a wolf's. It easily kept up with the horses, about one hundred paces behind them.

"Maybe it's a good sign that the horses aren't showing any fear," Aldan said at last. He faced forward, urging his horse on.

"We are so late," Sam said as he bent to avoid a limb overhanging the trail. "I'm sorry, Aldan. It took longer than I thought to reach the town. And of course, it's the same distance back. And now it's almost dark."

"It was still a good idea," Aldan said. "We were able to get fresh supplies and new information. I'd say it was worth the effort."

"Well, I'm still sorry. I think we're going to be in trouble with Her Majesty."

Aldan didn't reply immediately. There was sure to be friction with Srilani over their impulsive actions today. "You shouldn't call her that."

Sam chuckled. "You have to admit, Srilani was born to be in charge. She'd probably make a better ruler than her brother, if the laws of inheritance didn't work the way they do." He cleared his throat. "I'm not actually being insulting. She's got my respect."

"Her attitude toward you has mellowed too. You must have won her over while I was trapped in Minazor."

Sam's voice sounded like he was enjoying a secret joke. "We reached an agreement. But what's it to you?"

Aldan shrugged, even though Sam couldn't see him. "I care about everything that concerns Srilani, and I want her to like my best friend."

"You don't ask much, do you?"

"Before I met Joel, I didn't think I could expect anything much from life." He paused, trying to find the right words. "Since Joel gave me the words from El, I believe El will make his promises come true. Somehow. And I believe Srilani has a place in those plans."

"For your sake, I hope you get what you want."

The hillside took on a purple hue as Sol's last rays showed them the way. The horses picked their way up the incline, and the hound panted in their wake.

/̇\̇\̇

"Aldan. Sam. You're back!" Maelan hurried to take the horses' reins as the men dismounted. The day of rest seemed to have restored the younger princess to her regular level of energy. "Jamson, help me with Flame, Victor, and Stockings." She took Sam's reins and waited for Aldan to dismount.

Absently, Aldan handed Flame to Maelan. His gaze went to Srilani's face. Her eyes glittered in the firelight, but her face was otherwise devoid of emotion. She took in their appearance, the new bags of supplies, and then her gaze rested on the dog who stood at a distance.

"A wolfhound," she said. "Did you purchase a wolfhound too?" She left little doubt about her opinion of such a move. Slowly, she bent to retrieve her bow.

"Uh . . . no," Aldan said. "He followed us from the outskirts of town."

She strung the bow in her hand by touch and nocked an arrow, never taking her eyes from the animal. "Well, I hope he's trained. If so, it may be an asset. If he's vicious or a nuisance or untrustworthy, I'll have to kill him."

The flat note in her voice was disturbing. Had he imagined the subtle emphasis on "untrustworthy?"

A movement behind Srilani caught Aldan's attention. Linus balanced atop a tall rock beside their site and reached up to the tree above, frantically attempting to climb into its branches.

Aldan hurried over to the rock. "What are you doing?"

Linus didn't reply until he was perched, like an overgrown, featherless raven, high above the trail. His eyes focused on the wolfhound and his mouth opened in a rictus of fear.

Maelan gaped at Linus. "What's the matter with him?" The horses were forgotten for the moment as she seemed completely caught up in Linus's distress.

"I don't know," Aldan said. "Does the dog look vicious to you, Maelan?"

She swiveled around so that she could see it. "No. He's just watching us."

"Down," Srilani said in Norlan. She walked toward the dog, hands holding the bow ready. The wolfhound switched its attention to Srilani. She repeated the command and when it hesitated, she repeated the command again, with more force. Reluctantly, the dog lowered itself to its belly and flattened its ears to its head.

She approached the dog, eyes steady, projecting a tangible aura of power. When she got within a dozen yards, the great dog turned on its back, exposing its belly to her.

She released the tension on the bow and snapped her fingers. "Come."

The dog bounded up to her.

"Sit."

The dog plopped down, tail swishing, tongue lolling out of its mouth.

She reached out and scratched its ears. "Good boy." She kept her hand on the hound's head, at the level of her waist and faced the group. "Obviously, he's had some training, but I'd say he's fairly young. Young enough to wander away from home and lose his way." She gestured to

Maelan. "Please get one of the horses' leads."

"How did you know that it was tame?" Aldan asked.

"I took a chance."

Maelan brought a long rope lead and helped Srilani fashion a collar and leash for the dog. The dog sniffed Maelan's clothes and licked her hand before she led him away.

Srilani walked beneath the tree, stood beside Aldan and Sam, and looked way up. Linus's face had returned to its regular, hard-to-read expression. "Linus, I can tell you've had a bad experience with dogs. Please come down and talk with us. You're safe." Her voice was unexpectedly gentle and coaxing. She poked Aldan in the ribs with her elbow, sending him a speaking glance.

"Come on, Brother," he said. "I'll kill the dog myself if it offers to hurt you."

Linus warily joined his brothers and Srilani beside the fire.

Aldan spoke first. "Why are you afraid?"

Linus swallowed. His eyes followed the twins. Maelan and Jamson took the dog with them to care for the horses. The hound seemed at ease with the horses and didn't get underfoot.

"Dogs bite," Linus said. His eyes looked haunted. "Dogs chased me."

"When?" Aldan leaned forward, putting a hand on Linus's knee.

"When I met you." Linus shrugged. "Just before."

"When you were captured?" Aldan's voice was low.

Linus whispered, "Mother . . . killed."

"By dogs?"

Linus shook his head. "Dogs chased her. They *did* bite her, but the men—" A single tear trailed from the corner of his eye. "The men . . . they hurt her and then she died."

"You saw all this?"

Linus nodded again. "I climbed a tree."

Silence followed these revelations. Srilani and René looked especially sad and pale.

At last Srilani asked Aldan, "How old was Linus when he was sold to

Rozar?"

"I don't know for certain, but I always thought he was about four years old when he first came aboard. He was small. Rozar made me take care of him. I never figured out why Rozar bought such a small boy. Linus didn't talk much, and he could only tell me his name."

"That seems about right," Sam said. "When I was brought aboard, Linus seemed to me to be about five or six. He didn't speak to me for almost two months."

Srilani leaned over and took one of Linus's hands, and he went still, eyes focused on her face. Aldan watched her closely, but it was as if she'd shut out everything and everyone except Linus.

"We have a problem, Linus," she said. "Your fear is real and quite reasonable, and I'll understand if you can't overcome it. You decide. What's to happen to the dog?" She looked over her shoulder to check on the twins, and then back at Linus, lowering her voice. "If you can't have the dog around you, speak now. We'll get rid of it. But if you agree to let the dog live, then you need to take the dog as yours."

Aldan's head drew back. What was she up to? She seemed perfectly serious, but what she said made no sense.

"He will be yours," she continued. "You will name him. You will care for him and feed him. It's your decision — the dog's life is in your hands."

Linus stared into her eyes for an entire minute, and then he shifted his attention to the dog. The hound lounged at Maelan's feet while she combed Flame's mane.

Aldan opened his mouth to speak, but Srilani shook her head.

Finally, Linus pulled his hand free from her grip and stood. He bent and tore a strip of meat from the last rabbit on the spit. His footsteps were slow but resolute. The dog jumped to its feet as Linus approached and strained against the leash to meet the young man. Maelan held the other end and said something to Linus that Aldan couldn't catch. Linus put out his hand and the dog took the piece of meat he offered, wiggling all over with excitement. Linus squatted and the dog proceeded to lick his fingers and face until Linus stood up.

"That has to be one of the bravest things I've ever seen," Srilani said under her breath.

Maelan handed the leash to Linus. She said something else, and Linus nodded.

"Down!" he said.

When the dog obeyed Linus's command, Aldan let out the breath he'd been holding. The group by the fire continued to watch as the twins instructed Linus in all sorts of miscellaneous dog lore.

René pressed the men to eat the rest of the rabbit, and Srilani moved away, busying herself with distributing the new supplies among the packs. Aldan soon joined her, but there was none of the easy conversation he'd come to expect. Her comments were limited to the work at hand, and when Sam and René put out the fire, she mounted her horse and waited silently to begin the treacherous descent to the valley below.

CHAPTER FORTY-SEVEN

The next morning, Srilani pulled René aside and asked her privately to take charge of teaching the brothers the many things they needed to know before they reached Kaeson.

"But you know so much more than I do," René said, her eyebrows raised. "You've spent twice as much time with Elison and the other teachers."

"They'll like the lessons better coming from you. Besides, they don't need to know all the details that were drilled into me."

"But Aldan will need to know those kinds of things."

Srilani scrambled for a sensible reply. "Is there a better time to hunt? Jamson can teach protocol to Aldan. One future king to another. Jamson will benefit too, from reviewing what he knows."

René acted as though she wanted to argue further, but Srilani walked away.

When Srilani returned from hunting — the dog having killed the game before she could shoot — Jamson was starting the weapons drill, as he'd done at Nik's mill, and she joined the group to even up the numbers. She took turns sparring with Linus, Sam, and Aldan, but kept her comments to a minimum. Then it was time to catch sleep in shifts during the heat of the day.

They descended to the road as night fell, and Srilani rode beside René. This formed the pattern for the next four days, and a bare handful of words passed between Srilani and the brothers.

If Aldan asked Srilani a direct question, she answered — politely — but she didn't initiate conversations with him anymore. Rather than upset the equilibrium of the group with pointless arguments, she held back any hint of reproach regarding Aldan and Sam's jaunt to town five days before. Why bother? *Soon it won't matter anyway.*

Aldan didn't bring up the topic of the side trip, either. He probably wanted to avoid an argument. But the silence stretching between them seemed worse than having a fight. Srilani tried to seal off her emotions, wrapping them in a cocoon of indifference as she always had before, but despair nibbled away at her spirit. Separation from Aldan was inevitable. How would she survive it?

///\\\

Aldan watched Srilani leave their newest camp with her bow in hand and the dog at her heels. The twins tended the horses and his brothers arranged rocks for a fire ring. This was the fifth day since the fateful trip to the village. He had to talk to someone, and the best candidate was René. He joined her in gathering firewood a short distance from the others.

Without preliminary, he plunged right in. "Srilani's been avoiding me since Sam and I visited the town."

"Mmm." René glanced at him and kept working.

"She's turned the teaching over to you, and she's not acting like herself. The Srilani I know would have confronted us if she didn't agree with something we said or did." Aldan picked up a branch and added it to the others in the crook of his arm. "She hasn't said anything."

René nodded. "I've noticed. But you didn't see her first reaction."

"Was she angry?"

"Maybe, but to me it looked more like . . ." René bit her lip. "Srilani looked like she was fighting back tears."

Aldan stared at René. "Are you serious? Why?"

René averted her eyes and shrugged one shoulder in a noncommittal way.

"No, René, don't clam up on me now," Aldan said, coming to stand beside her. His voice roughened. "What did she say? Tell me."

René's face stiffened and her chin came up. "I don't think my sister would appreciate this discussion."

"I didn't mean to sound rude," he said. "Please, just tell me what happened."

After a moment, René relented. "It's probably better for you to know what you're up against." She told him what she'd seen that day, and he could only shake his head.

"You think we hurt her feelings?" he said. "Sam and I had the idea about visiting the village after she left camp, and we acted on it immediately because it would have been too late if we'd waited. We weren't trying to go behind her back."

"Maybe so, but I'm certain that's the way she saw it."

"So she's — What? Why hasn't she said anything?"

She shifted the branches in her arms. "I have a few ideas."

He gestured with one of the sticks he held. "Come on. Tell me what you think."

She took her load of firewood to the stone ring, and he followed. "We need more wood," she said. "Come with me."

When they were well away from the others, she spoke. "Srilani is First Princess, exactly like your older sister, Queen Yolani."

It wasn't a question, but he nodded.

"First Princess is an honorary rank that's given when a daughter is born before the heir, but it comes with lots of responsibilities. A First is groomed to be the ruler in case no male heir is born or he dies prematurely. Even if an heir is born, the First is trained to be regent in case the ruler dies before the heir is of age."

"Srilani told me all that."

René sighed. "But I'm sure she didn't tell you how it felt when our brother was born and she was brushed aside. It didn't affect me so much because I was only three and I'm the second child. She was Father's darling for almost five years before the twins were born. Our father is a really smart man — shrewd in business and good at ruling the barons — but he's a fool about his daughters, especially Srilani."

Aldan paused. Had *his* older sister experienced the same sort of loss as Srilani? His sister was twelve years his senior, according to what they'd told him.

She lifted her hand and let it fall. "I know Father loves us, in his way, but he tends to see his daughters as mere females. We've been raised to behave perfectly, remain pure, and marry well." René's mouth drooped, and she bent down to pick up a couple of pieces of wood.

Aldan broke a long stick with more force than necessary. Where was she going with this information?

"Ever since I can remember, Father has had a double-standard for Srilani and his other children. She spends her days with tutors and instructors. She's learned how to fight and how to manage the royal fleet of trading ships. She's learned our law, our history, and three languages."

René seemed to have forgotten the task at hand. "Jamson has tutors and instructors too, but the majority of his time is spent with Father. The rest of us get to follow our interests. I'm training to be a healer. Maelan is interested in plants and animals. Who knows what Audrilan will do? But not Srilani. Father dictates her life and makes all of the major decisions for her."

Aldan rubbed his neck as he puzzled over what she was trying to say. "What does your father have to do with Srilani's sudden change in behavior around me?"

René stopped working, and Aldan took the branches she'd gathered from her hands. "Up to now, you and Srilani have shared the decisions. You've encouraged her to say what she thinks. But the other day, you just left us without a word. That's what Father does. He makes decisions for Srilani without ever asking. She's brilliant and capable of deciding for herself, but he doesn't seem to see it."

"I didn't mean—"

"It doesn't matter." A steely note entered René's voice and she leaned forward. "Maybe she thinks it's pointless to say what she thinks if you're going to act like Father."

Aldan rocked back on his heels at the ferocity in René's amazing, jewel-colored eyes.

"You need to make it right with Srilani and devise a plan, Aldan." René pointed at his chest. "Because when we get back to Kaeson, you can bet our father will marry her off as soon as possible. She's already past the usual age of betrothal. Father will choose the man who seems to be the most advantageous match."

Aldan's jaw tightened and he squared his shoulders. "I have some apologizing to do."

René took all the branches from his arms and nodded toward the woods. "Do it now."

Aldan followed a deer trail in the direction he'd seen Srilani depart, and he found her within a few minutes. The dog announced Aldan's arrival, and Srilani jerked around, her hand flying to retrieve an arrow from the quiver on her back. She left the arrow in the quiver and hurried toward him.

"Is something wrong?" she asked. She sent a quick glance past him, her face taut and alert.

Aldan checked the impulse to say yes and shook his head. "Everything's fine. I didn't mean to scare you."

"Why aren't you with the others?" Her voice sounded breathless. Wary eyes met his for a brief moment before she focused on the wolfhound. The dog bounded around them in a circle, overly excited and out of control. She took a few moments to calm him down.

Aldan didn't take his eyes from her face. "I'm not with the others because I need to talk to you."

"I was just on my way back," she said quickly. Too quickly.

He stepped in front of her when she tried to skirt past him. "With only one kill?"

His question brought her up short and color bloomed on her face. She bit her lip, and his brows rose. She seemed . . . flustered. Unsure. And sad.

He folded his arms across his chest. "Surely you can come up with a better excuse for avoiding me." Reaching out, he took her free hand and bent to look closer at her face. "You can't run from me forever."

Her color deepened, and there was a tremor in the fingers he held.

"Can you forgive me for the other day, Srilani? I'm like that dog — sometimes I get excited and forget what's important." He smiled as she finally met his eyes. He enclosed her fingers with both hands. "I should have realized how it would look to you. Sam and I weren't trying to leave you out of the decision — we just saw the opportunity and took it."

"If something had happened to you, we couldn't have helped," she said. "You could have been captured or killed." Her voice quavered on the last word.

"I know. We went off without a real plan, and we won't do it again." He paused, trying to read her expression. "Can you forgive me? Can we still be friends?"

She nodded.

Slowly, giving her the opportunity to pull away, he raised her hand to his lips. She froze, like a startled doe, eyes wide. His smile returned, and he released her fingers. "Will you show me how to shoot the bow? I'll never learn if you don't let me practice."

⋀⋀

Srilani could hardly breathe. Teaching Aldan to shoot the bow required a fair amount of physical contact, and every time he looked her way, deviltry glinted in the depths of his eyes. He knew. Somehow he knew what he was doing to her.

She assumed her best teaching voice. "The most important part of shooting a bow is to always use the same anchor spot on your face. You'll never gain consistent accuracy until you form this habit. Let me show you how I do it."

He stood close to her and mimicked her form. Then she drew the bracer off her arm and held it so that he could put it on. Her fingers tingled from touching his arm, and she broke off the contact as quickly as possible. Next came her finger guard. "I wish we had more than one of everything," she said. "But we'll make do."

Finally, she handed over the bow and one arrow. She avoided looking into his face and concentrated on his hands. "We'll just work on the draw and repeat it until I think you're ready. Then I'll let you shoot."

"Is this right?" His first three fingers curved around the string and drew it back to the corner of his mouth.

"No. Don't lock your fingers on the arrow. It will stay where you put it." She loosened his fingers, placing them in the correct position. "Now stand like this."

She modeled the stance and watched him try, adjusting his shoulders. The memory of stitching his skin came to mind, and she tried to banish it. "All right. Now release the tension — like you've decided not to take the shot — and do it all over again."

"Again."

"And again."

At last, she pointed to a spot only a dozen paces away. "Aim right into the center of that bush. I don't want to lose any arrows. But first check around and make certain your field is clear. Where's the dog?"

The wolfhound slept soundly beneath a tree.

Srilani nodded. "Do as you've practiced, only this time, go ahead and make the release. After you release, hold your position until the arrow goes to the target."

His first shot was fair and on his fifth shot, he made it to the center of the bush for the third time. "With practice, you could become an outstanding archer."

Aldan's eyes glittered at her, and Srilani took a discrete step back. "We've been gone too long," she said, "and I shouldn't be alone with you at all."

"But I don't want to go back," he said. "I want to stay here with you."

She cleared her throat and took another small step away.

"Just for an hour," he coaxed. "You have enough to feed Sam, but one hare isn't enough to feed everybody."

Where was her brain? Sol was climbing high, and they needed to finish hunting soon so they could rest. "One hour only."

He removed the bracer and finger guard, handing them over. The dog sprang up, as though he knew the lesson was over, and started searching for quarry. Aldan seemed content to be with her. He respected the need for stealth and silence. He proved to be good company, but after she made her third kill, he touched her elbow.

"Do you smell smoke?"

She lifted her head, testing the air. The breeze had freshened and blew from the east. After a moment, the faint scent of a fire wafted past her nose.

"We have to go," she said.

Hurriedly, they retrieved the last unfortunate rabbit and broke into a run with the dog bounding at their heels.

CHAPTER FORTY-EIGHT

"Break camp!" Aldan called out. René hadn't lit the fire for cooking yet. Good. He strode forward and began dismantling the fire ring. René's eyes grew round, and she rushed to help him move rocks and dispose of the branches they'd gathered earlier.

Srilani hurried to the twins. "Pack up," she said. "We need to move camp right now."

"What's happening?" Sam grabbed a stout piece of wood, heaved it out of sight, and joined Aldan.

"Smoke." Aldan stopped working long enough to point. "From that direction. Thankfully, we're downwind from whoever's out there." Aldan handed several items to the twins. They needed no prompting to haul the gear to the horses and prepare the animals.

"Let me go back there," Linus said in a low voice.

Aldan gave Linus his full attention. "What?"

"Let me go back and find out who's behind us."

Sam stopped working, as did Srilani and René. They stepped closer.

The air seemed scarce, and Aldan labored to sound calm as he addressed the others. "What do you think?"

"It would be helpful to know where they are and how many," Srilani said. "But you know your brother best. Can Linus do this without being caught?"

"If anyone can find out who's back there without being seen, it's Linus," Sam said.

Aldan hesitated. If Linus were captured, he'd never forgive himself.

"You're sure you want to do this?"

Linus nodded. "You take my horse, and I will go on foot. I will catch up with you."

Srilani's mouth pursed and her brow crinkled as she paused to think it through. She sighed. "We ought to find a place we can stay before evening so Linus can catch up with us while there's still light. We'll have to switch to traveling during the days."

"We need to make the switch anyway," Aldan said. "In a couple of days, it will be the new moon. Too dark to travel at night."

She extended her arm to a forty-five degree angle pointing west. "Linus, when Sol is about there, you need to break off your search and find us. If you wait any longer, you'll be stuck in the hills by yourself after dark. Do you understand?"

Linus nodded and turned to go. He turned back to them. "Who will take care of the dog?"

René gave him a reassuring smile. "Don't worry. Maelan knows about dogs."

Aldan gave Linus's shoulder a squeeze. "You need to give your dog a name. You should think about it while you're away." His throat closed up and went dry. "Don't take unnecessary chances."

"Never." Linus pushed through the underbrush and was gone.

⋀⋀

Linus still hadn't caught up with them as night fell. Aldan took the first watch while the others slept. He perched on a rock overlooking the hillside and all its approaches. How could he possibly sleep when he didn't know what had happened to his brother? He'd wait all night if necessary.

Since the terrain had been so difficult, they'd been forced to keep the horses at a walk for most of the day, so Linus should have arrived by now.

A movement to the east caught his attention and his senses sharpened. Was it the breeze in the shrubs? An animal?

The tall form of Linus emerged from the shadows, and Aldan moved to intercept him. So did the dog, who couldn't contain his joy.

Linus addressed the dog in a stern voice. "Sit."

Aldan kept his voice low. "How did you fare?"

Linus stopped and endured Aldan's tight embrace. "I am well."

"What did you find?"

"Two soldiers are behind us. They have horses, and they're only one league away."

"So they passed our last position during the day?"

"They're on our trail, but they stopped for the night." Linus's words slurred together.

"Get some rest." Aldan climbed back to his perch. A sense of rightness crept into his core, and it didn't matter that soldiers were on their trail. This was how it ought to be. His gaze lingered on the camp below where Srilani rested with the others. His breathing returned to normal, and his heartbeat evened out. He was supposed to be here, watching over his new family. And nobody — not even King Terson — could keep him from claiming them as his.

Linus's news was passed with the watch from Aldan to Sam, from Sam to René, and from René to Srilani. She woke everyone before dawn while the stars were still the only source of light. They headed out on empty stomachs as Sol's first rays penetrated the forest canopy.

Sol rose in a crimson tide of light accompanied by a fierce wind from the southeast. The susurration of the pines surrounded them and oaks sent showers of leaves from the crags above. Needles and dust flew about, scenting the air with pine resin and making it difficult to breathe.

Srilani wrapped her headscarf over her mouth and nose. Here, at last, was a use for the hated headdress.

Sol reached his zenith, adding heat to the misery of the wind. Sam was on point, followed by René and the twins. Srilani was next. Aldan rode behind her with Linus as rear guard. To spare the horses, they continued the pattern of alternately walking and riding, and every time they were on foot, Aldan was beside Srilani.

"Tell me about your father," he said.

She pulled her scarf tighter around her face and lowered her head. "What do you wish to know?"

"Tell me about his plans for you."

She peered around the nose of her horse, trying to read Aldan's face. "Why do you ask?"

His dark brown eyes narrowed. "I'm asking the questions." His voice sounded gruff. "What does he intend to do?"

She hid from view behind the cream-colored mare and searched for a way to avoid the topic. How long had she known, deep inside, that Aldan would ask about her future?

She moistened her dry lips and stayed close to the mare's side. "My father intends for me to marry one of the barons or a son of a baron, preferably one who's been an officer in the Palace Guard. He has introduced me to most of those he considers eligible contenders for my hand."

"And what do you intend to do?"

"What do you mean?"

Something like a growl came from Aldan. He grasped her horse's bridle, brought the mare to a halt, and waved at Srilani to come around. "Walk between the horses with me. I don't want to misunderstand you, and your horse is in the way."

Linus stopped behind them, waiting as they sorted things out. She had no good reason to deny Aldan's request — this entire discussion was inevitable anyway.

They set off again, and he bent his head toward her. "What are you going to do about your father's plans?"

She shook her head. "Five weeks ago, I would have married the man my father selected without a question . . . unless the man were so elderly he was missing all of his teeth or so young, he didn't have whiskers."

"And now?"

"I don't know what I'll do. Believe it or not, there are times when I'd rather not return home to Kaeson."

She looked straight ahead. "In spite of the hardships we've faced since we were taken, I've been free to think my own thoughts and make my own decisions. At home, I only get to make decisions about minor issues. It will be difficult to go back to my old life."

She looked into Aldan's solemn face and then down at their entwined fingers. Which one of them had initiated the contact? What would the people of the court say? She was definitely breaking the rules now, but she didn't pull away.

"In my weaker moments, I've considered leaving my life in Kaeson."

Aldan's fingers gave hers a squeeze, and she continued. "I could renounce my title. I have a separate inheritance from my mother's mother so I wouldn't be without resources. But doing that would dishonor my parents, and poor René would have to be First Princess. The consequences of such an action would haunt me all my life."

"Do you favor one of the men your father has introduced?"

"I like some better than others."

"That's not an answer, and you know it. Is there one you favor?"

She sighed. Diplomatic double-speak evidently wouldn't work with Aldan. "There was one, but now . . ." Her steps slowed and she met his eyes. "Now they are all equally unacceptable."

There. She'd told Aldan the truth — all of it — even things she hadn't admitted to herself before.

But he said nothing as they continued on their journey. He just held her hand in a strong clasp, his calluses rough against her smooth skin.

Srilani ignored her aching body and growling stomach and kept a watchful eye on the worsening weather. The wind pushed them along, getting stronger at every hour. Forested hills gave way to rockier terrain with fewer trees. The upside of this change was more forage for the horses. The downside was less tree cover and greater exposure to the elements. The low mountains, pocketed with caves, thrust out of the ground at difficult angles and several times, they had to retrace their steps and work out a better route.

By late afternoon, soaring thunderheads were building in the southeast and moving closer. "We need to find shelter now," Linus said.

Driven to their limits, hungry and exhausted, the group chose to stop at the first large cave they found. There was a path to the mouth of the cave and numerous signs of previous, but not recent, human occupation. Below and off to the side of the cave was an overhang of rock that might provide the horses some protection from the approaching storm. They picketed the horses so they faced into the alcove and hurried to move their belongings into the shelter of the cave before the rain arrived.

"We're going to need light," René said. "If we could build a small fire, perhaps I could cook some porridge with some of the oats."

Sam groaned. "I swear, if you feed me, I will be in your debt forever. Just look at me. I'm wasting away to skin and bones." He peered out of the cave and back at the group. "Pray that I don't get struck by lightning. I'm going out to find some firewood."

"I'll help him," Maelan said. "There's no way I want to stay in a dark cave during a lightning storm." She left before Srilani could stop her, and Jamson ducked out after his sister.

"Aldan and Linus, could you please go with them?" Srilani asked. "We'll set things up while you're out."

The sky had darkened to tarnished silver, and lightning flashed in the distance.

René shook her head and chuckled. "I'm hungry, but all that effort for porridge. Can you believe it?"

Srilani smiled, too, and then the smile faded. "We could really use a couple of torches. It's too bad we didn't grab some from the stables in Dullon Bridge."

"Can't change that now. We'll have to put the fire close to the front of the cave so the smoke doesn't suffocate us. In the meantime, let's spread out the blankets."

"This is going to be tight," Srilani said, giving the floor of the shelter a measuring glance. "There's hardly room for us to stretch out. We may all have to sleep on our sides to fit."

René bit her lip. "How are we going to do this? It isn't a proper arrangement at all." She paused. "Speaking of which, what did you mean by holding hands with Aldan this afternoon?"

"I—" Srilani stopped. "He was encouraging me."

"Oh?"

"That's all I'm going to say."

※

Aldan herded everyone back into the cave as the lightning escalated. Thunder pulsed against the surrounding cliffs. The late afternoon turned evening dark in a matter of minutes, and the wind grew chilly. Everyone sat as close as they dared to the fire.

"There isn't enough wood to burn through the night," Aldan said, motioning to their pitiful collection of branches.

René stirred the meager pot of porridge steaming over the flames. "If we bank the fire, it will last until morning. Our eyes will adjust to the darkness. Since we'll be sleeping, we won't need the light anyway."

"As if we could sleep through this," Sam said. He sounded as gloomy as a sailor who'd been denied shore leave.

"You mean if we can sleep through your snoring," Srilani said. Her words held a touch of playfulness.

Sam straightened, turning toward her in surprise. "Grouchy princess."

She smiled. "Irritating pirate."

Aldan caught back a huge yawn. "I could sleep through the end of the world. I don't think we need to post a watch tonight."

"Indeed," Linus said. His dog clambered up into the cave just as the rain broke loose in a torrent. The animal crouched between Linus and Maelan.

Aldan gave the wolfhound a scratch behind one of his ears. "What have you decided to name your dog?"

A blinding bolt of lightning struck nearby, followed by a deafening crash of thunder. Maelan gave a little shriek, and the dog barked several times. Linus's slow grin seemed abnormally bright in the firelight. "His name is Kazka, after the lightning. Because he's fast and very loud."

Maelan giggled. "Kazka. I like it."

"The name fits," Aldan said. "A dog like Kazka needs a powerful name."

Srilani shivered, gesturing at the simmering pot. "Is the porridge almost done, René?"

"Yes. I'm going to take it off the fire and let it cool a couple of minutes. We really have no option but to pass it around and share."

Jamson gave an exaggerated sigh. "Sorry, Linus. Kazka has to go last."

Their laughter echoed strangely off the walls of the cave.

The twins slept in the middle of the group, facing one another. The rest lined up like planks in a floor, the sisters behind Maelan and the brothers behind Jamson, their feet pointing toward the embers of the fire. Kazka squeezed his bulk between Linus and the wall of the cave.

Eventually, the roar of the storm relented and turned into a soothing, steady rain.

Aldan adjusted to the low light and looked over the twins' heads. Srilani gazed back at him, and they continued to watch each other until sleep claimed him without warning. While he slept, her face stayed before him.

He woke at dawn and met her eyes, as if they'd never slept, as if the night and the storm had never been. A slow smile formed on her lips, and he returned the smile. Carefully, she slid from between her sisters and knelt near the fire ring, looking outside.

He lifted up on one elbow to watch her unwind her braid and comb it out with her fingers. Her hair flowed down her back like a length of burnished silk, the ends swinging just above the dirt floor. With swift fingers, she reformed the braid and pulled it forward over her shoulder to finish the end. She stood and smoothed down her clothes, twitching the tunic into place over her hips.

Aldan stifled a groan and turned his head away. She had no idea of her allure.

"Look," she whispered. She pointed to something outside the mouth of the cave.

Only Kazka stirred, raising his head to watch as Aldan moved to join her. He followed the direction of her gaze and strained to see anything out of the ordinary. He blinked and tried again.

"I thought I saw something flicker," she said.

"Wait a moment." He ducked back inside, pulled his pack out of the middle of the pile, and extracted Rozar's glass. Aldan returned to her side and surveyed every inch of the horizon until he reached the place he'd seen before.

He handed the instrument to her. "Here. Take a look."

Srilani moved closer, her arm brushing his. She trained the glass on the spot and caught her breath. "I see a campfire." She lowered the glass. "Is that what you saw?"

"Yes. And at least two men."

CHAPTER FORTY-NINE

Panic rode double behind Srilani, and he refused to leave. She glanced over her shoulder. There was no rational explanation for her certainty that they were being followed. There had been no clues since the cave, four days before, to confirm that the men they'd seen were still anywhere in their vicinity. But Aldan supported Srilani in setting a relentless pace, keeping to the hollows between hills as much as possible to avoid detection.

"The last thing we want is to be silhouetted against the sky," she told the group more than once.

Fortunately, there'd been no repeat of having to eat the horses' oats. Kazka proved his worth by hunting ahead of the party, and Srilani managed to bag plenty of quarry. They used the smallest fires possible to cook their meals and only lit the fires down in the valleys before dark.

On the morning of the fifth day, they arrived at a tributary of the Rhynder River and dismounted to let the horses drink. Aldan looked over Srilani's shoulder as she examined the map. According to it, the narrow stream originated in the north, made a bend to the west, and merged with the Rhynder before it reached the Great Gulf.

She measured the distance with her fingers. "Finally! This gives us a precise indication of our location. If this scale is accurate, we're about one hundred sixty leagues from the Cauldron fortress. So about eight more days."

"This stream should provide us with an easier source of water too," he said.

Sam rubbed his hands together. "And fish!"

Srilani rolled her eyes and her lips quirked. "And fish. Are you tired of meat, Sam?"

"No, but I like fish."

René let the water trickle over her fingers. "I just want to bathe in the stream."

"So do I," Maelan said.

"We're all filthy, but it's too exposed here," Srilani said. "We'll bathe after we cross and get away from this place."

They crossed the shallow stream and plunged ahead. The small river marked another change in the landscape to gently rolling hills covered in lovely, waving grasses. Here, though, they found another danger — pockets of human occupation. Little hamlets, connected by numerous wagon tracks, dotted the hills and valleys. The group skirted the settlements and plentiful herds of cattle.

"At this rate, I think it's going to take us more than eight days to reach the border with all of these detours," Aldan said. "If the soldiers are still behind us, they'll be able to pass straight through the villages."

Sam ran a finger under the neck of his shirt collar. "They have an advantage over us, for sure."

"Perhaps they'll waste time questioning people," Jamson said. "At least, I hope so." He gestured to the west. "Sol's going down. We should stop for the evening."

Srilani studied the terrain, turning her mare in a complete circle. The skin between her shoulder blades itched as it did when she walked to the dais each Third Day banquet, as if hundreds of eyes were fixed on her back. She shrugged. "Aldan, let's do a quick turn around the perimeter before we unpack."

"Good idea."

They left Sam and Linus to guard the others and rode forward a couple of hundred yards, turning back in a long arc, bypassing their party and ending their sweep behind them, in the path they'd just traveled.

"Seems clear," Aldan said.

Srilani fidgeted with her reins. "I just can't shake the feeling we're not alone."

Deep grooves appeared beside Aldan's mouth. "We'll have to stay on guard."

Within the hour, both fish and rabbit were roasting over the fire. Maelan, with help from Linus and Jamson, had gathered an amazing number of blackberries among the brambles by the riverbank. Srilani kept watch along the western side of the area, and Aldan took the eastern edge. When Sam and Linus took their place, Srilani and Aldan returned to the center to break their long fast from the day before.

"I'm happy you're a good hunter, Srilani," Aldan said. He took a bite and closed his eyes with an uplifted expression.

Srilani savored her perfectly roasted meat. The lack of seasoning didn't matter in the least. "Thank El that René has a knack for cooking. Killing prey isn't something I enjoy, but I certainly don't mind eating."

"Having food to eat is a good thing, believe me." He popped a handful of berries into his mouth, chewing with obvious relish.

A low rumble of sound drew their attention to Kazka, who abandoned his bone, rising slowly to his feet. He stood at rigid attention, his muzzle pointed to the west, where Linus had gone.

"Look at Kazka's ruff," Maelan said. "It's standing up from his neck all the way to his tail."

The hairs on the back of Srilani's neck stood up, too, and she set her food aside.

Kazka lifted one paw, like a runner preparing to start a race.

"Aldan—" Linus's yell was abruptly silenced, and Kazka took off, pelting through the grass in a straight line.

Aldan dropped everything and ran after the wolfhound.

Another shout rang out, and Srilani turned to René. Her voice was a hiss. "Quick. Hide with the twins."

She ran after Kazka and Aldan. She was within a few yards of Aldan when he drew his sword and engaged a large Norlan soldier. Kazka had his jaws wrapped around a shorter soldier's sword arm in a bone-crushing hold. Linus sprawled, motionless, on the ground nearby.

"Get clear!" The larger man shouted at Srilani. "Get clear!" The man wore the brown uniform of a Norlan soldier with its slash of red on each shoulder. His helmet had a sun-guard cloth that covered his neck and shoulders, also bordered in red.

The soldier met Aldan's attack with practiced skill and easily deflected the danger. The stranger went on the offensive, and it was Aldan who had to defend himself.

Srilani's heart rushed, and deep pain filled her chest as she looked for an opening, any way to help Aldan.

"Run, Princess!" The Norlander's voice was a roar in her ears. "Srilani, run!" The tall soldier pressed Aldan hard, and Aldan tried without success to disengage, to gain some distance from the man's flashing blade.

Srilani launched herself at the taller soldier, throwing all of her weight into his side. He staggered, and Aldan immediately took advantage of the opening she'd given him.

Aldan's opponent scrambled to recover his balance, yelling, "Are you daft, girl? Get clear, Your Highness!"

Srilani froze. Marstan. He was using Marstan, and his voice was familiar. She focused on the man's face.

"Olson?"

"Yes!"

"Olson, don't!" The words tore out of her throat, raw and urgent. "Don't strike him."

Olson didn't seem to hear her plea, preparing to attack again. A split second later, Srilani jumped between the two men. She caught Olson's wrist with both hands, hanging on for dear life. "Olson! No!" They overbalanced and fell together.

Sam chose that moment to appear, sword at the ready, looking like a wild man.

Srilani scrambled away from Olson. "Sam! Put your sword down. Friends!"

"Kazka! Down!" She waved to Sam. "Sam. Pull the dog off. These men are friends."

Sam hesitated, glancing between Srilani and the Norlan soldier. Then he grabbed Kazka's collar of twined rope. "Down, dog. Down!" At last, Kazka released his hold on the shorter man's arm but continued to struggle against Sam's hold, lunging and snapping at his victim.

"Kazka! Down!" And Sam forced the dog to the ground, shutting off his protests with ruthless force.

The silence after the sudden fury was shocking. Srilani held her hand out to the tall man. "Captain Olson, is it really you? Why are you wearing those clothes?"

"May El bless you, Your Highness." The soldier bowed low. He indicated his companion. "I'm sure you remember Lieutenant Edson." The other man stopped dusting himself off and bowed.

Olson gave her a quizzical look. "We wear these clothes whenever we cross the border on missions."

She bit her lip. "Of course you do." What a foolish question. "We thought we were being pursued by Norlan soldiers."

He crossed his arms. "To give you credit, we've had a difficult time catching up to you."

"You know these men?" Aldan asked.

"Yes." She looked past Aldan. "How is Linus?"

Aldan reached Linus in a couple of strides and bent over his prone form. Sam, still holding Kazka's collar, turned to look. "Is he dead?"

Aldan shook his head. "He's breathing."

This time Olson spoke in Norlan, "I struck him on the head with the hilt of my weapon." He turned back to Srilani. "Who are these men?"

"I'll introduce you in a minute." She hurried to kneel beside Linus. Aldan was pale and sweaty, and his hands shook. She ran gentle fingers over Linus's scalp. "He has a bump right here. Linus is stunned, but he'll probably wake up soon."

Aldan's fingers searched Linus's crown, and she guided his hand to the spot. "See?" He nodded, and she released his fingers.

"Princess, who are these men?" Olson seemed nonplussed by the situation. He still held his sword. Edson stood off to the side, wary eyes on the dog.

Srilani straightened to her full height and indicated the brothers with her hand. "Put away your weapons. These men are our friends, Captain Olson. We owe them a life debt."

<hr />

Aldan stared across the fire at Captain Olson. The soldier from the Northern Marst Palace Guard looked as tough as venison jerky. He had grizzled hair, closely cropped, and skin as weathered as the side of a barn. Fierce hazel eyes flashed from beneath bristling eyebrows.

Srilani had mentioned Olson's name before, as one of her many mentors. The man was old enough to be her father, but neither Olson nor Srilani stood on ceremony with each other. The captain felt free to speak his mind, even to the point of criticizing her decision to join forces with the brothers.

"Princess, this is going to cost you dearly," Olson said. "Norlan pirates, for the love of El! What were you thinking? And what of your sisters? What will people say of them when you return to Kaeson and your story gets out?"

"I've already told you — they aren't pirates. They were captives aboard the *Cathartid* just as we were. And they've saved us numerous times. If not for Aldan, Sam, and Linus, we wouldn't be here, alive and well."

Aldan looked down at Srilani. She sat next to him, at odds with the Marstan custom for unmarried ladies. Jamson sat on his other side. They were treating him as an equal, but so far, they hadn't shared his identity with their father's men.

Olson folded his arms across his chest. "It's good that we found you before you reached the border. Edson and I can take you home and none of this will have to be known except to your parents."

Srilani's hands folded into fists in her lap, but it was her brother who spoke.

"No. That is not our wish." Jamson's words were sharp, and both of the soldiers rocked back. The resemblance to his oldest sister was marked.

Aldan struggled to define the subtle difference. Jamson was acting as the heir to the throne.

The prince sat up straight, hands resting in his lap and face composed. "Our will is for the brothers to return to Kaeson with us as guests of honor. We owe them our lives. Our father owes them a reward. They are our responsibility."

Olson's eyes narrowed. He searched all of the faces around the fire before responding to Jamson's orders. "As you will, Your Highness." His words sounded reluctant. "We must think carefully on how your friends are to be presented to the court and to the Palace Guard to avoid unsavory rumors."

"What sort of rumors are you suggesting?" Srilani's voice was as smooth as ice, but there was no mistaking the heat that lurked beneath the cool tone.

Olson gave her a wary glance. "I think you can guess, my lady. You've been alone with these men for weeks."

"We — all of us — have been together for weeks," Jamson said.

Srilani tensed beside him, and Aldan couldn't resist a peek at her face. What Jamson said was true, except for the one night Srilani had spent alone with him as they kept watch together. Briefly, her eyes rose to meet his. Could it be that she was remembering that night too?

"You can say that until you run out of breath, Your Highness," Olson said. "But some will take this opportunity to blacken Princess Srilani's character. Hers, for sure, and possibly Princess Renélan's as well."

Srilani shrugged, and her voice sounded bitter. "Captain Olson, you know as well as I that there are some who love to spread rumors, lies, and innuendos about us. Undoubtedly, more people will believe their hateful stories. It cannot be helped. The truth tends to come out, for good or ill. If we attempt to hide from the truth, our evasions will only add fuel to the fire."

Abruptly, she stood up. "My sisters and I have some business to take care of in the river. We will talk more tomorrow."

⋈

Srilani handed her pack to Linus and bent to retrieve another. "How does your head feel this morning?"

"Hurts," he said. He lashed the pack onto Stocking's back.

"Today won't be pleasant for you," she said. "Neither will tomorrow or the next day. I ought to know after my experience aboard the ship."

René, who worked across from them, came around the mare. "If we pass any willow trees, we can harvest some of the bark. Why didn't I think of doing that before now? This evening, I'll brew you some tea to relieve your pain, Linus."

"Bend down and let me look at your eyes again," René said. She examined Linus's eyes in the dim light, holding his face between her hands. She released him and smiled. "You'll do. Let us know if you feel light-headed or drowsy. Don't try to tough it out."

René drew Srilani aside. "When are you going to tell Olson the truth about Aldan?"

"Today. But I won't be the one to break the news — I'm leaving that up to Jamson. I allowed myself to get angry and upset yesterday, and I don't trust myself not to say something I'll regret. Not yet."

"What he said was true," René said, a crease appearing between her brows. "But I agree with you — trying to hide what's happened to us and our relationship with Aldan . . . and the others . . . would be much, much worse for our reputation." Her eyes strayed to Sam and Aldan who were breaking down the campsite.

"What was I supposed to do?" Srilani spread her hands. "We needed help traveling across Norland. How many times have the brothers saved our skins?"

"I know."

"After we found out about Aldan, I felt that El had sent us across the Great Gulf to find him and bring him back with us."

"I agree." René's supportive words soothed like a balm. "Srilani, you did what you had to do, and I'm not second guessing your decisions. Give Olson time to think this through. He'll come around once he's spent some time with Aldan and his brothers."

⋈

Before Sol rose above the tree line, the entire party was ready to mount up. Aldan watched the officers approach on horseback. Olson and Lieutenant

Edson had taken over the watch duties so they'd stayed a fair distance away. Srilani and Jamson were engaged in a deep conversation off to the side.

Kazka growled as the men came nearer. Linus rested his hand on the wolfhound's head, and the dog subsided.

Captain Olson, impressive in his Norlan uniform, dismounted next to Aldan. Edson remained astride his horse, keeping his eyes trained on the horizon.

Olson nodded to the brothers and offered a slight bow to René and Maelan. "May El bless you."

René acknowledged his greeting, but her usual sweet smile was missing. "Captain, why are you wearing the Norlan colors this morning?"

"Prince Jamson agreed that we should continue in disguise. This way, Edson and I can pass through villages to gather more information. Given what we already know about King Dzor's activities, it seems prudent."

René clasped her hands together.

"You are troubled, Your Highness?"

"I hate to mention it, but as long as we are in Norland, do not continue to call us by our titles or in any way acknowledge our rank."

Olson's brows flew up. "Ah. You are right, Daughter. Edson, did you hear that?"

"Yes, sir."

The captain switched his attention to the brothers. Aldan returned the favor, studying this man who dared to criticize Srilani. Olson's shrewd expression, easy stance, and graying hair gave him the air of a man used to great authority. Edson, too, seemed confident although he appeared to be a score of years younger than the captain.

The silence, unbroken even by Maelan, grew onerous by the time Srilani returned to the group beside Jamson.

"Olson, there is something important you need to know," Jamson said. "And you too, Edson. You must swear to guard this secret until we have seen my father."

Olson nodded. "I so swear," he said, and Edson echoed the oath.

Jamson swallowed and cleared his throat. "In fact, there are two secrets.

You must guard the first secret until you die. You are not permitted to reveal it to anyone else."

Both officers wore puzzled expressions. "As you wish," Olson said. He looked even more curious when Srilani and her sisters moved away from the group.

Jamson removed his belt as he explained about the secret mark. "Mardan's Mark is a strictly guarded secret. My mark is here, but Aldan's mark is on the opposite side. Show them."

The cool morning air chilled Aldan's skin as he pulled up the hem of his shirt, raising goose flesh all over his body. Why couldn't Mardan have put the mark on his sons' ankles or somewhere else less personal?

As soon as the officers had had enough time to compare the marks, Aldan shoved his shirt back into place and made a production of strapping on his belt, prolonging the moment before he had to face them again.

Edson obviously hadn't figured it out yet, but under his bushy brows, Olson's eyes glittered with instant understanding. "All these years later, Baydan's son still lives. Amazing."

He stepped closer and peered at Aldan's face with renewed interest. "Ye-e-s. I saw your father a few times before he died, and you resemble him. Probably explains why I felt I'd seen you before." He blinked and stepped back. "Pardon me for staring so rudely. Extraordinary."

Olson cleared his throat and addressed Jamson. "We need to be on our way. Now it's doubly important to get you all safely across the border."

CHAPTER FIFTY

"That's the village marked on your map, Aldan," Olson said. He pointed to the south. "That means we're about . . . let's see . . . five days from the fortress at the Cauldron at our current rate of speed. I've been through there many times over the years as a spy."

Olson had proved to be an excellent teacher, and Aldan concentrated on everything he had to say. He flexed his sore shoulders. He'd sparred with the captain in practice sessions the past two evenings. Olson was stronger than any man his age had a right to be, and Aldan had been punished repeatedly by the hard blows he'd been forced to parry.

Olson continued his lecture. "The reach of Azor's priests isn't as strong this close to Northern Marst. Many of the people around here don't worship Azor at all."

Srilani rode on Olson's other side, bow at the ready, eyes on the path ahead. Olson's comment brought her attention back to the conversation. "Truly? I've never heard that before."

"It's true enough. So far from the swamps of central Norland, the pull of Azor isn't as strong. Who cares about a monster in the swamps when you've never seen one?" He glanced over at her. "I owe you a thousand apologies, Srilani."

Her brows rose. "Oh?"

Aldan hid a grin. She wasn't going to let the officer off the hook without a full confession.

Olson's saddle creaked as he twisted to face her. "Don't play dumb with me, Daughter. I'm well aware I offended you the evening we . . . ah . . . ran into each other."

"I'll recover."

Olson snorted. "And I shouldn't have been so blunt."

"But you were right — people are going to think the worst. Our people have little enough love for me, and they'll enjoy speculating about what happened while we were gone."

"I'm just saying, for the record, that it isn't fair. And I'm sorry that I wasn't fair to you." He faced forward again. "Now that I've seen the map you took from the pirate ship, I'm thinking we've got a traitor back home. A member of the court, perhaps, or an officer in the Palace Guard. Or both. It's too much of a coincidence that this map — a map created by one of our own map makers — was in the hands of the pirate who took you."

"The same thought has occurred to us," she said. She leaned forward in the saddle to look across at Aldan. "Do you know how Rozar came to be off our coast the day of the Solstice Festival?"

Aldan reviewed his memories. "Maybe. I know the map came to Rozar from the hand of King Dzor. Rozar went on and on about it because he was so pleased with the gift. But a few days before Rozar abducted you, he had a visitor aboard the *Cathartid*."

"Where was that?" Olson asked.

"Off the Marstan coast somewhere. A stranger in a green uniform boarded the ship from a sailboat."

Olson's exclamation was almost a yelp. "A *green* tunic? Are you sure?"

"Absolutely. He spoke Marstan, and so did Captain Rozar. Rozar was excited about the news the stranger brought, and we changed course immediately. A few days later, Rozar captured Jamson and his sisters."

One at a time Olson held up the fingers of his right hand, ticking off the facts. "First, a map made in Northern Marst is acquired by King Dzor. Maps are expensive and rare — that's suspicious. Second, King Dzor gives his friend Captain Rozar the precious map. Third, an officer from *Southern Marst* pays a visit to Captain Rozar. And fourth, a few days later the heirs to Northern Marst are taken on the only day of the year we give most of the guards a day off duty. Too many coincidences point to a plot."

"You've forgotten to mention one other thing," Srilani said. "The *Cathartid* also had the rightful heir to the southern throne on board as Captain Rozar's slave."

Olson rubbed his neck and shook his head. "Far too many coincidences. There's no denying Baydan's death and Aldan's disappearance were part of a treasonous plot. But how is it all tied together?"

Aldan tilted his head. "How do you know the officer was from Southern Marst?"

"Northern Marst colors are sapphire blue," Srilani said. "Southern Marst colors are emerald green."

"I feel stupid," Aldan said. "Green was the main color I saw in my visions. The officer had to be from Southern Marst."

"He might have been a Northerner wearing a disguise," Olson said. "Sorry. Once a spy, always a spy. It's the way we think." He sighed. "If we have a traitor in the Palace Guard or in the court, we need to keep this information to ourselves until we talk directly with King Terson. I think it's fair to say that Northern Marst is in danger from every direction."

Olson's bright eyes examined Aldan. "Son, you're returning to the Twin Kingdoms at a very dangerous time."

ᛗ

Srilani positioned the last spit of fish over the fire and stepped back from the heat. Aldan and Sam were on watch and René and Edson slept, even though it wasn't yet evening. Cooking duty wasn't so bad. And Sam was right — fish made a nice change. According to Olson and Edson, this was a space where they'd camped before, between settlements and off the beaten path.

"Jamson, Maelan, and Linus — you're in charge here," Srilani said. "I'm going to fill the water skins."

At this point, none of the three needed instruction on cooking fish on a spit. They'd all proved to be very capable. Jamson left off talking to Olson and took a spot by the fire ring. Maelan sat next to Linus, peppering him with questions about playing the flute.

Srilani gathered all the available water skins. This was the moment, and she might not get another opportunity. "Olson, would you please go with me to fill these?"

Immediately, Olson stood and sheathed the sword he'd been sharpening with his whetstone.

She handed him several of the water skins, and they descended toward the river. Fertile black soil muted their footsteps as they pushed through the dense vegetation near the water. The briskly flowing stream hissed and gurgled on its way to the Rhynder, drowning out all but the loudest birdcalls.

She glanced back, searching behind them. One of Olson's eyebrows quirked up. She perched on a small stone ledge and poured out the last few drops in the first water skin before plunging it under the fresh water.

"You've probably guessed I want to talk privately."

Olson knelt at her side to fill one of his water skins. "So? What's on your mind?"

"Uncle, I want a promise from you."

He gave her a sharp look but said nothing.

"You told us that a search party of guardian priests had reached the town you visited yesterday. That means they're in our vicinity." Her voice threatened to quaver, and she stopped to lick her lips. Why was it so hard to start this conversation?

"Yes."

"And you said there are soldiers looking for us too."

"Without a doubt. We reached Dullon Bridge the day after your *visit* there. The whole town was in an uproar. Smoke was everywhere, the entire wharf was gone, and soldiers were busy trying to retrieve their horses for many leagues along the main road."

Olson sat back on his heels and paused, a hint of a smile on his lips. "That was when Edson and I knew we were on the right track. Finally. That old groom you tied up in the stables was babbling to anyone who would listen about a blue-eyed lady. That story was also being passed around in the village yesterday." He paused. "Well done, by the way. It was a bold thing to do. Whose idea was it to release the horses?"

"Mine."

His hard face lit up. "My student has made me proud."

"Thank you." She plunged the next water skin into the stream. "The thing is—" Her throat closed off the words. "I've been thinking . . ."

"Princess, just ask."

"Promise me that you will put the safety of Jamson and Aldan first, before the rest of us." She said it all in one breath.

Olson's brows drew together. "Aldan isn't my responsibility, but you are. My charge from King Terson is to find and return his children."

She placed a hand on his sleeve and waited for him to meet her eyes. "But Father isn't here. He doesn't know the situation. Don't you see? Aldan's survival is important to both kingdoms."

Olson didn't seem convinced, and she plunged ahead. "Father's always believed that Habidan was behind King Baydan's assassination. We all know Queen Yolani has no control over her husband. I've heard rumors that Habidan is expanding his forces."

"That's not a rumor."

She squeezed his arm. "Then you have to agree that Northern Marst is the only possible target of such an army. It is in our kingdom's best interest to support Aldan's return to the throne. But we can't support him if he's dead." She removed her hand from his sleeve but continued to hold his gaze. "So I want your promise to put Aldan's survival ahead of everyone else's except Jamson."

"What about you and your sisters? What if I protected Aldan and you or your sisters were captured? Do you have any idea what happens to women captured by Norlan priests or soldiers?"

"We would die rather than be captured." She stood up straight and lifted her chin. "Do you think only men in the Palace Guard are willing to die for the good of the kingdom, Captain?"

"Brave words, Princess." Olson faced her with a solemn expression. "But there are things worse than death, especially for women."

Her heart skipped a beat. "We know that. Oh, believe me, we do know that. We've already decided what we must do in case of capture. My sisters and I have an agreement."

"Well, I haven't agreed to it." Olson folded his arms and stared at her. "Srilani, why are we having this discussion?"

His tone sounded reasonable. *So* reasonable. He sounded exactly like Father. Like lava beneath the earth, something hot and dangerous flowed through her, looking for a way out.

"There's little reason to think we won't escape Norland," he said, warming to his theme. "Edson and I know every path and secret place between here and the border. We have good information. Why invite trouble?"

I'm a man. You're a girl. I'm the teacher. You're the student. I'm right. You're wrong.

Pressure built behind her eyes and the tips of her ears grew warm. She copied his stance, crossing her arms to hold the heat inside, and refused to look away. "I'm not inviting trouble if I plan for disaster before it happens, Olson. You taught me that yourself. I want your promise."

"You won't get it."

They stared at one another for several seconds as her fever grew to a white-hot glow.

"Then your blood be upon your head, Captain Olson." She gripped her hands together to keep them from shaking. "I will not forgive you if Aldan is captured or killed, and I won't forget to bring disaster to your house."

The fish turned to ash in Srilani's mouth. Without a word, she passed the remainder to Sam. It was just as well that Olson was on watch so she didn't have to make conversation with him.

"We should reach the Cauldron tomorrow," she said. The twins nudged each other and René sighed. "What do you think? Should we take all our supplies with us or leave them behind?"

Stunned silence followed the question, and Aldan shifted at her side.

"Unless we know for certain that we're going to make it to the Cauldron, I think we should pack as usual," Sam said. "If we have another night out here, we'd be sorry not to have our supplies."

Aldan nodded. "We should take the supplies with us, but I think we should pack differently. We should be ready for anything. If we are pursued, we need to leave everything behind that slows us down."

"We aren't going to abandon Stockings, are we?" Maelan's voice rose. "We can't leave her behind!"

"Maelan . . ." Srilani hesitated. "I don't think that will be necessary."

"But you're not sure?"

Jamson came to Srilani's rescue. "If we release Stockings, she'll want to stay with the other horses, Maelan. She's slower than the rest, but she'll follow us. You worry too much."

Linus leaned in. "I can tie the ropes on the packs so it's easy to release. Stockings will be free to run. But what about Kazka?"

Srilani smiled at Linus. "Your dog is well able to stay up with the horses. And that's a clever idea to help the horse. Thank you."

"You are welcome."

Aldan stood and offered her his hand. "Let's do this now, while we still have light from the fire." She took his hand and let him help her to her feet. How was she going to do without him after tomorrow?

⋀⋀

The long gray fur on Aldan's neck stood straight up and a growl rattled in his throat. The vision was exactly as he'd seen it before. He threw back his head and pierced the darkness with a long howl. An answering call came from beyond the trees to his right, and he howled again. Others called, their cries echoing through the forest.

Paws thudded on the thick carpet of leaves, and Srilani entered the clearing, blue eyes narrowed. The pale light of midnight dappled her ghost-white fur. The rest of the pack joined them, circling about in a frenzy of excitement. They began to run.

The pack raced uphill, straining forward to reach the crest. But they weren't only striving toward a goal. They were running from an enemy.

Aldan woke with a start. The fire was a distant memory, its embers cold and dark. The moon's light spread a milky film over the sleeping figures of his friends. The only other gleam of light was the moon reflecting from Srilani's eyes. She was flat on her back, staring at the constellations above, one hand holding her grandmother's pendant. As if she sensed his scrutiny, she turned her head toward him, and he caught a glint of blue.

He pushed back his blanket and rose to a crouch. She lifted up on her elbow. He gestured to the south and moved away from the group. The grass tickled his feet. After a moment's hesitation, she followed him to the tree line.

"What is it?" she whispered.

He took her hand in his and drew her closer. He bent and spoke near her ear. "I know what my vision means."

"Which one?" Her fingers squeezed his.

"The wolves. Remember what I told you before?"

Her eyes widened and she nodded.

"I had the vision again tonight," he said. "We are the wolves, and we're being chased."

Silver moonlight washed over her face, molding itself to the planes of her cheekbones and her mouth. He raised his free hand to trace one of her brows. She caught his hand and pillowed it against the side of her face. Her eyes closed, and her voice sounded sleepy. "What does it mean?"

The skin of her cheek against his palm was too soft to be real. He shook his head to clear the fog. "What?"

The corners of her lips lifted and her eyes opened to slits. "The dream, Aldan. What does it mean?"

"It means we need to wake everyone and leave."

Her smile went into eclipse and she raised her head from his palm. "Now?"

"No. Not yet." His thumb ran across her lower lip. His voice sounded hoarse. "Just one more moment." His fingers slid under her chin, and he tilted her head to study her features again. Straight nose. Soft temples. Arched brows and twin pools of sapphire. "You are entirely beautiful, Srilani. May El bless you."

She swayed toward him. "May El bless you too."

Slowly, by torturous fractions, he lowered his head and her lashes fluttered down. She sighed softly against his mouth as he fit his lips to hers. The kiss was like spice, warm and sweet at once. His hand found her waist and her fingers clutched at his shirt.

He broke off the kiss and rested his forehead against hers. How had they come to this?

One of her hands lifted to his jaw. "Do that again," she whispered.

A low voice cut between them. "If you do that again, Aldan, I will gut you like a fish."

Srilani gasped, and Aldan's entire body jerked. They sprang apart.

"Captain Olson." Srilani sounded breathless.

"Princess." Olson managed to fit an entire world of disapproval into her title.

CHAPTER FIFTY-ONE

Aldan held out his hand, and Srilani grasped it like a lifeline. Her other hand rose to touch her lips. Had she actually begged Aldan to kiss her again?

Olson stood about ten feet away with his dagger drawn. His anger washed over them, and his lips twisted into a sneer. "How long has this been going on, Princess?" Her title sounded like a curse word. "Quite a cozy arrangement, don't you think?"

At least he kept his voice low. "It's not like that, Olson." *Oh, El — Help me!* "You know me better than to think—"

"After this afternoon? I'm not sure I know you at all." He adjusted his hold on the dagger. "You know the law."

"Don't. Olson, don't do anything hasty." She stepped closer to Aldan, as if to shield him, but Aldan released her hand and moved in front of her.

"Blame me, Captain Olson. I got carried away. She's innocent."

"Innocent?" Olson's brows knotted together. "Let me tell you . . . it didn't sound innocent to me."

Heat blistered her cheeks. *Do that again. Do that again!*

"I've never touched her like that before," Aldan said.

Olson advanced a couple of steps, and Srilani's throat went dry. They were unarmed. Barefoot. Not much chance of putting up a fight, and they couldn't run. Olson was a hardened soldier in full armor, and he seemed intent on carrying out the letter of the law this instant. *Do that again.*

Curse my tongue. She'd brought this disaster upon them both.

Aldan chuckled, and her head jerked up at the reckless sound.

"I've never touched her before," Aldan repeated. The corners of his eyes tightened. "Unless you count the night we spent alone together."

Olson stiffened, and Srilani's breath whooshed out in a hiss. "What are you doing?"

Aldan turned and drew her forward. He looped his arms behind her waist and pulled her close.

She pushed against his chest. "Let me go. You're making it worse."

Deep grooves bracketed Aldan's mouth as he held her gaze. "If we're going to die, let it be for doing something really wrong," he said. "Should we tell Olson that I held you in my arms all night long? Or what we told Nik and Drajna — that you're my woman?"

Srilani thumped him with her fist. "Are you mad?"

"Should we tell Olson it was *you* who discovered the mark on the bare skin of my back?"

At his damning words, all the fight went out of her. Why was Aldan telling Olson all of their secrets?

Olson stared at them for so long that Srilani forgot to breathe. Blackness threatened her vision. She gasped for air. Aldan held her upright — he seemed as steady as ever and his voice, though soft in volume, sounded firm and confident.

"What will you do, Captain Olson?" Aldan turned her in his arms so they both faced Olson. "Will you hear the whole story or just strike us down? Don't you want to know the reason we were out here talking when we'd rather be asleep?"

Olson snorted. "Talking, is it?" But he sheathed his dagger and crossed his arms over his chest. "Let's hear it, but don't think you're off the hook for the rest."

⟁

Aldan donned his boots, strapped on his belt and scabbard, stowed his blanket, and rushed to help saddle the horses. He grappled with the apparent enormity of his transgression with Srilani as he helped Linus load their gear.

"Quickly. It's too late to hide our tracks," Olson said. "Put your boots on and load up. Move, move, move!" Nobody questioned his orders. Olson's verdict for Srilani was deferred. At least the captain had taken Aldan's explanation of his vision seriously.

It wasn't as if Srilani had neglected to warn him about the traditions and laws that applied to female descendants of the king. He'd known the extreme care that was taken to preserve their modesty and virtue — even more so for the First Princess. And yet, outside the confines of the royal palace, those barriers had broken down.

Srilani didn't utter a word as she readied to leave, as if she'd lost the power of speech. Aldan glanced at her set face several times as they hurried through their tasks. He led Flame to stand near Srilani's mare, and when everyone was ready to leave, he stayed beside her.

Olson and Edson took a couple of moments to switch out of the Norlander uniforms and into northern tunics. The only conclusion to draw from their actions was that they planned to reach the fortress before the day ended. *Today.* Aldan's stomach turned over.

Olson motioned Jamson to ride at his side, and they took the lead, setting a jarring pace. By unspoken consent, René and Maelan were second in line. Linus and Sam rode behind the girls, leading Stockings, and Aldan stayed beside Srilani while Lieutenant Edson brought up the rear.

The moon was nearly full, the open terrain easy to negotiate. Half an hour passed as they posted over rolling pastureland, and then they reached the top of a hill overlooking the spot where they'd rested.

"Look!" Sam's low exclamation brought everyone's attention around. Below, among the trees near the river's edge, a dozen torches wavered.

René gasped. "El save us. They're so close."

Olson spurred his mount to a faster clip, and they pushed on through the waning moonlight. He led them into a shallow valley, across a little bridge, and down to the tributary's edge. "Let the horses drink, but not too much. We will ride beside the river for a few leagues and cross back over at a place I know."

The moon set, and soon after, dawn broke in a glory of golden light. They found the place Olson sought. He led them downriver for half a league, holding the horses to a walk through the shallow water until they reached a particularly rocky spot. Here they dismounted and trudged up the embankment to the plain above. As the terrain leveled out, they were all panting hard.

"How far?" Srilani asked.

Olson didn't look her direction as he answered. "We are half a day from the lip of the Cauldron, directly across from the fortress." He turned his back to her and led his horse away.

Srilani's head dipped as if it were too heavy for her shoulders, like a cut flower out of water. Aldan caught René's puzzled glance and ground his teeth. The captain could at least keep up appearances until they reached the fortress.

They left the trees behind at the river's edge and were at the mercy of the late summer heat. From there, they alternated walking with riding as Sol beat down on them.

The stirrup-high grass, bleached gold by Sol's rays, formed clumps between plentiful stony rises of volcanic rock. The soil was dark and full of small stones wherever it was visible. There were no signs of the men who'd found their camp, but Aldan didn't derive comfort from that seemingly hopeful sign. This land, like the rolling waves of the Great Gulf, was capable of hiding pursuers from view.

As the morning lengthened into midday, the party strung out enough to permit private conversation. Aldan and Srilani walked between their horses as had become their custom. She seemed distracted and remote, and Aldan searched for something to talk about.

"You made me name my horse," he finally said. "So what did you name yours?"

"Stella." Srilani fingered the mare's creamy mane.

Had he somehow lost all the trust she'd given him? He touched her arm. "Can you forgive me?"

She darted a glance at his face, not meeting his eyes. "For the kiss?" She looked away. "Of course I forgive you. I was equally at fault. For telling Olson all the rest?" She shrugged one shoulder. "Why did you do that?"

"I wanted to surprise Olson into giving us a hearing," he said. "He seems like a fair man, but I thought he might execute you immediately if I didn't do something. I just wanted to make him curious enough to listen to your side of the story."

"He was already angry with me, and then he found us in such a compromising situation. Olson is a very senior officer in the Palace Guard, and the older officers are almost a law unto themselves. Nobody — not even my parents — would have questioned his judgment."

"What about your sisters and brother? They know the truth."

"It wouldn't matter because none of them are of age."

"Will Olson listen to reason?"

She hesitated. "I believe so. He's been my mentor since I was six. Or maybe younger. But he was terribly angry yesterday. You're right. It could have ended badly."

"And now?"

"It may still end badly, but that seems less likely now. Let's talk of something else," she said.

He hunted around for a safer topic. "Assuming we both make it to Kaeson alive, what's the best approach to win your father's support?"

They focused on various scenarios until it was time to mount again. After a few minutes at a brisk trot, Edson spurred his horse to the front of the procession and spoke with Olson.

Olson waved Jamson forward with Edson and fell to the rear. He passed Srilani and raised his voice. "Priests are behind us!"

Linus slowed to a halt, dismounted, and approached Stockings in long strides. Kazka danced around Linus as he released Stockings from her burden and her halter. He remounted and spurred his horse to catch up with Sam. Aldan looked back. A large number of guardian priests, all in black armor like the set he'd taken in Minazor, were visible on the horizon.

Aldan wrinkled his nose. "What is that awful smell?"

"It's the Cauldron," Srilani said. "I've only visited the fortress once before, but the smell is unforgettable."

The rocky ground formed a gradual incline, rising and rising until it came to a sudden end. The group ranged themselves along the eastern edge and viewed their destination.

The Cauldron was a giant bowl spreading out to a diameter of roughly five leagues. Holes and vents pocked its surface. Some emitted sulfurous fumes. The Rhynder River meandered from north to south at the base of the eastern edge, cutting a valley through the southern end of the Cauldron. Directly across the giant basin, at the top of a rocky cliff, a fortress looked out toward them.

Aldan stared down the eastern face of the crater, a steep decline of at least a hundred feet covered in tiny volcanic gravel. "How are we going to get down to the river? Is there a path?"

"More than one path," Olson said. "But we don't have time to reach any of them. We'll have to go down the hard way." He took a few moments to study the situation behind them. "The guardians have split into two parties. They're still behind us a ways, but I believe they'll use the paths to get down. They've probably forced us to this point, hoping we won't dare to make the descent. Even if we do, they may try to use a flanking maneuver."

Olson pointed to the long course ahead of them. "Our only defense is to stay out in front of them and make our way to the base of the fortress. As soon as I get near enough, I will signal the outpost so archers can cover us from above."

Maelan spoke up in a small voice. "Olson, I don't think I can ride my horse down that hill."

"You'll be fine, Princess. Head your horse straight down, lean back slightly, and let her do the work. Don't get sideways. Trust the horse. Edson will descend with you after I go down with Prince Jamson." He scanned the entire group. "As soon as you reach the bottom, ride as hard as you can. Don't spare your horses."

Olson turned to Jamson. "Your Highness, let's go."

They made the descent look easy. Dust and scree flew everywhere as the horses headed down the long slope, sliding part of the way on their haunches and speeding up at the bottom of the hill. Aldan held his breath as Maelan followed, far enough from Edson that they wouldn't interfere with one another. Edson called instructions and encouragement to her as they took their turn.

"Here comes Stockings, at last," Sam said. "And the priests are getting closer. I think René and Srilani should go next."

Srilani turned to Sam. "Why don't you go with René? Then I'll go with Linus and Aldan. René and I have ridden down steep hills before, and we can coach you."

Aldan shook his head. "Let Linus go down with René. He's the next youngest."

Sam and Srilani instantly agreed. At that moment, Stockings took the initiative to head down the slope. René gave a nervous laugh. "I'm glad she decided to go now, instead of when we were halfway down. It's our turn, Linus."

Linus called to Kazka and urged his horse forward. The dog paced and whined as Linus's horse stepped over the lip.

"Go, you crazy dog," Sam said, but Kazka only grew more agitated. Finally, Sam dismounted and gave Kazka a gentle push over the ledge. After that, the dog had no choice.

"Let's spread out," Srilani said. "Straight down. Loose on the reins and stay upright."

Srilani's heart threatened to block her throat. The side of the Cauldron was the longest slope she'd ever attempted. As soon as Linus, René, and Kazka reached the base of the hill, they splashed across the Rhynder River. Fortunately, autumn was the dry season, and the river was at low stage.

"Ready?" Aldan asked.

Sam nodded and Srilani waved her hand.

"Go!"

Stella balked at the last moment, and Srilani slapped the horse's rump. The mare plunged forward and immediately began to slide. Ahead of her, both Aldan and Sam hung on for dear life as their horses braced on their haunches, skidding and jolting to the bottom.

"Loosen up on the reins!" Could they even hear her?

One after the other, with increasing speed, they splashed headlong through the river. Sam whooped, but Aldan was grimly silent, leaning over Flame's powerful neck.

She peeked over her shoulder. Her headdress unraveled and tore loose, flying off in the wind. To the north, a dozen priests rode single file down a path carved into the rock face. The path wound back and forth, keeping their pursuers from traveling quickly to the base. She looked to the left. Another group, half that size, was already in the basin to the south of them and getting closer. She bent low and urged Stella on.

Stella valiantly attempted to stay even with the two larger geldings, but Victor and Flame were created for speed and steadily drew ahead. They overtook Stockings and left her behind. In turn, Stella drew even with the packhorse and passed her as well.

Srilani checked the status of the hunting party to her left. Unbelievably, they'd drawn closer. The second group trailed far behind.

Jamson was ahead of her by a good ten minutes. Maelan rode close on his heels with the captain and the lieutenant.

A new noise was borne to her on the breeze — the blaring of horns. Olson and his lieutenant sounded an alarm to those in the fortress who watched over the plain. Tiny figures, like miniature toys, moved about on top of the edifice. More figures joined them. Praise El. They'd heard Olson's call.

We're going to make it.

Kazka lagged behind Linus and René, but his speed was astonishing. The dog's body bunched up and stretched out in long bounds. No wonder his kind could take down wolves.

Jamson reached the base at the far side and disappeared from view, followed closely by Maelan. One of the officers — she couldn't tell whom — stayed behind at the entryway while the other entered the hidden gateway. They blew their horns intermittently.

Srilani pictured the marvelous pathway leading to the fortress above the

Cauldron. Cut into the rock, it rose in a series of ramps twenty feet wide, suitable for men, beasts, and wagons to ascend and descend as needed. Guards were stationed all along the fortress road at a series of gates. Once past the first gate, they would be entirely safe.

The wind burned Srilani's eyes, and she brushed aside the tears that flooded her vision. The stench from the vents assailed her nose, and she resisted the urge to gag. Except for Stockings, she was dead last in this race. Aldan glanced back at her. He reined Flame in ever so slightly, probably so she could catch up with him.

"Don't wait for me!" A doomed protest. *Go on. Just ride.*

Stella stepped into a crevice, and Srilani shrieked as the horse stumbled and fell forward. She kicked free from the stirrups and concentrated on holding onto the reins. Her momentum, like a giant hand, pitched her over the horse's withers, and she fell hard on her back. The impact knocked every bit of air from her lungs. She was too stunned to breathe or move or think. Stella writhed, flailing her hooves in the air until she managed to right herself. The reins tore from Srilani's fist. She moaned and stretched to retrieve them, but the mare shied away and sped after the others.

"No!" The scream lanced through Srilani's chest. Frantically, she rose to her knees. Cold, dizzying pain engulfed her. A spiral of black dots spun in front of her eyes.

Perhaps she could catch Stockings.

She turned her head just in time to watch the old mare gallop past.

On the ground nearby, she spotted her shattered bow. It didn't matter — her quiver of arrows was attached to Stella's saddle. She still had her sword and dagger though. But half a dozen guardians bore down on her position in a cloud of gray dust. She didn't stand a chance.

Act. Her father's voice spoke in her ear. *Don't freeze because of fear.*

She struggled to her feet, and a fresh wave of vertigo struck. She swayed. *Get going. Go.*

She forced her uncooperative limbs to move, staggering toward the fortress. The thundering behind her increased in volume, and soon, she promised herself, she would turn and fight to the death.

CHAPTER FIFTY-TWO

Aldan fought Flame's instincts to stay with the other horses, and at last, the gelding obediently turned in a slow arc. Aldan urged the horse back toward Srilani. Even from this distance, he could tell she was hurt. She tried to run, but her gait was an unsteady lope. She stumbled forward, sword and dagger in her hands. The nearest group of guardians priests approached at a terrific rate of speed. They rode in an inverted V, three on a side, obviously intending to surround her. Could he possibly pull her up in front of him before they cut her down or took her captive?

She looked up, her white face strained, eyes wide. She'd seen him approaching, but instead of looking relieved, she seemed more terrified. The shouts of the men reached him, and he recognized two of them. Lector. And Bolz. The priests from Minazor.

Aldan arrived at her side seconds before the priests. No time to get her up on Flame's back. The bay drove his hocks deep into the volcanic dust as they halted. Aldan leapt from the saddle and drew his sword. Flame snorted in alarm, rearing up as the guardians drew even with them. The horse plunged through their ranks.

"You shouldn't have come," she gasped.

He didn't bother to answer, striking out at the closest man's thigh. He drew blood, and the man's horse reversed direction. Familiar battle-heat spread through his body as Lector shouted orders.

"Try to cover my back," Aldan said. He yanked one of their enemies from the saddle and slew him with a slice to the neck. He heaved the hapless man's body beneath the horses' hooves. The circle around them widened. The dead man's horse plunged into Bolz's mount.

Lector swung down, landing on his feet like a cat. He pulled a shield from his back and drew his sword. "Well, what have we here? Aldan, is it? And your lady. How exciting." He grinned. "Ah . . . she's injured."

Aldan resisted the impulse to glance at Srilani. "You're on the wrong side of the border, Lector."

One of the men laughed. An ugly sound.

Lector shrugged. "That border won't stand for long. You've put me to a lot of trouble, but I'll let you go if you'll surrender the lady."

Aldan lifted his brows. Not likely. He'd already killed a man and injured another. "And if I don't?"

"Why then, I'll have the pleasure of killing you." The priest paused. "And possibly the lady as well."

Srilani gave a feminine growl, and Aldan laughed. What a woman. He needn't ask what she planned to do.

At the same moment, they sprang apart, each lunging at their nearest opponent. In his case, the man was Lector. The head guardian deflected his blow with the shield, but Aldan had the satisfaction of wiping the grin from Lector's face. The priest answered with a counter-attack. Their blades scraped together. The priest shoved him away, and Aldan ducked as the man tried to brain him with the shield.

He scooped up a handful of the fine basalt scree and flung it in Lector's face. Then he swung his foot in a wide arc, catching Lector behind the knee and sending him onto his back.

Aldan risked a glance at Srilani. She was laboring against two henchmen who took turns trying to approach her.

A second man the size of a bear took Lector's place. Aldan feinted with his sword, and the man retreated a step. Aldan took the opportunity to kick Lector in the jaw as he tried to rise.

Bolz rode between them, aiming straight at Srilani. His mount struck her shoulder, spinning her around. She fell, her sword flying from her grasp.

Aldan narrowly missed a blow from his latest adversary. He parried the giant's strike and followed up with one of his own. Lector was on his feet again. Aldan ran a couple of steps to the side and kicked Lector's shield out of reach.

A low, rumbling sound heralded the approach of the other squad of guardian priests. Aldan faced Lector and the other man. Srilani was face down on the gravel. One of the guardians drove his boot into her ribs with enough force to lift her body from the ground.

Nausea welled up in Aldan's stomach, and bile coated his tongue. *Please don't let her die.*

With renewed zeal, he hacked at both Lector and the other man. Bolz circled around on his horse, and the injured man hung back, trying to staunch the blood flowing from his leg. At any moment, the other two would leave Srilani and attack him.

The giant beside Lector must have thought so too. He seemed to be biding his time. For an instant, he let his eyes wander to the others. Aldan sidestepped a blow from Lector and plunged his blade into the second priest's ribs. The brute tumbled into Lector, sending them both sprawling. Bolz lifted his weapon and urged his horse forward, ready to strike Aldan with a killing blow.

But a whirring of insect wings flew past Aldan. Blood bloomed from an arrow quivering in Bolz's shoulder. The priest bent over his horse's withers and clung to its mane.

Thud. Another arrow pierced the gravel near Lector. The head guardian pulled free of the dead man's weight and scrambled to recapture his horse's reins.

A third arrow pierced one of Srilani's opponents in the neck, and he dropped beside her prone form. His partner sprang into the saddle as the sound of swarming bees passed above their heads and a hail of arrows threatened. Lector and his remaining men whipped their horses into flight, racing toward the second squad of priests.

Aldan sheathed his sword and stooped over Srilani. Her eyes were closed. Gray dust coated her face and blood oozed from scrapes on her arms. "Srilani. Please—" Her blonde hair shielded part of her face, and he smoothed it back.

He placed his fingers on the side of her neck. A steady pulse beat under his fingertips. "Thank you. Thank you," he breathed.

More hoof beats returned his awareness to his surroundings. Sam guided Victor to Srilani's other side and dismounted before the horse came to a complete halt. "Is she alive?"

"Yes."

Flame stood several paces away, head hanging, pawing the ground and blowing hard. Sam slowly approached the animal and snagged his reins, leading him to Aldan. "Hurry. Mount, and I'll hand her up to you."

Every muscled protested as Aldan hauled himself into the saddle. Sam lifted Srilani from the Cauldron's floor and into Aldan's outstretched arms. Her head lolled in an alarming fashion, and Aldan struggled to position her body and control Flame at the same time.

Sam retrieved Srilani's weapons and remounted. The fleeing priests and those still in pursuit met in a confused tangle. Another flight of arrows left the heights of the fortress and persuaded all of the guardians to withdraw. Sam pulled ahead, and Aldan kicked his horse into a trot, trailing his brother through the treacherous terrain.

Aldan held Srilani so tightly his arm ached. She hung in his grasp, boneless and limp. They rode toward an opening at the base of the cliff where Lieutenant Edson waited.

The lieutenant guided his mount closer. "Is she alive?"

"For now."

Two soldiers in blue tunics waved them through the massive gate and barred the doors after they passed inside. Soldiers on horseback clogged the giant ramp leading to the fortress. Clearly, they were preparing to ride out after the trespassers. The crowd forced Sam and Aldan to slow their horses to a walk. Flame and Victor breathed hard, nostrils flaring and heads bobbing low. Officers shouted commands, and groups formed into squads as they attempted to pass.

Men surrounded Stella and Stockings to the left of the gate, and Stockings already wore a halter with a lead. Heads turned, though, at the strange sight of the young woman in Aldan's arms. A hush fell over those within their small radius.

"Make way for Princess Srilani!" Lieutenant Edson shouted.

A burly, red-faced sergeant hurried forward and waved a clump of men aside. "Here now, get outta the way, ladies! Can't you see the princess isn't well? Make way for the princess!"

Another man took up the sergeant's words and started to chant. "Make way for the princess! Make way for the princess!" Within a few seconds, the brothers were surrounded by a wall of sound. Like magic, the path opened up before them.

They rode through five or six gates, but none of these were barred like the gate at the base of the cliff. The cobbled street led up, zigging and zagging, first to the east, then to the west until it ended in the courtyard of the fortress.

René and Maelan rushed forward.

"What happened to Srilani?" René asked.

Maelan's eyes filled with tears. "Is she dead?"

Sam shook his head. "Not dead." He dismounted and strode to Aldan's side. "Her horse fell, and Srilani was thrown. The priests nearly captured her."

Aldan allowed Sam to take Srilani from his grasp.

"She's been injured," Aldan said. "Maybe she was hit on the head. At the very least, one of them kicked her in the ribs." He managed to alight from Flame's back without falling over. His knees threatened to buckle, and by sheer force of will, he stood up straight. Shock had set in, but he held out his arms and took Srilani from Sam.

René gave Srilani's head a cursory examination with her fingers. "I don't feel a bump. She's not bleeding except for the scrapes. We need a bed to put her in." Olson joined them, flanked by Jamson, whose face had lost all color. René turned to them. "Where can we go? We need to examine her for other injuries. Is there a healer who can help me?"

"Captain Ahn!" Olson raised his voice, and another man broke away from the crowd. He was tall and rangy but every inch in charge. "Where can we put Princess Srilani?"

"Follow me."

Aldan followed Captain Ahn into the shadowy recesses of the fortress, past corridors and doorways, guards and other workers. "Put her here. This is my wife's room, but she is away."

René and Maelan helped arrange the bedclothes and the pillow before Aldan laid her on the bed. René took his arm, pushing him toward the door. "Thank you, Aldan," she said. "I know you saved her life, but go away. Captain Ahn, if you have any healers, please send them to help."

They were dismissed. Aldan looked back, but René gave him another push. "I will send word after we know more."

Aldan reentered the corridor and found Jamson, the officers, and his brothers lined up against the wall.

Captain Ahn sized them up for a moment and then gestured at the hallway with a crooked smile. "Gentlemen, leave the women to their work. I think you all need something to drink. Olson, you know the way to the dining hall. I'll join you after I've located the healers."

Far in the distance, hunting horns echoed across the Cauldron.

CHAPTER FIFTY-THREE

"Srilani, are you awake?" Maelan's lips tickled her ear.

"I am now." But Srilani didn't open her eyes. If she held very still, the pain might stay in the corner of the room instead of sitting on her chest.

"I'm sorry I woke you. There's some soup for you if you're hungry."

Her stomach complained. When was the last time she'd eaten? The night the chase began. No. She'd given her supper to Sam. The fight with Olson had destroyed her appetite. So the night before that. The nasty confrontation with her mentor played again in her mind. She'd threatened Captain Olson, for the love of El. What had possessed her to do that? She'd only made things worse. And the kiss!

Maelan touched her shoulder. "Srilani? Do you want to eat?"

"Yes. Can you lift me up?" Facing the pain would be better than facing her thoughts. "You'd better get someone to help you."

Maelan sat on the end of the bed. "René will be here in a moment."

The spicy aroma of stew permeated the room, and her mouth watered. "How long have I slept?"

"About four hours. Six bells just rang. I think we arrived after noon, but everything got confused. You awoke during the examination, but then they gave you something to make you sleep."

"They?"

"René and the other healers — an old married couple. You have two cracked ribs. They say you fainted because of the pain."

Srilani processed this information. "How did I get here? My horse fell—"

"Aldan. And Sam. They went back and saved you. Aldan carried you here on Flame."

She suppressed a groan. Aldan seemed determined to put himself in harm's way.

※

Aldan looked across the dining hall table and cleared his throat. "Captain Olson . . . I mean, *General* Olson . . ." Oh, get the man's rank wrong. That would help his case. "We need to speak."

Olson's bushy eyebrows twitched upwards, and the gray thatch of hair on top of his head seemed to bristle. He ate another spoonful of stew. And another.

Olson was the general officer of the Palace Guard now. According to Captain Ahn, King Terson had named Olson to the office after he'd left on his mission to Norland. The king then sent notices of the promotion to all corners of Northern Marst.

Aldan tried again. "Would it be convenient to discuss our differences after you've finished your meal?"

Sam's fingers tapped on the tabletop, and Aldan met his eyes. Sam shrugged.

Aldan silently counted to ten. "Prince Jamson and his sisters have agreed to answer your questions, as have my brothers."

Slowly, Olson set his spoon aside and lifted his eyes to Aldan's face. "I don't need to hear what everyone else has to say. Only you." He shifted his gaze to Sam and Linus and back to Aldan. "It would be better to keep this between the two of us, believe me."

Jamson, on Aldan's other side, put down his cup. "General Olson."

"Yes, Your Highness?"

"Aldan has our support." Jamson had used the majestic plural, making his words an obvious command.

Olson nodded. "I understand." He stood up. "Aldan, please walk with me."

They ended up on top of the fortress overlooking the Cauldron. The sunset highlighted the steam, gases, and smoke emitting from the vents on the floor of the plain. In reality, there weren't more than a handful of fumaroles, and thankfully, the prevailing wind blew from the southwest so the fumes weren't bothersome to the fortress. They stood side by side in silence for several minutes.

"General Olson, I'm afraid that you have a poor opinion of me," Aldan said. "I would like to explain my statements from last night. The things I said could be . . . Misunderstood, and I don't want you to harm Srilani in any way because you don't have all the facts. Please, ask me anything you wish, and I promise to answer truthfully."

The general questioned him long into the evening, asking the same questions repeatedly and in several different ways, trying — it seemed — to trip him up or catch him in an untruth. They covered virtually every moment of Aldan's time with the royal children, from the day they were brought aboard the *Cathartid* to the present hour. Aldan's voice grew rough with fatigue.

Ten bells rang through the fortress, and Olson called a halt to the interrogation. "Young man, I'm satisfied that you aren't lying to me. Or at least, you don't believe you're lying."

"Does that mean Princess Srilani is safe?"

Olson shook his head. "Not necessarily. She, too, must answer my questions. If her answers agree with yours — and I hope they do — then she will arrive safely on the other side."

Aldan drew a deep breath and let it out. "Srilani has a habit of keeping secrets."

"A habit I encouraged," Olson said. He pushed away from the ledge. "I know it's late, but the princess slept all afternoon. Let's pay her a visit."

Srilani turned over the dispatch and added it to the small pile of parchments on the quilt covering her legs. News from Kaeson, even old reports, helped keep the pain in her side at bay. Captain Ahn deserved her gratitude for sending the messages to her. She chose another from the stack at her bedside.

"Your Highness, perhaps you should try to rest," Leanora said. The healer's anxious expression forced Srilani to bite back a hasty answer. The elderly woman sat near, sharing the lantern light, her gnarled fingers twined in the knitting on her lap.

"I rested so much this afternoon, I doubt I'll be able to sleep for some time to come."

"Are you in much pain, my lady?"

"It isn't too noticeable if I sit still and have something to occupy my mind." She bit her lip. "Aunt, if you need to rest, please do."

"No, no, I'm fine." Leanora shook her head. "When you get as old as I am, sleep is always a difficult matter. I never sleep when I want to." She held up her knitting. "The good news is I'm getting a lot of other things done."

Srilani nodded. The tiny room — big enough for a bed, a chest, and a couple of chairs — was cozy and the quilt was sewn from cheerful colors. But after sleeping under the stars for weeks, she couldn't shake the claustrophobic reaction to a room with four walls, a ceiling, and no windows. She switched her attention to the dispatch in her hand.

A knock interrupted her train of thought. Leanora set aside her work and answered the door. Srilani's stomach dropped as she recognized Olson's voice. A couple of minutes passed as Leanora conversed with the officer, and Srilani imagined all sorts of scenarios before the healer shut the door and turned.

"You have visitors. Let me put this robe around your shoulders and straighten your hair."

Visitors? Olson and who else? Srilani placed the dispatches on the chest beside the bed and sat forward to allow Leanora to help her into the borrowed robe. Thank goodness Ahn's wife was about her size. A shaft of pain radiated across her midriff, and she sucked in a sharp breath. Leanora smoothed the top of Srilani's hair.

Earlier, while she'd slept, René and Leanora had done their best to clean her hair and body before they'd dressed her in this gown. Srilani suppressed a shudder. It was too much like being laid out for a funeral. Carefully, she settled back against the pillows.

"Come in, General," Leanora said.

General? Surely she hadn't mistaken Olson's voice.

Leanora opened the door wider and stepped back. "And your friend too, of course."

Srilani's eyes grew wide as Aldan entered the room, stooping to clear the lintel. He took a place beside the door. He looked exhausted and anxious. Their eyes met, and he seemed to be trying to communicate something to her without words.

Olson bowed to Srilani and then to the healer. He wore a fresh uniform tunic with the newly applied golden collar of a general at the neck. "Leanora, I need to talk to the princess in private."

Leanora's brows lifted. "You know I cannot leave her, General."

"I am her teacher, Aunt." He smiled disarmingly. "This is important."

She hesitated. "Then I will leave long enough to brew her a sleeping draught. You may be private while I'm gone."

"Take your time." Olson closed the door. "Aldan, take a seat. You look like you're about to fall over."

Srilani's long-time mentor took Leanora's chair and fixed his keen eyes on her face. *General.* His promotion couldn't have come at a worse time.

He switched to Norlan. "This is a time for complete candor, my daughter. Aldan has told me everything, but if you fail to tell me all I would know, the consequences will be as dire as you imagine." His attention swung back to Aldan. "You are to hold your tongue. We shall see how well your stories match."

Leanora returned after a short time and refused to leave again. "General, you're speaking Norlan. The amount of Norlan I know would fit into a thimble. Pretend I'm not here." Aldan gave her his chair and perched on the very end of the bed.

Eleven bells rang, and then twelve bells. Leanora pressed the sleeping draught into Srilani's hand and she drank it without thinking, concentrating on answering Olson's questions. Her head grew muzzy and finally she sank into the pillows, burrowing under the covers. The velvety scent of lavender wrapped around her.

"Now I know why Father sends prisoners to you for interrogation." She yawned behind her hand and tucked it under her cheek. "I'm ready to confess to anything so you'll stop asking questions."

Olson's mouth quirked and he sat forward. "There's no need for that. I believe you. In fact, I believe both of you. Your tale is remarkable, but some of it needs to stay in this room, especially the part at the beginning with the pirates. We three are the only ones who know of the kiss, and this once, I will let it pass."

At mention of the kiss, heat flooded into her cheeks. Olson rose to his feet and put his hand under Aldan's elbow. "Let's go find a place for you to sleep, young man. May El bless you, Srilani."

She pried her eyes open for a brief moment. "El bless you." The click of the latch pulled her back to awareness. "Olson?"

"Yes?"

"I'm sorry for what I said."

The general's voice sounded far away. "I know, my daughter. Go to sleep."

※

"I don't understand, General Olson," Aldan said. Their footsteps echoed from the stone walls, floors, and ceilings of the rabbits' warren of hallways. The odors of men in enforced proximity assailed Aldan — sweat, food, torch smoke, and musty stone. The fortress was like a stone ship in the middle of a sea of land. "Why is it that you have the authority to execute a princess? What did we do that could possibly deserve death?"

"First of all, a princess is bound by the law to stay pure," Olson said. "The primary reason for this is our relationship to El, of course, but the secondary reason is to ensure a proper succession to the throne. The Palace Guard is responsible for guarding the monarchy in more ways than one."

Aldan pinched the bridge of his nose. That meant Olson was doubly powerful as the new head of the Palace Guard. The general led him past the dining hall where they'd eaten their last meal together six hours before. They entered the courtyard where about half a dozen torches flickered under the giant moon.

The general continued his explanation. "Other women don't face death for losing their purity, but there can be no questions about the lineage of a princess's children or of her loyalty to her people. The same goes for the behavior of royal sons, by the way. In our history, three princesses and one prince have lost their lives over these issues."

Olson's voice dropped. "There are no guarantees that Jamson will live long enough to have children or that his children will live long enough to succeed to the throne. Jamson might perish due to war, plague, or assassination. But with four sisters, he should have plenty of nieces and nephews in line for the throne."

Olson paused in front of a set of heavy oak doors. "What I saw the other night seemed to indicate an ongoing affair between you and the princess. Shocking, yes, and surprising too, given all the years I've known Srilani. But it looked bad. It was my duty to follow through." He grabbed the handle for the door but didn't open it. "Do you want the advice of an old man?"

"Yes, sir."

"Continue to pursue that young woman. She deserves to be happy, and you could not make a better match."

CHAPTER FIFTY-FOUR

The next day, Srilani held up one of the reports she'd been reading. "According to this, Queen Yolani and her mother are living in Kaeson Palace."

René dropped the tunic she was mending. "When did that happen?"

"Over a month ago." Srilani lifted the dry parchment closer. The metallic tang of ink transported her to the lovely maple desk at home where she wrote out her lessons, but the nagging pain in her side brought her back to the fortress. The pain wasn't only around her ribs. Her entire body hurt in places she never knew she had before. Even her bruises had bruises.

The bell in the fortress courtyard rang two bells in the afternoon. Time dragged by like a slug in the garden. The only distractions from the discomfort were her sisters and the dispatches.

She focused her attention on the words in front of her, sifting through the message to find what she needed to remember. "Mother accepted an invitation to Kaedan. Then she brought Yolani and Raslan back for a visit. But that's not the most interesting part. Listen."

"'*The cavalcade, on its way from Kaedan to Kaeson Palace, came under attack by a large gang of brigands at the Marstan River ferry crossing. Two men of Northern Marst were killed and Captain Raymon of Queen Yolani's Palace Guard was seriously injured as he protected the royal carriage containing Her Royal Majesty, Queen Yolani of Southern Marst; her majesty's mother, Lady Raslan; and the queen mother of Northern Marst, Lady Kaelan. None of the women were harmed. All but three of the attackers were slain, two escaped and one prisoner was taken. Further questioning has revealed evidence that points to an assassination attempt planned and orchestrated by Queen Yolani's husband, Lord Habidan. Signed by Lieutenant Greyson of Merripan.'"*

Her stomach performed a flip at Greyson's name.

René's eyes narrowed to slits. "I don't like anything I've heard about Lord Habidan."

"Don't you see?" Srilani said. "This means that Aldan can meet his mother and sister as soon as we reach Kaeson Palace."

"What if they don't agree that he's the heir?"

"They will." She crinkled the parchment close to her chest. "They must."

She lowered the dispatch to her knees and smoothed it out. Greyson. She tried to picture his face and failed. "I wonder if Greyson was in charge of the expedition or if his commander made him write the report."

René snipped the thread she'd been using and set her work aside. "What are you going to do about Greyson when we get home?"

"I don't know what I'll do, but I don't want to be more than friends."

A spark of amusement lit her sister's face. "Oh? What changed?"

Srilani snorted. "Like you don't know, Miss Matchmaker." She pulled her braid over her shoulder and shrugged. "I don't want to talk about Greyson. I want to get out of this bed. I want a real bath. I want clean hair and clean clothes."

⋀⋀

Aldan heaved himself out of the thermal pool in the lowest level of the fortress and grabbed the towel he'd been given. Goose flesh stood up on his arms and legs at the difference between the water's heat and the chilly air of the cavernous room. He dried the moisture from his skin with the rough material and squeezed the moisture from his hair. Nearby, his brothers and Jamson did the same.

"That was close to perfect," Sam said in reverent tones. "The water smells nasty, but the heat! I would bathe three times a day if I could use this pool."

"King Mardan built this fortress over the pools. There's more than one pool, you know." Jamson grabbed his shirt and pulled it over his head. "The cooks even have a well beside the kitchen where they draw up water for cleaning dishes." He chuckled and picked up his other clothes. "These pools are the only benefit of being posted here at the fortress."

Aldan pushed his legs into his new trousers. Actually, they were from a set of uniforms Olson had requisitioned from the fortress storeroom. Sam and Linus also had new sets of clothes. Naturally, they were the sapphire blue of Northern Marst. Any color other than black or brown seemed strange.

Kazka stood up and stretched. He looked like a new dog since he'd received a bath beside the stables the day before.

"Will we see General Olson or Lieutenant Edson this morning?" Aldan asked. He turned toward Jamson in time to catch the grin and wink he sent Sam's direction. What was going on?

Jamson instantly sobered. "No. The general will be leading worship for the men this morning. In fact, I've ordered that we should have the top of the keep to ourselves. This may be our last opportunity to be together — all by ourselves — for a long, long time. Besides, it's your first holy day."

"So your sisters will be there too?" Sam's question seemed disingenuous to Aldan.

The corners of Jamson's mouth quirked. "Yes."

"And Kazka?"

"Of course. He's nearly human."

The brothers followed Jamson up the spiral staircase to the level above and outside into the courtyard. Birds nesting between the fortress stones chirped even though the moon still shone in the slate-gray minutes before dawn.

"Are you anxious about seeing your mother and sister in a few days, Aldan?" Jamson asked.

"I'm nervous they won't think I'm who *you* think I am." He pushed his hair back, running his fingers through the damp strands. "That sounds as confusing as it is."

Sam clapped him on the shoulder. "No matter what your family does, you still have your brothers."

"And me," Jamson said. "I'll claim you too."

"Thank you."

Jamson's voice turned far too cheerful. "Brace yourselves. A large number of people are supposed to arrive tomorrow to escort us to Kaeson. Captain Ahn told me there will be at least two squads of soldiers. If you think it's crowded now, just wait."

They stepped through the enormous doors leading into the keep and wended their way to the dining hall. Jamson halted inside the large room and turned to Aldan. "You know your way to the top of the keep?"

His brows lifted. "I think so."

"Go up and make sure the coast is clear. If any of the guards are there, tell them to report here. My orders. While you do that, we'll arrange for food to be brought up after we finish prayers."

For certain, Jamson was up to something. His brothers too. But Aldan played along. There were too many people in too small a space here in the Cauldron fortress. A moment alone would be welcome.

⋀⋀

"El have mercy. Look at you." René's fingers brushed the blue and purple flesh over Srilani's navel.

Maelan's breath hissed. "Srilani, you're one gigantic bruise."

"Tell me something I don't know." Srilani carefully raised her arms so René could remove the nightgown.

"And you've lost entirely too much weight," René said. "I guess I didn't get the full impact down in the bathing pool last night." She shook her head. "It's a good thing you didn't hit your face or you would have black eyes to go with the rest."

"Ha!" Srilani grabbed her waist. "*Oh-h-h.* Please don't make me laugh. I sneezed earlier and almost died."

Maelan covered a giggle. "Well, don't die before you get your kiss."

Srilani's opened her eyes wide. "What?"

"Maelan." René blew out an exasperated sigh.

"Sorry." Maelan danced up and down on her toes as she held out the clean dress they'd borrowed from the captain's wife's wardrobe. "This is such a pretty color."

"Don't try to change the subject. What did you mean?" Srilani folded her arms and tapped her toe.

René's face flushed. "She's talking about the other night when Aldan kissed you and Olson interrupted."

Fiery heat prickled over Srilani, scorching every inch of exposed flesh. "You saw that?" Was it possible to pass out from blushing?

"We all saw that." Maelan hopped from one foot to the other. "Except for Edson. He was too far outside the camp."

"Sam and Linus too?" Srilani pressed her hands over her face and groaned. "Never mind. Don't answer that." She groaned again.

René was instantly solicitous. "Are you in pain?"

"Yes. Severe, emotional pain." Srilani uncovered her eyes. "You may as well put the dress away. I'm going back to bed. In fact, I may never leave this room again."

René's mouth formed a straight line. "Hand me that dress." She snatched it out of Maelan's fingers and advanced on Srilani. "Lift your arms again. You can't waste your last chance to wear color."

Srilani suffered through the process of donning the dress and ran her fingers down the skirt. If she were blind, somehow she would know the material was this beautiful.

René stood back and sighed. "It's exactly the shade of those dusky pink roses in Mother's garden."

Maelan wrinkled her nose. "After our maids arrive, it's back to white, white, and nothing but white until after we're married." She crossed her arms. "*Ugh.* I enjoyed not having to worry about getting dirty."

"You're right," René said. "But never say so to anyone else."

※

Their dresses rustled as they climbed the stairs. When they reached the dining hall, René led them inside. Jamson was already there with Sam, Linus, and

Kazka. He smiled. "Excellent. René, I need your help with something."

Sam and Linus rose to their feet and bowed to the sisters. Maelan stepped forward and made a beeline to Linus and the wolfhound. "Kazka looks so handsome, Linus."

Jamson moved to embrace Srilani. "I've been so worried about you."

She returned his hug. "Gently. Gently. It hurts a little, but I will recover."

"Aldan is up the stairs. He'd like to talk to you for a minute."

Butterflies fluttered in her midsection. "Oh?" But she advanced into the room, extending her hand to Sam. "First, though, I would thank you, Sam, for saving me. I will be forever in your debt."

He squeezed her fingers. "I think we're even, Princess. Without you, I would have starved to death in Norland."

"Do *not* make me laugh, Pirate."

He bent to whisper in her ear. "Go upstairs and talk to Aldan. He's waiting."

Between the floor-length dress and the aching muscles and ribs, climbing the stairs turned into a trial of mind over matter. Srilani arrived at the top of the keep slightly out of breath. The moon peered down at her from the still dark sky, and a rosy rim of light bordered the eastern edge of the Cauldron. At her step, Aldan turned and came to meet her halfway.

Without a word, she melted into his arms and rested her cheek against his tunic. He exerted no pressure at all and they stood there, still and solemn.

"You should not have turned back for me," she said at last. "But I'm happy you did. You were right — I couldn't do everything by myself." She leaned back to see his face, and her hand rose to stroke the hair beside his ear. "I need you so much."

"I couldn't live without you, Srilani."

"I love you, Aldan." She smiled, and her fingers touched his cheek. "Do that again," she whispered.

He bent and pressed his lips to hers. Her arms slowly, painfully reached up and around his neck, and she returned his kisses. Each one. At last, he trailed kisses along her jaw and drew away.

"I love you, Srilani, but I don't want to dishonor you in any way." He chuckled. "And I don't want to have another session with General Olson. Will convincing your father be as difficult?"

"Just don't let Father tell you no."

"Don't let your father make you say yes to anyone else." Aldan gave her another quick kiss. "All I have now are the clothes on my back, a horse, a few pieces of gold, a stolen map, and a strange mark on my skin." He drew her back into the circle of his arms. "But I believe the message Joel gave me, and I believe El means for us to be together."

She put her ear against his chest, listening to the strong beat of his heart. "El bless you, Aldan."

The sound of footsteps forced them to draw apart, but Aldan retained a hold on her hand. Only then did Srilani notice the benches grouped around a table near the edge of the keep. The arrangement overlooked the Cauldron. By common consent, they all gathered around the table with Kazka beneath.

"Take the hands next to you," Jamson said, and he led them in the King's Benediction. Afterward, they meditated in silence as Sol rose in an awesome, terrible display of scarlet. Dark clouds on the horizon piled up like waves of surf rolling in from a distance sea.

"There's a storm coming," Linus said.

Aldan squeezed Srilani's hand. "Yes, a storm is coming."

TO BE CONTINUED . . .

<<<<>>>>

Thank you for reading *Mardan's Mark*. If you enjoyed this story, let me know by leaving a review on Amazon and/or Goodreads.

DON'T MISS ANY OF THE ACTION

Sign up for my newsletter at **kathresemckee.com** to:

- Receive news about upcoming releases.
- Be eligible for prizes.
- Sign up for Advance Reader Copies.
- Vote on cover designs.
- Meet other fans.

AVAILABLE, SPRING 2015: *Healer's Curse*

What good is Elilan's gift of healing if she can't save those she loves? Elilan must risk failing once again or lose her gift, and the stranger she's learned to love, in *Healer's Curse*.

Thank you for reading! I appreciate you.

Kathrese McKee

ABOUT THE AUTHOR

Texas author, Kathrese McKee, writes epic adventures for young adults and anyone else who enjoys pirates and princesses combined with life's difficult questions. She is committed to exciting stories, appropriate content, and quality craftsmanship.

Mardan's Mark is the award-winning first book in the Mardan's Mark series.

Once upon a time, Kathrese worked as a systems engineer for EDS and various oil and gas companies. Then, she taught Reading and ESL at the middle school level. These days, she edits fiction, home schools her children, and turns a blind eye to the feral dust bunnies lurking beneath her desk.

Connect with her at **kathresemckee.com**.

NAMES LIST, ALPHABETICAL

A
Captain Ahn	commander of the Cauldron Fortress of Northern Marst
Aldan	Captain Rozar's slave, of Marstan descent, taken captive at age seven
Lady Angelan	orphaned daughter of Barthson and Jocelan, Baroness of Sea Watch
Princess Audrilan	fifth child and fourth daughter of King Terson
Azor	alligator god of Norland

B
King Baydan	King of Southern Marst, killed by an assassin's blade.
General Bertson	chief officer of the Palace Guard of Northern Marst
Biscuits	cook aboard the *Cathartid*
Bolz	a guardian priest

C
Cathartid	Captain Rozar's pirate ship
Cauldron	a massive caldera (volcanic basin), long dormant, pitted with fumaroles (vents), some of which emit sulfurous gases
Cauldron Fortress	the fortress overlooking the Cauldron primarily charged with guarding border between Northern Marst and Norland
Lady Cecilan	Corson's daughter and Greyson's sisterAna
Captain Corson	one of the senior officers in the northern Palace Guard, Baron of Merripan

D
Drajna	Nik's wife
Dullon Bridge	a Norlan fortress town in Norland named after its bridge over the Trahn River
King Dzor	king of Norland

E
Lieutenant Edson	an officer and spy for Northern Marst
El	God of all Creation, worshiped in the Twin Kingdoms
Lady Elilan	great-granddaughter of Judge Elison
Judge Elison	spiritual leader of Northern Marst, counselor to the king, chief minister of justice

F
Falcon	a rival Norlan pirate ship of the *Cathartid*
Flame	Aldan's bay gelding

Fratz	crewmember aboard the *Cathartid*

G

Gan	a Norlan village between the larger towns of Minazor and Dullon Bridge
Lady Goslan	Captain Corson's cousin
Great Gulf	a large sea forming the border of Norland, the Twin Kingdoms, and the Citrus Valley
Lieutenant Greyson	heir to the barony of Merripan, son of Baron Corson, captain of the Palace Guard

H

Lord Habidan	husband of Queen Yolani, ruler of the Kingdom of Southern Marst
Hanna	the daughter of the steward of Merripan
Histories of the Twin Kingdoms	a set of official chronicles of the kings of both Northern and Southern Marst
The Hole	a secluded bay on Norland's coast, east of the Trahn River and Port Azor

J

Prince Jamson	fourth child of King Terson, younger twin to Princess Maelan, heir to the throne of Northern Marst
Judge Jeridan	deceased spiritual leader of Southern Marst, formerly King Baydan's counselor
Jessi	maid to Princess Renélan
Joel	the angel, messenger from El

K

Lady Kaelan	king's consort, queen mother of Srilani, Renélan, Maelan, Jamson, and Audrilan
Kazka	Linus's wolfhound

L

Leanora	elderly healer stationed with the troops at the Cauldron Fortress
Lector	head guardian of the Minazor temple
Linus	Captain Rozar's slave, taken captive at age four, of unknown descent

M

Princess Maelan	third child of King Terson, older twin to the heir, Prince Jamson

King Mardan	Founding king of Marst, also known as the "Golden King" for his distinctive blond hair and blue eyes and his immense wealth.
Marst River	the river marking the border between Northern Marst and Southern Marst
Marstan	language of the Twin Kingdoms
Merripan	largest barony in Northern Marst, ancestral home to the indigenous people of Marst, location of Mount Merripan
Midnight Star	black mare
Minazor	largest Norlan city east of the Trahn River, a stronghold of Azor's priesthood, major trading hub
Mirza	witch of Azor

N

Nik	miller on the Trahn River
Norlan	language of Norland, term used to describe anything related to Norland
Norland	land at the north border of Northern Marst, all pirates welcome
Kingdom of Northern Marst	The kingdom given to Kaedan's twin, Kaeson, by their father, King Mardan, the "golden king" of Marst. Capital city is named Kaeson. Color of choice, "Northern blue."

O

Captain Olson	officer in the Palace Guard of Northern Marst, later promoted to General

P

Patience	nurse to the royal children of Northern Marst
Port Azor	capital city of Norland with a deep port

R

Lady Raslan	widow of King Baydan, queen mother of Southern Marst
Captain Raymon	officer in the Southern Marst Palace Guard, Baron of Vista del Mar
Princess Renélan	second child of King Terson
The Revelations of Elison	a record of Judge Elison's prophesies
Rhynder River	river forming the border between Norland and Northern Marst across the Cauldron (caldera) from the Cauldron Fortress
Captain Rozar	Norlan pirate, Captain of the *Cathartid*

S

Sam / Samazor	Captain Rozar's slave, of Norlan descent, given to Rozar by his father at age twelve, as settlement of gambling debts
Scar	First Mate of the *Cathartid*
Separatists	factions on both sides of the Marst River favoring separation of the Twin Kingdoms
Skylark	personal sailboat of King Terson
Sol	the sun
Sol's Light	King Terson's prize stallion
Solstice Festival	annual holiday celebrated on the day of the summer solstice
Soshi	Nik and Drajna's married daughter
Kingdom of Southern Marst	The kingdom given to Kaedan by his father, King Mardan of Marst. Southern Marst is one of the Twin Kingdoms. Capital city is named Kaedan. Color of choice, "Southern green."
First Princess Srilani	oldest daughter of King Terson, oldest child and second in line to the throne behind her younger brother
Stella	Srilani's cremello mare
Stockings	a mare, formerly owned by the baker in Trahnville

T

Telek	chief priest of Azor in Minazor
King Terson	current king of Northern Marst, married to Lady Kaelan, also the Baron of Kaeson
Trahn River	longest, widest river in Norland, effectively dividing the eastern third of the country from the western majority
Trahnville	a Norlan village near Nik's mill; obliterated by the hurricane
Triz the Tinker	a tinker from Norland
Twin Kingdoms	Both of the kingdoms of Marst founded by King Mardan.

V

Victor	Sam's black gelding, Aldan brought the horse out of Minazor

Y

Queen Yolani	ruler of Southern Marst, daughter of King Baydan and Lady Raslan

Z

General Zordan	Lord Habidan's older brother, chief officer of the forces of Southern Marst

NAMES LIST, BY CATEGORY

Characters from Northern Marst

Captain Ahn	commander of the Cauldron Fortress of Northern Marst
Lady Angelan	orphaned daughter of Barthson and Jocelan, Baroness of Sea Watch
Princess Audrilan	fifth child and fourth daughter of King Terson
General Bertson	chief officer of the Palace Guard of Northern Marst
Lady Cecilan	Corson's daughter and Greyson's sisterAna
Captain Corson	one of the senior officers in the northern Palace Guard, Baron of Merripan
Lieutenant Edson	an officer and spy for Northern Marst
Lady Elilan	great-granddaughter of Judge Elison
Judge Elison	spiritual leader of Northern Marst, counselor to the king, chief minister of justice
Lady Goslan	Captain Corson's cousin
Lieutenant Greyson	heir to the barony of Merripan, son of Baron Corson, captain of the Palace Guard
Hanna	the daughter of the steward of Merripan
Prince Jamson	fourth child of King Terson, younger twin to Princess Maelan, heir to the throne of Northern Marst
Jessi	maid to Princess Renélan
Lady Kaelan	king's consort, queen mother of Srilani, Renélan, Maelan, Jamson, and Audrilan
Leanora	elderly healer stationed with the troops at the Cauldron Fortress
Princess Maelan	third child of King Terson, older twin to the heir, Prince Jamson
Captain Olson	officer in the Palace Guard of Northern Marst, later promoted to General
Patience	nurse to the royal children of Northern Marst
Princess Renélan	second child of King Terson
First Princess Srilani	oldest daughter of King Terson, oldest child and second in line to the throne behind her younger brother
King Terson	current king of Northern Marst, married to Lady Kaelan, also the Baron of Kaeson

Characters from Norland

Aldan	Captain Rozar's slave, of Marstan descent, taken captive at age seven
Biscuits	cook aboard the *Cathartid*

Bolz	a guardian priest
Drajna	Nik's wife
King Dzor	king of Norland
Fratz	crewmember aboard the *Cathartid*
Lector	head guardian of the Minazor temple
Linus	Captain Rozar's slave, taken captive at age four, of unknown descent
Mirza	witch of Azor
Nik	miller on the Trahn River
Captain Rozar	Norlan pirate, Captain of the *Cathartid*
Sam / Samazor	Captain Rozar's slave, of Norlan descent, given to Rozar by his father at age twelve, as settlement of gambling debts
Scar	First Mate of the *Cathartid*
Soshi	Nik and Drajna's married daughter
Telek	chief priest of Azor in Minazor
Triz the Tinker	a tinker from Norland

Characters from Southern Marst

King Baydan	King of Southern Marst, killed by an assassin's blade.
Lord Habidan	husband of Queen Yolani, ruler of the Kingdom of Southern Marst
Judge Jeridan	deceased spiritual leader of Southern Marst, formerly King Baydan's counselor
Captain Raymon	officer in the Southern Marst Palace Guard, Baron of Vista del Mar
Lady Raslan	widow of King Baydan, queen mother of Southern Marst
Queen Yolani	ruler of Southern Marst, daughter of King Baydan and Lady Raslan
General Zordan	Lord Habidan's older brother, chief officer of the forces of Southern Marst

Place Names

Cauldron	a massive caldera (volcanic basin), long dormant, pitted with fumaroles (vents), some of which emit sulfurous gases
Cauldron Fortress	the fortress overlooking the Cauldron primarily charged with guarding border between Northern Marst and Norland
Dullon Bridge	a Norlan fortress town in Norland named after its bridge over the Trahn River
Gan	a Norlan village between the larger towns of Minazor and Dullon Bridge
Great Gulf	a large sea forming the border of Norland, the Twin Kingdoms, and the Citrus Valley
The Hole	a secluded bay on Norland's coast, east of the Trahn River and Port Azor
Marst River	the river marking the border between Northern Marst and Southern Marst
Merripan	largest barony in Northern Marst, ancestral home to the indigenous people of Marst, location of Mount Merripan
Minazor	largest Norlan city east of the Trahn River, a stronghold of Azor's priesthood, major trading hub
Norland	land at the north border of Northern Marst, all pirates welcome
Kingdom of Northern Marst	The kingdom given to Kaedan's twin, Kaeson, by their father, King Mardan, the "golden king" of Marst. Capital city is named Kaeson. Color of choice, "Northern blue."
Port Azor	capital city of Norland with a deep port
Rhynder River	river forming the border between Norland and Northern Marst across the Cauldron (caldera) from the Cauldron Fortress
Kingdom of Southern Marst	The kingdom given to Kaedan by his father, King Mardan of Marst. Southern Marst is one of the Twin Kingdoms. Capital city is named Kaedan. Color of choice, "Southern green."
Trahn River	longest, widest river in Norland, effectively dividing the eastern third of the country from the western majority
Trahnville	a Norlan village near Nik's mill; obliterated by the hurricane
Twin Kingdoms	Both of the kingdoms of Marst founded by King Mardan.

Other Names

Cathartid	Captain Rozar's pirate ship
El	God of all Creation, worshiped in the Twin Kingdoms
Falcon	a rival Norlan pirate ship of the *Cathartid*
Histories of the Twin Kingdoms	a set of official chronicles of the kings of both Northern and Southern Marst
Joel	the angel, messenger from El
King Mardan	Founding king of Marst, also known as the "Golden King" for his distinctive blond hair and blue eyes and his immense wealth.
Marstan	language of the Twin Kingdoms
Norlan	language of Norland, term used to describe anything related to Norland
The Revelations of Elison	a record of Judge Elison's prophesies
Separatists	factions on both sides of the Marst River favoring separation of the Twin Kingdoms
Skylark	personal sailboat of King Terson
Sol	the sun
Solstice Festival	annual holiday celebrated on the day of the summer solstice

Made in the USA
Middletown, DE
04 April 2015